CAGED IN SHADOW

OF DRAGONS AND FAE, BOOK THREE

JASMINE WALT

DYNAMO PRESS

COPYRIGHT

IMPORTANT NAMES AND PLACES

This is a list of some of the character names and locations from the previous books, to help refresh your memory.

MAIN CHARACTERS:

ADARA: Half-dragon, half-water fae, Adara is a rare fae who can wield both fire and water magic. According to a prophecy, she is the only one who can save Ediria, but only if she can master her powers and complete the sacred ritual that will allow her to unlock her final form.

EINAR: The last dragon in Ediria. The fae hunted his kind to near extinction, so he harbors a deep hatred for nearly all of them except Adara, who is his fated mate.

SECONDARY CHARACTERS:

LEAP: an orphaned air fae with the rare ability to wield lightning magic. His mother was Lord Oren's sister, and Leap was raised by him for a few short years until he ran away and fell in first with a gang of street thieves, then later was adopted by harpies. He joined Adara and Einar's band after the two of them saved one of his harpy friends.

MAVLYN: An earth fae with the ability to manipulate plant life. Mavlyn was raised in the same village Adara grew up in, and the two of them have been best friends for as long as they can remember. She is also a distant relative of Lady Mossi's.

SIDE CHARACTERS:

AVANI: Lady Mossi's granddaughter, and one of the three hostages taken by King Aolis to control the other houses. They helped Adara and her friends escape Kaipei Castle after defeating Aolis.

CASCADA: Lady Axlya's daughter, and one of the three hostages taken by King Aolis to control the other houses. They helped Adara and her friends escape Kaipei Castle after defeating Aolis.

DUNE TERRAN: an earth fae, and Adara's ex-boyfriend.

GENERAL SLAUGH: Leader of the Shadow Guard, formerly the right hand of King Aolis.

GELSYNE: Adara's adoptive mother, formerly the late Princess Olette's lady-in-waiting. Her body has been possessed by Nox.

KING AOLIS: the recently deceased king of Ediria.

KING CYRIAN: Adara's grandfather, and King Aolis's predecessor.

LADY AXLYA: Ruler of House Usciete and Lochanlee.

LADY MOSSI: Ruler of House Ithir and Domhain.

LORD OREN: Ruler of the House Reatha and the Gaoth Aire.

LORD TOR: ruler of the Bala Oighr and the ice fae who make their home there.

NOX, MOTHER OF SHADOWS: A powerful shadow demon who gifted King Aolis with powerful shadow magic, and who has been trying to possess him for decades. She now possesses Gelsyne instead, whom she has full control over.

PRINCE DARYAN: The dragon prince, and Adara's late father.

PRINCESS OLETTE: Adara's late mother, and the daughter of King Cyrian.

QUYE, THE ORACLE: Quye is a powerful air fae who can see the past, present, and future. The winds bring her whispers from all corners of the realm, and she also has a close connection with both the dream realm and the spirit realm. She is also a niece of Lord Oren, and Leap's cousin.

RYKER: Lord Oren's son, and current heir to the Gaoth Aire's throne. He bullied and abused Leap as a child, and threatened to kill Mavlyn when she and Leap fled Angtun.

TEMPEST: Lord Oren's daughter, and one of the three hostages taken by King Aolis to control the other houses. They helped Adara and her friends escape Kaipei Castle after defeating Aolis.

TAMIL: Lord Tor's heir. She helped Adara escape from Lochanlee and flee to the Bala Oighr, where she was killed in action fighting against Dune and his shadow soldiers.

TULIANA: The ice fae priestess. She was killed by Dune Terran and his soldiers before she could help Adara complete the Coming-of-Age ritual.

PLACES:

ANGTUN: The capital city of the Gaoth Aire, home of Lord Oren, leader of the air fae. Sister city to Wynth.

DOMHAIN: the earth fae realm, ruled by Lady Mossi.

EDIRIA: the kingdom this story is set in. It is made up of four realms—Domhain, Hearthfyre, Lochanlee, and The Gaoth Aire.

FENWOOD: The village in Domhain where Adara and Mavlyn grew up.

HEARTHFYRE: formerly the fire fae realm before it was taken over by the dragons. After King Aolis used shadow magic to defeat the dragons, Hearthfyre became a wasteland overrun by shadow creatures. Edirians now refer to it as the Deadlands, and few dare to travel there.

LOCHANLEE: the water fae realm, where Lady Axlya rules.

MOUNT FURIAN: a sacred mountain in Hearthfyre, where the portal the dragons used to escape is hidden.

TALAMH: The capital of Domhain, where Lady Mossi resides, and where Mavlyn was set to go to university.

THE GAOTH AIRE: the air fae realm, where Lord Oren rules.

WYNTH: a major city in the Gaoth Aire, where Leap is from, and where the Oracle makes her home.

1

Adara

"F*rom the waters we come, and to the waters we shall return.*"
       Tears slipped down my cheeks as the ice fae chanted
the refrain in unison, the final words to the funeral ceremony.
We were all gathered outside Linn Chrystail, a sacred lake ten
miles north of Fheir, where the ice fae sent their dead to rest.

Lord Tor, Tamil's father, cleared his throat as the chanting
died away. He was a tall, wizened fae with translucent skin and
snow-white hair, and though his imposing stature and the
majestic pelt draped around his broad shoulders lent him a
commanding air, the walking stick he leaned so heavily against
served as a reminder to everyone of his illness. Tamil's fiancé,
Havor, and her younger sisters, Lora and Nora, gathered close
around him, standing together in solidarity and grief.

In contrast, Einar and I stood on the outskirts of the clan,
Leap, Mavlyn, and Quye alongside us. The harpies who had

helped us defeat Dune and his shadow soldiers had departed, taking their dead with them. I wish I'd had more time to thank them properly, but it was probably for the best that they'd left so quickly. I didn't think the ice fae would feel comfortable having them here for the funeral.

The fae who had fallen in battle had all been laid out on ice floes perched at the edge of the lake, dressed in ceremonial robes or armor depending on their status. Tamil and Tuliana were in the center, the former dressed in battle armor, the latter in her high priestess robes. Both had been cleaned of all traces of blood and violence, the crowns and headdresses of their stations perched on their heads, their hands folded atop their weapons and amulets. Fanned out on either side of them, and stretching back behind them for several rows, were the soldiers and acolytes who had also perished.

The ice fae began to sing in the old fae tongue, a funeral lament about transformation and rebirth. We fae did not believe death was the end, but rather a cycle in which we returned to the loving embrace of the universe before being reborn once again in whatever form would best serve the cosmos.

After everything I'd seen and experienced with magic, I was inclined to believe it, too. But even so, it was hard to take comfort in the knowledge that Tamil was not truly gone when looking at the tear-streaked faces of her family and friends.

Lord Tor raised his hands, and the ice floes slid forward, gliding onto the ocean lake like ships setting out on a maiden voyage. Einar slipped his hand into mine, and I squeezed it tight as we watched the floes drift out to the center of the lake. The music swelled around us, the melody poignant and hopeful and heartbreaking all at once, and with a clap of Tor's hands, the ice floes melted. The bodies sank like stones beneath the lake's frigid surface, leaving only ripples behind.

Silence fell upon the clan, and all bowed their heads one last time in memory. The stillness was broken by the sound of ice reforming across the surface of the lake—Lord Tor had used his power to melt it for the ceremony, but it came rippling back now that his magic no longer held it at bay. The clan patriarch sagged, gripping his staff, and his children rushed to grab him before he toppled over.

"Stop this nonsense," he grumbled as more people surged forward, offering to help. "I don't need the entire clan to carry me. I'll be fine."

The other ice fae relented, but their concerned murmurs as they drifted away from the lake told me they weren't fooled. Their clan leader was hanging on by a thread, his heir had just been slain in battle, and their priestess had also been killed. The entire future of the Bala Oighr had been thrown into peril—and it was all because of me.

"It's not your fault," Einar murmured as we followed the clan back to the campsite. There was a nearby village, but it was far too small to accommodate us, so the ice fae had packed tents while Lord Tor and his family stayed with the village headman. If Tor had been in better health, we would have headed straight back to Whitecrest, but given his condition, we couldn't. We would stay here one more night and allow him to rest, then make the journey back home, where they would hold a proper memorial feast for the dead. "Tamil knew the risks involved. We all did, and we're still here with you."

"I know," I said heavily, my boots crunching through the snow. "It's just... if I was a better negotiator, maybe I could have convinced Lady Axlya to help me."

"Lady Axlya is a twat," Quye said. I jerked my head up in shock, not used to the acerbic note in her normally playful voice. "If this is anyone's fault, it's hers. The Bala Oighr, as she so often loves to remind them, are her responsibility, and as one of her descendants, so are you. She should have taken you under her wing and done everything she could to support and help you, not manipulate you into being another one of her pawns." Quye sighed.

"Also, Old Lady Axlya's got close to a thousand years on you," Leap pointed out. "You can't beat yourself up for not being able to beat her at her own game."

I snorted. "Thanks, you two. I'll try to keep in mind that almost everyone I'm up against is centuries older than I am and outclasses me in almost every possible way."

Einar clapped a hand on my shoulder, his fingers digging into the tense muscle. "Don't talk that way about yourself," he growled. "The House heads may all be older than you, but their age blinds them to both truth and reason, which is why Nox is so easily able to sink her claws into them. You outshine them all, which is why the Radiants are on your side, and why you were born with the power to defeat the Shadows."

He pulled me to a stop, gripping my other shoulder with his free hand so I was forced to meet his gaze. "But none of that matters if you don't believe in yourself, Adara. Defeatist self-talk is what creatures like Nox prey upon, getting their victims to tear themselves down from the inside before they even have to lift a finger. The more you doubt yourself, the more of a foothold she gains. You don't have the luxury of self-doubt, Adara. None of us do."

His tone was gentle, but the fierce look blazing in his golden eyes kindled a fire inside me. It burned through some of the grief fogging my mind, and I exhaled, letting go of that negative energy and inhaling some of his strength. My shoulders straightened, and I nodded as the self-pity finally sloughed off me.

"You're right," I said. It might not be my fault that Tamil and the others died, but it would be my fault if Nox succeeded. I had to be strong, had to trust in my own abilities and those of my friends if I wanted to see this through. We could do this. We had to.

The five of us made it back to camp, where the others were already making breakfast. I offered to pitch in, but the ice fae wouldn't hear of it. They shooed us away, pressing mugs of hot tea into our hands and sitting us down on logs near the fire to wait as they grilled fish and boiled porridge. They didn't seem to begrudge our presence—after all they were treating us like guests—and yet I still couldn't help feeling like an outsider.

But wasn't that right? I was an outsider—all of us were. It didn't matter that my water fae half strongly favored ice magic— I didn't grow up with these people, hadn't spent part of my childhood with them the way my mother had. A part of me had thought I might find community somewhere amongst the water fae, but Lady Axlya had denied me that. And while it might have been possible to find community amongst the ice fae if I'd succeeded in completing the ritual, that hope had died with Tamil.

Her death would always foreshadow my presence amongst the ice fae, whether I succeeded in my quest or not.

A shadow fell over me, disrupting my dark musings. I glanced up to see an ice fae soldier standing before me—one of the few that had survived the battle at the temple. "My apologies, Lady Adara, but Lord Tor requests your presence in the village. Along with your friends." His gaze shifted to Einar and the others.

"Of course." I stood at once, the thought of breakfast forgotten. The others exchanged glances but said nothing as they followed us. The village was a half-mile trek from the campsite, a quaint little cluster of cabins built along a slope that were dusted with snow and fringed in icicles. Perched at the very top was the headman's cabin, with a perfect view of the lake and surrounding areas.

"Welcome," the headman said as he opened the door, giving us a kind smile. We stomped our feet to shake the snow loose from our boots before we entered, then removed them before venturing further in. The house was large, more like a lodge than a cabin, yet it still had a cozy, rustic feel. The main room was spacious and well-lit, with a large stone hearth at one end, surrounded by comfortable chairs and cushions. On the other end of the room sat a throne carved from antler bones, and behind it was a large, woven tapestry depicting an ice fae hunt. A few simple shelves along the walls held leather-bound books and vellum scrolls, and there was a small writing desk in the corner, just off to the side of the throne.

I expected Lord Tor to be abed, given his condition, but he sat by the hearth in a rocking chair, the quintessential picture of an aging grandpa. The flickering firelight cast shadows on his translucent skin, highlighting the faint lines of age on his face. It struck me then that he had to be older than Lady Axlya, as only the most ancient of Greater Fae showed signs of aging. How much had those wizened eyes seen over the centuries? How much could I learn from him, if only I had the time?

"Lord Tor." I stopped a few feet away from him, inclining my head. Einar and my friends stood just a pace behind me, allowing me to take the lead. "I'm not sure I've had the chance to thank you and your people for their hospitality. We are very grateful you've given us sanctuary during these troubled times."

Lord Tor inclined his head. "It's Tamil you should be thanking," he said gruffly. Despite his age, his ice-blue eyes were sharp, missing nothing as they flicked between the members of our group. "It was her idea to defy Lady Axlya and bring you here, and one we spent many a night arguing about. But she believed in you, Adara, enough to give her life for you." His eyes flashed, knuckles turning white as he gripped the arms of his chair. "You must tell me now exactly what that sacrifice was for, and whether it was in vain."

I swallowed hard, glancing at Quye. "How much did Tamil tell you?" I ventured.

Lord Tor snorted. "She told me you are the girl in the prophecy that King Aolis had been blathering about for the last decade," he said. "The one who is supposed to cure our lands of the shadow magic infection. Yet we were forced to burn nearly half of our fallen this week because their bodies were riddled with shadow corruption. So tell me, was my daughter right about you?"

"Of course she was," Quye interrupted, stepping forward. All eyes in the room snapped to her, and maybe my eyes were playing tricks on me, but Quye seemed to glow a little brighter than everyone else, as if she'd been touched by the Radiants themselves.

Which I suppose, being the Oracle, she was.

"I prophesied her birth myself," Quye went on, waving an airy hand as Lord Tor's gaze narrowed on her, "So I think I know what I'm talking about. Adara is the only one who can drive shadow magic from our lands, but although she killed King Aolis, she failed to kill the Shadow corrupting him. That demon has since found another fae to use as a host, one far easier for her to manipulate, and she's been subtly influencing the other Houses, riling them up against each other to start a civil war. Her ultimate goal is to create enough chaos energy to rip a portal open to the shadow realm, and if she succeeds, the shadow infection we've been dealing with for the last twenty years will seem like a lover's caress. Shadow demons will devour our entire world, and there will be nothing left for the Houses to fight."

"A portal to the shadow realm?" Lord Tor protested. "That's insanity. Such a thing has never happened in our history!"

"Of course it hasn't." Quye rolled her eyes. "That's why we're all still here. In the past, the Champions have always kept the balance in our world, keeping the chaos energies in Ediria low so as to not open us up to a Shadow invasion. But since King Aolis allied himself with the Shadows, we are now close to that reality actually coming to pass. Adara is the only one who can stop it, but she can't drive Nox from our realm until she comes into her own powers. Lady Axlya refused to help her, which is why Tamil brought her here."

I stared at Quye, a little taken aback. Kiryan had never quite explained the situation like this—that it was through stirring conflict that Nox hoped to gain the power necessary to take over our world. I'd thought her shadow magic would be enough, but of course it wasn't—if that was the case, she would have accomplished her plan years ago. My stomach sank as I realized how close she had already come to succeeding—the three Houses had practically declared war on each other already, the day I'd fled Usciete.

"Well, I don't see how we can help her now," Lord Tor snapped. "My head priestess is dead, along with all her acolytes! It will take decades before we can train a new one, which also means that my daughters will have to wait decades before they can come into their powers!" He shook his head, disgusted. "Damn Axlya and her selfish ways for putting us into this situation! I would demand restitution from her, except that we don't currently have a king to enforce it."

He glared at me, as though that was my fault—which, of course, it was. But it wasn't as though King Aolis would have actually helped him if he'd still been alive.

"General Slaugh cannot be allowed to get away with killing my daughter," Tor continued, his voice a low growl. "The Bala Oighr will have our vengeance against him and his allies! We will mobilize our forces to fight—"

"No!" I interrupted, fear pumping through my veins. Lord Tor scowled, displeased at my outburst, but I charged on, undeterred. "Lord Tor, if you engage in the fighting, you will be feeding into the chaos energies, which is exactly what Nox wants. The only way to keep her at bay is to refuse to engage."

"Until what?" Lord Tor asked. "Until you convince Lady Axlya to help you? Because I can tell you right now how unlikely that is. I've known that female for centuries, and once she makes up her mind about someone, not even the Radiants themselves can convince her to change her mind. She'll never help you now that you've defied her."

"We don't need her help," Einar said. "There's still one more option for us, one more way Adara can complete the ritual. But until that time, we need the citizens of Ediria to resist Nox with everything they have. And that starts with you, Lord Tor."

"Harrumph." Lord Tor looked Einar up and down. "Never thought I'd be having a civilized conversation with a dragon, never mind the general responsible for killing so many of us fae." He shook his head, lips thinning with displeasure. "Still, I am a warrior at heart, dragon. I cannot sit by and let an act of war against my people go unanswered."

"My Lord," I said, gentling my voice. "I know what I am asking of you goes against your very nature. But we can't fight fire with fire, not in this battle. If you can't do this for me, do it for your daughter. Tamil believed in me, believed in the cause I am fighting for, enough to risk everything, including her own life. You said you wanted to know if her sacrifice was in vain. It wasn't, not yet, but it will be if you take up arms now. Don't throw away our only chance to win this for the sake of pride and vengeance. Please."

The ice lord's eyes flared with white hot anger, and for a second, I feared he'd taken offense to my words. But then his shoulders sagged, and he let out a great sigh.

"This goes against my better judgment," he said, meeting my gaze, "but I will do as you ask. The Bala Oighr will seal its walls against the outside world, and we will not take up arms to fight General Slaugh or any of the other fae. But you must do your part, Adara, and quickly. My people can only hold out so long, and my own days are numbered. You cannot fail."

2

Einar

After we finished meeting with Lord Tor, the five of us returned to camp, in desperate need of a meal. Thankfully, the ice fae had set aside some food for us, and we dug into the cold but welcome meal before retreating to our tent to discuss next steps.

"Quye," Mavlyn began as we settled into our furs. Snow flurries swirled in the air just beyond the confines of the tent—Quye, Mavlyn, and Adara were sharing this one, while Leap and I shared a smaller one—and I was glad for the insulation and the coverings. Adara and the ice fae might be immune, but Mavlyn and I weren't used to such temperatures. Even Leap and Quye, who as air fae, were used to the colder temperatures that came with flying at high altitudes, seemed relieved to be bundled up. "You told us that Adara needs to seek out the dragons for help with the ritual, but you still haven't explained exactly what that means."

"What it means," Quye said, pointing at me with a blue-tipped fingernail, "is that Einar here needs to open up the portal he and Kiryan used to help the dragons escape Ediria, so that Adara can go to the dragon's new home and ask their priestess to help her complete the ritual. Lord Tor was right when he said that Lady Axlya would rather eat her own arse—"

"I don't think that's exactly what he said," Leap pointed out, a smirk curling at the corners of his lips.

"—than help Adara, and there's no ice fae priestess who can help us. Adara doesn't have a drop of earth or air fae blood in her, so she can't ask the other Houses for help. The dragon priestess is the only one left."

Mavlyn stared at me. "Did I know this about you?" she asked, pinching the bridge of her nose. "That you and Kiryan opened a portal together to save the dragons, and that you're the keeper?"

"Yes," I said archly. "Kiryan explained the whole thing to you after we escaped Kaipei Castle, before Adara and I were taken captive by Prentis's soldiers."

"Well, that explains why I never heard about this." Leap scowled, crossing his arms over his chest. "So, let me get this straight. You've been able to open a portal to the dragon realm this entire time, and you didn't think to try that first? How come?"

"Because," I said, striving to keep my tone patient, "I can't go through the portal myself. I would have to send Adara through without me, and I have no idea what lies on the other side, or if my people would help her without me there to convince them. Plus, I can only open the portal from inside Mount Furian, and it's too dangerous to travel there."

"Not anymore," Adara said slowly. She met my gaze from where she was sitting directly across from me, a hopeful spark in her eyes. "You're immune to shadow magic now, same as I. We can travel to Mount Furian together."

"Right." I blinked as the realization rushed through me. I'd forgotten Adara had transferred that power to me during the battle with Dune. The bastard had poisoned me with his shadow magic, turning me into a raving beast who didn't even remember his own name. He'd nearly succeeded in getting me to kill Adara, but she'd brought me back from the brink by biting me, tapping into the bond between us so she could suck the shadow magic out of me and destroy it using the icefire she'd created inside her own body. She'd pushed the last of that power into me before severing the connection, leaving me with the ability to resist shadow magic on my own.

It was the most precious gift she could have given me... and right now, it might prove to be our salvation.

"Hang on," Mavlyn said. "We can't let Adara go through the portal and into a whole new realm all by herself. Yes, we know you're powerful and can kick ass," she said when Adara began to protest, "but none of us have any idea what is on the other side of that portal, and you're too important to the fate of our world. I'm coming with you."

"Me too," Leap insisted, eyes sparkling with excitement. "There's no way you're leaving me behind while the two of you go off to explore a whole new world."

"Absolutely not!" Adara exclaimed. "There's no way I'm putting you two at risk. Have you forgotten that dragons hate fae? Einar almost killed me himself when we first met—the only reason he didn't was because of my fire magic."

That actually wasn't true, but I kept my mouth shut. I wasn't about to announce to the room that the reason I hadn't torn Adara limb from limb was because the mating bond had tethered me to her like a dog to a leash. In fact, even she didn't know that was the true reason.

"The dragons might be willing to show me the same leniency," Adara went on, "if I can get enough time to explain my half-dragon heritage. But I'm almost positive that they'll kill you both on site."

"I hate to say it, but Adara is right," I said. "The only one of us who could safely travel with her is Quye. My people consider seers to be sacred, and they know of her—Ylena would never allow Quye to be harmed. And if I send you with a letter written in my hand, explaining the situation, she'll agree to help you."

"Ylena?" Adara asked. "Who's that?"

"Your aunt," I said with a smile. "Daryan's sister. She's also the high priestess, and the one who guides all dragons along the path of the Umnar—our own version of the coming-of-age ritual. She's the one you'll need to win over."

"This is unbelievable," Leap grumbled. "You've barely spent more than a handful of days away from the air temple in your entire life, Quye, and now you're going to go off to a whole new realm?" He shook his head. "Uncle Oren would have an apoplexy if he knew."

Quye laughed. "Uncle Oren is so busy with the war at his doorstep, he hasn't even realized I'm gone," she said. "Besides, this isn't the first time I've visited another realm—I visit the spirit realm and the dream realm all the time when I'm sleeping. That's how I was able to get messages to Mavlyn when you two were searching for me. If you think about it, I'm actually the perfect person for this task." She winked at Leap. "Besides, you and Mavlyn are needed here. The two of you need to spread the word about Nox and convince your respective people to resist."

"Convince them to resist?" Mavlyn scrubbed a hand across her face, looking a little overwhelmed. "I'm not sure how to do that, Quye. I don't have any influence in Domhain—I'm just a lesser fae."

"No, you're not." Quye took her hand, and something passed

between them as their eyes met. "You're brave and smart and resourceful. You wouldn't be part of our little band of heroes otherwise."

Mavlyn's expression softened, and some of the tension left her face. A small smile curled her lips as she looked over at Adara. "I'm just a loyal friend who would do anything for her bestie," she said.

A pang of envy hit me at Adara and Mavlyn's camaraderie. Most of my close friends were dead, and the ones who'd survived were in a realm I could never journey to. I wished I could cross over with Adara to see them, instead of being made to loiter in the Deadlands and wait while she met the people I had said goodbye to decades ago.

"You're a lot more than that," Adara said. "You're everything Quye said and more, and also, being a lesser fae is a strength here. You and I know how it was growing up in our village—we were disconnected from the Greater Fae, and our elders were downright resentful about our lack of representation. How many times did we hear our parents bicker about the amount we pay in tithes, only to have no say in how the realm is run? As a fellow lesser fae, you can tap into that resentment, but in a good way. Remind the people that they don't need to throw their lives away just because the Greater Fae say so, that they can choose peace instead of sending their children off to die."

"That's a pretty good point," Leap said. "I spent enough time as a street urchin in Wynth to know that the lesser air fae feel similar."

"There is one other matter to address," Quye said, looking at me again. "The bond between you and Adara."

A sense of unease rippled through me, and I saw Adara go still out of the corner of my eye. "What of it?" I asked cautiously.

"It hasn't been completed, that's what," Quye said, wiggling her eyebrows. "From everything I understand about dragons, it's emotionally painful for you to be separated from Adara until you two seal the bond... and you're about to send her off to another realm. Don't you think that's something the two of you should handle first?"

"Actually," an unfamiliar voice said as the tent flap opened, "they should not."

We all turned, startled, as an ice fae female—one of the matrons who'd been running breakfast—entered the tent. At first I couldn't fathom why she was interrupting us, but when I locked eyes with her gold-green gaze, I understood.

"Kiryan." Annoyed realization swept over me. "I see you've joined us again."

Kiryan inclined his head—or was it her? Did Radiants even have a gender? "And not a moment too soon," he said in the female's melodic tones, taking a seat next to Quye. "The Oracle usually gives stellar advice, but she was about to steer you terribly wrong with this one."

Quye huffed. "I do my best, but I'm not omniscient." She tossed a skein of curly white hair over one shoulder as she eyed Kiryan. "Why, exactly, is this terrible advice?"

"Because," Kiryan said, looking over at Adara, "once the two of you complete the mating bond, your lives will be tied together. That means that if Einar dies, you will die, and vice versa. We can't afford for you to take that risk, not until you've completed the ritual and defeated Nox."

The breath whooshed out of me as Kiryan's words struck, more powerful than a well-placed blow to the gut. Adara met my eyes from across the room, the stricken look on her face mirroring my own feelings. I hadn't had time to think about the bond much, what with everything else going on, but I would have wanted to complete it before sending her off to the dragon's new realm. Mated dragons could communicate telepathically over great distances, and though the bond had never been tested between realms, a part of me thought it would still work to some extent.

"When General Slaugh kidnapped you and shadow traveled with you to Kaipei Castle, I felt like a piece of my heart had been torn out," I said hoarsely. I held Adara's gaze as I spoke, wanting her to see the raw honesty in my face. "The only thing that kept me from losing my mind was that I had a way to get back to you —that, and that Leap and Mavlyn were by my side to help me." I cast them both grateful glances. "I can't imagine how much worse it will be if I send you to another world with the bond still incomplete... but I'll do it, if this is what you wish."

Adara bit her lip, clearly torn between Kiryan's logic and her desire to spare me the pain of separation. "Is there no way around this?" she asked Kiryan, turning to him.

Kiryan shook his head. "No, but it won't be as bad as Einar fears." He flicked a glance at me. "Because the two of you have exchanged blood, you've already partially completed the bond, so the pain of separation won't be as bad. However, because Adara has acknowledged the bond, unlike the last time you two separated, she will feel the pain this time as well. That's a burden you both must accept."

Adara blew out a breath, causing the strand of hair curling around her moon-pale cheek to flutter. I wished she was sitting next to me, so I could brush it from her face, then pull her into my arms and hold her close.

We'd come so far in our relationship, confessing our feelings, exchanging blood, power, and even pleasure. Why was it that just when we were on the verge of completing the bond, the Radiants had to send her away from me?

"Well," she said, meeting my eyes with a watery smile. "Guess that's just one more reason for me to complete this journey as fast as possible."

3

Mavlyn

Mavlyn rose before the dawn the next morning, her heart as heavy as the blanket of darkness still cloaking the sky outside. The group had already decided they would leave today—Einar, Adara, and Quye for Mount Furian, Leap and Mavlyn for Domhain to start a grass-roots campaign against Nox and Lady Mossi.

Already dressed for the journey, Mavlyn laced up her boots, then slipped out of the tent on silent feet so as not to wake Adara and Quye. They all had long journeys ahead, and if her mind wasn't so plagued by anxious thoughts, she would be trying to catch another hour of sleep.

But Mavlyn couldn't help worrying about the mission Quye had tasked Leap and her with. How could they start an anti-war campaign under Lady Mossi's nose, in her own realm, without being captured and killed? Adara had said Mavlyn's status as a lesser fae was an asset, that it would make the others more likely to listen to her, but Mavlyn wasn't sure that was true. After all, it wasn't as if she was anyone special amongst her people. She was barely an adult by fae standards, with hardly any life experience. Not to mention her family's distant connection to House Ithir was actually a liability, since she was about to ask the people of Domhain to stand against them.

The snow crunched beneath Mavlyn's boots as she walked away from camp, heading for the nearby woods. She always felt better when she was surrounded by plants, and the evergreen trees were no exception as she stepped beneath their verdant boughs. The scents of pine and fir enveloped her in a comforting hug, and she mentally wrapped the fragrance around her like a blanket as she walked, pondering the situation.

Leap and Mavlyn had both agreed that the best place to start was Fenwood, the village she'd grown up in. Unlike Adara, Mavlyn had many friends, and her family was respected there. She had little hope of convincing the headman, but her mother had backed her up in her decision to support Adara. Maybe she and her father would have some good ideas.

The snapping of a branch jerked Mavlyn out of her thoughts, and she whirled around, hand straying to one of the seed pouches around her belt. Her mouth dropped open at the sight of a white stag staring at her from between two trees. It was nearly twice Mavlyn's height, with magnificent fur that gleamed like starlight, and a majestic crown of antlers that looked as though they'd been wrought from pure silver.

The intelligence gleaming in its dark eyes was so fierce that for a heartbeat, Mavlyn wondered if the stag was a Greater Fae. They stood suspended in that moment for a long while, before a flutter of wingbeats broke the spell. Turning, they both spotted a snowy owl winging its way toward them, its silvery eyes gleaming in the waning moonlight.

The owl landed in the tree adjacent to the stag. It hooted,

and the two locked eyes, some kind of silent communication passing between them. Mavlyn watched with rapt fascination as the stag inclined its noble head, then retreated into the night, leaving the two of them alone in the woods. Satisfied, the owl hopped down from its perch, then transformed with a flash of light. Mavlyn's mouth dropped open as Quye stood before her, a playful grin on her face.

"Giant's teeth!" Mavlyn exclaimed, loud enough to startle a group of birds sleeping in one of the trees. They squawked reproachfully at her, but she was too flabbergasted to feel remorseful for disturbing them. "I... what... were you *following* me? And did you just have a conversation with a *stag*?"

Quye laughed, the sound like wind chimes tinkling through the trees. "Of course I followed you," she said, closing the distance between them. She took one of Mavlyn's hands, and Mavlyn's heart skipped a beat as she clasped it between both of hers. "I woke up and saw that you'd left the tent, and I wanted to make sure you were okay. And yes, I was talking to the stag. He's the guardian of this forest, and he didn't know what to make of an earth fae wandering around this far north. I assured him you meant no harm, and sent him on his way."

"I... well... thanks, I guess." Still flustered, Mavlyn dropped her gaze to their joined hands, not sure what to think. Her heart beat faster as she realized this was the first time she and Quye had ever been alone together in the physical world. Her mind cast around for some subject to latch onto, not wanting to read too much into the situation. "Does your beast form allow you to talk to other animals?"

"Yes, that's one of the perks of having an animal form," Quye admitted. "Though I don't actually need to shift to my owl form to understand animals. Because of my connection to the spirit and dream realms, I'm able to understand most creatures regardless of any language barrier. Which I think is going to come in handy when Adara and I travel to this new world. I doubt the natives there speak Edirian, and we're probably going to run into them before we find the dragons."

"Natives." Mavlyn scrubbed her free hand over her face, overwhelmed by the thought. "Right." The heaviness in her heart returned, and she struggled to keep the sadness from her voice. *"I wish you didn't have to go,"* she wanted to say. *"I wish we didn't have to be separated, just when I'd found you again."*

"I know," Quye murmured.

Mavlyn yanked her hand out of Quye's and clapped it over her mouth. "Radiants," she gasped, a furious blush heating her cheeks. "Did I say that out loud?"

"No," Quye said, gently removing Mavlyn's hand from her face and taking it again. Mavlyn sucked in a breath as Quye brought it to her lips, pressing her rose petal mouth against Mavlyn's knuckles. Her breath stuttered in her chest, and the flush on her cheeks spread lower, suffusing her entire body with heat. "You didn't have to, Mavlyn. I feel the same way. I have since the moment I met you."

Mavlyn opened her mouth to respond, but the only thing that came out was a puff of frosted air. Quye pressed Mavlyn's hand over her heart, right between her breasts, and held it there as she closed the scant distance between them.

"Did you know," she said as their frosted breaths mingled, her face so close to Mavlyn's she could nearly taste her words, "that even though I'm the Oracle, I can't see my own future, or the futures of those who are closely connected to me?"

"I... I didn't know that." Why was Quye telling her this?

Quye's lips curved into a soft smile, none of the usual mischief on her face. "Well, now you do," she said, releasing Mavlyn's hand. Mavlyn knew she should remove her hand from Quye's chest, but she couldn't, entranced by the sensation of her heart pumping beneath her palm. Though Quye appeared far more composed, as radiant and ethereal as the spirits themselves beneath the moonlight, her heartbeat was just as erratic as Mavlyn's own.

Was it at all possible that Quye felt the same way she did?

"I usually get flashes of a person's timeline when I first meet them—a few snippets of both their past and their future," she continued, reaching up to toy with a strand of hair near Mavlyn's face. Mavlyn tried not to let herself get distracted as Quye's knuckles casually caressed her cheek, trying her best to focus on what the Oracle was saying. "But I didn't see a shadows-damned thing when I laid eyes on you that night at the festival."

"You didn't?" Mavlyn asked, bewildered. "But... but you mentioned something to me about my future." She wracked her brains, trying to remember what it was. "Something about loyalties tested, and the Traveler's Grove."

Quye shrugged. "Hunches and suggestions, in your case," she said. "But what I'm trying to say is that even though I look like I have it all together, I'm worried too, Mavlyn. I have the utmost faith that you and Leap have what it takes to do this, but he's my cousin, so I can't see his future, or yours. I don't know how this is going to end for any of us. I have to do what's right, have to go with Adara, but that doesn't mean I want to leave you. Not when we just found each other again."

The sadness in Quye's voice tugged at Mavlyn's heartstrings, yet despite their shared heartache, Mavlyn smiled. "It might be true that you can't see our future," she said, "but the fact that you can't see it means that we have one, doesn't it?"

"I... yes." Quye blinked, caught off guard. A slow smile curved her lips, and she released the strand of hair she was playing with to cup Mavlyn's cheek. "It's not every day that someone manages to out-Oracle me, you know." Her silver-blue eyes twinkled, and something else gleamed beneath that mischievous look, something that made Mavlyn's skin tingle and her blood heat. "You're something special, Mavlyn."

Mavlyn opened her mouth to respond, but Quye pressed her rose petal mouth against Mavlyn's, silencing whatever she was about to say. Twilight suffused the sky above them, and Mavlyn closed her eyes against the impending dawn, savoring that first brush of their lips. Dropping her guard, Mavlyn wrapped her arms around Quye and hugged her tight the way she'd been yearning to. A fresh winter breeze drifted through the trees, whipping at Quye's snowy curls. Her hair wrapped around the two of them like a curtain, separating them from the rest of the world for one heart-stoppingly perfect moment.

Mavlyn knew she couldn't hold on to Quye forever. And that when she let go, they would break apart to set out on their separate journeys. But she could hold this memory close to her heart and draw on its strength when things grew dark. And that was enough, at least for now.

4

Adara

The next morning, we took our leave of the ice fae, bright and early. Lord Tor was still abed, but Havor and Tamil's sisters saw us off, gifting us with an abundance of rations for the journey ahead.

"Thank you so much," I told them, embracing Havor and the girls in turn. My heart ached at the smiles on their faces, still tinged with sadness, but I resolved not to let myself be dragged down by grief. I would stay strong and focused, and bring honor to these people who, in another life, might have been my kin. "I can never repay you."

"You will when you defeat Nox and liberate our kingdom from the shadows," Havor said with confidence. "Tamil believed in you, and so do we."

"We expect to see you in our halls again," Nora added.

"And the rest of you, too," Lora agreed, her gaze sweeping over Einar, Quye, Mavlyn, and Leap. "We'll hold a great feast in your honor, and you'll tell us all the story of how you slayed the Mother of Shadows."

"I will," I promised, then turned to Mavlyn and Leap. "I feel like we were just reunited," I said, giving them a wobbly smile. "And now I'm sending you away again."

"Hey," Leap shrugged, giving me a lopsided smile. "That's the story of my life." He gave me a brief hug before making way for Mavlyn. "Don't worry about us. I'll watch over Mavlyn and keep her out of trouble until you're back."

Mavlyn snorted, a smile twitching at her lips as she moved forward to embrace me. "Take care, Adara," she murmured into my hair.

I blinked back tears as I hugged my best friend hard. "You, too." Mavlyn and Leap's task, in some ways, was the most difficult of all of ours. "Do your best, but stay safe above all else. I don't want you to martyr yourself."

The rest of us exchanged our goodbyes, and then Einar shifted. His dragon form unfurled before us, terrifying and majestic all at once, and I took a moment to admire him in all his fire-breathing glory. He was at least twenty-five feet long from snout to tail, with iridescent ruby red scales and golden spikes that ran from the crown of his head to the tip of his tail. The snow steamed around him as he settled low onto his belly, spreading his wings wide so we could use them as ramps, and he huffed at us, his fiery gold eyes gleaming with impatience to be off.

"All right, all right," I said. "We're coming."

I climbed onto Einar's back, fitting myself in the largest gap between his spikes, just in front of his wings. Quye shifted into her owl form and fluttered up to sit on my lap—we'd decided this was the best way for her to travel with us, since direct contact with Einar's scales would weaken her magic.

Einar took a running jump, launching us into the wintry

morning sky. We quickly gained altitude, and I whooped as we burst through the cloud cover and into the azure sky waiting above.

Einar let out a noise that might have been a chuckle, and Quye hooted from where she was tucked inside my fur cloak. I grinned—despite the grim journey ahead, I couldn't help feeling joy every time I rode on Einar's back. I couldn't wait until I was finally able to shift into my own dragon form. Then I would be able to fly alongside Einar, instead of on top of him.

I wondered if I would be able to fly right away, or if there was a learning curve. I hadn't asked Einar about it—like fae, dragons didn't shift until after they'd completed the Umnar, their version of the coming-of-age ritual. The same ritual that I was going to embark upon. Giant's teeth, why hadn't I taken the time to ask about it? I think I remembered him saying something about a fasting period—was it the same number of days?

And then there was the bit about tattooing yourself in your own blood...

I shuddered a little, trying to imagine the process. Einar's tattoo was beautiful—the flames swirling from his left pectoral all the way down his arm were a work of art. I had no idea how he'd managed to tattoo himself with such painstaking perfection—were all dragons naturally able to do that? Or would my tattoo come out looking like a child's scrawl? I cringed as a vision of myself needling a stick figure onto my forearm popped into my mind, and then I shook my head at the ridiculousness of it all. I wished I could speak telepathically to Einar so I could ask him about it... but I guessed I would have to wait until we made camp for the night.

It took us the better part of the day to reach the Deadlands. We had to fly across Lochanlee and over the magical barrier that the three Houses had erected with their combined power to keep the shadow creatures from leaving the Deadlands. It was a high earthen wall set with hundreds of primal stones powered by all three Houses that had to be periodically recharged, and it emitted a shimmering violet field that spread from north to south as far as the eye could see. I could feel its power even though we were still half a mile out, and the hairs on the back of my neck stood straight on end as it rippled across my skin.

Still, the barrier was meant to keep shadow creatures in, not fae out. In theory, we should be able to pass through.

Quye nestled in closer against my chest as we approached the barrier, and I braced myself, gripping the spike in front of me tightly as Einar flew straight through. The barrier crackled as we passed through it, but though bolts of violet energy sizzled around us, we passed through harmlessly onto the other side.

The moment we did, the atmosphere in the room changed. The air here was thick and heavy with shadow magic, the sky tinged a bloody red that had nothing to do with the setting sun. The landscape below us was desolate, devoid of any normal signs of life. It was a land of smoking volcanoes and cracked earth, the rivers as thin as sewing thread, the vegetation blackened and oozing darkness.

The weight of it all threatened to send me spiraling into depression, and I had to fight against the dark thoughts pressing against my mind. How in the spirits did Kiryan expect me to undo all this damage? Even if I unlocked my icefire powers, did I really have enough magic to restore Hearthfyre to its former glory?

Einar's wingbeats slowed, as if he too found the atmosphere oppressive. I could sense his dismay through the bond—it had to be ten times worse for him, seeing his homeland reduced to shadow and ash. From the history books, I knew that Hearthfyre had always been a land of mountains and magma, bursting with volcanic activity. Back before the dragons had taken over, the fire fae had traded primal stones with the other realms. In exchange, the earth fae had used their magic to help them grow crops, the water fae rains for running rivers, and the air fae winds to help keep the skies clear. That magic was imbued deeply into the land, and the dragons had enjoyed some of the benefits, though they'd still been forced to steal from the other fae lands since we'd refused to keep trading with them.

I shook my head. How foolish it all seemed now, looking back at it. Why couldn't we have figured out a way to put aside our differences and work together? Why had it all come to this?

It didn't take long for the first wave of shadow creatures to attack us—flying beasts with leathery wings and razor-sharp talons that glittered menacingly even in the hazy, ash-tinted light. I kept Quye tucked tight against me while Einar spewed great gouts of flame from his mouth and slashed at them with his own claws. Now that he was immune to shadow magic, he was free to use all the weapons at his disposal, crunching them between his fangs and impaling them upon his spiked tail as he lashed it through the air.

The shadow creatures were relentless at first, darting in and out of our range with fluid, graceful motions and raking their claws across Einar's hide. Their sharp cries echoed across the landscape as they launched themselves at us, but Einar's roars of fury were louder yet. His rage pulsed through the bond as he tore them from the sky, and it was all I could do to hold on and keep Quye safe. Unable to attack the creatures myself, I focused on pushing energy into the bond, fueling Einar so he could fight for both of us.

Eventually, the shadow creatures realized their attacks were futile, and they retreated. I could still feel their eyes on us, watching from a safe distance, and held Quye a little tighter against me. Unlike us, she was vulnerable to their magic, and I had a feeling the bastards knew it.

"Let's set down for the night," I shouted, trying to be heard above the gusts of hot wind roaring around us. Even with our combined magic, the battle had taken a toll on Einar—his wing beats had slowed, and he was struggling to maintain altitude. "There's got to be someplace around here we can find shelter."

Einar rumbled his assent, and we descended, heading for a ruin perched at the top of a cliff. We landed in the remnants of a courtyard, cracked, ash-covered stone beneath our feet, the rubble from shattered statues scattered all around us. I hopped off Einar's back so he could shift, and Quye fluttered up to land on my shoulder as I turned slowly, trying to take the place in.

"Do you know what this place is?" I asked him. It seemed to be some kind of estate, though very little of it remained. What had obviously once been a proud and imposing structure lay in ruins before us, its once-grand buildings crumbled and shattered. The main house, which I imagined had once been a towering mansion, now stood only as a shell, its roof long gone, windows shattered and empty, walls knocked down in places. The outbuildings were in similar condition, and beyond them huddled a mangled entrance gate, its once-elegant bars snarled and tangled into rusted twists.

"Yes," Einar said bitterly. I turned to see him staring at the desolate ruins, raw anguish burning in his golden eyes. "This is my family home. Or at least, what's left of it."

I sucked in a breath as pain radiated through the bond—an old wound, long scabbed over, sliced open and made fresh once more by the surrounding desolation. I knew journeying to Hearthfyre would be difficult, but I hadn't considered the emotional toll it would take on Einar.

"This estate has been in my family for generations," he said hoarsely, looking around. The garden he stood in the center of was overgrown and unkempt, choked with weeds, the fountain looming behind him cracked and dry. "My great-grandfather ran through its halls as a child, and my mother played in the fountains that used to run in our garden." He scrubbed a hand over his face, his expression drawn with grief and exhaustion. "I thought I would raise my own children here someday."

Quye hooted softly, and I took Einar's hand, pulling his attention from the ruins. Pressing a kiss to it, I pushed a wave of reassurance through the bond, wanting to ease some of his inner turmoil. There was nothing I could do to change the past, to change what my people had done to his.

The only thing I could do was create a better future. For all of us.

"I'm sorry," I murmured against his skin. "Maybe we can rebuild it together, when this is all over."

He nodded, the lines of grief in his face softening a little. "Maybe," he agreed. He looked over the top of my head, scanning the horizon, and his grip tightened around my hand. "We should find another spot to make camp. This place is too exposed—it'll be a matter of time before another group of shadow creatures attacks us if we stay here."

Einar shifted back into dragon form, and we took off again. The sun had disappeared beneath the horizon, leaving us scant light to see by, but we eventually located a mostly intact tower nestled in a mountain valley. The windows had been smashed in, a portion of the roof was missing, and the rooms were littered with rotted wood and dried out skeletons. But the floors and walls were sound, and the location made it defensible, so we worked on clearing out one of the rooms so we could lay our bedrolls on the flagstones. There was no need to light a fire— even though we were well into the winter season now, the Deadlands were stifling hot. I already regretted bringing the fur cloak, and was considering leaving it behind altogether, since I couldn't carry it in my pack.

"We need to take turns keeping watch," Einar said, stifling a yawn. He cast a longing glance at his bedroll, then shook his head. "I can take the first watch while you two rest."

"Absolutely not," I insisted. "You've been flying all day—you're exhausted. I'll take the first watch."

"I agree with Adara," Quye said. She'd transformed back into her normal form, and was currently inspecting a smudge of dirt on her tunic. "In fact, I don't think you should sit watch at all, Einar. We need you to be at full strength so you can get us to Mount Furian in one piece tomorrow. Adara and I can take turns keeping watch while you sleep."

Einar crossed his burly arms over his chest, a scowl darkening his features. "And how is that going to work?" he demanded. "You don't have any protection against shadow magic, Quye. Adara or I will have to be on call if a shadow creature attacks while you're on watch."

Quye rolled her eyes. "Just because I'm not immune to shadow magic doesn't mean I'm defenseless." She strode to the door and threw it open. "Watch this."

Exchanging uneasy glances, Einar and I followed Quye outside. She marched a good thirty yards away from the tower, then lifted her arms, tilting her face to the ashen skies. Immediately, a strong gust of wind picked up, whipping her hair out behind her. It picked up speed, gathering dust and debris as it spun around her, and when it grew tall enough to swallow her whole three times over, she flicked her hand and sent it spinning across the valley.

Einar and I watched in open-mouthed amazement as she did it three more times, until there were small tornadoes spinning all around the edges of the valley. We watched as a flock of shadow creatures approached, winging their way around the edge of the mountain, only to get swept up by one of the cyclones and flung out of the valley entirely.

Quye propped her hands on her hips as she turned to look at

us, a cocky grin on her face nearly identical to Leap's. "Well?" she called, eyes twinkling as she looked at Einar. "Any objections, Einar?"

"I... no." Einar scratched the back of his head, looking a little sheepish. "I'm sorry, Quye. I shouldn't have discounted your magical abilities."

She huffed, blowing a few stray curls away from her face as she walked back to where we were standing. "Everyone does," she said, pouting. "They think that because I'm the Oracle and I spend all my days shut up in the temple that I'm some fragile flower whose only talent lies in visions and fortune telling. But I'm still an air fae, and a Greater Fae at that. I can command the winds as well as any of my people."

"And we are grateful for it," I told her, sincerely. The idea of camping out here in the Deadlands was nerve-wracking even with my shadow magic immunity, so having a magical barrier of sorts to defend us while we were sleeping went a long way to putting me at ease.

We returned inside, where we scarfed down a cold dinner, then bedded down. Quye took the first watch while Einar and I slept. As soon as the door closed behind her, Einar stripped off his tunic and trousers. I swallowed as the shaft of dim moonlight spilling through the window shimmered across his bare skin, highlighting his tall, muscular body. He was well-proportioned, broad in the chest and shoulders, slim in the waist and hips. His thighs were nearly as thick as my waist, and I jerked my head up and away from the bulge in his underwear, fighting against the blush in my cheeks. Einar and I might have been intimate with each other, but we'd been mostly clothed on both occasions. I'd never seen so much of his bare body before, and despite how tired I was, my blood began to stir with heat.

I met Einar's gaze from across the room, finding that same heat reflected in his eyes. His mouth kicked up at the corners in a sexy little grin, but then he sighed, shaking his head. "I can't believe you're looking at me like that and I don't even have the energy to take advantage of you." He dropped his gaze to the bulge I'd been studiously avoiding, giving it a disgusted look. "Not even a peep out of him."

I laughed, the sound breaking the sexual tension like the pop of a cork. "That might be for the best," I said, pulling my own tunic over my head. I tossed it on top of his, then reached for the waistband of my leggings. "Especially since Kiryan forbade us from completing the mating bond."

"What are you doing?" Einar asked. He groaned as I pulled my leggings off and threw them to the side. "Are you trying to kill me?"

I rolled my eyes as I squatted down, pushing our bedrolls together. "Don't be so dramatic," I said, grabbing his hand and tugging him down to the floor with me. "I'm just following your example. There's no way the two of us can snuggle together in this heat if we're fully clothed."

Einar growled as I tucked myself against him, nestling my cheek against his chest and tucking my head beneath his chin. "I want to do a lot more than snuggle with you," he said, draping his arm around me.

"I know." I traced the flames swirling across his left pectoral with a fingertip, wondering how he would react if I used my tongue instead. But if I did that, we definitely wouldn't be getting any sleep. And I needed Einar to rest.

Oh, well. I'd satisfy my curiosity another time.

Sighing deeply, I tossed my leg over Einar's, then rubbed my hand in soothing circles across his abdomen. He rumbled contentedly, and I smiled as a pleasantly sleepy fog descended over my mind. I'd never cuddled like this before with anyone, yet it felt so natural, so right. Smiling, I breathed in Einar's wood-smoke and crisp, starry night scent, and allowed it to sweep me away from my troubles, if only for a few hours.

"You guys!" Quye squealed, throwing the door open with a bang. I shot up from a dead sleep, and Einar leapt to his feet, body braced for a threat. I looked wildly around the room and toward the window, searching for any kind of threat, but there was nothing out of the ordinary. "You *have* to come and see what I've found!"

She made to dash out of the room, but Einar grabbed her by the wrist, lightning-quick. "Why are you only waking us now?" he demanded, using his free hand to point toward the window. "The sun is up!"

I blinked, realizing he was right—the sky had lightened from pitch black to a depressing grey. "You never woke me for my watch," I said, scrubbing the sleep dust from my eyes. "Why?"

Quye rolled her eyes. "You guys are seriously asking me this *now*?"

"Yes!"

Her lips twitched as we yelled the word in unison, some of the annoyance disappearing from her face. "I came in to wake you for your shift a few hours ago, but the two of you looked so cute snuggled up together that I decided to let you both sleep," she said. "I spent most of the day dozing anyway, so I wasn't tired, and I can sleep on the flight again." She gave us both a gentle smile. "This was your last night together for a while. I wanted to let you two spend it together."

A lump swelled in my throat at the compassion of that gesture, and I could feel Einar's gratitude through our half-formed bond. "Well, in that case," he said gruffly, a little thrown off by Quye's admission. "Show us what you found."

"Finally!" Quye spun on her heel and flounced through the door, leaving us to follow in her wake. She must have been telling the truth about not needing any sleep—she zipped through the hall and up the winding staircase, and we had to hustle to keep up with her.

"Don't you remember thinking this room seemed weirdly small yesterday?" Quye asked as she led us into what had once been a study.

"Yes," I admitted. It was spacious enough for its purpose, the remnants of a sitting area, desk, and chairs scattered across the space, but it was about a third smaller than the other tower floors.

"Well, there's a reason for that." Quye walked over to the far wall and rapped on one of the bricks. It retreated, and the wall swung open, revealing a dusty room lined with shelves beyond.

"A hidden library?" I asked as she disappeared through the door. Einar and I followed behind her, and I sneezed as a cloud of dust invaded my nostrils. "Giant's teeth," I coughed, fanning the dust motes away from my face. "This room needs to be aired out."

"I considered that, but most of the books have already crumbled to dust, so I didn't want to risk it." She rapped on the grimy window, which had miraculously managed to survive intact. "It's only thanks to this that any of the books have survived—they're all incredibly ancient, and no one has touched them for a very long time. In fact, I strongly suspect that whoever owned this tower didn't even know about this place, Einar."

"Why do you say that?" Einar asked, rubbing beneath his nose.

"Because..." Quye extended a hand toward the small desk located just beneath the window, stirring the air there. A letter slowly lifted from the wooden surface and drifted through the air to hover before her. "This letter was written by a fire fae."

Shock ricocheted through me, and Einar and I were at Quye's side in an instant, reading the yellowed parchment over her shoulder. It was nearly translucent with age, the writing faded and in old-fashioned script.

"I have no idea what this says," Einar complained. "It's not written in the modern tongue."

"Something about a ritual, I think?" I squinted, trying to decipher the words, but my grasp of the old fae tongue was rusty at best.

Quye, fortunately, had no such limitation. "It's a letter from the fire fae king to his cousin, Enbry," she told us. "They're discussing a negotiation with the witchlings—some kind of spell that will bring them more power, but that the witchlings insisted was too dangerous to perform."

Einar shifted uneasily. "We dragons have unearthed fire fae relics and pieces of history in the past, but we tend to avoid them," he admitted.

"Are you serious?" I stared at him. "But you could have found out the truth behind what really happened to them?"

"To what purpose?" Einar asked, shrugging his shoulders, his brows knitting in frustration. "Even if we had found out the truth behind their disappearance, it's not like the rest of the fae would have absolved us of wrongdoing. They just wanted an excuse to kill us all off so they could take Hearthfyre's resources for themselves." His mouth twisted, and I could feel his bitterness seeping through the bond. "Besides, our elders insisted that the relics were cursed, and given that the fire fae were wiped off the map of Ediria, we were inclined to believe that. It didn't seem worth testing the theory."

"Well, I'd say it's worth—" Quye began, then went rigid. Her head snapped back, eyes going white, and the letter fluttered to the floor as she lost control of her magic. I shouted, grabbing at her arm, but no sooner had the fit started did her head snap back up, her body relaxing.

"Huh." She blinked.

"Huh?" Einar repeated, incredulous. "What in the blazes was that?"

"A mini vision," Quye said, casually shrugging us off. She approached one of the shelves and used her magic to carefully remove a book. The two volumes on either side of it crumbled as it slid free, but this one held up as it floated through the air toward her. "About this book. Apparently, it's important."

"A notebook?" Einar asked as Quye used her air magic to turn the pages. Like the letter, it was written in the old fae tongue, and I couldn't make out much of it. "What's in it?"

"Notes on magical experiments." Quye's brow furrowed. "A lot of the writing is faded—I'm having trouble making it out." She closed the book, then gingerly took it in her hands. "I'll need to spend some time studying it, but not now. It's time for us to make the trek."

"Right." We left the hidden library, and Quye wrapped the book in a spare shirt, then stored it in her pack for later. I wondered if the secrets contained within would help us discover the truth about the fire fae—but how would that help us now?

After all... we'd already driven the dragons from their homeland. They'd joined the ashes of the fire fae before them... and they weren't coming back.

5

Einar

S ince Quye had not only allowed us to sleep in, but also waylaid us with her discovery of that library, we were forced to hurry through breakfast. Adara climbed on my back once I'd shifted into dragon form, Quye tucked beneath her tunic in owl form. We decided to leave our fur cloaks back at the tower--Adara didn't truly need them, and with any luck, the new realm would be warm enough that Quye wouldn't either.

I took to the skies in a pensive mood, thinking about the letter and the notebook Quye had discovered. I didn't actually know if fire fae artifacts were cursed, and I wasn't a superstitious person by nature. But still, I felt uneasy carrying around that ancient notebook through Hearthfyre. How was a book about magical experiments supposed to help us? Wasn't forbidden magic the thing that had created this catastrophe in the first place? It seemed foolish to meddle in whatever the fire fae had gotten themselves into nearly three thousand years ago.

But then again, I didn't have the direct connection to the spirits that Quye did. So who was I to judge?

A calming influence trickled into my thoughts, and I realized it was coming from Adara through the bond. She clearly sensed my annoyance and was trying to use our connection to comfort me. Guilt flared inside me—my emotions were affecting her, and now that I wasn't hiding our bond anymore, I wasn't making any effort to control it. I wished we could communicate telepathically so we could talk to each other along the journey, but that wouldn't be possible until she returned and we consummated the mating bond.

So instead, I pushed the negative emotions away and turned my attention to more pleasant thoughts. The first one that came to mind was of Adara in my arms last night, her nearly naked body tangled with my own. I wished I hadn't been too exhausted to take advantage of the alone time Quye had given us. True, I couldn't make love to her without sealing the bond, but I'd been fantasizing about making her orgasm again ever since that time she'd ridden me in the training room. A rush of heat flooded my veins at the memory of her grinding against my cock, and judging by Adara's sharp intake of breath, I knew she felt it, too.

Okay, maybe this isn't the best train of thought to be taking, I told myself ruefully.

We flew most of the day again, stopping once at midday for a quick lunch break which was rudely interrupted by another shadow creature attack. I kept to the skies, flying high above the clouds to avoid the notice of shadow creatures. But despite my efforts to avoid them, the bastards seemed to be able to sense us, and we had to fight off several flocks of shadow-corrupted fire bats. I felt bad about killing the creatures—before the shadow magic genocide, I'd enjoyed flying with them, watching their playful races and mating dances. All of Hearthfyre's native fauna had been corrupted—would they all survive when Adara came back and used her icefire to reverse the corruption? Or were these species lost forever?

The sun was more than halfway to the horizon by the time we reached Mount Furian. Dipping beneath the cloud cover, a rush of memories and nostalgia filled me as the sacred volcano that had helped thousands of dragons come into their powers came into view. The volcano had been dormant for as long as we'd been here, and was nearly thirty-thousand feet—the highest peak in the land.

The sacred temple was built into the mountain's base, and it was there that we landed. Several shadow creatures lurked in the area, and I scorched them with my flames, sending them scattering. To my relief, the temple seemed mostly intact, with only a few pillars broken. I used my claws to swipe away the debris covering the entrance, then let Adara climb off my back so I could shift.

"We aren't going to fly in through the top?" she asked, releasing Quye from beneath her tunic.

I shook my head as Quye landed on the ground, then transformed back into her fae form in a flash of light. "I've grown too large to fit through the volcano opening," I explained. "There is a tunnel that leads straight into the heart of the volcano, where the portal is. But we have to go through the temple to get there."

Adara cast an uneasy glance at the temple, which had seen better days. It looked almost sinister in the dim light, its stone walls rising up like the jagged teeth of some ancient predator. The coating of volcanic ash on the exterior gave it a dull, ashen sheen, and long, twisted shadows crawled across the temple's face, making it seem almost malevolent. I had to remind myself that before the shadow creatures came, this had once been a place of learning and light. A place where dragons came into their own. A place of passion and hope and love.

"How many shadow creatures do you think we'll have to fight through to get there?" Adara asked.

"Actually, we shouldn't run into any trouble," Quye said. "The temple is sacred, which means shadow creatures can't enter. We should get inside before the ones who ran off come back with their friends."

"Right." Adara shuddered, then lifted her hand, conjuring a ball of fire. She took a step forward, but I placed a hand on her shoulder, and she paused, glancing up at me.

"Let me lead the way," I said gently. "I do know the place, after all."

She relented, snuffing out the fire so I could conjure my own. I stepped through the rusted and decayed entrance doors, holding my fireball aloft to illuminate the space. Dust and cobwebs coated the walls and ceilings, and debris littered the stone floors. The air was thick with the smell of mold and neglect, and the only sound aside from our own breaths was the faint drip of water echoing through the halls.

"Giant's teeth," Adara said as we moved deeper into the temple. Statues of fire spirits and dragons loomed all around them, their once proud and gleaming forms covered in a layer of grime so thick, you could barely make out their features. "This place needs a good dusting."

"I'll get right on that," I said dryly. "Right after I send you through the portal."

Adara laid a hand on my arm. "I'm sorry—I didn't mean it like that," she said softly. "I forgot this is a sacred place for you."

"It's all right." I let out a breath, reaching with my other hand to interlace my fingers with hers. Adara was right—this place was in desperate need of love and care. But even with the clear signs of decay, I could sense the ancient power humming within the dark stone walls. It was dormant, waiting for a priest or priestess to awaken it through prayer and devotion, but the subtle vibration sparked hope within me for the first time. "Let's get going. The tunnel is toward the back of the temple."

The trek through the tunnel was dark and oppressive, with none of the fanfare and celebration I'd experienced the first time I'd made this journey. There were no flickering torches along the walls, no drumbeats from the priests or chanting from the acolytes as we climbed the interminably long staircase, no visions dancing in my head from the sacred tea the priestess had brewed for me before she'd sent me into the heart of the volcano. There was only the sound of my heartbeat pumping in my ears, along with the hum of the mountain's magma core through the walls. On and on we climbed, until our legs burned and our lungs ached. The higher we climbed, the hotter we got, until sweat soaked our clothes and our lungs burned.

"Squalls," Quye said as the sound of the bubbling magma grew louder. An orange light appeared up ahead, signalling the end of our journey. "How do you dragons survive this? I'm being cooked alive here!"

"You're telling me," Adara panted as we emerged. A sense of déjà vu swept over me as we stepped onto the bridge that spanned the length of the volcano. It was some fifty feet long and twenty feet wide, sturdy enough to bear the weight of a dragon. "It feels like I'm evaporating."

Had it only been twenty years since Kiryan and I had stood here? Since I'd said my goodbyes to Ylena, then used my blood to seal the portal my people had used to escape?

And was I really about to open that portal again?

"Dragons are built to withstand much higher temperatures than fae," I said, trying to bring myself back to the present. "Adara might be able to tolerate this if she was in dragon form, but as you both are now, you probably wouldn't last more than thirty minutes in here."

"Well, it's a good thing it won't take you thirty minutes to open the portal then," Quye remarked, stepping past me. She walked to the center of the bridge, stopping in the exact spot the portal had been, then crouched down and placed a primal stone Kiryan had given us there. It pulsed with the light magic the Radiant had imbued it with, which would help power up the portal again. "All you have to do is spill your blood over this and recite the incantation Kiryan told us to use, and we should be good to go."

I nodded, swallowing against a sudden surge of nervous energy. "Four weeks," I said to Adara as I placed my hands on her shoulders. "We'll meet back here in four weeks' time."

"Yes," she agreed. Her voice was firm with resolve, but the emotions that surged through the bond told a different story. Eyes bright with unshed tears, she threw herself into my arms, her lips finding mine. The kiss was hard and desperate, bursting with hope and love and longing, but with the sharp, metallic bite of fear at the edges. I held Adara tight as she clung to me, and though I never wanted to let go, all too soon, she was slipping from my arms, stepping aside so I could approach the primal stone Quye had placed on the ground.

Crouching down, I drew a knife from my belt, then slashed my forearm in the exact place I'd done all those years ago to close the portal. Blood welled immediately, and I turned my arm down so it could drip onto the primal stone. It flared to life the moment the first drop hit, and I slammed my eyes shut against the burst of blinding white light.

With no time to waste, I backed a safe distance away, then recited the incantation Kiryan had made me memorize. The language was clumsy and unfamiliar on my tongue, but I must have gotten it right, because as soon as I spoke the last word, a fey wind whipped through the inside of the mountain, stirring up a cloud of volcanic ash. The three of us ducked and covered our faces against the burst of debris, but the wind whipped it away from us just as quickly as it came, forming a vortex above the primal stone. It spun faster and faster, sucking the light magic from the primal stone into it, and the portal burst open in an explosion of violet light that shook the bridge and seared our eyes.

"Hurry!" Quye shouted, grabbing Adara's hand. "We only have a few moments!"

She raced across the bridge to the portal, tugging Adara along with her. My heart lurched, and I took an unconscious step after them before I forced myself to stop. Even if I wanted to, I couldn't cross the portal with them. I was the gatekeeper, bound by blood to remain on this side for as long as I lived.

Adara gave me one last lingering look over her shoulder as Quye stepped over the threshold, her expression fierce. *I love you,* she mouthed, the portal whipping the sound of the words away before they could reach my ears.

And then the two of them were gone.

Agony exploded in my chest, driving me to my knees. The bond between Adara and me stretched nearly to the breaking point, and I threw my head back and roared, desperate for an outlet for the pain. Tears ran down my cheeks, and if I could have, I would have reached into my chest and ripped my heart out just to relieve myself from the sheer torture.

A few heartbeats later, the portal closed with a deafening thunderclap as the last of my blood evaporated from the primal stone. A heavy silence fell upon the heart of the mountain, and I braced my hands against the stone bridge, panting hard. As the seconds passed, the pain gradually receded, until it reduced from searing agony to a dull ache in the center of my chest.

My breathing evened out, and I swiped a hand across my face, mopping at the sheen of sweat there. The bond was still there, stretched thin but stabilized, and I could still sense Adara's presence on the other end. The connection wasn't strong enough for me to feel her emotions, just that she was alive, but that would have to be enough.

At least for the next four weeks.

6

Adara

Traveling through the portal was unlike anything I'd experienced before.

The violet light pouring from the vortex fractured the moment we stepped through, splintering into a thousand rainbows that scattered all around us in a dizzying display of hues. Time seemed to stretch endlessly as we passed through it, and as I stared into the strands of color, random scenes flashed by depicting foreign landscapes and creatures. Were they figments of my imagination, glimpses into other worlds, or something else entirely? I snatched at them, wanting to know more, but they scattered into fragments of light, my fingers passing through them as if they'd never been.

I had no clue how much time had passed when the portal spit us out. One moment I was staring at an image of a huge, shaggy creature with tusks, the next I was flying through the air. My breath exploded out of me as I crashed into the ground, and only the grassy cushion beneath me kept me from breaking any bones.

A thud sounded next to me, and I assumed that was Quye's body also hitting the ground. My suspicion was confirmed when she groaned, the grass rustling beneath her as she rolled. "I think I'm going to throw up," she said.

I opened my mouth to respond, but a burst of agony cut my words off. Crying out, I rolled onto my back as I clutched at my chest, the pain so intense I felt like I was being cleaved in two.

"Adara!" Quye was at my side at once, snatching up one of my hands. "It's all right," she soothed, a cooling breeze carressing my sweaty forehead as she spoke. "It's just the bond between you and Einar. You'll adjust in a minute."

The bond. That's right. Kiryan had said I would feel the strain as well once we separated, but I hadn't imagined it would be this agonizing. I pulled in deep breaths, forcing myself to relax, to breathe through the tearing sensation. Was Einar feeling this too? He had to be, but unlike me, he was all alone in that mountain. My heart ached at his absence, but as the pain faded into a dull ache, I realized I could still sense him through the bond. It was a bit like having a scrap of clothing in my pocket with his scent on it I could pull out whenever I needed comfort. The thought eased me, and I opened my eyes, looking up into Quye's worried face.

"I'm all right now," I said, releasing her hand so I could push myself up into a sitting position. "That was just... intense."

"Looked like it," Quye agreed. She got to her feet to inspect our surroundings, and I followed suit, doing a slow turn to take it all in. I'd expected the location of the portal in this world to also be in a mountain, but instead we stood atop a grassy knoll amongst a landscape of rolling hills. The elevation, though much lower than Mount Furian, nevertheless gave us a good view of the land below—miles of fertile fields, and beyond that, a big, broad river glinting beneath the sun. A small town nestled along the far side of the river, the bright blue rooftops of the buildings a welcoming sight.

"Well, this is disconcerting," Quye said. "This hill we're standing on is identical to the others. It's going to be a pain to find the exact location when it's time to return."

"That's easy enough to fix." Crouching down, I lit a small flame at my fingertip, then used it to burn a large patch of grass. I snuffed the flames out with a snap of my fingers so that it wouldn't cause a wildfire, then made a show of dusting my hands. "Not quite an x marks the spot, but it'll do."

Quye grinned. "I like it," she said, admiring my handiwork. "An x would be a little too on the nose, anyway. This is more discreet."

We made our way through the hills and toward the river, aiming for the town we'd spotted. The dull ache in my chest from the bond continued, but the excitement of setting foot in a new world and the prospect of meeting the dragons overshadowed my discomfort. This realm was different from Ediria—the sky was teal, rather than blue, and the air was more humid and carried scents of foreign vegetation. I was thankful we'd left the fur cloaks behind, and as we continued our trek, Quye and I stripped off our tunics and tucked them into our packs, wearing only our undershirts and leggings.

We kept a lookout as we descended from the hills and into the farmlands, on the alert for any predators. But the only ones we found were these tiny, biting flies that made annoying buzzing sounds and left itchy welts on our skin. I was tempted to put my tunic back on just to keep them away from my flesh, but they were easy enough to kill, and besides, the sun shining overhead was bright and hot, beating down on us with the full weight of summer.

I wondered if they had seasons here, like we did, or if the weather was the same year-round.

We passed farmers working the fields, along with beasts of burden we didn't recognize. The people here were similar in stature to fae, but with golden skin, rounded ears, and flaxen hair. They stared at us in open suspicion as we walked by, and at one point, a small beast similar to a dire wolf, but with much shorter fur raced up to us from his master's side. I yelped, nearly conjuring a fireball, but Quye dropped to her haunches, cooing at the barking beast and holding out her hand. The animal stopped to sniff her hand, then promptly licked her face and trotted back to its master, its whip-like tail wagging.

The farmer, however, was staring at us in open-mouthed shock. His face turned pale, and he dropped to his knees where he stood, pressing his forehead into the ground.

"I... why is he doing that?" I asked Quye, unnerved.

"I'm not sure," she admitted, biting her lip. "Should we check on him and make sure he's okay?"

"Absolutely not." I grabbed her hand and tugged her forward. "The last thing we need is for him to freak out even more and call for help."

We picked up the pace, putting as much distance between the farmer and his strange behavior as possible. "Are you sure you aren't part earth fae?" I asked her, thinking back to her inter- action with the wolf-like beast. How did she know it wouldn't attack her? "You've got such a way with animals."

"Well, you know how it is with the Greater Fae," Quye said. "We're always marrying into each other's Houses, though there hasn't been a marriage alliance between Ithir and Reatha in a long time. I'm pretty sure one of my great aunts was an earth fae, but I don't think that has anything to do with it. I'm good with living creatures in general, animal or fae." She shrugged.

"Well, I hope that talent extends to the people here," I

muttered as another farmer side-eyed us from a distance. He was a big, burly male holding a pitchfork, the type that wasn't afraid to use it as a weapon. "Because I have a feeling we're going to need it."

We left the fields and made it to the river, which was a welcome sight. Taking a minute, we took off our shoes and hiked up our leggings so we could wade in and splash water on our faces and arms. The cool water soothed our heated skin and the irritating bug bites, and I drew energy from the rushing current, revitalizing myself the way I had when I was fasting.

Finished, we walked along the river until we found a small house along the bank with a dock and boat floating in the water. A male was sitting on the porch, and he leaped to his feet as he saw us approach, a wary expression in his dark eyes.

"Greetings!" Quye called, giving him a friendly wave. "Would you mind helping us out? We're looking for someone to take us across the river."

The man's eyes widened, his wary expression replaced by a look of awe similar to the farmer's. He dropped to his knees and pressed his forehead to the dirt, and I realized in shock that he was genuflecting, as if we were *important*.

"No, no, no," I said, rushing to help him up. "Please, don't do that."

The man squawked as I touched him, a furious blush racing over his cheeks. Flustered, I backed away, unsure how to approach him. How were we going to talk to him if we couldn't even speak his language?

The man began babbling, and I glanced helplessly at Quye. "Do you have any idea what he's saying?" I asked, frustration bubbling inside me.

Quye cocked her head as she listened. "I'm not sure. He's talking about some kind of lizard deity, I think? Or asking if we're deities?" She preened a little at that. "I wouldn't say no to being treated like a goddess."

"A goddess?" I didn't even know what that meant. "Is that like a spirit?"

"Kind of, except more powerful, and they tend to have their own temples and followers," Quye explained. She shrugged when I stared at her, nonplussed. "The dream realm gives me glimpses into other worlds and cultures sometimes. I know a lot of weird things."

"Right." I blew out a breath, not sure how to interpret this. "Is it a good thing if they think we're goddesses?"

"Yes," Quye said cheerfully. "Unless this happens to be the type of culture where they sacrifice deities. Then we're in trouble."

I groaned. "This is really not helpful," I said, glaring at her.

The man glanced rapidly between us as we talked, wringing his hands. He probably thought he'd displeased us somehow, and I gave him a friendly smile, feeling guilty about the impression we were making.

"Look," I said, spreading my hands in what I hoped was a peaceful gesture. "We just need your help to get to the town across the river." I pointed to him, then to the boat tethered to the dock, then to the town beyond as I spoke. "We can pay you."

I pulled a coin from my pouch, hoping that even though we didn't have local money, the precious metal would still be of some value. The man's expression cleared, understanding dawning in his eyes. He shook his head violently, refusing the coin, then held up his hands in a "wait here" gesture. Quye and I shared a glance as he hurried into his house, then returned a moment later with a wide-brimmed straw hat. I sighed in relief as he led us down to the boat, helped us board, then unfurled his sail. Within seconds, we were gliding across the river, heading toward the city.

The male chattered as we set out across the river, uncaring that we couldn't understand him. He glanced back at us several times from the prow of the boat, his entire being vibrating with excitement. His enthusiasm made me uneasy— it felt like we were some exotic find or discovery, and I wondered if we'd made the right choice in trusting him. Perhaps we should have taken our chances and swam across— I could have made it easily enough, and had enough control over my water magic to help Quye across as well. She could have also flown across in a pinch, though that would have been a last resort. Quye had told me the people here might not use magic, and we didn't want to alarm them with overt displays of power.

Soon enough, the fishmonger steered his boat into the town harbor, drawing it up alongside one of the docks. The dock-worker greeted him with cheerful familiarity, but he pulled up short at the sight of us. The fishmonger spoke rapidly to him, and whatever he said must have put him at ease, because he allowed us to dock, and sent us on without a fuss.

We made to part ways with the fishmonger, but he gestured for us to follow him, refusing to take no for an answer. Discon-certed, I looked to Quye, but to my surprise, she looked delighted by whatever he'd said.

"He says he's going to take us to someone who can speak our language," she told me, her eyes sparkling. "That's got to be the dragons!"

"Or it could be a trap," I argued, but she had already started off, following the fishmonger through the harbor square. I hurried after her so I wouldn't lose them in the throng—this was a busy place full of market stalls selling mostly seafood, but also various trinkets and wares. The fishy smell mixed with the scents of sweat and people, as well as other foreign smells I didn't recognize. As we left the harbor, the fishy scent faded, replaced by the scents of strange spices and an underlying note of urine.

The buildings here were sand-colored, with spade-shaped doorways and windows bordered in geometric patterns. The roofs were tiled in the same azure as the stones that formed the city's footpaths, winding through the capital like glittering streams. We followed the fishmonger through the winding streets, past fountain squares and market stalls and other places of business. Everywhere we went, people leaned out of doors and windows to stare, but unlike the farmer, they weren't afraid to approach. We quickly attracted an entourage, and by the time the fishmonger led us into the plaza in the center of the town, hundreds of townsfolk surrounded us.

"I'm definitely going with the deity theory," Quye said with a grin as they began pressing small gifts of food, soaps, and candles into our hands. Not wanting to offend, I tried my best to smile and thank each person, but it was becoming a struggle. My arms were nearly full to bursting with items, and there was no room to even set them down so I could put them in my pack. Panic started brewing inside me at having so many strange people pressing in close, and I began turning this way and that, desperately looking for an escape.

A piercing whistle cut through the din, and the crowd quieted, the sea of heads turning away from me and toward the sound. A path opened up to reveal a tall, muscular man striding through the crowd toward us. His bald head gleamed in the sun, and his torso was bare save for a gold torque inlaid with blue gemstones that draped across his neck and chest. He wore a cream-colored garment that swished around his legs as he walked, covering him from waist to ankle, and carried a wooden staff carved with geometric symbols similar to the ones we saw on the buildings.

"I'm guessing this guy is a priest or something," I muttered to

Quye as the people bowed, the crowd rippling like a wake as he passed by.

The priest stopped a few feet in front of us and addressed the fishmonger. The male bowed deeply, then began to speak, practically tripping over his words as he pointed and gestured at us. Unlike the others, the priest didn't react at all, his expression stoic as he patiently waited for the fishmonger to finish. But something about the set of his face told me that our presence disconcerted him.

The priest said something to the fishmonger that made him smile wide, then bow again. He gently tapped his staff against the man's shoulder, and the crowd cheered. Then he turned to us, and my mouth dropped open as he addressed us in our own language.

"Welcome to the Kingdom of Palmyria," he said, his words heavily accented but completely understandable. "I am Iman, High Priest of Sobek-Ra. It must have been quite the journey to get here from your realm. What are your names, and what has brought you here?"

"I... I'm Adara," I said, scrambling for my composure. "And this is my friend, Quye. We're looking for our kin... the dragons who came here twenty years ago." Or at least I hoped it was twenty years ago. Did time pass the same in this place as it did back home? My stomach lurched as I realized I hadn't thought about that. What if we returned to the portal, but missed Einar because of the time difference? How would we get back home then? "Do you know where they are?"

"Your kin?" he repeated, his jade eyes sweeping over us. They were lined in some kind of black pigment, making them stand out even more against his tanned skin. "You don't look like kin."

"Ahh, but that means you do know them," Quye said, wagging a finger at the priest. "You're right that I'm not kin, but Adara is."

The priest cast a glance at the crowd, who were watching us with bated breath. It occurred to me that in their eyes, they were witnessing their high priest talk with living, breathing, in-the-flesh gods. This was a historic moment for them—probably the most exciting thing that had ever happened in their lives.

"Perhaps we can discuss this further in the sanctity of the temple," the priest said carefully. "With some refreshments."

"That sounds perfect," Quye chimed in. "Please lead the way, High Priest."

We followed the High Priest to the temple looming above the plaza, the crowd parting for us once more. They all bowed low as we passed, and the back of my neck prickled under the weight of their stares.

I couldn't help but be impressed as I took in the temple's facade. It was built of stone, with tall pillars carved into crocodile heads lining the entryway. The entrance was a massive archway, flanked on either side by towering obelisks. The walls were covered in intricate hieroglyphs and depictions of crocodiles, all painted in gemlike blues, greens, and golds.

"My apologies for the commotion," the priest said once we were inside. A hushed silence filled the space, and the cool, shadowy atmosphere was a welcome relief after the heat we'd endured. "As you might surmise, my people are unused to foreign visitors such as yourselves. They believe the gods have sent you to us."

I glanced sidelong at Quye, whose eyes were gleaming with suppressed amusement as we followed the priest through the hall. The torches lining the walls flickered in the dim light, casting long shadows across the floor. Each breath I took filled my nostrils with the smell of incense, and as we ventured further in, the sound of faint, rhythmic chanting reached my ears.

At the end of the hall, the priest stopped to address a temple servant. The servant bobbed his head furiously at whatever the priest told him, then bowed low before scurrying off.

"I've ordered the servants to prepare a feast to celebrate your arrival," he explained at my quizzical glance.

"That's very kind of you, but unnecessary," I said, feeling uneasy again. Unlike Quye, I wasn't comfortable with the idea of these people treating me like a deity. I might come from royalty back in my own world, and I had strange and powerful magic, but that didn't mean I wanted to be an object of worship or allow these people to become attached to me. I just wanted to get what I came here for and get home to Einar.

A wave of heartsickness hit me at the thought of Einar, but I shoved it back as the priest led us into a sitting room off the main hall. It was a small, but opulent space, fit for a high priest or visiting dignitary. I supposed Quye and I technically qualified as both. Oil lamps lit the space, illuminating the comfortable chairs and couches scattered throughout the room. They were all upholstered in rich fabrics and piled high with very inviting-looking pillows.

We'd only just sat down when two servants bustled into the room, carrying a golden tea service and a platter of fruit, bread, and dried meats. My stomach growled at the sight of the food, and it was all I could do not to snatch several pieces off the plate and stuff them in my mouth all at once.

"Please, help yourselves," the priest said once the servants had poured our tea. "I'm sure you are hungry from your travels."

"Thank you for your hospitality," Quye said as we loaded up our small plates. The servants shut the door behind them, giving us privacy. "We appreciate your kindness, especially given that we're strangers."

"Of course," the priest said. He studied us over the rim of his teacup as he sipped his drink, his dark gaze unfathomable. "Now, what is it you came here for?"

"I'm trying to find my kin, the dragons," I told him. "They have important information I need to solve a problem in my home world. Many lives depend on it. Can you tell me where they are?"

The priest lowered his teacup. "I'm afraid I can't give you that information."

"Why not?" I demanded. "You speak our language, so obviously that means you've met them."

"I am but a lowly village priest," the male demurred. The dull ache in my chest throbbed, and my fingers twitched with the urge to reach out and shake the priest until he told us what I wanted to know. "Such mysteries can only be discussed at the capital, with the head priest of Sobek-Ra Temple. You will need to travel there if you want your answers."

"How far is the capital?" Quye asked, surreptitiously nudging my twitching fingers. I realized I was clenching my teeth, and forced myself to relax.

"It's a three-day journey by camelback."

"Camelback," Quye repeated. "What's a camelback?"

The priest gave her a bemused look. "I will show you tomorrow," he said, getting to his feet and brushing the crumbs off his hands. "I have other matters to attend to, so I will leave you now. The servants will show you to your quarters when you're finished with your tea, and we can discuss the journey during the feast tonight."

"You're saying you'll help us get there?" I asked.

"Of course." The priest rose an eyebrow. "The high priest there will want to meet you. It will be my sacred duty and honor to deliver you to Kemet-Nefer."

7

Leap

The stench of rotting carcasses drifted to Leap's nostrils, yanking him from his thoughts and back to the present.

"Is everything all right?" Mavlyn asked sleepily as Leap jolted upright. They'd been flying atop Cirra for the last couple of hours, heading from the Bala Oighr to Fenwood so they could start their anti-war campaign.

Leap was more than happy to accompany Mavlyn to the earth realm. He'd never been there, and he was none too eager to return to the Gaoth Aire, not after breaking out of Angtun and then breaking in and out of Windhelm to rescue Quye. His uncle would be livid once he found out Leap had stolen his precious Oracle away, and would likely order the lightning riders to strike him down on sight.

He briefly thought of Gale, and wondered how the older rider was faring. Had Ryker punished him for helping Leap escape? Did the other riders support his decision? He wished he'd had a chance to thank Gale for helping him escape—he'd risked his career, maybe even his life, so that Leap could get away.

He would have to repay the favor someday, once this was all over.

"I smell something strange," Leap told her, still looking down. Unfortunately, all he could see were the clouds blanketing the earth below. "Cirra, take us beneath the cloud cover," he ordered.

His cloud familiar dipped beneath the cloud line, revealing a battlefield just on the outskirts of a smoking village. Mavlyn sucked in a breath beside him as they took in the blood-soaked grasslands. Hundreds of dead fae littered the burnt and torn up ground, their glassy eyes staring sightlessly as snowflakes drifted onto their lifeless faces.

"Giant's teeth," Mavlyn swore as Cirra brought them to the ground. Leap hopped off her back and helped Mavlyn down, his stomach clenching against the reek of gore and rotted flesh. Slowly, the two of them picked their way across the prairie, trying not to throw up their breakfast as they inspected the battlefield. He'd seen dead bodies before, but nothing like the carnage before him. Flies buzzed around the dead, some with arrows sticking out of their chests, while others had their guts slashed open by blade wounds. Many of the death blows had been inflicted by magic as well. Leap saw a body covered in thorny vines, another leaking watery blood from various orifices, and many others who had been crushed or frozen or trapped in the earth.

"Most of the dead are water fae," Leap said, crouching down to examine one of the bodies. It was of a lesser fae with sea green hair and patches of scales on his pale skin. He clutched a farming scythe in his cold, dead hand, and wore battered leather armor that looked like it had been worn by several generations of his family. The body next to him was an earth fae female, dressed in brand new, forest green armor with the House Ithir emblem stamped in the center of her breastplate. "Have you seen any air fae amongst the dead?"

"No." She spoke through gritted teeth, her eyes burning with angry tears. "This is General Slaugh's doing. He must have sent troops to attack this village." She kicked at a pitchfork sticking out of the ground. "They didn't even have proper weapons to fight with."

They searched the field and the village for survivors, but found only death and destruction. The earth fae had used their magic to destroy the village—there were deep cracks in the roads from where the earth had split open, and the houses and buildings had all collapsed in on broken foundations.

"What was the point of this?" Leap asked. His head spun with the senselessness of the destruction. "It's not as if this is an important village. These people could barely even defend themselves!"

Mavlyn shook her head. "This is part of Nox's plan," she said, her voice heavy with sadness. "By ordering General Slaugh to attack water fae villages unprovoked, she's hoping to force Lady Axlya to retaliate. I'm sure she plans on doing the same with the air fae too, if she can manage it."

Leap clenched his fists as he looked toward the Gaoth Aire mountains. They loomed in the distance, their shadowy peaks veiled by thick clouds. It would be snowing heavily up there now, which was a good thing, as it would make the mountain passes nearly impossible for the earth fae to traverse. But Leap knew better than to trust the snow would hold the earth fae off forever. He wished he could travel back there and warn his people.

But he already knew what would happen if he tried. The best thing he could do right now was to help Mavlyn.

Searching the battlefield one last time for any clues, they found tracks leading away from the village and into the forest. "They've headed back to Domhain then," Leap said as he traced the edge of a particularly large footprint. The prints were at least a quarter inch thick, made by heavy military boots. "Do you want to follow them, try to take them out before they do any more damage?"

He glanced up at Mavlyn to see her staring at the boot print, indecision written all over her face. Eventually, she shook her head. "We shouldn't engage if we can help it, or put ourselves in a position where we could be captured or killed. Getting back to Fenwood has to be the priority."

"All right. We'll keep going, then."

They took off on Cirra, but as the battlefield shrunk behind them in the distance, Leap couldn't help wondering if they were really doing the right thing.

8

Lord Prentis

"I cannot believe this," Lady Axlya fumed. "The audacity of General Slaugh, to come into my territory and attack my people so brazenly!"

Prentis watched his aunt as she paced back and forth in her sitting room, her pale face stark with rage. Her aura pulsed with frenetic energy, lifting her unbound hair from her shoulders so that it writhed through the air like a living creature. Prentis knew that if he looked outside right now, the garden pond would be frothing. The water features in Usciete were linked to Axlya's emotional states, and while she was usually in control, she was furious enough to raise a hurricane right now.

"We knew this might happen when Lord Oren declared he was leaving the Edirian alliance," Prentis reminded her. "We should have taken the opportunity to form a new alliance with House Ithir, and launch a joint attack on the Gaoth Aire instead."

"Yes," Lady Axlya agreed tersely. She stopped pacing for a minute to stare into the crackling fire. Outside, a chill wind rattled the panes—the first true sign of winter. "But tempers were high, and none of us were feeling particularly friendly at the time. Besides, we would have had to wait until springtime to attack the air fae. It would be suicide to attack the Gaoth Aire during blizzard season."

"True," Prentis relented. As water fae, they might be able to mitigate the actual snowstorms, but there was little they could do against the terrifyingly high winds the air fae used to shut down their mountain passes.

"Do you not have anything to add?" Lady Axlya demanded, rounding on Cascada. His cousin was sitting by the window, a wan expression on her haunted face. Prentis's gut clenched at the sight of her—she'd been found unconscious in the cellars, outside the secret entrance Adara and Einar had used to make their escape. When she'd woken, she claimed that she'd tried to stop them from escaping, but some dark entity had taken over her mind, and she had no memory of what had occurred after that.

Cascada shrugged. "I don't know why you think I'd have anything of value to add," she said. "I've been a pawn for the last twenty years, and I'm not foolish enough to think anything has changed now that I've returned home."

Lady Axlya clenched her jaw. Prentis knew she was struggling to control her temper—Cascada was her youngest and only remaining child, and aside from the fact that she'd been through quite a lot, Lady Axlya had always had a soft spot for her. But Axlya was not the type to tolerate insolence from anyone—she might be a water fae, outwardly fluid and serene, but beneath that she was driven by an iron-clad compulsion to maintain control by any means necessary.

"I will let your attitude slide for now, given that you are still recovering from your ordeal," Axlya finally said in a cool voice. "But you are my heir, and you need to start acting like it."

Cascada said nothing, merely turning her head to stare out the window. Ignoring her petulance, Axlya rounded on Prentis again. "Has there been any news from the Bala Oighr?" she demanded. "Have they responded to our request for aid?"

"No," Prentis replied. "They have sealed their borders completely, and are refusing to answer our missives. My spies report that Adara and her friends are no longer there, and that the ice fae are mourning Lady Tamil's death."

Lady Axlya shook her head. "Foolish male. General Slaugh is responsible for his daughter's death, and his response is to cower behind his ice wall rather than make the earth fae pay for their crimes. I should have him stripped of his title."

"Perhaps Lord Tor will reconsider once this initial wave of grief passes," Prentis suggested. It was too bad the ice fae were determined to remain neutral—they could really use the additional twenty-thousand troops the Bala Oighr would have supplied. "But then again, his refusal to support us likely has more to do with our treatment of Adara than anything else."

"Yes, I'm sure the ice fae were hoping that Adara would grant them their independence once she was on the throne," Axlya said. She rested her hand on the back of the armchair near the fire, a pensive expression on her angular face. "The truth is, I'm glad we are no longer backing Adara as the heir to the throne. I've never felt at ease about that decision."

"Really?" Cascada turned away from the window, suddenly interested in the discussion. "Why is that?"

"Because." Lady Axlya pursed her lips. "The ease with which she wields her fire magic reminds me too much of the fire fae."

"The fire fae?" Prentis frowned. "What do they have to do with all this?"

Axlya sighed, taking a seat in the chair. "You are both too

young to know this, but before the dragons came, there was a war raging between the fire fae and our realm. The fire fae believed we weren't paying a high enough tithe in exchange for the primal stones they supplied us, so they cut us off, which influenced our ability to trade with the earth and air realms. My grandfather told me we were in talks with the air fae about forming an alliance against them, but the dragons arrived and wiped them out before we could, solving the problem."

Prentis stared at his aunt as though seeing her for the first time. "Are you telling me that our war against the dragons had nothing to do with avenging the fire fae?"

Axlya laughed. "Of course not," she said. "The other Houses were thrilled the dragons had solved the problem! Unfortunately, my grandfather was a little too greedy, and he convinced the others to launch a full-scale attack on the dragons and wipe them out so we could take over the primal stone mines ourselves. By the time we realized dragon hide is immune to fae magic, it was too late to make peace."

"So the entire dragon-fae war was based on a lie," Cascada said flatly. She shook her head, her lower lip curling in disgust. "No wonder Ediria is in this state. The spirits are punishing us for our sins."

Axlya scowled. "The dragons have committed plenty of sins against us as well, child," she pointed out. "And anyway, they are gone now, except for that pesky Einar, so this situation is not about that." She got up from her chair and began to pace again. "We cannot let General Slaugh's attack go unanswered. If we intend to maintain our position, we must rally our own forces and beat the earth fae into submission before the winter season finishes. Once we have their forces under our control, it should be child's play to conquer the Gaoth Aire and bring Ediria under one banner again."

Cascada's face darkened, but she said nothing as she turned

back to the window. Prentis remained silent for a long moment as he mulled this over, trying to find the most tactful way to express his opinion on the matter.

"My Lady Aunt," he finally said. "I am grateful for your support, and I very much want to be the next king of Ediria. I recognize we must unite the Houses in order for that to happen, but I don't think killing thousands of earth and air fae is the answer. We cannot conquer Domhain and the Gaoth Aire without sustaining losses of our own, and given that they will not submit easily, our reign will be unstable and difficult to hold. It would be far better if we could work out a truce with Lord Oren and suggest a compromise with Lady Mossi."

Prentis thought Lady Axlya would argue, but to his surprise, she nodded. "A truce would be ideal," she admitted. "Perhaps if you agree to marry an eligible female from House Reatha, Lord Oren will be more amenable to continue the alliance. And if the two of us unite, it will be that much easier to convince Lady Mossi to stand down. But," she warned, her expression darkening, "if they reject my proposal, we must prepare for war. I will not allow General Slaugh to march across my territory unchecked."

"Agreed," Prentis said. "I will order the border patrols to be strengthened."

"Yes, and you will also prepare our troops for battle." Lady Axlya's eyes gleamed as she stared off into the distance, and something about that look made Prentis's stomach clench. "Make sure to choose a terrain where we can use our strongest weapons."

"Strongest weapons?" Cascada narrowed her eyes on her mother. "Surely you're not considering the poison rain."

"I will use whatever force is necessary to bring Lady Mossi and her impudent nephew to heel," Lady Axlya said smoothly.

She pinned Prentis with an icy stare. "Any objections, Lord Prentis?"

"I will do as you command," Prentis said, bowing his head. But even as the words came out of his mouth, he wondered just what he'd gotten himself into. He prayed that the negotiations were successful, because if they had to go to war and the Houses were prepared to use such deadly magic, he wasn't sure the kingdom would survive.

9

Adara

T hree days later

"I have to say," Quye said as we mounted up, "my ass has never been so sore in my life."

The priest—who was already astride his camel—gave Quye a scandalized look, but I just shook my head and laughed. "Riding is a great way to develop your muscles," I said as I swung my leg over my mount. Privately, I had to admit I was sore as well. It had taken me a few days to get used to the camel's odd side-to-side gait, which was very different from a horse's, not to mention its strange, lumpy back. "And no offense, Quye, but you could use some work in that department."

Quye huffed as she lifted her slender arms and pushed up her sleeves. "I have muscles," she said, flexing her pitiful biceps. When I merely raised an eyebrow, she snorted and dropped her arms back to her sides. "Fine, I don't have muscles, but who needs them when you can command the winds to do your bidding instead?"

That was a fair point, I thought to myself as we set out across the desert. Part of the reason I'd trained so hard as a warrior was because I'd never been able to use my magic. Would I have spent so much time on strength and conditioning if I'd been able to wield my powers from the get-go?

Who are you kidding? a voice in my head snarked. *If you'd been using your magic, King Aolis would have snatched you up and turned you into a child bride. You'd have been locked up in Kaipei Castle and groomed into being his puppet.*

The very thought of that fate made me shudder, and for the first time, I found myself grateful that Olette and Gelsyne had bound my powers when I was born. True, I still wished my mother would have told me the truth instead of leaving me blind to the threat hanging over my head. But at least I'd been raised by a parent who loved me and genuinely cared for my well-being, and not a mad king who only wanted to use me as a tool to maintain his shaky hold on the kingdom he'd failed.

Our journey through the desert had been fairly silent—the only person Quye and I could talk to was Hamond, the priest traveling with us. He'd been assigned to take us to Kemet-Nefer by High Priest Iman, who had informed us that though he wished he could escort us to the capital personally, he had to remain at the temple. Unfortunately, Hamond was just as tight-lipped as Iman, and since he refused to give us any information about the dragons and their whereabouts, Quye and I had decided to keep our own counsel. If they didn't trust us, that meant we couldn't trust them, either.

"Look," Hamond told us as we climbed yet another sand dune. "You will see the city when we get to the top."

We crested the sand dune, and Quye let out a low whistle as we beheld Kemet-Nefer for the first time. The city was split down the middle by a majestic river, its shimmering waters reflecting the teal sky above. In its center, a limestone palace sat, tall and proud and gleaming like a star fallen to the earth. Even from this distance, I could see the golden ornaments and gemstones that adorned the walls and towers, glittering beneath the rays of the powerful sun.

The buildings on each side of the river seemed so different, they looked like they were two separate cities. On the west side, sundried brick buildings gathered, almost blending into the sandy landscape save for the smoke rising from their chimneys. To the east, the buildings were more majestic—grand temple and pyramids decorated with precious stones and metal reaching toward the sky.

"I don't think I've ever seen such a massive city in my life," I muttered to Quye, trying not to make my astonishment too obvious.

"You could fit Wynth in there four times over," she agreed, shaking her head. "These people must procreate at a much faster rate than we fae, if they can justify having such large cities."

It took us another three hours to reach the city, and by the time we stood before the city gates, I was exhausted and struggling not to sway in my saddle. Shaking off the fatigue, I craned my neck to take in the massive gates, which were at least thirty feet tall. They were made of sandstone blocks reinforced with iron bands, and adorned with carvings of the crocodile god as well as other figures I didn't recognize, but assumed were deities. The gatehouse itself was an impressive structure, with several levels, and arrow slits for watchful archers to defend their city. Beyond, I could see the hustle and bustle of the city, hear merchants hawking their wares and animals braying, and smell the musky scents of sweat and spices.

The guards standing watch at the top of the gatehouse stared at us in open astonishment, the grips on their spears growing slack as they took in me and Quye. One of them shouted down to Hamond, who shouted back, presumably to explain who we were. The guards exchanged glances, and after a brief discussion, one of them left his post and ran off into the city.

"He is informing the temple of our arrival," Hamond explained as the remaining guards waved us through. We passed through the gates and onto a paved road, and he smirked a little as I craned my neck, twisting this way and that to take into the city. "The capital is impressive, is it not?"

I nodded, too busy taking it all in to speak. The streets were packed with people, horse-like creatures with long ears and short legs, and carts carrying goods to and from the market. We ventured deeper, following the winding roads past the clay and sandstone buildings, many of which were adorned with ornate carvings and paintings. This was a residential area, the air filled with the scents of cooking fires and incense from personal altars, but as we continued down the street into the artisan, the scents changed to wood smoke, leather and clay.

"Ooh," Quye said, her eyes sparkling as she drifted toward a jewelry store. Intricate pieces dangled behind the glass storefront, tantalizing her with their natural gems and minerals, and her gaze landed on an ornate butterfly necklace made of gold and lapis lazuli.

"Not now," I said firmly, grabbing the reins of her mount. I pulled her away from the shop before we lost Hamond, who was already five steps ahead and disappearing into the crowd. "We have a temple priest to visit."

"It's so pretty though!" Quye whined as I led her away. "Can't we just—"

I stopped in my tracks, the rest of whatever she was about to say fading away at the sight of the two well-dressed males walking along the street toward us. The shorter one looked much like everyone else we'd seen so far, with tanned skin and golden hair, but the male he was talking to stood out like an oasis in the desert. He was a good head taller than his companion, with flame colored hair that would have been unusual enough in these parts. His gaze flicked toward mine, and my breath caught as his golden eyes flew wide open at the sight of us.

There was no mistaking it—he was a dragon.

"Wait!" I cried, even as the two males walked down a side street. I yanked on the reins, pulling my camel to an unceremonious halt and causing a bit of a stir as I leaped off my mount. Hamond yelled after me, but I ignored him as I dashed down the side street and straight into a bazaar. The narrow street was full to bursting with colorful stalls, people shouting and jostling each other as they haggled, and they barely even seemed to notice me. Struggling to get through the crush, I scanned the crowds for any sign of the flame-haired man, but there was no sight of him.

I felt something brush my hip, and my hand instinctively darted toward it. My fingers latched onto a wrist, and I looked down to see a small boy staring fearfully up at me, his face pale beneath his tanned skin. He clutched a pouch in his hand—the same pouch I'd tied around my belt this morning after stuffing it with a few pieces of dried jerky.

"Keep it," I said with a sigh, releasing his hand. He darted off immediately, and I shook my head, returning to the main boulevard.

"Miss!" Hamond shouted as he caught sight of me. He and Quye were still on their mounts, and he clutched the reins of my abandoned camel in a white-knuckled fist. His expression was torn between relief and anger as I approached, thick brows drawn into a thunderous scowl. "Miss Adara, you cannot run off like that by yourself! Kemet-Nefer is not a safe place for a foreigner to walk around alone. There are pickpockets and thieves looking for targets just like you!"

"I know." I raked a hand through my hair, frustrated at the situation. "I caught one trying to steal my food earlier."

Hamond gave me a pained look, and a wave of guilt rippled through me. The priest was just trying to do his job, and I was acting like an entitled brat. "I'm sorry," I said, throwing him a bone. "This city is a very exciting place, and I got a little carried away. It won't happen again."

"Good," he said gruffly. He handed me the reins. "Stay close, and let's keep going."

Quye gave me a sidelong look as I mounted up, but I shook my head. I remained tense and alert as we continued through the city, looking for any other signs of dragons. But though there had to be more here, I didn't catch sight of any other golden-eyed denizens walking the streets.

Eventually, we reached the bridge spanning the river that connected the two halves of the city. Leaving our camels at a stable just outside, we crossed the bridge on foot. It was both beautiful and functional, with broad arches and tall pillars, and statues of gods and goddesses tucked into alcoves along its length. I could feel the power of the rushing river below, and for a heartbeat, I wished I could reach down and run a hand through the water, to feel the current and take in that divine strength.

As we crossed the bridge and into the temple city, the atmosphere shifted. The streets here were broader, the buildings taller, various depictions of gods and goddesses adoring their walls in the form of intricate carvings and murals.

The scent of burning incense was stronger here, mingling with the aromas of spices, herbs, and exotic foods from street vendors. Towering structures of various shapes, sizes, and colors dominated the area, each devoted to a different god or goddess.

The streets seemed fairly busy with priests, acolytes, citizens, and visitors going about their day, yet a sense of peace and serenity pervaded the air that wasn't present in the main city.

"What's this?" I asked as we stopped outside an inn.

"You will be staying here for the evening, as well as the duration of your visit," Hamond explained. "The High Priest has been informed of your arrival, and will call for you when he is ready to receive you. I would expect that to be tomorrow at the earliest."

"And what about you?" I asked.

He raised an eyebrow. "I am a priest," he said. "This inn is for non-clergy members only. I will stay in the temple housing with the other priests and acolytes."

With that, he led us inside the inn, which was a simple, but cozy sandstone building. The lobby had a few simple chairs and tables for guests to lounge in and sip tea, with a fountain in the corner that added a soothing, bubbly sound to the space. A friendly female innkeeper awaited us behind the reception desk, and to our relief, she spoke perfect fae. Hamond left us with her, promising he would return for us in the morning, and after taking down our information, she led us to our quarters.

"Here is your room," she said in her musical accent as she slipped a heavy brass key into the lock. She opened the wooden door to reveal a comfortable-looking room with two twin beds. The walls were painted a warm beige, the floors covered with intricately woven rugs, and the beds were made of dark wood and adorned with plush pillows and soft blankets. Gauzy white curtains covered the two windows, diffusing the warm, natural light that poured into the space, and there were also heavier curtains tied back, in case we wanted more privacy or darkness.

"Do you have any recommendations for where we might go shopping?" Quye asked, her eyes sparkling with excitement. She clearly hadn't forgotten the jewelry store from earlier. "I'd love to try some of the snacks we saw at the stalls, and also get some clothing," she added ruefully, looking down at our travel worn clothing. The high priest had given us hooded cloaks to protect us from the sun, but we really did need more suitable clothing for the weather. Not to mention, having local garments would help us blend in a bit more.

"Of course! There are several shops here on the temple grounds, as well as a few others outside the temple district that are cheaper, if you prefer."

She gave us some recommendations, and after taking a minute to unpack our meager belongings and splash some water on our tired faces, we set out. With limited funds, we decided to try one of the cheaper bazaars the receptionist had recommended, but to our dismay, the guards refused to let us back across the bridge.

"The High Priest has ordered for you to remain on the temple grounds until he meets with you," the guard explained when we demanded to know why. "For your safety."

"I see," I said, though judging by the way he stood, arms folded across his broad chest and feet planted wide as he blocked the entryway, it felt more like he was trying to protect the city from us, rather than the other way around. But then again, Hamond had warned us that Kemet-Nefer could be dangerous to foreigners, and I *had* been pickpocketed today. The citizens here didn't seem nearly as in awe of us as the villagers had, so perhaps the guards really were just trying to keep us safe.

"I still don't like it," Quye said as we walked away from the guards. "What's the point of visiting a new world if we can't go out and explore?"

"To find the dragons and convince them to help us so we can save our own world?" I suggested.

Quye rolled her eyes. "Sure. But that doesn't mean we can't have some fun while we're at it."

I sighed, worried that Quye's capricious nature was going to get us in trouble. But then again, maybe I was being a bit of a stick in the mud. I felt guilty about having fun while my friends were still fighting back home... but was there any point in feeling guilt? After all, we were stuck here until the priest could see us. There couldn't be any harm in finding some entertainment while we waited on him... right?

10

Einar

Exhausted from the day's travels, I spent the night sleeping in the heart of Mount Furian, falling into a deep, dreamless slumber and waking with the dawn. As an adult dragon, I was too large to fly out of the volcano opening, so I had to climb back down the tunnel and go through the ruined temple in order to leave.

Somehow, making the journey without Adara by my side was even worse. The hollow ache of her absence echoed with each step, and the scattered remains of my culture only served to emphasize my loneliness.

Once again, I was the last dragon in Ediria. And this time, there was no enchanted slumber to take away my pain.

On my way out of the temple, I picked up a fallen sword and scabbard I found strapped to the skeleton of one of the temple guards. I felt a little guilty as I secured the weapon at my hip, but I had a hunch I was going to need it once I stepped outside.

My hunch proved correct the moment I emerged from the temple ruins. A low growl rumbled through the air, and I leaped aside just in time as a shadow creature lunged at me from behind a fallen pillar. Howls tore through the early morning air as six others peeled away from their hiding spots and raced toward me, and I roared an answering battle cry as I ripped my sword from its scabbard. Anger surged through me, driving the first swing of my weapon, and black blood sprayed everywhere as I sliced clean through the first beast, then hacked off the head of the second one.

Once, the sight of that blood would have sent me running scared in the other direction.

But now that I was immune, I tore through the creatures, gladly unleashing all my pent-up emotion as I gave myself over to battle rage. I cut down ten of them in a matter of minutes, though not without sustaining minor cuts from their teeth and claws. The scent of my blood drew even more of the bastards, sending them swarming from the hills and straight toward me.

Eventually, I was forced to shift into half-dragon form and fly away before their sheer numbers dragged me down. The creatures howled as I took to the skies, but I didn't look back as I winged away from them. Killing them would solve nothing, and aside from that, there was a chance Adara could bring them back to their former selves once she mastered her icefire ability. If they wanted to restore Hearthfyre to its former glory, they would need to revive the natural flora and fauna that had flourished here all those decades ago.

Once I was out of danger, I shifted into full dragon form, then headed west, toward the nearest primal stone mine. Before we'd left on our journey, Quye had pulled me aside and told me to collect as many of the stones as I could. *We'll need them to defeat Nox,* she said when I'd asked her why. *At least a dozen, if you can manage it.*

I didn't know how Quye planned to charge a dozen primal stones, nor what she hoped to do with them. But she'd yet to steer us wrong before, and with so much time to kill, I needed to do *something* useful.

As I flew, my mind couldn't help but drift back to the night we spent in the tower and the secret library Quye had found. That notebook... what experiments had the fire fae been doing that led to their destruction? Was there truly a curse on the artifacts they'd left behind, and if so, who was to say that curse didn't extend to the whole of Hearthfyre? Perhaps that was why these lands were so torn by war and strife, even all these years after the fae had defeated us. Nearly every place I flew over was infested with shadow corruption. My heart grew heavy as I passed over what had once been a crop field, but was now infested with thorny, tentacle-like plants that would sooner eat me rather than nourish me, were I to make the mistake of getting too close.

As I swept my gaze across the desolate landscape, an ancient ruin caught my eye. Recognition flared inside me at the sight of headstones jutting out of the barren earth—this was a fire fae cemetery, one of the few remaining above-ground archeological sites the fire fae had left behind. With our aversion to all things fire fae, my people had always stayed well away from such sites, especially ones that housed the dead.

I knew I should continue on to the mines, but curiosity nagged at me, and I found myself banking in the cemetery's direction. Like the temple, this place was devoid of shadow creatures—it seemed this still counted as a sacred place, though it had been millennia since anyone paid homage to the dead or make offerings to the spirits. Shifting back into bi-pedal form, I drew my sword and scanned the area, on the lookout for predators.

But there was nothing here, save for the dead beneath my

feet.

A hushed, almost reverent silence hung in the air as I slowly made my way through the rows of headstones. Many of them were cracked and crumbling, most of the names inscribed into them worn away by time. A hulking mausoleum crouched in the center of it all, the names of long-dead fire fae royals inscribed on the entrance.

I wished I could talk to them, get them to spill their secrets. But though something otherworldly seemed to whisper on the winds here, I did not have the ears to hear it. I was no Oracle, able to see the future and commune with the spirits of the afterlife. I was a dragon warrior, capable only of dealing with physical realities.

I took my time wandering through the graveyard, reading what legible inscriptions I could find. From a few of the more well-preserved memorials, I gathered that many of the fire fae here had died in battles against both the water and earth fae. But what were the three races fighting over, and why? And was it not hypocritical for the fae to be angry at us for supposedly killing off the fire fae, when they were already busy murdering each other before our arrival?

Shaking my head, I took to the skies in dragon form again, this time heading for Cloudfang Manor, Hearthfyre's royal family estate. We hadn't started keeping written records until about two hundred years after our arrival, but even so, those historic records might have some clues. The royal library had the most extensive collection in all of Hearthfyre, and if the books had survived the collapse of our realm, I needed to get my hands on them.

I just hoped Cloudfang was still standing. Because if the fae had destroyed it the way they'd done my family home, that meant our history was lost forever. And we would never find out the truth.

11

Adara

With no other choice left to us, Quye and I spent the afternoon wandering the temple city's shopping district. The outfits they sold here were rather modest, with high necklines, long hems, and muted colors. Not the clothing I preferred to wear in the heat of summer. But the fabric was light and breathable, and I had to admit that with the sun beating down on us, it was best we keep as much of our skin covered as possible.

"I'm famished," Quye announced as we walked out of the shop in our new clothing. "We should go back to the inn and eat."

"I'm hungry too." I scanned the map of the grounds that the innkeeper had given us and found a building marked with a fork-and-knife symbol. "I think this place sells food. Why don't we check it out? We might meet some people who are more willing to talk to us."

The building turned out to be a canteen that served a variety of foods, all laid out on a long table set against the wall. Eager to try more of the local fare, Quye and I grabbed plates from the left end of the table, then spent the next ten minutes piling them high with grilled meats, spiced vegetables, flatbreads, tangy sauces, and spreads. The aromas were like nothing I'd ever smelled before, and my mouth watered as I looked around the canteen for a table to sit at.

"Are you going to eat all that?"

I turned to see a female staring at me, one brow raised skeptically as she studied our plates over her round spectacles. She wore plain, sand-colored robes, and had a thick book tucked under one arm while she balanced her own plate on the other. Unlike us, she'd filled it with a modest amount of food—two skewers, a salad, and a single piece of flatbread. The tips of my ears heated as I realized how ridiculous we must look.

"We're going to do our best to try," Quye said cheerfully as she wedged a piece of cake between two hunks of hard cheese. "I know we look like idiots, but we've never tried any of these foods before, so we don't know what's good."

"Oh." The girl shifted on her heels, her expression clearing. "Well, you should have asked me. I could have saved you the trouble of putting the grilled liver on your plate." She made a face as she pointed to the brown lump in the middle of my plate. "That stuff is disgusting."

I bit back a smile at that. "Can we sit with you?" I asked, glancing around to see if she was with any friends. Most of the tables were filled with people wearing similar robes to her, though there were a variety of colors. They pretended to ignore us, but even though I couldn't understand their language, I could tell we were the primary subject of conversation based on the way some of them kept sneaking glances at us. "We don't know anyone here, and we could use a friend. Or at least someone who's willing to warn us about kidney pie, and anything else we should avoid."

"Sure." The girl shrugged, then led us to her table. Her name was Nysa, and as we talked with her, we learned she was a religious scholar. Like many of the acolytes here, she'd been abandoned by parents too poor to feed or care for her, and left at one of the temples as an offering—in her case, Setros, the god of change and chaos. In exchange for housing and food, she served as a temple attendant, assisting with the ceremonies and maintaining the grounds and buildings whenever she wasn't occupied with her studies.

"So, what's the difference between you and the acolytes?" I asked, tilting my chin toward a boy across the room who was staring straight at us. His face reddened, and I hid a smile as he glanced away.

"The difference is that unlike the acolytes, Nysa here doesn't want to give her life in service to Setros," Quye said, a knowing look in her eyes. "They've probably told you that you have to take part in religious studies until you come of age, correct?"

"Yes," Nysa admitted. She pushed her spectacles up her nose and glanced at the thick tome sitting off to the right. "I do love reading, and the lore is interesting enough," she said. "But I wish they'd allow us to read non-religious texts, too. A visitor gave me a fiction novel once, about a boy who befriended a trio of benu spirits who took him on grand adventures. They taught him how to play pranks and hijinks on bullies and villains to get justice for the weak. It was such fun! But the priests confiscated it before I could finish it." Her face fell. "They said it was too frivolous and portrayed the benu inappropriately."

"That's horrible," Quye said. She patted the girl's hand and added, "I hope you show those fuddy-duddys up by leaving this place and going on your own grand adventure someday."

Nysa snorted. "I would love to," she said, and there was no

mistaking the longing in her eyes. "But I'm not sure what adventures would be accessible to a woman traveling alone. I'd have to find a husband, and he'd saddle me with so many babies I wouldn't have time for adventures." A bitter smile stretched her lips, and she shook her head. "I've resisted putting on the acolyte robes so far because there's still a stupid part of me that thinks it's possible. But I know one day I'll be forced to choose between serving Setros in his temple, or a mortal man in his bed."

She shuddered, and I glanced sidelong at Quye, curious to see her reaction. Her expression was carefully blank, and I suspected that Nysa's words struck a little too close to home. After all, as the Oracle, she'd been sequestered in the air fae temple at Wynth for most of her life. I knew from what Leap told me that she'd snuck out of the temple often, posing as a lesser fae so she could get a taste of what it was like to live amongst them, but in the end, she always had to go back. Always had to choose duty over desire.

I wondered if she'd ever been in love. As I understood it, the Oracle wasn't allowed to take a husband or bear children. I wasn't sure why that was, but it seemed unfair to me that Quye was banned from partaking in the pleasures most of us seemed to take for granted. Perhaps that was why she had such an irreverent attitude and mischievous outlook on life. Because she was trying to cope with the ivory tower life her abilities had forced her into.

Looking at Quye and Nysa's lives made me a little more grateful for my own situation. True, I was also forced into a destiny I hadn't asked for, but once I unlocked my powers and vanquished Nox and the shadow creatures, I could move on. I would live a normal life, with Einar at my side, building a life filled with adventures and babies and anything else we saw fit to enjoy.

After we finished lunch, Nysa offered to take us on a tour of the temple grounds. She led us through the wide streets and bustling squares, pointing out the various temples and structures and explaining their functions.

"Wow," Quye said, her eyes shining as Nysa led us toward a magnificent temple. The building was crafted of black marble with opaque white veins that mimicked threads of starlight, and adorned with silver accents representing various phases of the moon and other celestial bodies. "Who is this temple dedicated to?"

"Aahuti," Nysa said proudly. She gestured to the twin foxes guarding the entrance, each with crescent moons on their furry chests. "Goddess of the Moon and patron of the desert fox. She is the twin sister of Montu-Ra, the god of sun and war, and the second most powerful deity in our pantheon." A wistful look entered her eyes. "Sometimes, I wish they had given me to her temple instead of Setros," she said, so quietly I almost didn't hear it.

We made to follow Nysa inside the temple, but the sounds of children squabbling drew my attention away from the foxes. Following the commotion, I rounded a corner to see three teenage boys playing catch with a rag doll. A girl no older than ten ran between them, trying to catch the doll, but the boys were too quick, snatching it out of the air before she could reach it.

The girl screamed something at the boy, tears streaming down her round face. She jumped up and down, trying to reach the toy, but the older boy held it just out of her reach. He sneered something back at her, gesturing toward her overlarge teeth, and the girl responded with a swift kick to his shin. The boy howled, clutching his leg, and the girl reached for the toy again, but one of the other boys stepped in and yanked her by the pigtails with such force, she went sprawling to the ground.

A red haze clouded my vision, and before I even realized

what I was doing, I was across the clearing. The children shouted as I grabbed the offending boy by the back of his collar and lifted him in the air until he was eye-level with me.

"Adara!" Nysa and Quye yelled in unison. But I disregarded their warning cries as I glared at the boy clutching the doll, who glared right back from where he stood just a few feet away.

"Give the girl her doll back," I said in an even tone. His eyes widened as he took in my foreign features and strange language, and he threw the toy in my direction, then ran away, the second boy hot on his heels. The third boy raced after them the moment I dropped him, shooting fearful glances over his shoulder at me as he went.

Good. Let them be afraid. Maybe it would teach them a lesson about bullying defenseless girls.

Crouching down, I picked up the doll, then turned to face the girl. She was still sitting in the dirt, frozen in place as she stared up at me with equal parts fear and awe. A wave of sympathy swept through me—the village children had teased me in a similar fashion, yanking on my braids and stealing my toys and alienating me in every possible way.

"Here," I said, pressing the toy into her hand. She trembled a little, and I gave her a reassuring smile. "It's okay. You're safe now."

Rushing footsteps drew my attention away from the child, and I turned to see a priest round the corner on the opposite end of the temple. He was a tall, olive-skinned male with sharp cheekbones and a thick mustache, his lean body clad in a white linen kilt and a long, flowing robe of pale blue silk. His scalp was bare save for a thin black strip of hair that ran down the center of his scalp, which was braided and tied at the nape of his neck with a thin blue ribbon. He carried a staff of polished ebony topped with a silver spear that leant him an air of authority, and the simple, woven reed sandals he wore slapped ominously against the ground as he strode toward us. The three boys were with him, and they pointed at me with shaky fingers as they babbled.

"I'm pretty sure you just landed us in hot water," Quye said under her breath, coming up to stand behind me as I got to my feet.

"I'll deal with it," I muttered back.

The priest strode up to me, his heavy brows drawn into a thunderous scowl. He dragged the boy I'd grabbed behind him, who looked very much as though he was regretting the decision to tattle-tale now that he was being brought within spitting distance of me again.

"Nysa," he snapped. "Who are these strangers, and what are they doing, attacking my acolytes? This is a sacred place—there is no violence of any kind allowed here!"

"My apologies, Brother Khufu." Nysa bobbed her head, her face growing pale. "This is Adara and Quye, honored guests of High Priest Bakare. I was showing them around the temple grounds when we heard the children shouting and came to investigate."

"These boys were bullying that poor girl," I said in a hard voice, drawing the priest's ire away from Nysa and back to me. "They stole her doll, and when she tried to get them to give it back, they yanked her by the hair and threw her to the ground." I crossed my arms and leveled a glare at the priest. "I don't know about you, but where I come from, we don't allow our children to treat each other this way."

The priest narrowed his eyes, then turned to face the children. He spoke rapidly, and all four of them began to shout at once, likely hurling accusations at each other. The priest listened for all of five seconds before he shouted them into silence, then shooed all four of them into the temple. The girl shot a glance at me over her shoulder before she disappeared around the corner, and I bit my lip at the worried look in her eyes. I hope I hadn't ended up causing more trouble for her in the long run.

"Can you corroborate your friend's story?" the priest asked Nysa.

Nysa nodded. "The boys were harassing her. I would have called for you myself, but Adara does not know our ways, and she stepped in before I could stop her."

The priest frowned, but before he could say anything, a group of priests emerged from the gardens to our left. My mouth dropped open—I didn't recognize any of them, but the one in the middle wearing long, golden robes embroidered with the image of a reptilian beast, was clearly a dragon. His orange-gold eyes widened in alarm as he caught sight of us, but I hardly noticed as I rushed toward him, the priest and the children forgotten.

"Finally, a dragon!" I crowed, stopping just short of him. "Please, where is the Princess Ylena? I must speak with her!"

"Princess Ylena?" The dragon bared his teeth, hatred gleaming in his eyes. "What is the meaning of this?" he demanded, rounding on the priest I'd been speaking with. "Why have you allowed our enemies access to sacred grounds?"

"The enemy?" the priest echoed, shocked.

"But aren't they from your world?" Nysa protested, confusion stamped over her pretty features. "They speak your sacred language!"

"They may speak our language, but they are not my people." The dragon jabbed a clawed fingernail at me and Quye, fangs glinting in the sunlight. "These two are enemies of Sobek-Ra, and must be put to death. Guards, kill them!"

12

Mavlyn

"A re you sure you're going to be okay on your own?" Leap asked.

Mavlyn tucked a strand of auburn hair behind her ear as she surveyed Fenwood from atop Cirra, Leap's cloud familiar. They'd arrived with the dawning sun, and the villagers were stirring, tending their gardens, drawing fresh water from the village well, exchanging the usual greetings with their neighbors.

She'd never seen it from above before, and after zooming all over Ediria, it hit her just how small her childhood home was. Compared to Wynth and Angtun and Kaipei, it was just a tiny blip on the radar. It would take a lot more than convincing the residents of Fenwood to stand against Nox if she wanted to make a real difference... but she had to start somewhere.

"I'll be fine," she said to Leap, giving him what she hoped was a reassuring smile. "I grew up here—these people are my neighbors, my friends." She scanned the village again, looking for anything out of the ordinary, but the only difference she noted was the plot of land where Gelsyne and Adara's house had once stood. The villagers had razed the house, removing all traces of it. Sadness welled inside her at how easily they'd ripped out her friend's childhood roots, as if she'd never existed, never frolicked through their woods or trained with their warriors or played with their children.

The fae here might very well be her neighbors, as she'd told Leap, but were they truly still her friends? Could she trust people who turned their backs on one of their own as easily as Fenwood's residents turned on Adara?

"Okay." Leap searched Mavlyn's face, then surprised her by throwing his arms around her midsection in a tight hug. "Don't do anything dumb when I'm gone."

Laughing, she ruffled his spiky hair. "I'll be on my best behavior."

"All right." He twirled his finger, and an icy air current swirled around them. "I'm going to have the wind take you down so they don't spot me. Just hop off and it'll do the rest."

"Umm." Mavlyn peered over Cirra's scalloped, golden rim and peered down at the several-thousand-foot drop. "Can't you just drop me off at the lake or something?"

Leap snorted. "I could, but this is faster. Come on, Mavlyn, don't be a baby. I won't let anything happen to you."

Mavlyn glared at Leap, but she did as he said, getting to her feet and standing at the edge. She hesitated, but just as she was considering taking a step back, Cirra bounced, pitching her forward. Mavlyn swallowed a shriek as she pinwheeled through the air, but a second later, the wind current whipped around her, slowing her fall from a sharp plummet to a gentle descent.

Leap's laughter drifted to her on the air, and she glared up at Cirra, biting back a string of curses. She wasn't sure if Leap had ordered his cloud familiar to push her off, or if she'd done it of her own free will—both were equally possible. She'd learned from the time she'd spent traveling with Leap that though Cirra mostly followed his orders, she still had a mind and will of her own.

She sighed in relief as her boots touched down on the bare earth, just on the outskirts of the village, with the forest at her back. Glancing up, she caught sight of Leap waving down at her, and she lifted her hand and made a rude gesture. He grinned, and then he and Cirra jetted off, back to the battlefield they'd stumbled upon the other day. They'd decided his time would be better spent tracking General Slaugh's soldiers, and that he would meet back up with her here once he'd found where they'd gone.

Squaring her shoulders, Mavlyn set off along the path, heading into the village. Her boots crunched against the fine dusting of snow that covered the ground and frosted the rooftops. Smoke billowed from the chimneys, and the familiar scent of burning cedarwood calmed her a little. The villagers paid her little mind—she'd chosen to wear the hood of her cloak up, so that she wouldn't draw too much attention from the villagers. She wanted to speak to her parents before she talked to anyone else.

Taking a deep breath, she stepped onto her porch and lifted a hand to knock on the front door. But before her knuckles could make contact, the door swung open.

"Mavlyn!" her mother cried, her face lit with joy and relief. Tears sprang to Mavlyn's eyes as they embraced, and her hood fell away from her face. "Kaid, our daughter is home!"

Footsteps thundered from inside the house, and Mavlyn lifted her head to see her father appear in the doorway. Her stomach clenched at the tightly wound expression on his face— his jaw was clenched, his brows drawn together, his mouth a thin line.

But when Mavlyn's mother stepped back, he didn't hesitate to draw her against his broad chest in a crushing embrace. "Welcome back," he said gruffly. "I'm glad to see you made it home in one piece."

They ushered Mavlyn inside and set her down at the kitchen table, demanding to hear a full account of everything that had transpired. Mavlyn's mother fussed over her the entire time, tucking a strand of hair away from her face, adjusting her collar, repeatedly refilling her mug of tea even though Mavlyn was only taking tiny sips of the hot liquid. In contrast, her father was still as stone, sitting in the chair across from her with his brows drawn and his massive arms crossed as he listened to her tale.

"You're lucky to be alive," he finally said, shaking his head. His auburn ponytail swung with the motion, and a ray of winter sunshine glinted off the single silver ring in his left earlobe—a ring he'd forged himself, just like he'd forged every other metal tool and decoration in this house. "Very, very lucky."

"Kaid!" Mavlyn's mother snapped. She placed a supportive hand on Mavlyn's shoulder as she leveled a glare at her husband. "Is that really all you have to say?"

"Do you want me to applaud our daughter for leaving without our permission?" Mavlyn's father demanded. "For dropping out of university to help a wanted fugitive, then falling in with two *more* fugitives and engaging in acts of rebellion against the crown?"

"Fugitives?" Mavlyn echoed, clenching her hands beneath the table. She knew her father hadn't been pleased about her decision to go after Adara, but she hadn't thought his enmity ran this deep. "Father, you watched Adara and I grow up together. She's not a criminal, and you know it."

"It isn't my place to decide whether she's a criminal," her father said. "Just as it isn't my place to stand against the crown." He shook his head. "Do you have any idea what it's been like here since you've been gone? General Slaugh garrisoned a few of his shadow guard here to patrol the village in case you or Adara came back. Those cruel bastards made our lives miserable, setting unreasonable curfews, conducting frequent searches of our homes unannounced, and fining us for even the smallest infractions. People tried to speak out, but that ended after the soldiers started dragging dissenters into the square and whipping them."

"That's horrible!" Mavlyn sat back in her chair, aghast at the cruelty her father described. "Where are those soldiers now?"

"They were recalled after Adara killed King Aolis," he said. "The only good thing to come out of that."

"How can you say that?" Mavlyn's mother argued. "Didn't you hear what Mavlyn said? King Aolis was responsible for the shadow magic infection that has been spreading through our lands. He couldn't be allowed to continue to rule!"

"And what now?" Mavlyn's father demanded. He slammed a fist against the wooden table, and the mugs jumped from the force of the blow. "King Aolis might be gone, but rumor has it Lord Oren is threatening to withdraw the Gaoth Aire from the Edirian alliance, and both House Usciete and Ithir are preparing to attack. Just this past week, we had recruiters banging on our doors, looking for more of our children to enlist!"

"They were doing that anyway!" Mother argued. "That was how all this trouble started in the first place—how General Slaugh found Adara!"

The two of them fell silent, glowering at each other over their daughter's auburn head. Mavlyn shifted in her chair, not sure how to break the stalemate. She'd never heard her parents fight like this—they had squabbles, of course, just like any other couple, but even then, they rarely raised their voices when they fought.

Eventually, Mavlyn's father broke the staring contest and

turned to Mavlyn with a sigh. "So what is your plan, now that you're back? You can't return to university—you're a known ally of Adara's, and Lady Mossi will likely have you arrested if she gets wind of your presence."

"The headman also isn't your biggest fan right now," Mavlyn's mother admitted. "I'm not entirely sure he won't send word to Mossi once he finds out you're here."

Mavlyn's heart sank, and she struggled not to let the trepidation she felt show on her face. "I didn't come here because I wanted to return to university, or to my old life," she told them. "I came here because I need your help."

Her father scowled. "Help with what? More sedition?" He shook his head. "If you think—"

"If I think what?" Mavlyn snapped, her temper boiling to the surface. "I don't know what's gotten into you, Father, but you're a fool if you think sticking your head in the sand is going to solve anything. Yes, Adara created a power vacuum when she killed King Aolis, but Aolis was covering up a gaping wound in the heart of our kingdom, a wound that needs to be healed if we expect to survive. The rest of the country might think that shadow magic has disappeared, but I know better. The Shadow that possessed King Aolis is still at large, and if we don't stop her, she's going to bring other demons here and destroy everything!"

Mavlyn's parents exchanged glances. "Sweetheart," her mother said, taking Mavlyn's hand in hers. "We understand you want to do something. But what can we hope to accomplish against Lady Mossi and this Nox demon?"

"I'll tell you," Mavlyn said, straightening her shoulders and doing her best to sound authoritative. "But first, I need you to talk to the headman and convince him to call a meeting. This is something everyone needs to hear."

Her parents did as she asked, visiting the village headman and asking him to set up a meeting in the village square. The three of them agreed not to tell him that Mavlyn would be the one speaking, and the next evening, she stood behind her father with her hood up, trying not to wring her hands as he addressed the crowd.

"My fellow villagers," he said, raising his hands. "I've asked the headman to bring you all together to discuss the impending civil war, and what we can do to protect our village and our families."

Murmurs swept through the crowd, villagers exchanging worried glances. "Impending civil war?" one of them shouted. "I thought that was just a rumor. No one has declared war, have they?"

"Not yet," another person piped up. "But we all know it's been coming since General Slaugh announced his candidacy for the throne."

"What can we do about it, though?" A female asked, clutching her two-year-old against her chest. The child squirmed against his mother's fearful grip, but she was heedless of his protest, her eyes wide and anxious. "Fenwood is far from the borders—it's not as if we're going to see much fighting, are we?"

Mavlyn's father cleared his throat. "To be honest, I am not the expert on this situation. That's why I brought someone else to speak to you who is."

He moved aside, and Mavlyn stepped forward to address the villagers. The crowd gasped as she pulled her hood back, revealing her face, and Mavlyn fought against the urge to shy away from their shocked stares.

"You!" the headman jabbed a finger at Mavlyn, his eyes bulging with anger. He swiveled his gaze in her father's direction. "You didn't tell me your wayward daughter would be the one speaking to us today," he growled.

"Our wayward daughter has a name," Mavlyn's mother called. She was standing in the crowd as well, just a few feet away from the headman. "It's Mavlyn, and seeing as how she's the only one of us who's seen what transpired firsthand, I think you'd be wise to let her speak, Headman."

The headman pursed his lips, but said nothing, and the crowd quieted, waiting with bated breath for Mavlyn to address them. A wave of nausea swept over her, and she cursed herself for her weakness. After all the dangerous escapades she'd been through—breaking into sacred temples and fortresses, facing off against thieves and soldiers, *this* was the thing threatening to bring her to her knees? Addressing her peers, the very people she'd grown up with?

No. She would not let these people intimidate her. Not when she'd already come so far.

"Citizens of Fenwood," she said, addressing them in a firm voice. "I've asked my father to gather you here today because you deserve to know the truth about what's happening in our kingdom. As lesser fae, the Houses that rule over us keep us in the dark, giving us only the barest pieces of information while they demand our loyalty and our coin. It's time for us to change that, to arm ourselves with information and make our own decisions, instead of being told what to think and how to act."

Many of the villagers stared at Mavlyn with skepticism, but a few were nodding their heads in agreement. Taking heart, Mavlyn forged on.

"You all remember the day that General Slaugh came to our

village and kidnapped Chaya." She decided not to rehash Adara's own narrow capture, or the fact that half the villagers had tried to assist in it. "His target was Adara, because although she was raised as Chaya's daughter, her parents were of royal blood. She is the daughter of the late Princess Olette, and the late Prince Daryan."

The village square erupted into a cacophony of shouts. Myriad emotions flickered over the villagers' faces—outrage, surprise, disbelief, comprehension. Some of them refused to believe it, while to others, it made far more sense that the child who'd never been able to use a drop of earth fae magic but could suddenly wield fire was secretly the child of a dragon.

"Is that why she was with a dragon that day?" someone shouted.

"Where did he even come from?" another asked. "King Aolis said all the dragons were dead!"

"There isn't time to explain all that!" Mavlyn shouted, trying to get the meeting back on track. "The dragon is Adara's protector, but where he came from isn't important. What is important for you to know is that Adara is a child of prophecy, foretold to have the power to end the shadow magic infection in Ediria and return our kingdom to its former glory. That's why King Aolis ordered General Slaugh to take her—he wanted to use her powers for himself."

She went on to explain the truth—that Aolis himself was the cause behind the shadow magic infection, and that he'd had a Shadow inside him who'd given him his power. The audience listened intently as she told them about how they'd stormed Kaipei Castle and used Adara's fire magic to kill Aolis, but unwittingly released the demon in the process who was now possessing Gelsyne and using her magic to influence General Slaugh and the Houses and their rulers.

"Nox's ultimate goal is to get us all to fight each other—

earth fae killing water fae, water fae killing air fae, and so on, until the earth is soaked with the blood of all three races and the air is poisoned with darkness," Mavlyn continued. "She's already nearly gotten what she wants—the air fae are threatening to withdraw from the kingdom, and Lady Axlya and Lady Mossi are both fighting over the throne. It won't take much to push them over the edge, and if that happens, Nox will use the dark energies we create to summon more Shadows."

Mavlyn took a deep breath, and then said, "The only way we can stop Nox from winning is to refuse to fight our fellow countrymen. To resist Lady Mossi and General Slaugh's call-to-arms, and do everything we can to sabotage the war effort."

The crowd exchanged doubtful and low murmurs at this. "You're asking us all to become rebels?" the headman asked, incredulous. "To go against the crown?"

"There is no crown right now," Mavlyn reminded him. "And while Lady Mossi would have you believe we are fighting to install General Slaugh as the next king, the truth is far more sinister. If we fight, it won't be for the glory of Domhain. We'll only be ushering in an era of darkness!"

"This is ridiculous," one of the elders protested. "If what you're saying is true, then why has all the shadow taint disappeared?"

"Yeah," someone else chimed in. "Shouldn't it be spreading even faster if this Shadow is on the loose?"

"That's not—" Mavlyn started, but the crowd was arguing amongst themselves now, their shouts drowning her out. "Please," she said desperately, addressing the headman. "You've already lost one of your sons thanks to Nox and her machinations. Are you going to allow Lady Mossi to sacrifice even more of us?"

"Lost one of my sons?" the headman barked. His face grew

pale beneath his dark complexion, and his wife clutched at his arm. "What do you mean by that?"

Sweat broke out along the back of Mavlyn's neck. It hadn't occurred to her that news of Dune's death hadn't reached the village yet, or that she would have to be the one to break it to him.

"I'm sorry, Headman Terran," she said quietly. "But Dune was killed in battle."

A heavy silence fell upon the square, and Mavlyn wished she could make the earth swallow her whole. "Killed?" Dina, the headman's wife, echoed. "How?"

"I..." Mavlyn swallowed hard. Radiants, how was she supposed to tell them? "Nox turned him into one of her minions and ordered him to assassinate Adara. He failed."

"Are you saying," the headman said in a low, deadly voice, "that Adara killed my son???"

"It was self-defense," Mavlyn tried to say, but the crowd was shouting again, and the headman took a step toward her, his fist raised.

"You dare ask us to support Adara when she's brought nothing but trouble to this village?" he roared, eyes bulging. He whirled to face the villagers, flinging his hand in my direction as he shouted, "This child claims Shadows have corrupted Lady Mossi and General Slaugh, yet she is the one who is addled! She is asking us to help a murderer, a bloodthirsty monster who not only assassinated our king, but killed my son in cold-blood!"

The crowd roared their agreement, and Mavlyn's heart jumped into her throat as they surged forward. "Throw her in the gaol!" someone shouted, reaching for her arm.

"Back off!" Mavlyn's father snarled. He jumped in front of her and shoved the male away, but the crowd kept coming, grabbing him and pulling him down to get to her. Mavlyn backpedalled, frantically searching for a way out, but the exits leading away from the square were blocked. She reached for one of her pouches, heart sinking at the thought of having to fight when that was the opposite of what she'd been preaching...

A thunderclap shook the sky, and the crowd screamed as electricity sizzled through the air. The hair on Mavlyn's arms stood straight on end, and she look up to see Leap whizzing through the air toward her on Cirra's back.

"Come on!" he shouted, leaning forward with an arm outstretched. The crowd tried to grab her, but he summoned a powerful gust of wind, knocking the ones closest to Mavlyn to the ground. Heart hammering, she leaped forward and grabbed his arm as he swooped in. Someone tried to grab her leg, but they were yanked away, and she looked back to see her father pulling her attacker down to the ground. His eyes blazed as they met hers, and she held them for a split second before Leap hauled her onto the cloud and whisked them away from the village.

"Are you all right?" Leap asked as she stared at the receding village. She tried to get one last glimpse of her parents, tried to see if they were okay, but tears blurred her vision, making it impossible. "What happened?"

Mavlyn shook her head, swiping angrily at her tears. "I was an idiot, that's what happened."

She waited for Leap to make some sarcastic quip, to tell her he'd warned her not to be dumb, but to her surprise, he gave her a sympathetic look. "We knew this wasn't going to be a walk in the park," he told her. "I had a hunch the villagers might not be receptive to you, so I decided to come check on you instead of waiting by the lake like we agreed on."

"Well, I'm glad you did," Mavlyn said, unable to keep the bitterness out of her voice. "If you hadn't, I'd probably be rotting in the gaol right now." Guilt twisted like a knife in Mavlyn's chest, and she swiped more tears from her face. "Instead, it's my parents who are going to suffer that fate instead."

Mavlyn told Leap what had transpired, and he shook his head when she'd finished. "It didn't sound like the Headman was going to side with you anyway, even if you hadn't mentioned Dune," he said. "He was already pissed at Adara, and the news that she killed his son was just the nail in the coffin. He just doesn't realize it's his own casket he's nailing shut." Leap shrugged. "You can't fix stupid."

Mavlyn laughed a little at that, but her heart was still heavy as she glanced back at Fenwood. It was a mere speck in the distance now, and she felt removed from it in more ways than one. Her time in the outside world had changed her, and while she was sad that the villagers had turned against her, she wasn't sure she wanted to fit in there anymore. For the first time, Mavlyn understood how Adara must have felt, growing up in a community where everyone made her feel like an outsider.

It only made her even angrier on Adara's behalf.

"Were you able to track the soldiers?" Mavlyn asked, desperate to change the subject.

Leap nodded. "They went to Talamh. I was going to ask if you also wanted to go, and see if we can drum up some support there. It'll be more dangerous... but I think we'll find more people willing to listen in the bigger cities."

"It's worth a shot," Mavlyn agreed, latching onto the idea. She couldn't give up now—not when Quye had put her faith in them to stall the war effort for as long as possible to give Adara the chance to succeed. They would have to use disguises, or Lady Mossi would catch them, but it was better than not doing anything else. And if they couldn't convince the people to help, maybe they could at least sabotage the troops. After all, if the soldiers couldn't fight, that meant they couldn't make war. Right?

13

Adara

"Now wait just a damn minute!" I yelled as the temple guards peeled themselves from their posts in the garden and along the temple walls, steel ringing through the air as they drew their swords. "We're not the enemy! I'm one of you!"

"One of us?" the dragon sneered. "Don't make me laugh. You're a fae! How could you be one of us?"

Quye swept a hand wide and spun in a circle, knocking back the guards before they could reach us. Unfortunately, she knocked the priests over as well, and they all landed in a heap of tangled limbs. Knowing I only had seconds before the dragon unleashed his rage on us, I drew a circle in the air and snapped my fingers. A ring of fire sprang up around the group, and they began shouting frantically, scurrying as close as they could to the center to get away from the rising tongues of flame.

"Fire magic?" the dragon stared at me through the flames, his face slack with shock. A few seconds passed before he remembered himself, and then he banished the ring of fire with an angry flick of his hand. "That's impossible. You're a water fae!"

"I am," I agreed, igniting another flame in the palm of my hand. I casually bounced it from one hand to the other, watching his face for any reaction. "But I'm also the daughter of Prince Daryan, which makes me half-dragon. And therefore, makes me one of you."

The dragon's eyes narrowed as he got to his feet. "Stand down," he told the guards, and they reluctantly sheathed their swords. He crossed the distance between us until we were mere inches apart, and I tried not to betray my nerves as he studied me closely.

"You don't bear much resemblance to Daryan," he finally said.

"Maybe not," I agreed, pushing the sleeve of my dress up to reveal the golden cuff clasped to my bicep. The dragon sucked in a breath as the red primal stone set in the center glinted in the afternoon sunlight, and I resisted the urge to give him a smug smile. "But I think you'll recognize this."

"I don't believe this," the dragon snarled. He tried to snatch the cuff from my bicep, but I jumped back, out of his reach. "You must have stolen that cuff somehow, along with the fire magic inside it. Guards!" he yelled again.

"Stop!" a feminine voice cried, and the guards came to a halt. A hushed silence fell as a priestess stepped out of the moon goddess temple, and my breath caught as I took her in. She was the most regal female I'd ever seen, with deep, piercing silver eyes, elegant features, and power that radiated from the crown of her midnight hair to the tips of her violet-painted toenails. She wore a flowing robe that seemed spun from moonlight, embroidered with intricate silver embroidery depicting the moon in all its phases, and around her neck hung a crescent moonstone pendant.

"That's Anuket," Nysa hissed in my ear. "High Priestess of Aahuti!"

"These two may not be children of the Sobek-Ra," the high priestess said in her melodious voice, "but they are clearly powerful in their own right. We dare not risk offending the god or goddess they serve. I will take them into my custody and question them beneath the light of the moon goddess, so that I may discern the truth."

"This is preposterous!" the dragon spluttered. "These two aren't servants of the moon goddess, they are—"

He cut himself off, as if realizing he had said too much. The other priests stared at him expectantly, but he clenched his jaw and shook his head. "There will be a reckoning for this," he warned the moon goddess priestess. "You should hand these two over to the Cult of Sobek, before it's too late."

"My goddess will protect me," the priestess said coolly. "And as you are currently on her temple grounds, you have no authority here. Please leave at once."

Cursing under his breath, the dragon stalked away, but not before leveling me with a malevolent glare that threatened to singe the hair on my exposed arm. Hastily, I yanked my sleeve back down, covering the golden cuff he'd tried to rip off me moments ago. The other priests reluctantly dispersed as well, but I knew they'd come sniffing for information later, once the priestess had finished speaking to us.

"Come," she told us, then turned away in a swirl of silvery-white robes. Her long hair rippled in glossy waves behind her as she walked toward the temple. "You may take shelter in here until nightfall."

Nysa, unfortunately, could not accompany us, so we said farewell to her, then followed the priestess past the twin foxes guarding the entrance and into the temple. The air inside was cool and musty and quiet, the only sound the soft whisper of the priestess's sandals on the floor as she glided ahead of us. We walked past rows of statues of the moon goddess, some seated, some standing, some with outstretched arms, while others held objects like the moon, the stars, or the desert fox.

But none of these compared to the statue rising from the center of the temple, a fifteen-foot tall depiction of Aahuti in gleaming white marble. Her serene face was tilted skyward, her arms spread wide in welcome, offerings of flowers and candles gathered at her feet. I followed her gaze to the massive oculus set into the center of the ceiling. The oculus was fitted with a glass window, and there was a tarp draped over it to shield the temple from the harsh sunlight. But I imagined that when the acolytes removed it at night, moonlight would bathe the goddess's face.

As we walked, I noticed various rectangular doorways were set at intervals along the hall, leading to prayer and meditation rooms. Between these doorways were colorful murals depicting scenes from the moon goddess's mythology.

"This is a beautiful place of worship," Quye told the priestess, her tone filled with a reverence I'd never heard from her. Her silvery eyes, similar to the priestess's own irises, sparkled as she took in a mural of the moon goddess holding back the tide of chaos with a crescent-shaped shield. "Thank you for giving us sanctuary."

"You are more than welcome." The priestess smiled, turning to look at Quye over her shoulder. "If I didn't know better, I would think you were a child of Aahuti yourself."

Quye grinned. "I'm a child of air, not night. But I appreciate the compliment."

The high priestess handed us off to a temple attendant, a tiny female called Tuya. "Unfortunately, I cannot allow you to roam through the temple at this time," she told us, "So I will leave you in Tuya's care. She will attend to your needs and ensure you are kept safe."

I wanted to balk at that, but really, what choice did we have? I wasn't certain about Anuket's motives, but at least she wasn't trying to kill us. "Thank you," I said instead. "We appreciate your hospitality."

The high priestess left us in a swirl of silvery robes, and the temple attendant led us to a salon off the main hall. The salon was inviting enough, but the guard posted outside the door reminded me we were not honored guests. He was there as much to prevent us from leaving as he was to keep us safe.

"Well, this is a mess," Quye said as she reclined on one of the couches. At least our prison was a comfortable one, and the temple attendant had provided us with tea and snacks. "It looks like the dragons who moved here are now affiliated with the Cult of Sobek, and they're not at all keen on helping us."

"Well, we knew we'd meet some resistance," I said, sipping on my tea. It was hot and fragrant, but I hardly noticed the flavor, too preoccupied with my nerves. "The dragons fled Ediria to escape the fae, yet here two of us are, looking for them. It's only natural for them to be suspicious."

"Yes," Quye agreed, "but there was something off about that dragon in his fancy gold robes. He was afraid of us, yes, but he was also hiding something, something he didn't want the priests to find out. I wonder if our presence is threatening to expose whatever this secret is, and that's the real reason he tried to have us killed on sight."

"Well, that's disturbing." I wracked my brains, trying to think what that might be, but I couldn't come up with anything tangible. "I wish Nysa had given us more information about the Crocodile God and his followers."

We speculated on it for another hour or so, but eventually lapsed into a drowsy silence. I wasn't sure when I dozed off, but when a temple attendant came in and woke us, the room was completely dark.

"Come," she said in clumsy fae. "The High Priestess will see you now."

Quye and I straightened our rumpled clothing and fixed our hair as best we could, then followed the attendant out of the room. We expected her to lead us down to the main temple floor, but instead, we followed her up a flight of stairs and into a dome at the very top of the temple. My eyes were immediately drawn to the oculus in the center of the dome, which gave us a perfect view of the moon hanging in the sky. Rays of moonlight poured in through the circle, illuminating the entire room.

"Greetings," the high priestess said. She stood directly behind the shaft of moonlight that fell through the oculus, her silvery robes rippling in the gentle breeze. "Please, step into the light."

We did as she asked, though my steps were hesitant as we crossed the smooth marble floor and stepped into the shaft of moonlight. The moment we did, power rippled over my skin, sending a frisson of energy down my spine. I was struck by the eerie sensation that I was being watched, but when I glanced above me, toward the source of the feeling, I saw nothing but the waxing moon shining above us.

"You are standing in the Eye of Aahuti," the high priestess explained to us. I glanced down to realize I was standing on the glass disc I'd seen from the lower level earlier, directly above the massive statue of the goddess. From a distance it appeared to be a clear pane, but now that I was standing on it, I could see the hieroglyphs etched into its surface. "The goddess's watchful gaze protects you from outside influence, but it also compels you to speak the truth. You must answer my questions truthfully while you stand in the eye. To do otherwise is a sign of disrespect to the goddess and will incur her wrath. Do you understand?"

I snapped my gaze back up to the priestess. "Yes," Quye and I said in unison, the word compelled from me almost without thought. My stomach clenched—I'd been interrogated before, but never like this, and though I had no idea if this Aahuti was real, the power humming in the air around me definitely was.

"Good," Anuket said. She studied us for a beat, then said, "I am High Priestess Anuket, devoted servant of Aahuti and guardian of this temple. Tell me your names, and what brings you to our realm."

"I am Adara, daughter of dragons and fae," I told her. "My companion is Quye, a fae and a powerful seer. She is very well respected in our realm for her ability to listen to the winds and see the future, and she has the power to commune with both the dream and the spirit realms as well."

"I see." The high priestess's elegant brows rose as she studied the Oracle. "That is a very impressive talent. Do you also have the ability to walk between the physical realms?"

Quye shook her head. "Not normally. We were only able to cross over to your realm with the help of the spirits."

"So you do commune with the gods, then," she said, studying her closely. "Why have they sent you to us?"

"We are looking for Princess Ylena," I told the priestess. At her nonplussed look, I added, "She is the leader of the dragons who came to this realm from ours twenty years ago."

The priestess shook her head. "I have never heard of a Princess Ylena," she told us. "Nor the term 'dragons'."

"The male wearing golden robes is from the same realm that we came from, and is of a race of fire-breathing reptilian creatures we call dragons," Quye explained. "Adara here is half-dragon, but the other half of her lineage is fae, which is what I am. We do not serve a god or goddess, as you and the others think, but rather our powers come from the land itself, and therefore are elemental in nature."

"So these dragons are not sons and daughters of Sobek-Ra?" The priestess asked.

"Not that we're aware of," I said. I thought back to the note-book and the secret library Quye had found, wondering if any of those books had mentioned a Crocodile God. For all I knew, the dragons *were* descended from some sort of reptilian deity. "They certainly never worshipped him back when they were in our realm."

Quye and I spent the next hour explaining the history between the dragons and fae, and the events that led to the dragons fleeing Ediria and coming to this new realm to find a haven. The priestess listened intently, nodding to herself at certain points, but content to let us tell the whole of it without interruption.

"You say you don't serve the gods," she said when we finished, "and yet it seems the both of you work to execute the will of these 'spirits', as you call them."

I shook my head. "It's not like that," I told her. "The spirits offer us guidance so that we may keep the elements and the balance of light and dark in harmony. They advise us, but they don't make demands of us."

The priestess shrugged. "Any demands that our goddess makes of us are for our own good," she said. "Our offerings, prayers, and rituals give her the energy she needs to watch over and protect us. Is it so different from your relationship with the Radiants, as you call them?"

"Perhaps not," Quye allowed before I could argue. "But you didn't bring us here to discuss the nature of our religions."

"True," the priestess agreed. "I brought you here to discover what your connection with Sobek-Ra was, and you have uncov-ered some very interesting information." She tapped her chin thoughtfully, studying our faces for a long minute before she spoke again. "High Priest Inatol has been lying to us."

"About what?" I asked.

The priestess shook her head. "Twenty years ago, Inatol came to Kemet-Nefer with a man he claimed was the avatar of Sobek-Ra, the Crocodile God. The citizens and the king were skeptical, but when the avatar transformed into his reptilian form, they all tripped over themselves to acknowledge him as a deity. He took up residence in the temple, along with the hundred or so other foreigners he claimed were his sons and daughters, and they have grown shockingly fast since then. Many of the parishioners of the other gods and goddesses left those temples for Sobek-Ra's, since they are the only temple claiming to have a god in residence, and as a result, the Cult of Sobek has eclipsed all the others. They receive more gold and offerings than the rest of us, and as such, they have the most power."

Quye raised her eyebrows. "That seems very unfair."

"It will be of great interest to the other priests—and not to mention the God-King—to learn that this man is not, in fact, the avatar of Sobek-Ra, and that he and his 'children' are not even crocodiles, but a different beast entirely." The priestess's silver-painted lips curled into a satisfied smile. "I've long suspected that Inatol has not been truthful with us. This is our chance to expose him."

"I'm pleased that we could help you bring this truth to light," I said carefully, not wanting to take sides on this issue. On the one hand, it seemed wrong for the dragons to impersonate a deity. But on the other, I could see how the idea of being worshipped as gods after being hunted to near extinction for thousands of years, was a hard bargain to pass up. "But it is imperative that we find Princess Ylena. She is the only person who can help me unlock my abilities, abilities I need to drive away the dark entity that is trying to kill everyone in my world."

"I do not know what has become of your Princess Ylena," the

priestess said ruefully. "The dragon impersonating Sobek-Ra has established himself as the leader, and there is no female ruling alongside him. The only ones who would know of her whereabouts are the dragons themselves, or High Priest Inatol. And since they want you dead, I'm not sure they will be forthcoming."

I sighed, scrubbing a hand over my face. "Well, we're going to have to convince them it's in their best interest to help us." I looked helplessly at Quye. "Do you have any ideas on how to do that?"

"I might." Quye tilted her head, a considering look in her eyes. "What do you plan to do with this information, now that you know the dragons are imposters and that Inatol has disgraced his station by lying to the public?"

"I'll call a council meeting with the other priests, and we will discuss it," the high priestess said. "But if this goes the way I intend, this will end with Inatol losing his position as high priest, and the dragons losing their venerated positions as children of Sobek-Ra. As for the imposter himself... there are very severe penalties for impersonating a deity. And he is about to find out what they are."

14

General Slaugh

"Well? Have you located Adara yet?"

General Slaugh shut the door to the war room, then turned to face Lady Mossi and Mistress Nox. The two sat on the far side of the round table, a large map of Ediria spread out before them. Flags representing the three Houses were scattered across the map's surface, indicating the locations of the various troops.

"No." Frowning, Slaugh leaned over the map, then plucked one of the blue water fae flags and moved it closer to Domhain's border. He also adjusted a few of the air fae flags—the Gaoth Aire had made no move to attack, but had sealed off their borders, making the mountain passes nearly impassable with ferocious blizzards. "I sent a few more shadow soldiers to Bala Oighr in disguise and had them search, but Adara and her friends are no longer there. Dune did kill their priestess as well as Lady Tamil before he met his own end, so at least we know Adara didn't complete the ritual."

"Good, then Dune has served his purpose." Mistress Nox waved a hand, dismissing him from the discussion as though he were of no more consequence than a fly. Slaugh felt a brief twinge of anger at that, but the emotion was quickly eclipsed by the darkness inside him. It was impossible for him to hold any ill will against his mistress. Not when she had given him so much, and was working so hard to give him even more.

"Well, if Adara can't complete the ritual, then she is of little danger to us," Lady Mossi remarked. She toyed with the water fae flag Slaugh had moved toward her border, her lips pinching in annoyance. "We should continue searching for her and her little band, just in case, but in the meantime, perhaps we should resume negotiations."

"Negotiations?" Slaugh scowled at his aunt. "I thought we already agreed that it was time for House Ithir to take the throne. The other Houses have rejected my claim already. House Usciete has put Lord Prentis forward as a contender for the throne, and House Reatha has refused to back either of us. How are we to win if we don't corral them into submission with a proper show of force?"

"There is more than one way to prune a shrub," Lady Mossi said, her voice sharp with rebuke. "Lord Prentis is not as stubborn as King Aolis—he would be far easier to treat with if he were on the throne, and I could marry Avani to him, or even Gelsyne." She patted Mistress Nox fondly on the shoulder. "As much as I loathe Lady Axlya, I would rather see our Houses united than torn apart."

A wave of fury rose inside General Slaugh, and this time, the darkness eagerly fed it, allowing him to work himself into a towering rage. "How dare you?" he snarled, slamming his fist on the table. The flags toppled over, scattering themselves all over the map, but he hardly noticed. "I have sacrificed too much for you to betray me by giving the throne to that spoiled dandy. Do not cross me, Lady Aunt, or there will be consequences."

Lady Mossi's eyes flashed, and she rose from her chair. "Are you threatening me, nephew?" she asked, the air around her crackling with power. "Perhaps the power I've allowed you to keep has gone through your head, and you've forgotten who you're dealing with?"

"Grandmother," Mistress Nox said, laying a hand on top of Lady Mossi's before Slaugh could respond. The fight went out of Mossi in an instant, her eyes going blank. "I understand your desire to protect your people and minimize the loss of life, but General Slaugh is an experienced soldier. He will end this war as quickly and efficiently as possible to prevent needless death."

"Of course," Lady Mossi said, her voice sounding very far away. Nox withdrew her hand from Mossi's, and the older fae blinked, her eyes returning to their normal color. "My time would be better spent at the family seat, ensuring Domhain remains protected while you conduct your campaign."

"Precisely," Mistress Nox said, beaming. "I will accompany you and make sure all is well."

General Slaugh's eyebrows rose. "You wish to return to Talamh? Don't you think you should remain here at Kaipei to hold down the fort?"

"I don't believe that's necessary," Nox said. She placed a hand on Lady Mossi's shoulders, whose eyes turned blank again. "Grandmother, might I speak to my fiancé alone for a moment?"

"Of course." Lady Mossi rose from her chair and drifted out of the room. Slaugh noticed the slight imperfection in her shadow as she walked past him—a tiny piece of Nox's power she'd planted in Lady Mossi in order to control her, just as she'd done with the hostages before they'd sent them back to their own homes.

As soon as the door shut behind them, Mistress Nox rose from her chair. She sauntered around the table, her shadows snaking behind her, and pressed her willowy form against General Slaugh's. Her scent—an intoxicating mix of florals and midnight stars—enveloped Slaugh, and his ire evaporated, replaced with servile adoration.

He'd never felt this way about anyone he'd served. Not even King Aolis when he'd been at the height of his power.

"My fierce, handsome general," Nox purred, tracing the ruined flesh on the left half of his face. He tried not to flinch away from her touch—he'd always hated it when anyone touched his burns, even her. "I hope you're not losing sight of our mission. We need Lady Mossi to cooperate with us if we want her to continue to give us access to her soldiers and resources."

"I know." General Slaugh swallowed as her hand moved lower, past his jawline and down to his throat. "I haven't forgotten. But I'm two hundred years old, Mistress, and it chafes at me that Lady Mossi still treats me like a child."

"Then let her," Nox said, hooking her forefinger into the collar of his shirt and yanking. The top button popped off, and hunger surged like a living beast within him. "Let her continue to underestimate us until we've brought this world to its knees, and she sees you for who you truly are."

She kissed him then, driving all thoughts of Lady Mossi from his mind. A part of him knew that the sweet, decadent darkness that made up who she was would kill him, would kill all of them.

But like any addict, he was too far gone to care.

15

Mavlyn

"I still can't believe I let you dye my hair green," Leap grumbled as they walked through the bustling streets of Talamh. Cirra followed them from a discreet distance, high enough above in the clouds that her distinctive golden coloring wouldn't be spotted, but close enough to swoop in and rescue them should they find themselves in real danger. "How long does it take for this dye to wash out?"

Mavlyn laughed as Leap raked a hand through his spiky hair. She'd mixed up plant dye—an old trick she and Adara used to do during their childhood dress up days—and used it to turn Leap's white hair a moss green color, and darken his pale skin to a clay red color. Unfortunately, she didn't have Adara's potion making skills, so there wasn't much she could do about his silver-colored eyes. She'd instructed him to tell everyone he'd changed the color on purpose if they asked.

"The dye will last about a week on your skin, probably two

weeks in your hair," she informed him as they walked through a market square. She'd only been to Talamh a handful of times in her life, but it seemed like there were more city guards on patrol than usual, hands toying with the pommels of their swords as they kept a watchful eye over the citizens. "You need to stop fidgeting with your hair and skin so much, though, or it will come off faster."

"Squalls," Leap swore under his breath. "I have to walk around looking like a carrot for two weeks?"

"If you don't want to get arrested, then yes." Mavlyn nudged Leap's shoulder as they passed through an archway, drawing his attention to the guard posted by the entrance. "I'm not sure if you've noticed, but I haven't seen a single water or air fae here since we've arrived. That means they've either made themselves scarce because of the impending war, or been imprisoned as spies."

"I did notice," Leap muttered. He glanced around as they moved away from the shopping district and into a more residential area. "Where are you taking us, anyway?"

"An old friend."

Mavlyn quickened their steps as they turned down a street lined with old, expensive houses. Small snowdrifts were piled along the sides of the streets, and a chill wind whistled around them, making Mavlyn shiver. She still wore the fur cloak the ice fae had given her, the hood drawn up around her face not only as a deterrent against the cold, but in case the guards had been told to look out for her.

Eventually, they came to an old brownstone at the end of the block. Mavlyn's stomach churned with nerves as they walked up the path and onto the wide porch so she could knock on the door. It had been a long time since she'd last seen Emelie, and given recent events, she wasn't sure how well she would be received.

A servant answered the door, and Mavlyn explained who she was. "Miss Troth isn't home right now," the servant said, a little snootily as she eyed Mavlyn and Leap's shabby, travel-worn clothes. "But if you'd like, I can leave a message for her, and—"

"Mavlyn? Is that you?"

Mavlyn whirled at the sound of the familiar voice. Her heart beat faster at the sight of Emelie Troth hurrying up the sidewalk toward them, her honey-brown eyes wide with excitement. Mavlyn remembered her as a plump girl, with long, wavy red hair she wore in chin-length, corkscrew curls around her round face, and a pair of thick glasses perched on her button nose. But while she still had the glasses and the apple cheeks, she'd slimmed down, and she wore her fiery hair waist length now. She'd also traded her colorful dresses for a Talamh University school uniform—a button-up white shirt with the university's crest embroidered on the breast, and a green and gold plaid skirt. She wore black leggings and boots beneath the skirt to keep her warm, along with a black cloak and matching bookbag.

"Emelie!" Mavlyn raced up the path to greet her old friend. The two embraced, and a wave of giddiness rushed through her. She and Emelie had been close, once, but her father had moved them from Fenwood to Talamh five years ago for business, and they hadn't seen each other more than a handful of times since. "How are you?"

"Drowning in homework, as usual," Emelie huffed. She slid her bookbag off her shoulder and onto the ground, then stepped back to give Mavlyn a good once over. "Where have you been all this time? I thought you were supposed to start university this year! I was looking forward to helping you settle in."

Mavlyn winced at the hurt expression on her friend's face. In her last letter to Emelie, she'd asked her friend for help in finding a place to stay and introductions with the various university clubs and organizations. Emelie had enthusiastically agreed, even offering to let Mavlyn stay at her home for a few weeks while she searched for accommodations. But when Adara had fled from the village on Einar's back, everything had changed. Mavlyn had penned a brief letter to Emelie before she'd left with her aunt for Wynth, but she hadn't explained the circumstances, only telling her an emergency had come up and she wouldn't be arriving for the start of the semester.

"It's a long story," Mavlyn said. "Maybe we can tell you about it inside, over a cup of tea?"

Emelie glanced over Mavlyn's shoulder, to where Leap and the servant were waiting on the porch, and raised her eyebrows. "Yeah, I think you'd better."

Emelie led them inside, and Mavlyn and Leap hung up their cloaks on hooks by the door, then joined her in the sitting room. Her parents were both away—her mother visiting a friend, her father working at the family trading company—so they had the house to themselves, if you didn't count the servant. She still didn't seem pleased about having them here, but she served them tea and biscuits, then disappeared into the kitchen, where she would undoubtedly eavesdrop on every word.

"So," Emelie said after they'd taken their first sips. "Who is your friend, and what brings you both here? Are you hoping to get a late start in this semester?"

"Not exactly," Mavlyn said. She introduced Leap, then told Emelie about the situation with Adara, Einar, General Slaugh, and the Shadow. Emelie listened with an open mouth, hardly touching her biscuits as she absorbed the tale.

"I think the only good thing out of everything you've said so far is that Dune is dead," Emelie said when Mavlyn paused to take a breath. "I never liked him—he used to tease me about being fat, and he was horrible to Adara." She wrinkled her nose as she picked up another biscuit. "When you told me the two of them were seeing each other, I nearly asked Father to borrow a horse so I could travel back to Fenwood just to slap some sense into her."

Mavlyn laughed. "That would have been a sight." Adara and Emelie hadn't been as close as Mavlyn had been to her, but they'd still been friends. Mavlyn half-wished she'd been able to convince Adara to attend university—the three of them would have had such fun together! But then, Adara's powers might have been unleashed in the capital instead, and it would have been far more difficult for her to escape Lady Mossi's and General Slaugh's clutches. She also likely would have never found Einar, either.

Fate was a funny thing.

"How have things been here in Talamh since King Aolis's death?" Leap asked. Emelie started at the sound of his voice—Leap had stayed silent for most of the conversation, nursing his tea as he curled up onto the settee by the window, and Mavlyn suspected she'd forgotten he was there.

"Not good," Emelie said darkly. "Things were good for a while when the shadow creatures disappeared, but now that civil war is brewing, shipping companies are far more reluctant to travel. The supply routes have stalled, and it's difficult for anyone to move goods in and out of the city. My father has been working long hours trying to manage it all, and Mother is stressed. So, if there is something I can do to help, I'm all ears."

"Well, now that you mention it," Mavlyn said hesitantly, "Leap and I do have a plan. We came to Talamh to raise awareness about Nox and General Slaugh, and to convince the people to protest the war. If enough citizens refuse to fight, Nox won't be able to tip the balance from light to dark. We only need to hold her off long enough until Adara returns to Ediria."

"Where exactly did she go?" Emelie asked. "I can't imagine where she could find another priest to help her, given that she's public enemy number one."

"To the Deadlands," Leap said before Mavlyn could answer. "There's ancient magic hidden in the ruins that the Radiants said can help. But it's going to take her a few weeks to find it."

"The Deadlands?" Emelie shuddered. "May the Radiants watch over her, then. I wouldn't wish anyone to set foot in that horrid wasteland, not even my worst enemy."

Emelie convinced her parents to let Mavlyn and Leap spend a few days with them, and the next day, she took them to Talamh University. Mavlyn felt a pang of longing as they entered the campus grounds, taking in the grand buildings and the excited chatter of students as they walked from one class to the next or sat together in the common areas, studying or working on projects together. She nearly wept when they walked by the massive greenhouse—she'd visited it on her campus tour, and the collection of plants there rivaled Lady Mossi's arboretum. She would have to sneak in there at some point to get a look at some of the rarer specimens.

"Are you okay?" Leap asked in a low voice. "You seem... sad."

Mavlyn blinked at Leap, surprised at the concern on his face. "I'm fine," she said. "It's just... I can't help wishing things were different, that I was here as a normal girl going to university for her first semester, not as an activist."

"You will get to attend as a normal girl one day," Leap said. "That's why we're doing this, right?"

"Well... yeah," Mavlyn said, though privately she was still unsure. "But I'll probably be older than the other first-year students, and I won't fit in as well."

"Fitting in is overrated," Emelie said, tossing a curl over her shoulder. "Besides, activists go hand-in-hand with universities, so you'll fit right in here."

She winked, and Mavlyn cracked a smile. But as her friend led them into the campus café, she couldn't help feeling nervous.

"Emelie," a handsome male said, rising from a couch by the window to greet them. He was lanky, with long, jet-black hair and skin nearly as dark. His eyes were a startling jade green against all that inky blackness, and his white teeth flashed as he smiled at them. "Are these your friends?"

"Yes." Emelie gave him a peck on the cheek, then turned to introduce them. "This is my boyfriend, Roylan. Roylan, this is Mavlyn, my childhood friend, and her friend, Leap."

Roylan invited Leap and Mavlyn to sit with him, and they explained in low voices what they were trying to accomplish. Roylan listened intently, interrupting to ask questions every so often, and when they were finished, his expression was downright grim.

"To be honest, I was a little suspicious when I heard the reports that all the shadow creatures had disappeared," Roylan said when they'd finished. "It seemed too convenient, and I would have thought the Houses would want to make peace and negotiate, rather than going to war after the losses all three realms have sustained over the years. The idea that the Shadow behind all this is stirring the tensions shines a light on the true nature behind what is going on here... and also gives me hope that we lesser fae might be able to do something about it, rather than just blindly follow the Greater Fae as we have always done."

"Does that mean you're going to help us spread the word?" Mavlyn asked, hope rising in her for the first time since she and Quye had parted ways.

"Of course," Roylan said. "I'm president of the Earth Guardians Club, and my sister Tulia is the editor of the Talamh Tribune. I'm sure she would be delighted to print an article about this, and you can come speak at the next club meeting to see who else we can recruit for the cause."

"The Talamh Tribune?" Emelie asked, a little nervous. "Roylan, are you sure that's wise? Nearly three-thousand people read that paper every week. Word will get back to Lady Mossi quickly if we publish an article."

"We don't need to run it right away," Roylan argued, "but time is of the essence. As Mavlyn said, General Slaugh has already struck the first blow in water fae territory—it's only a matter of time before they retaliate. There are already rumors circulating that a general draft of university fae is imminent, so now is the time to let the students know the truth before they agree to fight a war that's going to doom us all."

"I would almost rather publish an article anonymously in the paper than speak to your club," Mavlyn said. "The last time I tried to speak publicly about this, my fellow villagers tried to arrest me. I had to make a run for it."

"That won't happen here," Roylan said. "I can't promise that all the members will believe or agree with you, but I'll be there to make sure you're given a fair hearing."

"Come on." Leap nudged Mavlyn in the ribs when she hesitated. "This is what we wanted, right?"

"It is," Mavlyn agreed. She squared her shoulders and met Roylan's stare. "I'll be at the meeting," she promised.

She just hoped she would walk out of it in one piece.

16

Adara

"Are you seriously feeling guilty right now?"

I raked a hand through my hair as I paced the main chamber in the suite the High Priestess had given us to sleep in tonight. She had ordered her attendants to fetch our meager belongings from the inn—we couldn't risk going back there tonight, not when we were wanted by the Crocodile God priests.

"I know I shouldn't," I said, staring into the fire. "But I can't help feeling like I just betrayed the dragons by outing them to the High Priestess last night." I bit my lip. "I wish there had been a way to get her to help us without exposing the truth about them."

Quye huffed. "Not unless you wanted to get zapped by a moonbeam," she said. "I almost told a lie just to see what would happen, but the moment the words formed on my tongue, my skin started heating up. I probably would have lost all my arm hair last night if I'd kept going."

I snorted. "What a tragedy that would have been."

"Thank you." Quye sniffed. "I'm glad you agree."

I resisted the urge to smack her on the shoulder.

We retired to bed not long after that, but I remained up for a long time, tossing and turning and wrestling with my conscience. What would Einar think if he knew what had transpired? Would he be angry with me for exposing the dragons' fraudulent behavior? I wished he could have come with me—my encounter with that dragon in the garden would have gone very differently if Einar had been by my side. But it wasn't as if I'd tried to make an enemy of him. In fact, I'd done my best to convince him we were kith. He just hadn't been willing to listen to reason.

Then again, neither had Einar, I reminded myself. I was pretty sure that if the mating bond hadn't stopped him, he would have killed me on sight. Had it really only been a few months since I'd stumbled upon his stone form in that tower ruin and accidentally broken the sleeping enchantment Kiryan had placed upon him?

I miss you, I thought, closing my eyes and reaching for the bond. It was thin and fragile as gossamer, but I tried to push the thought down it anyway, hoping he would get the message. The hollow ache in my chest pulsed, and I curled into myself, trying to hold on to someone who wasn't there.

I wasn't sure if I was dreaming, but I could have sworn phantom arms slipped around my waist from behind. *I miss you too,* a voice whispered, and that was the last thing I remembered before I fell asleep.

The next morning, I awoke groggy, but also lighter, the heartache and guilt in my chest no longer pressing down as heavily as before. A temple servant brought us breakfast and a set of fresh clothes, and once we'd bathed, dressed, and eaten, she led us back to the east wing of the temple.

"Are we meeting with the priestess again?" I asked as we passed the salon Quye and I had spent most of the previous day languishing in.

"Yes," the servant said. "As well as a few others who would like to question you as well."

The servant stopped outside a pair of heavy wooden doors carved with celestial symbols. The door on the left opened, and she led us into a large meeting room dominated by a long, oblong table in the center. I froze at the sight of half a dozen priests seated around it, all from different temples if the varying colors and symbols on their robes and headdresses were anything to go by. My heart pumped faster as I scanned the lot of them, looking for any crocodile symbolism.

"Relax, child," High Priestess Anuket said. She smiled at us from the head of the table. "High Priest Inatol is not here."

"Do you normally exclude him from council meetings?" Quye asked, approaching the table. Her white curls were pinned up, exposing the length of her swan neck, and I had to admit she looked regal, ethereal even in her all-white attire. In contrast, I felt frumpy and out of place, and more than a little nervous about being the center of attention amongst all these religious leaders.

"Not at all," the priest to Anuket's left said. "However, given the circumstances, we thought you might be more comfortable giving your testimony without him present. He can be... intimidating."

"Testimony?" I asked. "I thought we already did that last night."

"You did," the priestess said, "but the council would like the opportunity to ask their own questions. You are not standing in the goddess's eye today," she added gently, "so you do not need to answer any questions you do not want to. But we would appreciate it if you could shed some light on this matter, as it seems High Priest Inatol has not been honest with us."

"Very well," Quye agreed.

We spent the next thirty minutes telling the priests everything—about the war back home in Ediria, why the dragons had fled, the shadow magic infection, and the reason we'd come for their help.

"So these refugees are shape-shifting dragons?" a priest wearing green robes embroidered with golden sheafs of wheat asked. "Not children of Sobek-Ra?"

"I'm afraid not," I said. "And dragons aren't the only ones who can shape shift in our world either."

I gestured to Quye, and she grinned. A white flash of light eclipsed her body, and the priest cried out in astonishment as she transformed with a flutter of wings into a snowy white owl. In true Quye fashion, she did a lap around the room, skimming the tops of their headdresses with her wingtips before landing on the edge of the table and hooting proudly.

"I... that..." the priest spluttered as he stared at Quye.

"The white owl is a sacred animal amongst our people," the moon goddess priestess said, turning to me. "Are all of your people capable of shifting into beasts?"

"No," I said. "Only the most powerful amongst us." A memory flashed in my mind—the vision of that ice dragon staring back at me, my inner beast waiting to be freed. I nudged Quye, and she hopped off the table, then shifted back into her fae form.

The priests turned away, arguing amongst themselves about what to do. They were furious at the deception—

evidently High Priest Inatol had been using the dragons to his advantage, converting many of the citizens away from the other temples. The Crocodile Cult has become immensely wealthy thanks to their booming patronage over the last twenty years, while the other temples had been losing followers and struggling to find the funds to maintain their buildings and feed their staff.

"Inatol must be brought to justice!" one of them shouted. "He should be stripped of his titles and banished!"

"Banished?" another argued. "That is far too kind. He should be drawn and quartered, along with everyone who aided him!"

"And what about the imposters?" someone else asked. "These dragons have been raking in the gold as well, living like kings while the rest of us struggle!"

"Now hang on," I said, my skin tingling with alarm. "I know you're angry, but remember that the dragons are refugees just trying to fit into this new world. You can't blame them for going along with Inatol. I think most would have done the same in their situation."

"That is true," the priestess said, "but they still need to be held accountable for impersonating religious figures. At the very least, they should pay the gold back."

"Of course," Quye said smoothly. "Justice must be served, and we would especially never tell you what to do with your High Priest. But if you are going to kill him, we beg that you first allow us to speak to him. We must find out what has become of the Princess Ylena, as she is the only one who can help us."

"You can question him when he is behind bars," a priest snapped. "Let us confront him now, while he is still here in the city!"

The priests dispersed, each heading back to their own temples to gather their personal guards to accompany them to Sobek-Ra's temple. "It might be best for you to stay here," the moon goddess priestess said, pausing beside us on our way out. "It will be safer for you."

She left in a swirl of silvery robes, and I turned to Quye. "This is spiraling out of control," I said, my stomach churning with anxiety. "What if they kill the High Priest before we can talk to him? We'll never find Ylena then!"

"They did seem rather bloodthirsty," Quye admitted, glancing toward the open doorway. "Perhaps we should investigate before the priestess thinks better of it, and orders her guards to hold us prisoner again."

Agreed, we left the temple, making a quick stop in our room to grab our belongings in case we couldn't return. I didn't need to consult the map to figure out where the Crocodile God's temple was—acolytes, scholars, and temple attendants crowded the streets, all headed in the same direction. Anxiety clawed at me, and I pushed my way through the crowds, gripping Quye's hand as I dragged her behind me.

The Crocodile God's temple was one of the grandest in the temple district. Made of white sandstone that glowed in the bright sun, it rose in tiers, each level adorned with columns and carvings that depicted Sobek-Ra's power and majesty. A golden spire glittered at the very top, and two massive, intricately carved crocodile statues flanked the entrance. Making my way through the crowd of people gathered in the temple courtyard, I braced myself for some kind of violent display, expecting to see the high priest being dragged out of his temple.

What I didn't expect was to see a contingent of soldiers surrounding the perimeter of the temple.

"What is the meaning of this?" High Priestess Anuket demanded, addressing what appeared to be the highest-ranking soldier of the group. They wore gold and purple armor, with a sigil of a river snaking between two mountains stamped on their breastplates. "Why are you shielding High Priest Inatol from the scales of justice?"

"Because meting out justice is the responsibility of the government," the soldier said. "We have already taken the High Priest into custody, as well as the so-called avatar of Sobek-Ra, and their supporters. There will be a trial in one week's time, which the King Ramsenan will preside over."

"The God-King himself?" a familiar voice asked, and I glanced over my shoulder to see Nysa standing there. Relief swept over me at the sight of a familiar face in this sea of chaos. "That's a rare occurrence—he rarely involves himself in such affairs."

"God-King?" I repeated. "What does that mean?"

"Right, you wouldn't know." Nysa said. "King Ramsenan and his fathers before him are descendants of Montu-Ra. He is the god of sun and war, and the most powerful deity in our religion, so we refer to him as the God-King."

"And is he really a God-King, then?" I asked, pitching my voice low so that the others wouldn't hear. "Or is it... you know... like the situation here?"

"I'm not sure," Nysa admitted. "But he does command the skies. That's why our crops are so fertile here in the desert. He brings the rains which allow the river to overflow, bringing the rich black sand we plant our crops in."

"Interesting," Quye said. Behind us, the priests were still arguing with the soldiers, but since the high priest and the dragons weren't here, I only listened to them with half an ear. "Do you find him to be a just king?"

"I would like to think so," Nysa said, glancing at the temple. "But I wouldn't say the king is a neutral party in this situation. He and Inatol have been at odds these last few years, as the Crocodile priest's power and influence has become dangerously close to rivaling his own. If I were a betting woman, I would put money on him using this situation to get rid of Inatol and the dragons altogether."

"This isn't good," I said to Quye. "We can't let the God-King kill the high priest or the dragons. We need to be at the trial."

Quye raised an eyebrow, her gaze fixed over my shoulder. "Somehow, I don't think that's going to be a problem."

I turned around just in time to see four of the soldiers marching toward us. My palms grew sweaty, and I grabbed Quye by the elbow, trying to drag her into the crowd so we could disappear. But the crowd, seeing the soldiers coming their way with spears in hand, parted before we could take more than two steps, leaving us directly in their line of sight.

"You." One of the guards jabbed his spear at us, nearly poking me in the chest. "Come."

"Why?" Panic rose inside me, and I glanced around, looking for the moon goddess priestess. But she'd already left, along with the others.

The guard said something to me in his language, and I shook my head, feeling helpless. "He says that the God-King commands that you attend the trial, since you are persons of interest," Nysa translated for us. "They will take you to the palace, where you will be kept until the trial for your safety."

"This isn't what I had in mind when I said we needed to be at the trial," I growled at Quye.

She shrugged. "The universe doesn't always give us what we need in the exact manner we ask for," she said. The guards surrounded us, and we reluctantly allowed them to herd us away from the temple and back toward the main city. "All we have to do is survive a week in the palace without being assassinated by any of the high priest's co-conspirators." She winked at me. "How hard could it be?"

17

Einar

As I suspected, the royal palace was also destroyed, reduced to ash and rubble by King Aolis and his soldiers. However, though the fae had burned the aboveground structures, it seemed they cared very little about the foundations of the palace... or the treasures that lay beneath.

"Here we go," I grunted, moving a giant slab of wall away to reveal a staircase. If memory served, this stairwell led to the royal library's archives—those many books and scrolls considered too precious to be stored in the main library above. Conjuring a fireball to light my way, I descended the staircase, stopping several times to clear the rubble away.

There were three levels built below the main palace—the cellars, where food and wine were stored, the dungeons, and then at the very bottom, the archives. I stopped off at the first level to see if I could salvage any of the food stores, and a trio of shadow creatures ambushed me. Swearing, I slayed them with my sword, then burned the carcasses before continuing on. There hadn't even been anything worth eating—the creatures had devoured all the pickles and preserves, and the seals on the wine casks had been compromised, spoiling the contents.

"What I wouldn't do for a drink right now," I muttered. I did a sweep of the dungeons and killed another two shadow creatures lurking there, then made my way to the lowest level, bracing myself for another attack.

But it seemed the shadow creatures possessed no love for dusty books and scrolls. That, or perhaps there was some other magic at work down here, protecting the precious literature and keeping the shadows at bay. Whatever it was, I whispered a grateful prayer of thanks to the Radiants as I made my way into the cavernous space, careful not to let my fireball touch anything. Spying a torch in the bracket next to the entrance, I lit it, then used it to light the sconces set at intervals along the walls. The tiny flames flickered in the darkness, illuminating the rows of bookshelves and tables. The shelves cast long shadows across the stone floors, and though nothing stirred, I couldn't help feeling there was a haunted quality about the place—the ghosts of the past watching as I walked between the shelves, looking for the answers they'd taken with them to the grave.

I cleared off one of the study desks, then scanned the shelves, looking for any books about the early history of my people. An hour later, I'd piled the desk with yellowed scrolls and fragile, leather-bound volumes—the oldest texts I could find.

I sat down to read, and the next few hours passed in a blur of history and legends—family trees and tales of epic battles, noble warriors, and wise leaders. It seemed that not all of the fae had been hostile to us—we'd invited a few exiles to seek refuge in Hearthfyre, in exchange for using their magic to help us maintain the lands. One of the early dragon princes had even married a fae, though the two had borne no children. I frowned at that... did that mean Adara and I wouldn't have children? But no, Adara herself was proof that dragons and fae could produce offspring.

A wave of fierce longing blazed through me, and I closed my eyes, pressing a hand to my chest. Adara and I had only been separated for a few days, but I missed her with every breath I took. I wondered how she was doing, if she'd found Ylena yet, and how my people had received her. I'd sent a letter along with her for Ylena's eyes only—Daryan's sister would recognize my handwriting, and the letter would explain Adara's parentage and her status as my future mate. Ylena would be suspicious, of course—Adara had no dragonlike features, after all—but she wouldn't deny Adara help if I asked on her behalf. Not after the sacrifice I'd made for them all.

Shaking my head, I pushed the thought of Ylena from my mind and refocused my aching eyes on the text in front of me. The handwriting was cramped and tiny, written by a dragon scholar over two millennia ago who had interviewed the oldest dragons alive at the time. I suspected this wasn't the original copy—there was no way these yellowed pages had survived that long, even in the archives—but I still handled the pages with care as I read.

"My grandfather told me of the day of our arrival," the scholar wrote, speaking of his interview with an ancient dragon called Mirastis. *"He said that he woke in a ruin of fire and brimstone—a crater that stretched a good hundred meters wide, along with a dozen others. Similar craters were scattered all over Hearthfyre, each with their own dragons, amongst the ruins of towns and villages and big cities alike. But there were no fire fae in the whole of the realm, no matter where they searched. And they had no memory of who they were, or how they had come to be."*

I shook my head, confusion brewing like a storm behind my

eyelids. How was that possible? And where were all these supposed craters? He'd never seen or heard of them before— had his ancestors covered them all up, built new towns and cities atop them and buried the evidence of their arrival? And how was it they had neither memory of where they'd come from, nor of what happened to the fire fae? Was there some larger force at play?

Sighing, I closed the book, then organized the texts so I could come back to them another time. The hour was getting late, and I needed to visit the primal stone mines and get out of the Deadlands before the sun went down.

Even with my newfound shadow magic immunity, this place was not safe for a dragon alone.

18

Adara

"Well," Quye said on our fifth day in the God-King's palace. "We've managed to avoid being assassinated so far, but if something doesn't happen soon, I might just die of boredom instead."

I snorted, turning away from the book I was reading. Well, reading might have been a bit of a misnomer, since I couldn't actually understand the text. But since Quye and I were trapped in the suite of rooms the palace steward had assigned to us, I'd requested that the servants bring me any picture books the royal library was willing to lend. The one I had in my lap seemed to be a collection of historical figures, filled with portraits of important warriors, generals, and rulers throughout the ages.

"I think you can hold out for one more day," I said, glancing to where Quye stood by the window, staring longingly at the gardens below. I had to admit they were breathtaking-rows of palm trees, fragrant flowering bushes, and intricate topiaries lined the pathways leading to the palace, the ground was covered with lush green grass, and elegant fountains and small ponds filled with koi fish were scattered throughout.

I couldn't blame Quye for feeling put out. We'd never gotten the opportunity to explore the grounds, or even get a good look at the God-King's palace from the outside. High Priestess Anuket had insisted that we be taken to the palace via the network of catacombs that ran through the city, so that we could avoid any assassination attempts by the dragons and the Crocodile Cult priests. It had been a rather morbid journey, walking through tunnels surrounded by the bones of the dead, but after five days of being cooped up in these rooms, I almost wished I was back there instead.

Quye was about to respond when the door flew open, and our servant, Musat, rushed in. Her eyes widened at the sight of us in our dressing gowns, and she clapped both her hands to her face in dismay.

"Great spirits!" she cried in thickly-accented fae. "Did no one tell you? The two of you must get dressed at once!"

"What's going on?" Quye asked, her eyes sparkling with excitement. "Are we finally going to meet the God-King?"

"Yes," she snapped, yanking on the bell pull near the door. "He's moved the trial to today."

My stomach lurched. "How much time do we have until it starts?" I asked, my hands flying to my rumpled hair.

"Less than an hour."

Three more servants rushed into the room, and the next thirty minutes passed in a blur of scrubbing, primping, and fussing. The servants dressed us in fine gowns of silk—Quye's an ivory embroidered with silver thread, and mine in blue damask. I felt stifled by the high collars and long sleeves, and the servants wound my braids so tight around my head that my temples ached.

"Is this really necessary?" I demanded as a servant applied some kind of red powder to my cheeks.

"Yes." Musat inspected my face, her brow furrowed. I flinched as she patted both of my cheeks, hard enough to sting. "You don't want to appear before the God-King looking like a corpse. He'll think you're a ghost from the afterlife, here to haunt him!"

"One would think a king descended from the gods would be able to tell a real ghost from a fake," Quye quipped. I snorted, but we both fell silent beneath Musat's death glare. The woman might have been all of five feet tall, but she had a way of cowing us both into submission with a single look. The one time I'd tried to sneak out of our rooms to snoop around the palace, she'd been waiting right outside, hands propped on her ample hips. The expression on her face had been so terrifying, I hadn't even tried to explain myself. I just turned around and shut the door in her face, then pretended like nothing happened when she came to help us dress the next morning.

"There." Musat took a step back to survey us, clucking her tongue. "I wish we had more time, but you are presentable enough. Hurry now, you don't want to keep King Ramsenan waiting."

We followed her out of the room, where an escort of guards waited to take us to the throne room. Quye craned her neck as we were led through a maze of halls and stairwells, taking in all the expensive art and furniture that we hadn't gotten to see when we'd arrived under the cover of night. But I could barely focus on my surroundings, my stomach churning, my palms damp with nerves. What if the God-King didn't believe us, and he sided with the dragons instead? Would he allow us to return to our home world, or would he have us imprisoned, or worse, executed?

We turned a corner, and I sucked in a breath at the sight of the double doors at the end of the hall, already opened to the throne room. I could already see the massive audience that had gathered within—the gallery was packed, and the sound of their excited chatter drifted through the hallway, growing louder the closer we got.

"Breathe, Adara." Quye slipped her hand into mine and squeezed it. "It's going to be all right."

I let out the breath I didn't realize I'd been holding, and slowly pulled in another one. Quye released my hand as we passed the threshold, and I composed my features, not wanting to betray my nerves. The throne room was a grand chamber that exuded power and majesty. The guards led us down the center of the gallery, which was filled with nobles seated on colorful cushions. Their expressions ranged from curious to bored as they gathered to watch the oncoming spectacle. Behind them, the walls were adorned with intricate murals depicting the sun god and his achievements—on one side, images of him bringing light and life into the world, and on the other side, depictions of war and conquest as he raced through the battlefields on his blazing sun chariot.

The gallery opened out into a wide, polished floor, where petitioners and supplicants stood when coming to speak with the God-King. Beyond that was a grand dais, where King Ramsenan sat, elevated on his golden throne. It was a towering structure made of gold and precious stones, with intricate carving of the sun and moon on its backrest, and the male who sat on it looked as though he was born to be there. Regal and stern, he sat straight-backed as he looked down at his subjects through the golden mask he wore. His muscular body was clad in ornate robes made of silk and cloth-of-gold, with a crimson cape that draped majestically across his broad shoulders. His piercing violet eyes fell on me, and I hastily remembered to look away. Musat had warned us that looking directly into the God-

King's eyes was an act of hubris and disrespect, and to avoid it at all costs.

The guards led us over to the right side of the audience chamber, where High Priestess Anuket waited for us, along with the other high priests. On the opposite side stood a male who I assumed was High Priest Inatol. He looked to be in his mid-50s, with a thick build and a broad, weathered face sporting a hawk-nose and neatly trimmed beard. His hair was shorn close to his scalp, and he wore a white linen robe with crocodiles intricately embroidered along the hem and neckline. Gold rings set with precious gemstones winked at me as he flexed his fingers, and though his haughty expression betrayed nothing, I had the distinct impression that if he could, he would have launched himself across the room and fastened those fingers around my neck.

Next to Inatol stood the same dragon I'd encountered outside the moon goddess temple. Unlike Inatol, he made no attempt to conceal his rage—his amber eyes blazed as he glared at me, his swarthy face twisted with fury. His outfit—a set of elaborate cloth-of-gold robes encrusted with jewels—was even more ostentatious than the last time I saw him, but I supposed it was befitting of a male impersonating a god. The two pretenders were surrounded by several other priests and dragons, all united in their avarice and greed as they glared at me.

"Adara, Quye." High Priestess Anuket smiled. "I would like to introduce you to High Priest Kidmat. He is a servant of Tomaras, the God of Knowledge, and he has a gift for you."

"A gift?" I echoed as the priest stepped forward. He was an old man, his head oiled and shaved, his weathered face a mass of wrinkles, his eyes milky and unseeing. "What kind of gift?"

The priest gave me a kind smile and held out both of his hands, palms down. "The gift of language," he said. "Come closer, children. This will only take a moment."

I hesitated, but Quye stepped forward at once, allowing the priest to place his hand on her head. Reluctantly, I followed her lead. His hand settled atop my head, a warm, oddly comforting weight that took the edge off my anxiety.

"Very good," the priest said. "Now close your eyes and relax."

I did as he said, and a moment later, there was a flash of light that lit the insides of my eyelids red. A strange tingle rippled through my brain, and I gasped, my eyes flying open.

"Can you understand me?" the old priest asked.

"Yes," I said, puzzled. "Should I not be able to?"

"Order!" the herald cried, banging his staff on the floor. The sound reverberated through the throne room, and everyone fell silent. "Now that all parties are here, the trial shall begin!"

"King Ramsenan has agreed to convene this trial at the request of High Priestess Anuket," the herald went on, "who today brings some very serious accusations against High Priest Inatol. High Priestess," he said, turning to Anuket, "come forth and tell us the nature of these crimes."

The High Priestess stepped forward in a swish of robes, bowing deeply. "Your Eminence," she said, her dulcet tones carrying throughout the chamber, "it disturbs me to speak ill against any of my fellow High Priests, especially one so venerated as High Priest Inatol. But I have discovered that he has not been truthful with us. Recent information has come to light that the man Inatol claims to be the avatar of Sobek-Ra, is in fact not Sobek-Ra at all, but of a race of beings from another world called dragons. And that his so-called children are not his children at all, but his fellow people, who he brought to our realm to escape genocide."

Shocked whispers rippled through the crowd. "That is a lie!" High Priest Inatol spat. High spots of color marred his tanned cheeks, and he jabbed a finger in Anuket's direction. "High

Priestess Anuket has fabricated these allegations! She has long been jealous—"

"Did I give you permission to speak, Inatol?"

The God-King's voice rumbled through the throne room like rolling thunder, silencing everyone. He turned toward the high priest, his violet eyes hard as diamonds as he glared at Inatol through his mask.

Predictably, Inatol quailed beneath the God-King's ire. "I apologize, your Eminence," he said, bowing his head. "I allowed my temper to get the better of me."

The God-King ignored him, turning back to Anuket. "High Priestess Anuket," he said, "these are very serious accusations. Do you have any proof to back them up?"

Suddenly, it hit me like a thunderbolt—I could understand every word being spoken—by the herald, the God-King, and the priests. There was no way they were all speaking fae—the priests might use the language, but I couldn't imagine the God-King himself would, being that he was a self-proclaimed deity himself. Wide-eyed, I turned to Quye, who grinned at me.

"Took you long enough to catch on," she said, and I resisted the urge to stick my tongue out at her.

"As a matter of fact," Anuket said, indicating us with a sweeping wave of her arm, "these two witnesses can verify my claims. They both come from the same world these dragons fled from."

The crowd buzzed with excited whispers at this, and the herald had to call for order. "Come forward and state your names," he commanded, pointing his staff at us.

Quye and I did as he commanded, bowing low before the God-King. His eyes glittered as he stared at us through his golden mask, and I tried not to be unnerved at my inability to read him.

"Your Eminence," I said, clasping my hands behind my back

to keep from fidgeting, "my name is Adara Greenwood, and this is my friend, Quye. We are from the kingdom Ediria, and have traveled across realms searching for the dragons who left our realm almost twenty years ago." I turned to point at the imposter, ignoring his hateful glare. "These men who have been pretending to be the children of the Crocodile are the dragons we have been searching for. We moderns recognize them by their distinctive eye color, and also the stylized flame tattoos they have."

I hid a smile as the imposter's hand automatically went to his own flame tattoo, which was conveniently inked down the front of his neck. He yanked his hand down the moment he realized what he'd done, but it was too late—everyone's eyes were now upon the evidence stamped across his skin.

"This is a bald-faced lie," the High Priest snapped, his dark eyes sparking with anger. "These two foreigners may be from the same realm, but they are clearly neither kin nor kith of Montu-Ra or his children. And if they fled to escape that other world, as this girl claims, then that must mean they are enemies! Why should we believe anything she says?"

"I've always found it strange that I wasn't able to communicate with Sobek-Ra or his descendants upon their arrival," the God-King said, stroking his chin beneath his mask. The gleam in his eyes turned calculating as he stared at the dragons. "Considering that I, too, am descended from the gods and speak their divine language, I was always puzzled as to why the Crocodile God would have his own tongue."

The High Priest opened his mouth, then closed it again. Ignoring him, the God-King turned back to me. "Why did these dragons flee your homeland, and why did you risk coming to this realm to find them?"

I cleared my throat. "Because we were at war with the dragons, and our previous king used dangerous magic to kill nearly all of their race." A wave of guilt washed through me as I looked at the dragons again. "I understand why the dragons are not happy to see me, given the history between our people. But my mate, Einar, is the one who helped create the portal that allowed them to travel to your realm. And he is the one who sent me here, to find Ylena."

Shock rippled through the High Priest's group, and one of the dragons stepped forward. He was taller than the rest, with dark red dreadlocks gathered into a queue at the nape of his neck, and a golden hoop winking from his earlobe.

"You are Einar's mate?" he demanded. "Truly?"

"Yaggir!" the imposter grabbed the other dragon by his sleeve and yanked him back. "What are you doing?" he hissed.

"Yes," I said, speaking over the other dragon. "I am, though we have not completed the bond yet." I pushed my sleeve back to reveal the golden cuff on my bicep. "Einar gave this to me, not as proof of our bond, but because it is mine by succession. The late Prince Daryan was my father, and therefore, you all are my kith."

"No," one of the other dragons barked. "This is impossible! You cannot be Daryan's daughter! He and the Princess Olette were killed!"

"Forgive me," King Ramsenan drawled. We whipped our heads around to see him staring at us with something like amusement, his head propped in his hand as he watched the back and forth. My cheeks heated as I realized I'd forgotten he was there. "But based on this exchange, it seems there must be some truth to Adara's claim. Or else you would be as clueless as I am as to what she's speaking of."

Yaggir shook off the imposter's hold on his arm, then stepped forward and bowed low to the God-King. "Forgive me, Your Eminence," he said, keeping his head bent even as he straightened his spine. "I have been complicit in this charade, but given what has come to light here, I can no longer continue."

"So it is true, then?" the God-King demanded. "You are dragons, and not descendants of Sobek-Ra?"

"Yaggir," High Priest Inatol pled, his voice sharp with desperation. "Don't do this."

Yaggir whirled to face Inatol. "How can I not?" he said, throwing up his hands. "We are dragons, creatures of fire, who have pretended to be the descendants of a water-dwelling reptile for twenty years just so we could be accepted by your people!" He spun to face the God-King again and dropped to his knees, assuming a posture of humility. "Adara wasn't exaggerating when she said that the Edirian king nearly killed us all off. There used to be thousands of dragons, and those of us who came here are all that are left. We were home-sick and battle weary, and terrified of the possibility that we might repeat history and find ourselves fighting to exist again. So when the opportunity arose for us not only to assimilate into your society, but be venerated as deities, we could not say no."

The God-King tapped his golden nose as he considered this. "And why are you coming forth now, after all these years?"

Yaggir turned to look at me, his eyes brimming with emotion. "Because Adara's mate, Einar, was a close friend of mine. He was the general of our army, and I was his deputy. If he sent her to us, then I am honor-bound to do whatever is in my power to help her." He looked over his shoulder at his fellow dragons. "And so are all of you."

The other dragons shifted, looking down at their feet. Even the imposter seemed ashamed. The High Priest, for his part, had turned a sickly shade of green beneath his tan. He knew his days were numbered, and while I felt bad for the dragons, I couldn't bring myself to feel an ounce of pity for him. He had brought this upon himself.

The audience held their breath as they waited for the God-King to speak, and I half-expected him to smite Yaggir where he stood. But to my surprise, he nodded his approval. "I admire your courage and loyalty, even if that loyalty is to your dead comrade, rather than to me, your sovereign." Yaggir flinched. The God-King turned to me, then asked, "Who is this Ylena to you? I have never heard of her."

I blinked at that. "You should have. Her mother was the queen of the dragons, which means she should have inherited her title. She is also the priestess of the dragons, and I need her to help me with a sacred ritual that only she can perform." My stomach sank as I glanced toward the imposter, who must have taken up her role as the leader of the dragons. "What did you do with Ylena? Why is she not here?"

The imposter clenched his jaw, but Yaggir answered for him. "She is not here because she refused to be complicit in the High Priest's scheme," he admitted with a sigh. "She found the idea of pretending to be crocodiles an affront to our ancestors, and she wasn't the only one of us who felt that way. The High Priest had her, as well as the other dissidents, banished to an island so that they would not expose us."

The audience went into an uproar over this, and it took several tries for the herald to calm them down again. "Silence!" he roared, his voice echoing through the packed chamber. "The God-King needs a moment to confer with his advisors. You will all wait here until he returns."

The God-King exited the throne room, leaving us alone. As soon as the door shut behind him, the audience broke out into excited chatter, speculating over what verdict their king would hand down. Would he have the dragons executed for their hubris? And what of the High Priest who had orchestrated this scheme? Surely he deserved something worse than a mere hanging!

"Are you okay?" Quye asked, laying a hand on my arm.

I glanced at her, wondering how she could stay so calm during all of this. "I just hope they aren't really going to execute the dragons," I said, my stomach churning. "I don't think I could bear it if I was responsible for their deaths, even if they don't feel the same way about me."

"King Ramsenan is not a tyrant," Anuket said. "I cannot promise he will spare the lives of your kith, but given his favorable response to Yaggir, I suspect he will offer them an alternative to death." Her mouth thinned as she glanced toward Inatol, who was conferring with the dragons in low voices. "I cannot say the same for Inatol, however. The God-King will punish him to the fullest extent of the law for this."

I nodded as I stared at the dragons, noticing that Yaggir stood a little off to the side of their group. The others had clearly shunned him for his betrayal. The dragon gave me a small smile when he noticed me staring, and I felt a twinge of pity for him. It was very brave of him to speak out, especially since he didn't know me. I would have to express my gratitude to him if the God-King decided to show him mercy.

An agonizing twenty minutes passed before the doors opened and the God-King strode back in with his advisors. I held my breath as he took his seat again and the room quieted down, all waiting in anticipation for their king to speak.

"High Priest Inatol," the God-King said in his rumbling voice. "Come forward."

The High Priest reluctantly did as the king commanded, bowing low. I caught a glimpse of his trembling hands before he tucked them into their opposite sleeves. "Your Eminence," he said, "I—"

"Save your excuses," the God-King said. "I have made my decision. You have been found guilty of committing fraud against the crown and the gods, and will undergo the Rathkir as punishment."

Gasps echoed through the chamber, and the High Priest fell to his knees. "Please, Your Eminence," he croaked. "Anything but that. I have been your most faithful—"

"You have been anything but faithful," the God-King growled, his grip tightening on the arms of his chair. "Not only have you deceived me and the good people of this city, but you have robbed your fellow High Priests and their temples of their acolytes, and insulted Sobek-Ra by installing a false god in his temple!" His voice boomed throughout the chamber, and the walls themselves seemed to vibrate with his rage. "How dare you claim to be faithful to anyone, when you don't even believe in the god you serve! Get this sniveling coward out of my sight," he snapped to the guards, "before I kill him myself."

The guards moved in at once, seizing Inatol by the arms and dragging him away from the platform. "What is the Rathkir?" I whispered to High Priestess Anuket, confused.

"It is a punishment worse than death, reserved for the most heinous of criminals," Anuket said as she watched the guards haul Inatol away. I expected her to look triumphant, but her expression was grave as she looked on. "Inatol will be bound from head to toe in white linen, then locked inside a coffin and buried alive in a tomb."

"That's... gruesome," Quye said, looking both horrified and impressed. "What if someone tries to break him out?"

"There is no chance of that." Anuket smiled grimly. "Guards patrol the burial grounds to discourage grave robbers, and the God-King's priest will place booby traps on the tomb. Should anyone try to free Inatol, they will suffer a terrible curse that will be passed down through their family. No one would dare."

A chill ran down my spine, and as I looked up at the God-King again, I was thankful that I was, at least for now, on his good side. I expected him to call the imposter forward next, but to my surprise, he summoned Yaggir.

"Because you came forward and confessed, I will exempt you from punishment," he said. "As for the rest of your kith, they may choose between either banishment or twenty years of service. Except for the imposter," he added, pointing at the dragon in question. "He must die for his crime."

Yaggir's face paled, and the imposter snarled, his wings bursting from his back. "I don't answer to you!" he roared as his fangs punched through his gums and his claws sprouted. The crowd screamed as he launched himself at the God-King, eyes wild, fists blazing with fire, and I yelled, jumping forward to intervene.

But before I could take more than a step, Anuket raised her hand. A silvery-purple energy field flared to life in front of the king, swirling with strange runes I did not recognize, save for the moon-shaped symbol in its center. The imposter slammed into it, and blinding light flared, forcing everyone to throw their hands up and shield their eyes. A horrifying scream tore through the chamber as the energy field sizzled, and when I lowered my hand, all I saw were flecks of white ash floating in the air, settling into a pile before the God-King's throne.

"Well then," Quye said under her breath, sounding impressed. "Looks like these people have magic of their own."

"My apologies, Your Eminence," Anuket said, bowing before the God-King. "I should not have allowed him to get so close to you."

The God-King waved his hand. "That duty falls to my guards, not to you," he said, giving a mild look to the guards who had already rushed forward, but a little too late. "Please escort the dragons back to the Crocodile Temple. They have one day and one night to make their decision... and if any of them attempt to flee, they will join Inatol in his fate."

19

Adara

A fter the trial was dismissed, King Ramsenan's advisors kept us at the palace for another few hours, questioning us thoroughly about the world we'd come from and the nature of our mission. Once we'd assured them we posed no threat, and that the shadow creatures from our realm would not be coming through to infect theirs, they released us.

Yaggir was waiting for us on the steps of the palace entrance.

"Ahh, there you are," he said, a hesitant smile coming over his face. "I was hoping to speak with you before you leave."

"Me too," I confessed. "I wanted to thank you for coming forward. I don't know if the God-King would have believed us if you hadn't backed up our story."

Yaggir shook his head. "I should have joined Ylena in exile," he said, leading us further down the steps so we could sit and talk away from the entrance. We sat down on the wide marble steps, looking out over the vast gardens. "It never sat well with me, what we were doing, but I couldn't leave Myras in charge on his own. He's too hot-headed and impulsive."

"Myras?" Quye asked.

"Right." He laughed a little. "The imposter Sobek-Ra," he explained. "His real name is Myras, and he's one of Ylena's cousins. He's never been fond of her, and when Inatol approached him with the offer to make him a god, he jumped on the opportunity to wrest the leadership from her. But he doesn't have the temperament to lead, and I worried what he might do, so I told myself I needed to stay behind and act as the voice of reason." He shook his head. "But in reality, I was just being a coward. I should have gone to the island with the others."

"Perhaps," Quye said. "But I'm glad you didn't."

His head snapped up. "You are?"

"Of course I am," she said breezily. "If you hadn't been here, then you wouldn't have been able to corroborate our story, and Inatol and Myras wouldn't have been brought to justice." She winked. "One might even say your decision to stay behind was influenced by divine intervention."

Yaggir gave Quye a wry smile. "That would be letting myself off the hook a bit too much," he said. "But I am glad I could be here for you." He shifted to face me. "And I was wondering if I might offer you my help once more."

"In what way?" I asked, a little wary despite myself. I hated that I was becoming so jaded, but after my time in Usciete, I'd come to learn most people didn't offer help without strings attached.

"Well," he said, reaching into his pocket and withdrawing an envelope, "while you were being questioned by the advisors, I was interrogated by the God-King himself. Which, let me tell you, was not pleasant." He shuddered a little as he handed the envelope to me. "But at the end of it, he gave me this letter and told me to deliver it to Princess Ylena. It's a writ lifting her banishment, and that of the other dragons, so that they may leave the island and settle wherever they wish."

I lifted my eyebrows as I beheld the envelope, which was sealed in red wax and stamped with the royal seal—a round disc surrounded by a ring of lines I assumed represented the sun and its rays. "So why are you giving this to me, then?"

"Because I was hoping to take you with me, so you can deliver it to Ylena yourself."

"You're offering to give us a ride?" Quye asked, her tone brightening.

"Yes." Yaggir smiled. "The island is a five-day journey that is normally completed on camelback and by boat. I can get you there in less than half that time. Besides," he said, his gaze sweeping across the grounds, "it is not safe for you to stay in the city. The other dragons will seek revenge against you, and even High Priestess Anuket may not be able to protect you. It's best we get you out of the city as soon as possible."

After taking a few minutes to weigh the pros and cons, Quye and I agreed to travel with Yaggir. He escorted us, along with a trio of palace guards, back to the Moon Goddess temple so that we could collect our belongings, change into travel-appropriate clothing, and say goodbye to the High Priestess.

"Thank you for everything," I told her. "Is there anything we can do to repay you?"

The High Priestess smiled. "You helped us bring Inatol and the imposter to justice," she said. "It is I who should thank you. Please, take these with you. You will need sustenance on your journey."

A temple servant stepped forward, holding a sack in her arms, and I did a double-take. "Nysa? Is that you?"

Nysa smiled at me as she held out the package. "There's no need to look so shocked," she said teasingly.

"But... you're wearing acolyte robes." I stared at the white robes she was wearing, the symbols of the moon goddess embroidered in tiny silver thread along her sleeves and throat. "I thought you intended to remain a scholar?"

"I had a change of heart after everything that transpired between Inatol and the other priests," she said. She smiled at Anuket and added, "The Crocodile Cult might have been corrupt, but High Priestess Anuket is a shining example of what it means to be a religious leader, and I admire her greatly. I hope to follow in her footsteps someday."

Quye grinned. "I think you'll make an excellent priestess," she said. "You'll keep these boys in line and show them who's boss."

We thanked Nysa and the priestess one more time, then left. The sack was filled to the brim with pork dumplings, and Quye and I chowed down a few as we walked back to the main square of the temple district, where Yaggir was waiting for us.

A shadow fell across our path, and I looked up just in time to see a dragon descending upon us in half-dragon form, his wings spread wide. He unleashed a blast of fire upon us, and I shoved Quye out of the way, then threw both my palms up to block the flames. Drawing on my magic, I caught the giant ball of fire, then absorbed the energy into my body so the nearby buildings wouldn't go up in flames.

The dragon's eyes widened as he landed in the street in front of us. "How did you do that?" he demanded.

"She's half-dragon, you idiot!" Quye snapped. She flung out a hand and hit him with a gust of wind, sending him tumbling down the street. Turning, I raised my eyebrows when I saw her glaring at him in an unusual fit of pique. "He made me drop the dumplings," she said by way of explanation, indicating the food strewn all across the ground.

Shaking my head, I turned my attention back to the dragon, who was getting to his feet. Pissed, I stalked over to him and shoved my boot into his chest, pushing him back to the ground.

"Get off me!" he snarled. He tried to fight me, but I conjured an ice stake and drove it through his right wing, pinning him to the ground.

"How about we make a deal," I said, leaning over him and pressing my boot even harder into his chest as he screamed in agony. "You agree to stop trying to kill us, and I'll agree to stop trying to kill you. Is that agreeable?"

He spat in my face. "Fuck you! You're the enemy!"

I sighed, then pulled back my fist and punched him square in the jaw. His eyes rolled back into his head, and his head lolled to the side as he passed out.

"You sure we shouldn't kill him?" Quye asked dubiously as she walked up beside me. She clutched the sack of dumplings— which was about half its size now—to her chest as she stared at the unconscious dragon. "He didn't agree to your terms."

I shook my head. "Enough dragon blood has been spilled on my account already," I said. "I won't add more if I can help it."

We hurried out of the alleyway and onto the main street, sticking to the sides of the buildings and trying our best to stay out of trouble. I sighed in relief as I caught sight of Yaggir waiting for us next to the fountain in the square, and quickened my stride to reach him.

"Thank the Radiants you're alive," I said fervently.

"Of course I'm alive. This place is surrounded by guards." Yaggir frowned, noticing our flushed faces. "Did something happen?"

"A dragon attacked us," Quye said, glancing over her shoulder. "You were right that this place isn't safe for us—we should have asked High Priestess Anuket for an escort here."

"Can we leave right now?" I asked, feeling a little anxious. "Before something else happens?"

"Of course." Yaggir glanced around. The square wasn't particularly busy right now—there were a few people milling about, but there was plenty of space for him to shift. "I've always wanted to do this here," he admitted with a grin.

We took a few paces back, and Yaggir transformed, his body lengthening as scales rippled across his tanned skin. The people in the courtyard shouted in alarm as he grew, his body taking up a good third of the square as his tail and spikes sprouted from his spine. Despite his red hair coloring, his scales were green, glittering like emeralds in the afternoon sun. Stretching his neck, he lifted his head to the sky, then let out an earth-shaking roar that sent everyone running for cover.

"Yaggir!" I scolded. "You're scaring the humans!"

"I think that's the point," Quye said with a chuckle as he snorted. "You should be glad he didn't breathe fire at them while he was at it."

"That sounds like a good way to get banished," I said darkly.

Yaggir lowered his belly to the ground, then extended his wings so I could mount. His neck was slimmer than Einar's, so I was able to settle more comfortably astride him, using a notch between two of his dark blue spikes. Quye shifted into her owl form and perched on my lap, and then the three of us were off, winging our way toward the coastline.

We expected the dragons to pursue us, but to our relief, none followed. I hoped that meant the rest of them were being detained inside the temple as the God-King had commanded, and that the one who'd attacked us had been a one-off who'd snuck through the guards. If they attacked us in great enough numbers, they could overwhelm us.

You and Yaggir are both immune to fire magic, I reminded myself. *And Quye can use her air magic to protect against fire attacks. You'll be fine.*

We made it to the coast by nightfall, then found a sleepy

seaside inn to spend the night before continuing our journey the next day. I marveled at the sparkling sea below us as Yaggir flew tirelessly through the day—it was a strange, deep green color, far different from the crystal blue of Ediria's oceans.

I was dozing off on Yaggir's back when a movement in the sky caught my attention. Sitting up, I looked to my left—and my breath hitched at the sight of three dragons flying in formation toward us. Their scales glinted purple, indigo, and blue in the setting sun, and I braced myself, expecting a confrontation. Were these enemy dragons, sent by the Crocodile Cult to kill us? Or were these the exiled dragons we'd been searching for?

Yaggir turned to face the approaching dragons, answering my unspoken question. He let out a low-pitched warble, and something primal fluttered inside me in response. The dragons pulled up short, about ten yards from us, and they hissed as they took in our presence atop Yaggir's back. Quye hooted uneasily from her perch on my lap, and I held her close, drawing on my well of magic but holding back, at least for now.

The four dragons made no other noise, but their gazes shifted between one another, and I had a feeling they were communicating telepathically. Several long minutes passed before they reached an agreement, and then the strange dragons took up a formation around us, two of them flanking Yaggir while the other one brought up the rear.

Sweat slid down my back as our group descended through the cloud cover, revealing a group of islands below. There were five total, forming a sort of S-shape, and as we grew closer, I saw the largest one had a village, built along the island's eastern shore. Other dragons were coasting along the air currents, and they called greetings to us as we passed.

We landed on the beach, about half a mile from the village. The moment Yaggir's clawed feet touched the sand, I hopped off his back and Quye shifted back into her fae form. The dragons also shifted, and my heart began to beat faster—all three of them were female, with hair that matched their scales. They were dressed in colorful short-sleeved crop tops and loose, flowing wrap skirts made of some kind of natural woven fiber, stylized flame tattoos on full display, eyes gleaming with distrust.

"Yaggir." The purple-haired one stepped forward, a thunderous scowl on her face. She marched right up to the male and fisted her hand in the front of his shirt, bringing them nose to nose. "Tell me right now why I should not have your hide flayed and hung on the wall of my hut for turning your back on us."

"First of all," Yaggir said, raising his hands in a non-threatening gesture, "my hide is far too big to fit on your wall. And second of all, you already know why I'm here, and why you should spare my life."

"Yes, but your friends did not have the benefit of listening to our conversation." The indigo-haired dragon approached Quye, her head tilted to the side as she examined her. "You are the seer, I presume," she said, before turning to me. "Which makes you... the hybrid."

I tried not to bristle at her tone. "I have a name," I said evenly. "It's Adara."

"A very *fae* name." She wrinkled her nose. "I am Isador. The purple-haired one is Diyani, and my other sister is Rysla."

Rysla folded her arms beneath her chest as she stared at me. "Yaggir told us you are Daryan's daughter, but you barely look like him. How do we know Olette wasn't tupping someone else at the same time they were together?"

"Because if she was, I wouldn't be able to do this," I said, then chucked a fireball at her, lightning-fast. Rysla's eyes widened as she caught it, then tossed it from palm to palm, staring at it with great interest before snuffing it out.

"Your fire smells different," she informed me.

I blinked at her. "It does?"

"Absolutely." She rubbed the tip of her nose. "It's a strange scent, one I can't quite place, but it reminds me of winter."

"Really?" Diyani released Yaggir and came over to me. "Show me," she demanded.

Bemused, I lit a flame in my palm and held it out for her. She sniffed it, and her eyes widened as she looked toward her sisters. "It *does* smell different."

The three of them took turns sniffing for a moment, but we were interrupted by the arrival of several young children, who had spotted us from wherever they were playing. Isador intercepted them before they could get too close, and she herded them back toward the village, shooting glances at us over her shoulder along the way.

Clearly, we weren't to be trusted around the children. Or at least, not yet.

"Come," Diyani commanded, waving me forward. "We will bring you to Ylena, so you can deliver this letter and make your request for aid. Whether she will accept is another matter, especially given the company you keep." She shot Yaggir a nasty look over her shoulder, then marched off, leaving us to follow.

"Is it just me," Quye said in a low voice as we trudged through the sand, "or is her vendetta against Yaggir personal?"

"Diyani served alongside me and Einar in the army," Yaggir explained in a heavy voice. "She and I were close once, and she has a strong bond with Ylena. She was heartbroken when I chose Myras's side over theirs."

"Heartbroken?" Diyani scoffed from up ahead. "Don't make me laugh. I just get angry when I see trash littering the island."

"Yup," Quye said brightly. "Definitely personal."

I elbowed her in the ribs. "Are you trying to get us killed?" I hissed.

"What?" Quye complained, rubbing the spot I'd struck. "I

live for this kind of drama. Besides, they're not going to kill us. We're far too interesting for that."

We entered the village, and my skin prickled with a strange combination of self-consciousness and excitement. Everywhere I looked, there were dragons of all ages and sizes—children playing in the streets, adults talking or doing chores. All of them turned to look at us as we passed, their curiosity turning to shock and fear as they beheld Quye and me, taking in pointed ears and fae coloring. My heart sank—I knew I couldn't expect to be welcomed with open arms, but it would have been nice not to be viewed with suspicion, hostility, or fear. Aside from the ice fae at the Bala Oighr, my time at Usciete had taught me that my water fae family only saw me as a pawn to be played in their sordid game of chess. It was a little disheartening to realize that neither halves of my heritage might ever see past what I represented, and to the person who lay beneath it.

But then again, I didn't come here to make friends. I came here to complete the ritual and get back to my world. Back to Einar, and the friends I already had, so I could save our home from Nox and her shadow cohort.

Isador rejoined our group, her face flushed with exertion. "I've informed Ylena of our visitors," she told Diyani. "She is waiting in her hut for them."

My heart beat faster as we stopped outside a hut located toward the edge of the village closest to the jungle. This one was bigger than all the rest, with a sturdy wooden frame and walls crafted of bamboo and palm fronds. The roof was thatched with palm leaves that sloped gently downward, and the entrance was marked by a wooden door, also woven with palm fronds, that hung on leather hinges. The door was flanked on either side by large, tropical flowers, their colors bright and striking against the hut's earth tones, and more palm trees loomed from behind, casting welcome shade across the dwelling.

Diyani knocked on the door, and a female voice told her to enter. A frisson of nervous energy shot down my spine as she opened the door and we stepped over the threshold. The inside was shadowy and cool, with a fresh breeze from the ocean blowing in from the many open windows. A fearsome-looking spear tipped with a curved blade hung on the wall above the sitting area, the other walls adorned with woven baskets, seashells, and other small trinkets. Woven mats made of natural fibers covered the floors, and a large wooden table with a few chairs gathered around it dominated the center of the room. Toward the back was a curtained-off area that I surmised was Ylena's private sleeping chambers.

My eyes zeroed in on the tall female standing by one of the windows, staring at the clear blue ocean lapping at the shoreline that lay a mere hundred yards away.

"Ylena," Diyani said. "I have brought the visitors."

Ylena turned from the window. She was as majestic as a dragon queen should be, with long, golden hair falling in waves down her back, save for the two sections along the sides of her scalp that had been braided away from her face. Tall and well-muscled, she wore a sleeveless garnet dress that gathered in tight below her bust before falling in a long curtain down to just above her ankles. A more delicate, feminine version of the gold cuff I wore on my bicep encircled her left wrist, the red primal stone catching the fiery sunset and throwing its rays against the far wall.

"Well," she said, raking us with her fiery-gold gaze. "This is a surprise."

I cleared my throat, trying to work past the ball of nerves attempting to rob me of speech. "I'm not sure how to address you," I said. "Should I call you 'Queen Ylena', or would 'Auntie' be more appropriate?"

Ylena raised an eyebrow as she approached. She did a slow

circle around me, ignoring Quye and Yaggir. "I have not taken the title of queen, though it is mine by right," she said. "And yet, I am not sure I am willing to allow you to call me auntie, given that there is no true familial bond between us."

"Familial bond?" Yaggir asked. "She is your niece, Ylena. What more do you need?"

"Just because my brother's blood runs in her veins doesn't mean she is family," Ylena snapped, whirling on Yaggir. "Family isn't just about shared lineage, Yaggir. It's about the people who are truly there for you, who have your back during the good times and the bad, who stick by you when their loyalty is tested. Something you would know nothing about."

Yaggir flinched. "I had my reasons for doing what I did," he said. "They may not have been the right reasons, but I cannot undo my decision now."

"As far as loyalty is concerned," I said before Ylena could respond, "Yaggir could have kept his mouth shut and allowed the High Priest to defame me in front of the God-King. Instead, he risked his life not once, but twice, by revealing the truth about Myras and then bringing me to you." I paused for effect. "I think that deserves some credit."

"Perhaps." Ylena turned away from Yaggir to face me again. "I was told you have a letter. Hand it to me, please."

"Actually," I said, smiling as I reached for my pack. "I have two."

I pulled out the envelope from the God-King, and a second one that I'd brought from Ediria, and handed them over. Ylena frowned as she looked at the first one, but her eyes widened as she beheld the second, and she tossed the God-King's missive aside as if it were no more consequential than a piece of packaging.

"This is written in Einar's hand," she said, ripping the letter open.

"Yes," I confirmed. "He could not come with me himself, so he asked me to give you this letter instead."

Ylena's eyes scanned the letter, then read it over again, slower this time. My stomach clenched as the seconds ticked by. I had no idea what the contents of the letter were, only that Einar told me he hoped it would convince Ylena to accept me as her kin.

Finally, Ylena gently folded the letter, tucking it into her pocket like it was a priceless treasure. "You're his mate," she said, meeting my gaze. "And yet, I can scent that the two of you have not consummated the bond. Why?"

"We decided it was too dangerous to complete it now, when he was about to send me to your realm," I explained. "If I were to be killed, Einar might die as well, and then the portal to this realm would be torn open. Given that the Shadows are on the verge of taking Ediria, it would only be a matter of time before they tired of our world and found their way into your new one. We couldn't allow that to happen."

"I see." Ylena picked up the God-King's letter and read that next. A conflicted look passed over her face as she took in the news, and she looked over at Yaggir. "This is your doing?"

He shook his head. "I cannot take credit for the God-King's mercy."

"What mercy?" Diyani demanded. "What is this letter?"

"The God-King has lifted our exile." Ylena held out the letter so Diyani could read it herself. "We are free to leave this island and settle wherever we wish."

"Hmm." Isador tapped her chin from her post by the doorway. "Seems to me that the God-King wouldn't have made that decision if Yaggir and Adara didn't speak up on our behalf."

Diyani glared at her sister, but Ylena nodded thoughtfully. She spread her arm wide, waving toward the sitting area. "Einar mentioned the Shadows, but he has a way of being frustratingly brief with his missives. Please, explain to me what has occurred in Ediria since me and my people have left."

Quye and I did as she said, spending the next several hours debriefing Ylena about everything that had occurred in Ediria since she and her fellow dragons had left. We told her about General Aolis taking the throne, about the shadow magic infection spreading throughout the kingdom, about the prophecy and my role in it, and his efforts to find me before I came into my powers so he could control the outcome. About the Shadow I'd accidentally released when I killed him, and how she was manipulating the other fae into starting a civil war so she could tip the balance of light and dark in our realm and bring other Shadows through.

"So, you have come here to ask me to help you perform the Umnar, so that you might return with this hidden power and defeat the Shadow?" Ylena said when paused to drink some coconut water. I'd never encountered the milky beverage before, but it was served inside the shell of the nut it had come from, and was curiously refreshing.

"That's the plan," I said.

"And if I refuse?"

A chill of foreboding rippled down my spine. "Why would you refuse?" Diyani asked, a suspicious note in her voice. "Einar himself has asked us to help her. You don't think we owe him our loyalty?"

"Absolutely we do," Ylena said, "but Adara here is not Einar, and I do not know her. That she and Einar did not complete the mating bond before parting ways tells me that on some level, they do not trust each other, which means I do not trust her either."

"Now wait just a minute—" I started, indignant, but Ylena held up a hand.

"Hush. You may think you have everything figured out, but

you are barely out of your childhood years, and you know nothing of dragons and our ways," Ylena said, her voice as harsh as the winter winds of Bala Oighr. She did not move from her chair, and yet somehow she seemed to tower over me, her presence swelling to fill the entire room. The scents of fire and sweet cedar thickened the air as her eyes glowed with power. "I will not prepare you for the Umnar, at least not until I have had a chance to take your measure. Until then, the three of you may stay on the island as guests."

20

Mavlyn

Mavlyn tried not to betray her nerves as she walked into the basement of the Earth Guardians Club one week after Roylan had invited her to the next club meeting. The place was packed with students—all earth fae, since the water and air fae who had been attending had returned to their home cities once rumors of civil war began circulating.

Mavlyn wasn't certain whether it was because all these people were packed into a small room, or because she'd already had an unpleasant experience with public speaking, but she could feel a panic attack coming on. Her heart was palpitating, and beads of sweat slid down her spine to gather at the small of her back.

"Mav," Leap said in a low voice from behind her. "You're sprouting."

Mavlyn glanced down and nearly swore at the sight of the dream weed unfurling from a pouch on her belt. Wrestling for control, she used her magic to undo the rapid plant growth, then forced her power into a box inside her and clamped it down with several heavy locks.

Thankfully, no one was paying any attention to her, as they had no idea who she was or that she had come to speak.

"Do you need a minute?" Emelie whispered. The three of them were hanging back by the entrance, so they hadn't been noticed yet. Several students shuffled into the room, and Mavlyn pressed her back against the wall so they could pass by. "I can ask Roylan to give you some time."

Mavlyn shook her head. "The longer we drag this out, the more nervous I get," she said. "I'd rather do it sooner than later."

"Good evening, my friends!" Roylan called out in his booming voice. The room quieted at once, and he gave everyone a beaming smile. Mavlyn wished she had even an ounce of his charisma—Roylan had a way of lighting up a room, drawing everyone's attention regardless of what they had been occupied with before he'd entered. "And welcome to the weekly Earth Guardians Club Meeting!"

Roylan took a few moments to address some general news, announcing a few new members as well as the general agenda for the meeting. "Before we get into this week's projects," he said, "I have a special guest I've invited to speak. Please welcome Mavlyn of Fenwood!"

The audience clapped politely as Mavlyn walked up to the front of the room to address them. There weren't as many people here as there had been in Fenwood when she'd addressed her fellow villagers, yet because of the room's compact size, the audience before her seemed larger. Trying not to be intimidated by the dozens of eyes on her, she focused her gaze on Emelie, who gave her an encouraging smile from her place in the audience.

"Hello everyone," Mavlyn said, and she took pride in the fact that her voice didn't crack when she spoke. "I've come to talk to you about the upcoming draft. Many of you will have heard by now that Lady Mossi is calling for more able-bodied fae to join the army because the water fae are planning to invade and take over our farmlands." She paused for effect, then said, "But I have come to warn you that House Ithir has been lying to you about not only the reason for the draft, but the conflict between the fae realms in general."

Mavlyn went on to explain that the true conflict between the fae centered on the line of succession, and also the truth about King Aolis's use of shadow magic and the demon he'd loosed into the world upon his death. The students reacted predictably to this news—most shocked, many angry, others skeptical or disbelieving.

"How can you be sure Lady Mossi is lying to us, and that the water fae aren't planning to invade?" a female student called from the back.

"Because during my journey here from Lochanlee, I ran across a water fae village destroyed by General Slaugh and his army," Mavlyn said. Shocked murmurs rippled through the students as she added, "There have been no reported attacks on Domhain from either the water or earth fae, which means Lady Mossi, or rather Nox through her, has struck the first blow. She aims to antagonize the water fae so that we will fight each other."

"But doesn't that mean the water fae are going to retaliate?" someone else asked. "We can't just allow them to destroy one of our villages in return! We have to be prepared!"

"Lady Mossi has plenty of soldiers in the earth fae army already, and not to mention the Griffin Riders," Roylan interjected. He'd retreated a few paces away to give Mavlyn the floor, but he stepped forward now, commanding the room's attention. "She does not need to draft the fresh young minds here at

Talamh University to patrol our borders. And while the water fae may try to retaliate, the answer is not to redouble our attacks against them."

"How do you know this Shadow really exists?" another student challenged, "and that she is manipulating Lady Mossi? Mossi isn't some pushover—she's centuries old, and one of the most powerful fae in Ediria. I find it hard to believe a fae as ancient and powerful as her could be taken over by a Shadow."

"Lady Mossi hasn't been possessed," Mavlyn said. "At least not yet. Nox has the power to use her shadow magic to influence the minds of others to a degree, and the fact that she is impersonating one of Mossi's own granddaughters makes it that much easier to manipulate her. But if Nox can get us to kill each other, she will use the dark magic generated by that bloodshed to bring others of her kind into our world. And if that happens, she will be unstoppable."

"That still doesn't explain how you know all of this," the student said, sounding exasperated. The others nodded and voiced their agreements. "How do you expect us to trust your word over Lady Mossi's?"

"I don't," Mavlyn said simply. She'd thought the disagreements from the students would discourage her—instead, she found their skepticism strangely motivating, some hidden part of her rising to the challenge. "What I do expect is for you to think for yourselves. Even if you don't believe me regarding Nox and the shadow magic infection, it's easy enough to see the throne is true conflict here. Are you all willing to risk your lives just to make General Slaugh the next king of Ediria? Why does Slaugh even deserve to be king? King Aolis before him was also a general, and that didn't make him a fit leader. Look at where we are now, because of him!"

The room exploded with chatter, the students arguing amongst themselves and shouting more questions at Mavlyn.

Excitement thrummed in her veins as she fielded the questions as best as she could—this kind of discourse, the exchange of ideas and debates, was something she could handle. It was why she'd enrolled at Talamh University in the first place, why she'd been so eager to attend and get away from the close-minded villagers she'd grown up with. And while there was no guarantee she would be able to convince the students of her argument, at least they were actually *discussing* what she'd said, rather than threatening to imprison her for daring to challenge authority.

"Oi!" a voice shouted, and Mavlyn started as she realized Leap was standing at her elbow. She'd been so caught up in the room's energy, she hadn't noticed his approach. When none of the students responded, he puffed out his chest, then tried again. "OI!"

The sound exploded from his mouth, along with a blast of wind that knocked everyone against the backs of their chairs. The students stared open-mouthed at Leap, who crossed his arms over his chest and smirked.

"Now that I have your attention," he said, "I wanted to add to what Mavlyn was saying about supporting General Slaugh earlier. Even if you decide to fight for him, it's going to be the earth fae against both the air and water fae. The water fae have their own candidate, and the air fae have declared that they are going to withdraw from the Edirian alliance, so they aren't supporting Slaugh either. And in case it's escaped you," he added with a drawl, sending another gust of wind around the room, "the reason I know about this is that I'm an air fae myself. So you could say I have some insider knowledge."

"And how do we know that the air fae didn't send you to spread lies and disinformation?" the same student from earlier challenged. "That you aren't trying to get us to lay our arms down, to make it easier for the Gaoth Aire's army to invade?"

Leap snorted. "I'm fourteen years old," he pointed out. "Don't you think Lord Oren would have sent someone of age to infiltrate the university, someone who would fit in, instead of sending in a kid with dyed green hair?"

"He has a point," one of the other students said.

The students debated this for another ten minutes before Roylan called them to order again. "We've got to get on with the rest of the agenda," he said, pointing to the black board where he'd written said agenda out. "But if anyone would like to talk to Mavlyn about joining the anti-war effort, and what they can do to help, she'll be here at the end of the meeting."

Mavlyn thanked the students for their time, then rejoined Emelie. Her friend gave her hand an encouraging squeeze, but even though the meeting moved on, Mavlyn could feel eyes on her from all around the room. Had she done the right thing by coming here in person to spread this message? Or had she just painted a target on her back?

21

Adara

The following week passed on the island with excruciating slowness. While the other dragons—eager to hear news of their homeland and fascinated by the presence of both a half-dragon and a seer—had warmed up to us, Ylena had kept her distance. She'd suggested that I make myself useful, so I'd been spending my time on chores around the village, winning over the dragons by helping them with various tasks and projects.

"There has got to be an easier way to do this," Quye complained as we sat beneath the awning of Isador's hut, shelling peas. We had two baskets in front of us, one for the discarded pods, and the other for the fresh peas. "Isn't there a device or machine? Or some magical way we could do this?"

"Why, because you have something better to do?" I said, meaning only to tease. But there was a sharp edge to my voice, because in truth, I was only half-joking. "If Mavlyn was here, she could probably get these peas to wiggle out of their pods all on their own. But since she's not, we're on our own."

Quye huffed. "Of course I have something better to do," she said. "I could be performing readings right now, or telling stories to the children by the fire. You know, the things a seer is expected to do."

I rolled my eyes. Quye had been eating up her seer status since we'd arrived on the island. The dragons had mistrusted her at first since she was full fae, but she'd won them over by doing a few dream readings and fortune tellings, and had become a favorite of the children, who had not grown up with an inherent dislike of fae as their parents had. There were fifty or so dragons on the island—most of the original thirty who had been exiled here were still alive, and they'd had many children over the last twenty years, nearly doubling their numbers. At the moment, the island was large enough to sustain them, but they would outgrow the place in another decade.

"I could also," she added as she sprinkled a handful of peas into the basket, "be deciphering that fire fae journal."

"Aha," I said. "The real reason you've been trying to palm off chores on me." I shook my head, not sure whether to be amused or irritated. "Have you found anything of interest in that journal?"

The sound of the door opening interrupted us before Quye could answer. "Have you two finished shucking the peas yet?" Orga asked, stepping onto the porch to join us. She was one of the dragon elders, her face lined with age and her jet-black braid liberally streaked with silver. The beads embroidered on her skirts tinkled a little as she joined us, and the wind shifted, bringing her patchouli scent with it.

"Not yet," Quye said, glancing down into the bowl. "We're about halfway through, though. I think we can finish it in another thirty minutes."

Orga nodded approvingly, resting a wizened hand on Quye's shoulder. "I'm glad you two stopped by to help," she said. "My hands can still do the work, but they're not as nimble as they used to be. Would take me twice the time."

"Elder Orga, do you mind if I ask you a question?" I said, pausing my work for a moment so I could meet her eyes. They were golden, like most dragon's, but with a jet black rim on the outside of her irises that made it feel like her attention was focused solely on you.

"Of course," she said, nodding her head. "So long as you keep shucking those peas."

Chagrined, I snatched up a fresh pod from the basket. "Forgive me if the question is offensive, but were you alive when the dragons first arrived in Ediria?" I didn't know enough about dragons to understand how they aged, but since only ancient fae showed signs of aging, I took a guess that the dragons might be the same.

Orga laughed. "Radiants, no," she said, shaking her head. "I am old, it's true, but I was born five hundred years after."

I nearly choked on my spit. That meant Orga was twenty-five hundred years old... longer lived than any of the fae. "How are you... I mean..."

"How am I still alive?" she finished for me, and I nodded. A knowing twinkle sparked in her eye as she answered, "Being an elder has its perks. Back when I was a child, female dragons didn't fight in the wars, only the males. We were expected to stay behind and protect and rear our children. By the time that changed, I was considered 'too old' to join, so I was never drafted. I have always served my people in an advisory capacity."

"I'm sure you've still seen and done a lot, even if you never fought in the war," I said. "Did your parents ever tell you any stories about the early days, when dragons first arrived?"

Orga's gaze grew distant, her nose wrinkled as she dredged

up long-buried memories. "It is difficult to remember," she finally said, "but I don't believe my parents ever spoke of our arrival."

"So you don't know how you got to Ediria?" I asked, a little incredulous. "Or what happened to the fire fae?"

Orga shook her head. "No. None of us do. And, if I'm honest," she said, her eyes narrowing thoughtfully, "I've always suspected that the reason my parents never spoke of that fateful day is because they don't remember it."

"How is that possible?" I shucked another pea, my movements jerky with frustration, then cursed as the tiny green vegetables scattered all over the floor. Quye saved me from having to pick them up with a wave of her hand, conjuring a gentle breeze to lift the peas from the floor and deposit them into the basket.

"I've been spending the last week translating a journal I found in the ruins," Quye said. "The writer was a fire fae named Pyros, and he was obsessed with a summoning spell he'd stolen from the witchlings and tried to modify."

"Pyrios?" Orga said, frowning. "What an interesting name. Very similar to my father's name, Pyrgos."

"Really?" Quye raised her eyebrows. "Do you think there's some connection?"

"I don't see how, since they didn't live at the same time. Besides, my father was a dragon of honor—he would never dabble in stolen magics. What was this fire fae hoping to accomplish with this spell, anyway?"

"I haven't gotten to that part of the journal," Quye admitted, "but I suspect he was trying to summon—"

"Adara?" a young dragon—Linos, I think his name was—approached the front porch, carrying a basket in his right hand and balancing an enormous fishing rod on his left shoulder.

"Miss Ylena told me to come find you. She says you're to help me with the fishing today."

"Fishing?" Quye wrinkled her nose. "Sounds horrid." She took the mostly empty basket of pea pods from me and placed it in her lap. "I think I'll stay here with Orga and discuss the journal a bit more."

I rolled my eyes, then left the two of them and followed Linos out of the village and toward the shoreline. The dragons had set up a dock along one of the beaches, where a large, sturdy wooden boat bobbed in the water, waiting for us.

"I'm surprised you're using fishing rods," I said as we loaded our supplies into the boat. "Can't you just fly over the ocean and catch fish like the sea birds?" I gestured to a large, grey and white bird with an enormous, bucket-like beak as I spoke. I'd been watching the strange creatures all week, flying over the waves and dipping into the water with their open bills to scoop up prey.

Limos gave me a wry grin. "If I were the size of that bird, it might be effective," he said, "but the shadows we dragons cast are too big. The fish see us coming and they scatter before we can get close enough to grab them. Also, our mouths might be bigger, but we have way too many gaps. Even if we caught a fish, they'd slip right out."

"Huh." I took Limos's hand, allowing him to help me into the boat. "Well, I guess that makes sense. Dragons aren't meant to be fishers."

"No," he agreed with a laugh. "But there's not too much else to eat on this island, so we've had to make do."

Picking up the oars, Limos rowed us away from the shoreline, heading for the open ocean. As we moved farther and farther away from the beach, I privately wished I'd completed the ritual and unlocked the rest of my powers. If Cascada were here, she'd probably scorn me for my inability to use my water magic to move the boat or control the current in other ways. I was certain water fae didn't use fishing rods. They probably dove into the water and caught them with their bare hands, manipulating the currents to bring the fish right to them.

But then again, if I'd completed the ritual, I wouldn't be on this boat right now.

"All right, this is far enough." Limos stopped rowing. "Can you drop the anchor?"

"Sure."

I grabbed the heavy metal object attached to the boat by a chain, and heaved it overboard while Limos prepared the fishing line. He reached into the basket and withdrew a bait fish, then attached it to the hook and lowered it into the ocean.

An hour passed with very little activity aside from the sea birds calling to each other over the spray of the ocean. A cool breeze caressed my skin, taking the edge off the sun blazing overhead, and I had to struggle against the urge to drift off.

I was about to pinch myself for the third time when there was a giant tug on the line, and the boat rocked forward.

"Help me!" Linos cried, seizing the rod. I grabbed hold of it as well, struggling to keep it from flying overboard. But whatever creature had latched onto the other end meant business, tugging ferociously on the other end and forcing us to retreat to the other side of the boat to keep from capsizing.

"We've got to cut the line!" Linos said, his tone pitched high with panic. "Or else we'll go overboard!"

He let go of the rod with one hand to draw a knife from his belt sheath. But just as he was about to cut it, the boat pitched forward, and the blade went spinning into the ocean.

"Hang on tight!" I shouted as Linos spewed curses from his mouth. "I'll get it!"

Before Linos could protest, I leaped overboard. Linos yelled something, but his words died away as the ocean current rushed around me, muffling the world lurking just above the surface of the waves. This time, my gills opened on either side of my neck without effort, allowing me to breathe. I propelled myself deeper, following the fishing line to see what was caught on the other end.

To my horror, I found a large, orca-like creature tethered to the line, the hook sunk deep into its mouth. Her calves swam around her, crooning anxiously, but they were too young to figure out how to free their mother, and the orca herself seemed unable to bite the line off herself, the hook caught at an odd angle.

Knowing I would never be able to find the knife before she capsized the boat, I seized the line and drew on my ice magic. The line hardened, and I grabbed it with both hands and snapped it in half, severing the connection.

The orca, suddenly freed, flew backwards several feet through the water before she righted herself. I watched as she shook her head, trying to get her bearings while her calves bumped her with their snouts, their fins wiggling with joy.

When the orca didn't make an immediate move to leave, I cautiously swam toward her, keeping my movements slow and deliberate. She stilled as she saw me coming, and I stopped a few feet away, then pointed to the piece of fishing line still hanging from her mouth.

For a few seconds, I thought she didn't comprehend what I was trying to say. But then she turned to her calves and made a cooing sound, motioning with one of her fins. The babies retreated behind her, and she turned back to me, opening her mouth and waiting.

A wave of nervous energy prickled across my skin as I approached. Placing one hand atop her head in reassurance, I slowly reached inside her mouth with the other and tried to pretend I wasn't sticking my hand in between two rows of long, dagger-like teeth that could snap my arm in two. I grasped the fishing line and slid my fingers along it until I located the hook, which was jammed into the roof of her mouth.

"I'm very sorry about this," I mouthed to her, then yanked it out in one swift motion.

The orca flinched, her mouth snapping shut a millisecond after I'd cleared her mouth. Clouds of blood filled the surrounding water, and the calves darted forward, circling frantically around their mother. I backed a safe distance away, in case her maternal instincts kicked in, but after a moment, she calmed, nuzzling the calves to reassure them.

The mother lifted her head to meet my gaze, and I could have sworn she nodded at me. Then she turned and swam away, her babies following at her sides.

Bubbles clouded the air in front of me as I let out a breath I hadn't realized I was holding. Heart racing from the thrill of that encounter, I stared after the creatures, watching as they grew smaller and smaller in the distance until I remembered Linos was still waiting for me on the boat, probably worrying himself to death.

Angling my body toward the ocean floor, I propelled myself downward, searching for the dagger. I found it lodged in a large piece of orange coral, and yanked it free, careful not to touch it in case the aquatic plant was poisonous.

I was halfway back to the surface again when I sensed movement out of the corner of my eye. Turning toward it, my heart leaped in my throat at the sight of a long, wicked looking fish with silver scales hurtling toward me through the water. It had glowing yellow eyes and a diamond-shaped head, and fear shot through me as it opened its mouth to reveal several rows of serrated teeth.

I dodged to the left as it attempted to take a chunk out of my arm, then drove the dagger clutched in my fist into its side.

Blood spewed into the water, clouding the air between us as the fish thrashed, and I hissed as one of its sharp fins scraped against my forearm, cutting it open. Rage overtook me, and I struck blindly, landing another lucky hit. The fish stopped moving, and as it sank, dragging me down with it, the blood cleared away to reveal that I'd stabbed it right through its vicious yellow eye.

Yanking the dagger out, I swam beneath the fish so I could position myself underneath it, then wrapped one arm around it to hold it against my back while I swam to the surface. The aquatic beast, while significantly smaller than the orca, was still heavy, and by the time I broke the surface of the water, my arms and legs were leaden.

"Limos!" I yelled, spotting the boat several yards away. "I caught something!"

Limos quickly rowed the boat toward me, stopping a foot away from me. His mouth dropped open when I lifted the enormous fish above my head, my arms trembling from the effort.

"That's a giant barracuda!" he exclaimed, his eyes bulging. "How are you holding it above your head while treading water? It must weigh at least two-hundred pounds!"

"I'm stronger than I look," I grunted. "Now, are you going to take this thing off my hands or what?"

"Right." Sheepish, Limos tossed the fishing rod he was holding aside, then leaned over the side to take the fish from me. It was a struggle for us to get it into the boat without capsizing it, and when it was finally done, the young dragon shook his head, his boyish face filled with disbelief.

"Here," I said, holding his knife out to him. "I got this back for you."

Limos shook his head. "You should keep it. You earned it." He glanced back at the fish, then at me again, and winced. "I'm not sure if there's room in the boat for you, though."

"That's fine. I can swim back. Just take this thing so I don't accidentally drop it. I went through way too much effort to get it back."

"What was on the other end of the line?" he asked, leaning over the boat to take the weapon from me.

"A mother orca and her two babies." I smiled as his face paled. "Don't worry, I freed her and removed the hook from her mouth. All three of them are safe."

Limos gave me a strange look. "I can't tell if I admire you or if I think you're crazy," he said.

I gave him a crooked smile. "Why not both?"

Limos snorted. "I'll meet you back at the beach."

Nodding, I dove beneath the waves, activating my gills again. Despite my ordeal with the barracuda, the ocean current reinvigorated me, and I cut through the water with ease, making it back well before Limos.

The two of us secured the boat, then carried the fish up the sand and back to the village. The other dragons cheered, and Ylena came out of her hut to watch from her porch as we approached. We laid our massive catch at her feet, then stepped back so she could inspect it.

"A giant barracuda." Ylena gave Limos a pleased smile. "You caught this?"

Limos ducked his head. "No, Miss Ylena. Adara did."

Ylena's eyebrows winged up as her gaze flicked toward me. "Did she now?"

"Yes." Limos told Ylena the whole story while the other dragons gathered around to listen. Her expression remained impassive as he told her how I'd rescued both the orca and the fishing boat, then used the knife to slay the fish and swim back to the surface with it, but the other dragons were impressed by the feat.

"I'm surprised you weren't able to use your water magic to

carry the fish back to the boat," Ylena said to me when he finished.

I shrugged. "I know I look like a water fae, but it's much easier for me to wield fire magic. Once I complete the ritual, I should be able to access a wider range of abilities, but right now, ice magic seems to be the only type of water magic I can reliably use."

Ylena nodded. "Well, I hope you're not too tired to put that knife to good use again. That fish needs to be gutted and filleted before we can cook it."

She turned away, and I buried a sigh as she walked back into her hut. Limos gave me an apologetic glance, and Yaggir stepped forward, clapping a hand on my shoulder.

"Ylena can be a cold fish sometimes," he said, pitching his voice low so that the dragoness wouldn't hear. "Try not to let it get to you. I've known her long enough to tell when she's warming up to someone, and you definitely left a good impression today."

I nodded, though I wasn't entirely sure whether I believed his words. Limos and a few other dragons hefted the fish up, then brought it to the communal kitchen area, where several others were already at work skinning and chopping vegetables. They laid the enormous creature on one of the counters, and I hesitantly approached, not sure where to start.

"Here." I started as Ylena came up beside me, a long, thin knife in her hand. "Let me show you what to do."

She taught me how to clean and fillet the fish, and we worked alongside each other in silence. I was a little surprised she'd decided to teach me herself—I'd seen her doing village chores alongside the others, but she could have delegated this task to someone else. Yet she'd taken it upon herself to show me what to do. Perhaps Yaggir was right after all.

Once we'd finished filleting the fish, we wrapped the individual portions in leaves, then set them atop hot coals to roast them. Within no time, the aroma of sizzling fish filled the air, and my stomach grumbled loudly.

"Mmm." Quye entered the outdoor kitchen, her eyes gleaming with interest as I worked with the others to remove the freshly-grilled fish. "Is this the sea monster you caught?"

"I wouldn't call it a sea monster," I said wryly as I set one of the fillets on the counter. "Just a really big, mean fish."

Quye snorted. "I saw that thing when you brought it to Ylena's hut. It looked like a monster to me." She reached for the fillet I'd set down, which was still wrapped in the leaves, then snatched her hand back at once, hissing. "Squalls, that's burning hot! How can you touch it with your bare hands?"

"I'm half-dragon," I reminded her. "Fireproof."

Quye tapped her chin in thought. "I wonder if it's your dragon side that allows you to touch burning things, or if your water fae side protects you." She waved a hand, and the remaining fillets all sailed off the coals and onto the counter, startling the other dragons.

"You could have given us some warning," Ylena said mildly, raising an eyebrow at Quye.

The Oracle grinned. "I could give warnings about lots of things. But where would the fun be in that?"

Finished, the dragons all came to take helpings of fish and vegetables, thanking those of us who'd prepared the food for the meal. Someone had built a bonfire, and everyone gathered around it to eat and talk.

"You did good today," Diyani said, plopping down next to me on the log I was sitting on. "Catching and cooking a fish like that is no mean feat."

"And you saved that mother orca, too," Isador said, sitting down on my other side. She wiggled her eyebrows at Diyani. "Looks like Yaggir was right about her."

Diyani huffed, but I noticed her gaze stray to where Yaggir sat a few paces away, in deep conversation with Quye. His gaze flickered our way, and a slow grin spread over his face as he caught her staring.

"Cheeky bastard," she grumbled, yanking her gaze away, and I had to hide my grin at the spots of color riding high on her cheeks.

"Looks like your soft spot for Yaggir hasn't gone away," Isador teased.

"Do I look like I have any soft spots to you?" Diyani growled, raising an arm so she could flex her well-toned biceps.

"Not on the outside, maybe, but—"

A shadow fell over us, and we turned to see Ylena standing behind us. Her tall, lithe form was backlit by the setting sun, the flames from the bonfire lending a fiery glow to her golden hair so that it matched her eyes. She looked every bit as regal as the day I'd met her, even though her hair was mussed from the long afternoon of work, and there were a few smudges of coal on her cheek and arms that she'd missed.

"I would get seconds if I were you," she said, indicating my empty leaf with a tilt of her chin.

"Seconds? Why?"

"Because," she said, her lips curling into the first genuine smile I'd seen, "You'll be starting your fast for the ritual tomorrow."

22

Mavlyn

M avlyn experienced a rude awakening when she joined Leap, Emelie, and her family for breakfast the next morning.

"Good morning," Emelie's father greeted her from his seat at the breakfast table. He was reading a copy of the Talamh Tribune as he sipped on his morning coffee, his bushy eyebrows barely visible from behind the paper. "Did you know you made the news today?"

"What?" Mavlyn froze in the doorway, her eyes darting to Emelie. Her friend flinched, then dropped her gaze to her bowl of porridge. Leap, on the other hand, seemed pleased. "What do you mean, I made the news?"

"Your little political rally from last night made the papers," Emelie's father explained. He folded the newspaper over, then handed it to Mavlyn, who barely refrained from snatching it out of his grip. Heart thundering in her ears, Mavlyn unfolded the paper and read the article, which took up half a page. Apparently, one of the students who'd attended the club meeting last night worked for the paper, and had done a write-up and submitted it just in time for printing. Mavlyn braced herself for harsh words or criticism, but to her surprise, the piece only reported on the facts she herself had presented. It didn't take sides, but it did urge viewers to consider the information and do their own research, while also reminding them army drafts are mandatory and that any legal consequences incurred are their own responsibility.

"Well," she said, setting the paper down. "This isn't as bad as I expected."

"Bad?" Leap's eyes sparked indignantly. "Mavlyn, this is exactly what we wanted!"

"You're not mad, then?" Emelie said, the relief evident in her voice. She took the paper from Mavlyn, a hopeful look on her face. "I know you said you wanted to wait on the article, so I wasn't sure how you'd react. One of the Tribune's associate editors was at the meeting last night, and when Roylan's sister heard about the story, she'd seized it and sent it to print right away."

"That's right." Mavlyn had forgotten that Roylan's sister was the Talamh Tribune's editor. "I do wish she'd spoken to me first —I would have liked to have some say about what was printed. But, Leap is right. Putting articles in the paper will help spread the news far quicker than any speeches I might do."

The trio finished breakfast, then headed to the campus, hoping to help fuel the gossip fires. Within minutes of sitting down at the coffeehouse, one of the club members came up to Mavlyn and Leap with three of his friends. She ended up fielding a steady stream of questions all morning from dozens upon dozens of students. Some were belligerent and stubbornly patriotic, refusing to believe that Lady Mossi had anything less than their best interests at heart, but most of the students were surprisingly open to what she and Emelie had to say. Many already held anti-war sentiments, and happily latched onto the message Mavlyn was promoting, while others were prepared to fight, but wanted to make sure they were going to war for the right reasons.

Emelie rushed in at around mid-afternoon, her face grim. "University authorities went by the Tribune's office and confiscated the remaining papers," she said in a low voice as she joined us on the couch.

Leap and Mavlyn exchanged uneasy glances. "Maybe this is a good time for us to head home," she suggested.

"Probably," he agreed, glancing toward the counter. "But not without some sandwiches."

The three of them took their to-go orders, then hurried out of the campus and back to Emelie's house. They were just removing their cloaks when a loud knock sounded at the door, and Mavlyn and Leap froze, their hearts hammering.

"Good afternoon—" the housemaid began as she answered the door, then gasped. "Giant's teeth, what is all this? I wasn't told we were expecting company!"

"We're dropping in a little last minute," Roylan said, his voice pitched so that Emelie could hear him from down the hall. "My apologies. But my friends are eager to meet Emelie's new friend, and they wouldn't take no for an answer."

The disgruntled servant reluctantly let the group in--ten more university students Mavlyn hadn't met yet, including Roylan's sister, Rina. "I can't *believe* the campus guards had my paper confiscated," she said in what would have been an indignant voice if her eyes hadn't been sparkling with so much excitement. "I've been the Tribune's editor for three years, and they've *never* done that, not even when I reported on that scandalous affair between Professor Thornbloom and Professor Barkley!"

"Are you really Adara's best friend?" one of the other students gushed, looking a little star-struck as she pumped Mavlyn's hand. "I heard you were there with her when she fought King Aolis. What was *that* like?"

"I was there, yes," Mavlyn said, though she felt a little uncomfortable admitting that. She spent a few minutes answering questions about Adara and Aolis, then tried to turn the conversation back to the anti-war campaign. "Do you all have any ideas about what else we can do to spread the message? Not just here, but in the other fae realms as well?"

"I could always publish another article," Rina suggested. "Perhaps one spotlighting the truth about King Aolis. And perhaps I can talk to some of the other paper editors I know. I've developed some good media connections in the last year."

Roylan shook his head. "That will bring the authorities straight to your door," he said. "We need to find safer alternatives, one that doesn't point directly to us."

"What if we printed pamphlets and distributed them door to door?" another student suggested. "Perhaps under the cover of night? That way, no one will know it was us."

"Or perhaps we could stage a protest?" someone offered. "It's unlikely they will arrest us, especially if we get large enough numbers."

The group was still debating when the servant rushed into the room. "Miss Emelie," she said, a harried look on her face, "I don't mean to interrupt, but I spotted a troop of soldiers coming down our street while I was cleaning the windows. I believe they are from Lady Mossi's personal guard."

"Squalls!" Leap cursed, jumping to his feet. He grabbed Mavlyn's hand and yanked her from the couch. "We need to get out of here, *now*."

The two of them raced up the stairs just as someone started banging on the door. Heart hammering in her chest, Mavlyn followed Leap into one of the bedrooms. Leap yanked open the window, then put two fingers in his mouth and let out a piercing whistle. A moment later, Cirra pulled up right outside, and Leap hopped onto her back, then helped Mavlyn out.

"Wait!" someone shouted. Mavlyn turned back to see two students enter the room, their panicked faces glistening with sweat. They were the two from earlier who'd asked about her friendship with Adara. "Take us with you!"

They dove through the window before Leap could say anything, forcing Cirra to expand so the four of them could fit on her back. Leap swore under his breath, and Cirra took off like a rocket, propelling them well out of eye and earshot. They hovered over the house, peering anxiously over the cloud familiar as they watched the guards march the remaining students out of the house, all in handcuffs.

"No," Mavlyn groaned, her heart sinking when she saw that Emelie, Roylan, and Rina were among them. She felt a sickening lurch in her gut when one of the guards shoved Emelie into the armored carriage outside, fitted with iron bars on the windows. "Leap, we have to help them!"

"What do you want me to do?" Leap demanded. "Kill the guards? We'll be wanted for murder if we do that!"

"That's a bad idea," Lyra said, shaking her head. "The citizens won't listen to you if you've been accused of murder. It's better if we just let them go, at least for now. My father is a barrister—he can help get them released. It's not like they actually did anything wrong, after all."

"How likely is it he'll be able to do that?" Mavlyn asked, fighting against the urge to use her magic to stop the guards. Even from this distance, she could toss some of her nightshade tangle seeds to the ground and use them to tangle up the guards' legs so the others could get away.

"Pretty likely," Tora said confidently. "If they detain them for too long, their parents will cause an uproar, and that will only lend credibility to your claims."

"Exactly." Lyra's eyes gleamed as she nodded to the neighbors, who were all filing out onto the street to watch the commotion. "In fact, this display is proof that Lady Mossi is taking your claims seriously. She wouldn't do this if you weren't a threat, and these people know that."

"That's all well and good," Leap said as they watched the guards load the last of the students into the carriage. Mavlyn wondered what Emelie's parents would say once they returned home and realized their daughter had been carted off to jail. Shame filled her—they'd taken her in, and this was how she'd repaid them. "But what are we going to do? We can't go back to Emelie's house."

"You can stay at my aunt's house," Tora declared. "She's out of town right now, so there's nobody living there. It's perfect timing."

"Can we at least leave a note before we go?" Mavlyn asked, a pleading note in her voice. "Emelie's parents deserve to know what happened."

"It's too risky," Lyra said. She gave Mavlyn's shoulder a sympathetic squeeze. "But don't worry. I'll send a servant to the trading post to let Emelie's father know after we get you two to safety."

"All right," Mavlyn relented.

Tora gave Leap directions to her grandmother's house, which was a small cottage by the river. Vines and flowering plants climbed its rough-hewn stone walls, its roof thatched with sedge leaves. Tora didn't have a key, but Leap was able to get in through the garden window and let the others in through the front door.

"Phew, this place is dusty," Lyra said, wrinkling her nose as they walked in. The windows were shuttered, the meager light coming through the front door and the one window Leap had opened revealing a living room full of furniture that had been draped in white sheets. "How long has your aunt been away for?"

"A few months now," Tora admitted. She whipped off the sheet covering the sofa, then sneezed violently as a cloud of dust hit her in the face. "She's been taking care of my grandmother, who lives on the southern coast and has been ill. I don't think she'll be back anytime soon, so Mavlyn and Leap should be safe here."

The four of them spent the next fifteen minutes going through the rooms, removing the furniture sheets, clearing away the dust, and lighting a few of the wall sconce candles. "Much as I hate the idea of spending all our time in the dark," Leap said as they folded the last of the sheets and put them away, "I think we should leave the windows shuttered."

"I agree," Tora said. She closed the shutters of the window Leap had climbed in through. "My aunt's neighbors are busybodies. They'll start snooping around if they see someone else is living here, and the last thing we want is for one of them to report you to the authorities for squatting."

Lyra opened the cold box in the kitchen and clucked her tongue. "Your aunt hasn't left much in the way of food," she said. "We should bring them some supplies while they lie low."

"Here," Leap said, digging some coins out of his money pouch. "You can use these to buy us some food."

"But not too much," Mavlyn said. "We aren't going to stay long."

"You're not?" Tora raised her eyebrows. "What are you going to do, then? You can't be seen around town right now, not when Lady Mossi's got her guards on the lookout for you."

"I don't know yet," Mavlyn admitted. She tried to ignore the helpless feeling rising in her gut, tried to stay positive. "But I do know that we can't just sit in here and hide forever. I promised... I promised I would do my best to thwart Nox's plans, and I can't do that if I'm shut away."

The two friends exchanged glances. "We'll brainstorm some ideas on how we can sabotage the war effort while keeping you out of danger," Lyra said. "I don't want the two of you to have to go on the run, especially since you're the only two who will tell us lesser fae the truth about what's really going on."

They left Mavlyn and Leap then, promising to come back tomorrow with food and a plan. The two friends made themselves a meager meal out of the items Tora's aunt had left in the pantry and cold box, then settled in for a long and restless night.

"Did you get any sleep at all?" Leap said with a yawn as he stumbled out of his room the next morning.

"Maybe an hour," Mavlyn said with a groan, sitting up from where she was lying on the couch. She'd tried to sleep in the bedroom she'd claimed, but after startling awake with every creak and groan the old house made, had given up and moved to the living room. She'd spent the rest of the night with one eye on the door, ready and waiting in case Lady Mossi's guards broke down the door to arrest them.

"Same." Leap flopped into the armchair next to her. He ran a hand through his spiky hair as he stared up at the ceiling, making it stand on end. "Maybe we should just leave today. Travel from town to town and spread the message, get ahead of the recruitment officers."

"That is an option," Mavlyn mused. "We could ask Roylan's sister to print more pamphlets, and you could use your wind magic to spread them through the towns and villages."

"That could work for one or two towns, but we can't carry enough for the entire realm," Leap pointed out. "We'd have to keep coming back to Talamh to restock. It would be better if we could attend more town hall meetings and convince the mayors and village leaders to let us speak."

"I don't know about that." Mavlyn shuddered, remembering what had almost happened to her in Fenwood. "It sounds like a good way for us to get arrested. What about going to the Gaoth Aire and trying to spread the word there?"

"It's too dangerous to travel into the Gaoth Aire right now," Leap said. "The mountain passes will be snowed in, and even though we're flying, we'll have to go through snowstorms. My magic is pretty strong for a youngling, but even I can't battle blizzards." He scowled, crossing his arms over his chest. "I wish I was old enough to do the coming of age ceremony."

"You're only a few years away," Mavlyn said encouragingly.

"Yeah, but still." Leap sighed. "Anyway, I don't think I want to go back to the Gaoth Aire anytime soon, given what happened the last time." He curled his lip. "If I see Ryker again, I don't think I'll be able to stop myself from killing him."

Mavlyn nodded absently, her mind drifting to Adara and Quye. She wondered how the two of them were doing, if they'd found Princess Ylena yet, and if the dragons had agreed to help them. Close to two weeks had passed since they'd left with Einar... she hoped they'd made it to Mount Furian safely, and that they hadn't run into too many shadow creatures along the way.

"They're fine," Leap said drowsily, and Mavlyn realized she'd spoken the last part aloud. "If they weren't, Kiryan would be hounding us right now."

"That's right." Mavlyn had forgotten about the Radiant. She wondered where he was, if he had retreated to the spirit realm, or if he was out there influencing the fae to counteract Nox's efforts. She wished she had his ability to possess other people's bodies—if she could, she would impersonate high-ranking officials, mayors, and other leaders and have them tell their people to take a stand against the draft and the war.

Tora and Lyra returned later that afternoon, bringing not only a large supply of food, but a few friends as well. "Emelie!" Mavlyn cried, flying off the couch to greet her friend. "I'm so glad you're safe," she said, hugging the other girl tightly. "Did they hurt you?"

"No, but you're going to if you don't let go of me," Emelie croaked.

"Sorry!" Mavlyn quickly released her friend. She was relieved to see Roylan and Rina were there, too. "You're all okay?"

"We're fine," Roylan said, shooting a grin at Lyra. "Lyra's father showed up bright and early this morning and gave the jailer a dressing down. Said he'd have a story running in the paper about corruption and student harassment if they didn't let us go. We were released thirty minutes later."

"Our parents were another story," Rina groused, taking a seat in one of the living room chairs. "They scolded me for being reckless and tried to ground us both from leaving the house after school hours."

"My parents weren't too happy either," Emelie admitted. "I had to sneak out of the house to come see you."

"Is it okay for you guys to be here?" Mavlyn asked, her insides squirming with guilt. "I don't want to get you into trouble with your families."

"Are you kidding?" Lyra scoffed. "We're talking about the potential end of our world here if this Shadow succeeds. I think that's worth rebelling against our parents a bit."

"It's not just our parents," Roylan warned. He met Mavlyn's gaze, his dark eyes serious. "Wanted posters have been put up around town with yours and Leap's names. They don't have sketches on them—yet—but it's only a matter of time until they get your likenesses out there, and they've listed sizable bounties for you both." He looked at the others. "We might find our own faces up there too, if we're not careful."

"It's okay if you guys don't want to help us," Leap offered. "Mavlyn and I were talking, and we were thinking of leaving Talamh and spreading the word in the other towns and villages, maybe distributing pamphlets if you'd be willing to help us get them printed."

"No," Lyra shook her head. "From everything you and Mavlyn have told us, it's clear that the war effort is being gener-ated here in Talamh. Even if you go to the other cities, we can't give up here. We have to convince the citizens to take a stand against General Slaugh and Lady Mossi, instead of laying down and letting these Greater Fae throw our lives away so carelessly."

"That's right." Tora fisted her hands in her skirts. "I've already lost my cousin to the shadow creatures when General Slaugh recruited him for King Aolis's army, and I know others who've lost family members, too. We can't keep blindly following the Greater Fae, not when they won't even tell us the truth about why we're fighting in the first place."

"All right." Mavlyn squared her shoulders as she faced the group. "If you guys really want to help, I have some ideas for how to make a stand without putting ourselves too much at risk. Here's what we're going to do..."

Lady Mossi

"Oh, it is so good to be home!" Gelsyne gushed as they entered the arboretum. A delighted grin spread over her face as she turned in a slow circle, taking in the sparkling glass dome and the greenhouse within. Towering trees with leaves in nearly every shade of green imaginable rose up toward the glass ceiling, casting dappled shadows across the plush grass floor. Vines and creepers snaked their ways up the trunks, while colorful flowers and exotic fruits dotted the foliage. The air was warm and humid despite the chilly winter winds whipping just outside, and the sound of trickling water leant a soothing air to the atmosphere.

"It is, isn't it?" Lady Mossi said, her own lips curving into a smile. It had been nearly thirty years since the last time her granddaughter had set foot in the arboretum. "We used to spend nearly every day in here together. Do you remember the time you accidentally flooded the arboretum with sweets by accidentally over-watering the sugar sprouts?"

"The what?" Gelsyne blinked as she turned to face Lady Mossi.

"The sugar sprout bushes." Lady Mossi stared at her. "Please, you can't tell me you've forgotten. They were your favorite!"

"Oh yes, that's right," Gelsyne said carelessly. She reached a finger toward one of the electric blue flowers dangling from a tree to her left, and Lady Mossi reacted lightning fast, smacking her hand away before she could make contact.

"Have you lost your senses?" she demanded, grabbing Gelsyne's arm and turning her granddaughter around to face her. "Siren blooms are poisonous!"

"I... right." Gelsyne's face flushed, and she pulled her hand from Lady Mossi's. "I'm sorry, Grandmother. It's been a long time since I've been here."

"You've spent many more years in this arboretum than you've spent away from it," Lady Mossi said as she studied Gelsyne's face. Their eyes met, and for a split second, a dark shadow passed across her granddaughter's retinas, turning them completely black.

"Yes," Gelsyne said, taking Lady Mossi's hand in hers again. Her voice deepened, and Lady Mossi's mind turned hazy, her suspicions slipping away like an oil slick moving down a rushing river. "You'll have to forgive me, grandmother. King Aolis had me tortured for information about Adara when I arrived, and the experience seems to have addled my brain somewhat. I'm hoping you'll be able to refresh my memory."

"Yes, of course," Lady Mossi said, her voice sounding far away to her ears. Gelsyne let her go, and the world came rushing back, the sights and sounds of the arboretum thrown into sharp relief. For a split second, her senses were too overwhelmed to gather her thoughts. "It's only natural that you'd still be recovering from the ordeal."

She led Gelsyne to the audience chamber in the center of the arboretum, which housed Lady Mossi's throne as well as a sitting area for more informal meetings. To her surprised delight, Avani was waiting for them. She sat at the edge of the koi pond with her skirts tucked under her, skimming the surface of the water with her fingers and allowing the giant koi to nibble at her nails.

"My dear," Lady Mossi said, sweeping toward her other granddaughter. She took Avani's hand, who rose to her feet. "I'm so glad to see you're out of bed." Avani had returned several weeks ago after General Slaugh had released the hostages, travel worn and extremely withdrawn. The healers had put her on bedrest for several weeks, and though Lady Mossi had visited several times, Avani had spoken very little to her.

"Thank you, grandmother." Avani smiled, and Lady Mossi tried not to notice that the gesture didn't quite reach her eyes. Her leaf-green hair, which had once been lush and vibrant, hung listlessly around her pointed ears, barely able to hold up the weight of her butterfly clips, and her rust-colored skin was dull and waxen. Still, her eyes had a bit more life in them, and Lady Mossi tried to take heart in that. "The healing tonics seem to have finally perked my spirits up a bit."

She glanced over Lady Mossi's shoulder, and a shadow flickered in her eyes. "Cousin Gelsyne," she said. "I didn't realize you would be here."

"I thought it would be best to return to my ancestral home, given these troubling times," Gelsyne said. She took a seat at the table, where an afternoon tea had been laid out. "Should we eat, Grandmother? I'm starving."

The three of them settled in at the table and dug into the food. Lady Mossi was surprised when Avani chose to sit next to

Gelsyne rather than her, but she tried not to make too much of it. One of the servants came in and delivered a sheaf of reports, and she turned her attention to those instead, taking sips of tea as she read through them.

"Are those the war reports from General Slaugh?" Gelsyne asked, surreptitiously leaning in.

"Yes." Lady Mossi lowered the paper a little so she could meet her granddaughter's gaze. "Would you like to read them?"

"Yes please." Gelsyne held out her hand. At Lady Mossi's raised eyebrow, she added, "As the future queen of Ediria, I feel I should take an interest in these matters. Especially since it's my future husband who is leading the troops."

"True enough." Lady Mossi finished reading the report, then handed it over to Gelsyne. "The war seems to be going well, though I do worry General Slaugh is being a bit too heavy-handed. He's wiped out four water fae villages in their entirety."

"Then he's doing well," Avani said.

"Well?" Lady Mossi glanced at Avani, surprised at the vehemence in her voice. "He's certainly effective, but I'm not sure it's necessary for him to be killing females and children."

"Those females can still fight, and those children will grow up wanting vengeance if they are left alive," Gelsyne pointed out, reaching for another report. "Better to eradicate their family lines completely, and cow the other villages into submission. If word spreads, perhaps they will surrender instead of fight, and this will end quickly."

"Or perhaps they will fight harder," Lady Mossi snapped, "and we will suffer greater casualties as a result."

Gelsyne waved a dismissive hand at that. "There is a more pressing issue," she said. "I spoke with the guard captain this morning, and it would seem that the draft is being met with resistance here in Talamh. An article appeared in the Talamh University's student paper reporting on a student speaking out against the draft. I had the guards confiscate them all, of course, but the damage has been done."

"You gave my guards orders, without consulting me first?" Lady Mossi stared at Gelsyne, shocked by her granddaughter's audacity. "Where are these papers? I demand to see a copy."

"I had them all burned." Gelsyne took Lady Mossi's hand, and once more, that strange, dark haze descended upon her mind again. "Grandmother, you don't need to worry about the paper or what it said. But we do need to find the girl who is spreading these rumors. I had her friends arrested, but she herself has escaped. We cannot allow her to keep sowing dissent amongst the city folk."

Lady Mossi frowned, trying to think past the fog in her mind. "Aren't we only lending credibility by giving her so much attention? I'd think it would be best to ignore her."

"I disagree," Avani said. "We have to make an example of those who speak out against us. If there are no consequences, the other lesser fae will think it's okay to rebel."

"Yes, you're right." Anger flared in Lady Mossi at the thought of those impertinent lesser fae questioning her. After all the centuries she'd spent tirelessly leading and protecting them! Whoever this upstart girl was, she wouldn't let her get away with her little rebellion. Turning away, she called a servant to her side. "Fetch the guard captain at once. I have orders for him."

24

Einar

On my way back from the royal palace ruins, I made a pit stop at one of the primal stone mines to gather the stones Quye had requested. Unfortunately, the mine shaft had collapsed, making it impossible to dig for stones, so I was forced to travel to a second mine, then a third much farther out of the way before I finally found one safe enough to enter.

To my surprise, there were very few shadow creatures lurking in the mine shaft, and I cleared it with relative ease. The carts and pickaxes the miners had left behind were still in good condition, and I unearthed a good two dozen stones. They were roughly hewn, and I didn't have the talent or the tools to cut or polish them, but that didn't matter. They could still store magic, and that was all we needed.

Exhausted, I found a sack to store the primal stones in, then climbed out of the mines. Shock punched me in the gut when I saw that only a sliver of weak daylight lit the skies—I must have been down there longer than I realized.

"Blast it," I swore. I shifted back into dragon form and flew toward the border as fast as I could, trying to outrace the dying sun. But even as the mountainous divide between Hearthfyre and the Gaoth Aire loomed closer, I realized I wouldn't make it. I was starving, my energy nearly depleted by a day full of flying, fighting, and mining.

It wasn't safe to spend the night here, not without Adara and Quye to watch my back. But I needed to rest, at least for an hour, if I was to make it back over the border safely.

The last of the sunlight disappeared, replaced by the watery light of a full moon obscured by the thick layer of ashes clouding the sky. Normally, I flew high above the cloud cover so I wouldn't have to breathe in the noxious fumes, but since I actually needed to see the landscape, I was forced to fly low. Anxious, I scanned the terrain, looking for a safe place to land before I was spotted.

This will have to do, I thought as I settled on a desolate, arid hill overlooking a plain. The hill was dotted with large boulders, but not large enough to hide a dragon, so I shifted back into bipedal form, then hunkered down between two of them, the sack of primal stones clutched to my chest.

I remained awake for a long while, my senses on high alert for shadow creatures. But as the minutes ticked by and nothing approached, I grew drowsy, my eyelids sliding to half-mast. Yawning, I leaned my head against the bolder, allowing my eyes to close.

I'll just take a little catnap, I told myself.

And then I was asleep.

The wind howled around me as I trudged through snow, fighting against the raging snow storm as I headed toward Fheir, the town we'd traveled to for Tamil's funeral. The storm was so bad I could barely see more than three feet in front of me, but I pushed on, anxious to get back to Adara. I knew she was waiting for me—I could feel her through the bond, feel her fear and worry for me.

The ice fae town wasn't far—I'd only left to go for a short walk in the woods—yet the journey seemed to stretch on forever, until my breath came in sharp pants and my legs trembled with exertion. I wished I could shift into dragon form, but it wasn't safe to fly in these conditions, so I pushed on, struggling through the snow as the drifts piled higher and higher.

I'm so cold, I thought, my teeth chattering. I bundled my fur cloak around me tighter, trying to stay warm, but the cold seemed to penetrate my very bones. Even my inner fire could do nothing against it, which was extremely unusual. I could feel cold in my bipedal form, but this was worse than anything I'd ever experienced before. It was as if my blood were about to freeze over.

My stride grew sluggish, my limbs slowly giving into the frigid temperatures. A sense of desolation spread through me, opening an abyss wider and darker than even the one I'd felt after I'd sent my fellow dragons through the portal and sealed it shut, forever separating myself from them. I tried to force myself to move, tried to take another step, but my arms and legs refused to budge. It took everything I had just to stay upright.

"Einar…" a voice that sounded like Adara's shouted, the words barely audible over the roar of the wind. At first, I thought it was my imagination, but the next shout was loud and clear, reverberating in my ears. "Einar, wake up!"

My eyes flew open, and I bolted upright. A horrified yell tore from my throat as I realized small, worm-like shadow creatures had attached themselves to every inch of my exposed skin, leeching the energy from my body. No wonder I was so cold! Swearing, I ripped the little bastards off me and stomped on them, crushing them into the dirt, then spent a frantic ten minutes yanking off my clothes and checking every inch of my body for more.

Only when I was sure there were no leeches left did I pull my clothes back onto my shivering body. The cold wasn't just a figment of my dreams—those shadow creature leeches had drained my inner fire, robbing me of nearly all my strength. I was in even worse shape than I'd been when I'd laid down to take that nap in the first place.

"Idiot, idiot, idiot!" I swore, running down the hillside. If Adara hadn't reached out and woken me through the bond, those leeches would have killed me. As it was, I didn't have enough energy to shift into my dragon form, which meant I had to travel the rest of the way on foot.

If only I had Daryan's cuff with me, I could have drawn on the primal stone to restore my energy. But I'd given it to Adara— who was its rightful owner—and the primal stones I carried now were all empty, useless trinkets with no power.

I'd nearly given up hope when the breeze shifted, and a familiar stench, one I hadn't scented in a long time, reached my nostrils.

Sulfur.

Heart beating faster, I changed direction, following my nose toward the rotten egg scent. I could barely see where I was going —the light of the moon was too far away—so I moved carefully, straining my ears for the sounds of nearby predators, stumbling over rocks several times.

But eventually, I turned a corner, and there it was, nestled between a trio of massive boulders.

A hot spring.

Excitement buzzed through my veins, and I stripped off my clothes, flinging them aside as I waded into the scalding water. The temperature would have been unbearable for a fae, but I groaned, sinking into the bubbling depths as the heat penetrated my bones. I hadn't sought the springs before, afraid that they might have been corrupted by the shadow creatures, but it seemed this was one of the few places their taint hadn't been able to compromise. The hot springs might smell terrible, but the waters had special healing properties, and the high temperatures worked wonders to rejuvenate exhausted dragons.

I wished I could stay in the hot springs forever, but I only allowed myself to enjoy the waters until I had enough energy to fly. The springs were rejuvenating, but they couldn't sustain me forever. I still needed to find food. Sighing, I reluctantly left the water and dressed, then shifted back into dragon form and headed for the border.

I would make it to the Gaoth Aire, where I hoped to find game to sustain me for the next few weeks. And then, when the time came, I would return to Mount Furian to open the portal for Adara and Quye.

25

Adara

"Einar!"

I shot upright in bed, my eyes flying open as the shout burst from my lips. Heart pounding, I looked around the dim interior of the hut, trying to make sense of my surroundings. It took me a minute to remember that I was on the dragon island, staying in a hastily erected shelter with Quye.

"Adara?" Quye asked sleepily. She sat up as well, rubbing her eyes. Moonlight streamed in through the window, setting her white hair and pale skin aglow. "Are you all right?"

"Yeah." I scrubbed a hand across my face, anxiety still clawing at my insides. "I just... I think Einar is in danger. I had a dream about him. He was covered in these disgusting black worms... and... and..." A wave of nausea swept through me, and I swallowed. "I think they were draining him of his life force."

Quye's eyes flickered with concern. "What do you feel through the bond?"

"I'm not sure." I closed my eyes, concentrating on the connection. I could feel Einar's presence still, but it was faint, weaker than normal. "I can barely sense him."

Quye came over and pressed a hand to my chest, closing her eyes. Several seconds passed before she opened them again. "He's still there," she said. "Whatever he was fighting must have drained him, but he's a tough old dragon, and he's been through worse. He'll survive."

"How can you be so sure?" I asked.

Quye gazed steadily at me. "Because his love for you is stronger than any shadow creature. He'll do whatever it takes to make sure he's ready and waiting for you when we return. I'm far more worried about Mavlyn."

The conviction in Quye's voice filled me with shame. What did it say about me that Quye had more faith in Einar's love for me than I did? Was I even worthy of such steadfast adoration?

"Wait a minute." The rest of her statement caught up to me. "What do you mean, you're more worried about Mavlyn?" I seized her hand. "Did you see something?"

Quye shook her head. "Not exactly. My vision is clouded when it comes to certain matters. But I know from checking in on her in the dream realm that she is in Talamh, and that Nox is there too."

My stomach sank. "Do you think she's in danger?"

"We're all in danger of some kind," Quye reminded me. "There's no sense in worrying about Mavlyn or Einar or anyone else. You need to focus on your training with Ylena so you can prepare for the Umnar."

I knew she was right, but even so, it took me a long time to fall back asleep, my mind churning with worry for my friends. I was several days into the fasting period, and the humidity and constant heat made it even worse this time around.

Only a few more days, I reminded myself. Only a few more

days, and you'll be back in Einar's arms again. I held that vision close to my chest, sinking into the faint but steady bond that tethered me to Einar. My last thought was of him before I finally fell asleep.

"Concentrate," Ylena said sharply.

I opened my eyes and turned to see her glaring at me from the open doorway. She'd been having me come to her hut every day to prepare for the Umnar, assigning me daily tasks either mental or spiritual in nature. Today's task involved visualizing the future, something I was having a lot of trouble focusing on given how insistently my body was protesting in the present. I'd decided to sit outside on the porch so I could smell the ocean breeze, but even that didn't seem to help much.

"How can you tell I'm not concentrating?" I asked, frowning back at her.

"Because I could hear you muttering swear words under your breath from inside," she said dryly, and I blushed. Her expression softened a little as she came to sit beside me, crossing her legs the same way I was. "I know it's difficult to focus when you're hungry," she said, "but that is part of the challenge."

I let out a gusty sigh. "Can't I try this in the ocean?" I asked. The water would take the edge off and make things easier—it helped me get to sleep at night when the hunger pangs would have otherwise kept me awake.

"No," Ylena said sternly. "The ability to clear your mind even when you're experiencing pain and discomfort is an important skill that you must learn before completing the Umnar. A weak mind cannot bond successfully with the inner dragon—the beast will dominate you instead, and you will be left a slave to its urges, rather than the other way around."

"Oh," I said, taken aback. I hadn't realized such a thing was possible. "Have you ever seen this happen before?"

"Yes," Ylena said softly. A faraway look entered her eyes. "My younger sister, Celi."

"I'm sorry," I said. I hadn't known Ylena had a younger sister —that I had another aunt on the dragon side of my family. "What happened to her?"

"The beast swallowed her mind," Ylena said. Pain tightened her regal features, her lips pressing together as she relived the memory. "She lost the ability to speak and interact with the other dragons, as well as much of her empathy and compassion. She killed livestock and razed several crops before my father eventually ordered her to be chained. She withered away in captivity, and passed away a year later."

"That's horrible." Pity welled inside me, and my fingers flexed with the urge to reach out and offer Ylena comfort. But even though we'd grown closer since she'd agreed to help me, the bond between us was more student and teacher than it was familial, so I wasn't sure a hug would be well-received.

"It is," Ylena agreed, "and I don't want that to happen to you. So shut out your earthly woes, and focus on the task I've set for you today."

She left me on the porch, and I closed my eyes again. The hunger pangs hit me, loud and insistent, but I focused on my breathing, trying not to allow my body to distract me. Eventually, the pangs faded away and my mind cleared, enabling me to think once more.

Be specific about your future, Ylena had told me when she'd first explained what she wanted me to do this morning. *What deeds do you want to accomplish, what goals do you hope to achieve over the next hundred years? What do you want your life to look like, and who do you want in it?*

That last part was easy enough. I knew I wanted Einar in my life, as well as my mother, Gelsyne, and Leap and Mavlyn. I wanted children, once Nox and the shadow creatures were vanquished and the world was safe. But was defeating Nox and having children all I wanted to accomplish?

"I continue to serve my people and safeguard my realm, because the Radiants gifted me with my power for a purpose." Lady Axlya's voice echoed in my head. *"That purpose was not to hide away in a pocket of safety, where my abilities and my mind are of no use to anyone. And that is not your purpose either."*

I shook my head. I couldn't believe I was taking advice from that conniving biddy, after everything she'd done. Yet, now that I was sitting here trying to envision my future, I realized she had a point. I hadn't been given these powers, been born a daughter of dragons and fae, only to slink off after I fulfilled the terms of the prophecy. It would be a waste if I didn't use my spirits-given talents to make the world a better place, not just for myself and my friends, but also for the future generations.

I was a child of dual abilities, dual races, dual perspectives. There had to be a way to use that as an advantage, to bring everyone together and create a better version of Ediria than the one we struggled under. I just needed to figure out how.

26

Mavlyn

Three days later, Leap and Mavlyn quietly crept out of the house, using the back garden entrance to avoid the neighbor's attention. The two were dressed in heavy disguises—Mavlyn as an elderly fae woman, dressed in elegant clothes she'd found in Lyra's aunt's closet, and Leap as her grandson, his signature spiky hair tucked beneath a cap.

"I can't believe you actually came up with this idea," Leap said, sounding almost gleeful as they headed up the street. They turned a corner onto the main road, which would lead them to the city center. "It's a lot ballsier than I gave you credit for."

"I don't think it's ballsier than anything else we've done," Mavlyn said, tucking her hands into the pockets of her cloak. The snow flurries that had plagued the city over the last few days had finally stopped, so people were out and about, running errands or visiting friends and family. "We've stormed and broken into castles, temples, and fortresses. This should be child's play compared to that."

"Yes, but we had the element of surprise in most of those scenarios," Leap reminded her. "And the one where we didn't, the temple break in, was where we got caught."

Mavlyn raised her eyebrows at Leap. "I never thought you'd be the voice of caution."

He shrugged. "I'm just saying, we need to be prepared to bail the moment we get a whiff of any guards coming our way. We almost got arrested last week."

"We will," Mavlyn promised.

In truth, she was more nervous about doing this than she'd let on. As Leap pointed out, they didn't have the same element of surprise they'd enjoyed in their other endeavors—Lady Mossi had been alerted to their presence, which was why they'd decided to wait a few days before putting their plan into action. It would have been prudent to wait longer, but the recruitment drive was ramping up today, so they couldn't. They needed to act.

It took them twenty minutes to reach the square where the main recruitment center was located. The square was relatively busy, but she was still able to spot the two people she was looking for next to the fountain in the center, their hoods drawn over their heads to hide their features.

"Good morning," Mavlyn said, strolling up to them. "Fine weather we're having, aren't we?"

The taller of the two grinned at her, lowering his cloak. It was Roylan, but he'd hidden his midnight hair under a cap, and had used herbal magic to lighten his skin and change the shape of his mouth. "Fine weather indeed," he told her.

Rina lowered her hood as well, revealing striking red hair and golden-brown eyes. "You do the 'posh, elegant old lady accent' very well," she said, sounding amused. "Are you going to be able to keep it up all morning, though?"

"Oh, don't worry," Leap said, smirking. "She's been practicing it for days."

"Do you have the pamphlets?" Mavlyn asked Rina.

"Of course." She reached under her cloak and produced a thick stack, bound with twine. "I'm a professional."

"Good. I'll be right back."

Mavlyn left the others by the fountain and strode toward the recruitment building. She could see there were people inside, but they were preoccupied, so no one noticed her surreptitiously tossing seeds by the doors and windows. She did a quick walk around the building to make sure she'd covered all possible exits, then retreated a safe distance away and called on her power.

The seeds sprouted immediately, unfurling into thick, thorny vines that crawled up the sides of the building. They covered the doors and windows, preventing anyone from going in or out, or even being able to see outside. The fae standing outside the building began to shout in alarm, and Mavlyn returned to the fountain at an unhurried pace, rejoining her friends so she could take some of the pamphlets from Rina.

"Come on," she told them. "The vines aren't going to keep them in forever."

The three of them strode into the growing crowd outside the building, many of whom had shown up for the recruitment drive, and began handing out the pamphlets. The pamphlets Rina had printed were filled with information on the true reason behind the war, as well as information about General Slaugh, Nox, and her nefarious plans. Mavlyn had tried not to give too much information, only the salient points, and Rina had done a wonderful job editing what she'd written, adding helpful headers in bold and bullet points beneath them for easy reading.

"What is this nonsense?" a hulking brute snapped, ripping a pamphlet out of Mavlyn's hand. His lip curled into a sneer as he scanned the contents with his beady eyes. "Did the water fae hire you to write this nonsense propaganda?"

"I'm not the author," Mavlyn lied, affecting a snooty tone. She attempted to look down her nose at the male, which was no mean feat considering he was nearly a foot taller than her. "Merely a concerned citizen trying to save you young people's lives before you throw them away for a lie."

"I dunno, Nitan," another fae said, reading the pamphlet over his friend's shoulder. "I've been hearing some pretty strange rumors about General Slaugh. Word is that he's been abusing his power over his soldiers, forcing them to commit war crimes that would normally get them court-martialed. And then there was that article in the university paper—"

"That article was probably written by the same sniveling pacifists who made these pamphlets." He crushed the paper in his meaty fist and tossed it to the ground. "Go home and cry to your mother if you're scared. I'm still signing up."

Predictably, there were other Nitans in the crowd, staunch patriots loyal to Lady Mossi and General Slaugh who would hear no ill talk against them and fully bought into the false narrative the recruiters were pushing. But many more already read the article Rina published, and even better, there were other rumors trickling down the grapevine that General Slaugh *had* ordered unprovoked attacks on Lochanlee's border towns and villages. Roylan, Rina, Leap and Mavlyn spent the next thirty minutes answering questions and telling the others how they could spread the word, and with each person they converted, Mavlyn felt her spirits buoy.

Perhaps Quye was right, and she really could make a difference here.

"Mav." Leap tugged on her sleeve, drawing her attention away from the girl she was talking to. "There are guards coming."

Mavlyn turned in the direction Leap jerked his chin to see a troop marching through the square, carrying wickedly sharp axes to cut away the vines trapping the recruiters inside. She whistled to Roylan and Rina, and the four of them immediately dispersed, heading in different directions. Mavlyn darted into an alley on the square's east side, her heart pounding as she forced herself to keep an unhurried pace. The four had already decided ahead of time that they would split up if the soldiers arrived, so that they wouldn't all be caught if the soldiers pursued them.

Mavlyn took a long, circuitous route through the city before finally heading to the ice cream shop located across the street from the university campus. To her relief, her other friends were waiting for her, Leap and Roylan slurping ice cream cones while Rina shook her head at them.

"I don't understand how you two can enjoy a frozen dessert in weather like this," she said. She gave Mavlyn an imploring look. "Please tell me you're not about to order ice cream, too."

Mavlyn shook her head. "I agree with you. I'd sooner order hot chocolate."

"You're the one who told us to meet you at the ice cream shop," Leap pointed out around a mouthful of ice cream.

"Besides, we deserve a celebration treat," Roylan said. He lifted his half-eaten cone to Mavlyn in a toast. "I think we did quite well today, don't you?"

Mavlyn opened her mouth to answer, but the sound of a rumbling carriage distracted her. She turned around, and an icy chill swept over her as a large, golden carriage pulled up in front of the university building, House Ithir's Tree of Life crest emblazoned in green on the outside. Her breaths shortened as the doors swung open, and a second later, Nox came into view.

Time slowed as she watched the Mother of Shadows walk toward the university gates. A sense of surrealism came over Mavlyn as she studied the Shadow—it was so strange to see her in Gelsyne's body, which she'd made subtle changes to, dressing it in a form-fitting black gown, and darkening her hair to a greenish-black color. There was a sensual sway to her movements Gelsyne had not possessed, and as Mavlyn looked closer, she saw that Nox's shadow had a life of its own, slithering over the cobblestones in a manner similar to a snake's flickering tongue.

"Is that her?" Rina whispered. "The Shadow?"

Nox twisted her head in their direction, and the four ducked their heads together, pretending to be in deep conversation. Mavlyn's heart beat wildly in her chest as she felt Nox's eyes burning a hole in the side of her head, and her body braced for a confrontation. But a few seconds later, the Shadow turned away, resuming her trajectory toward the campus.

"I'm surprised she came to the campus herself," Roylan said once Nox had disappeared from view. "Seems like she's taking you seriously, Mavlyn."

"A little too seriously," Leap said darkly. He glanced at Rina. "You should probably stay home the rest of the week. I have a feeling your printing press is about to be shut down... permanently."

27

Leap

After their close call with Nox, Mavlyn and Leap's new friends decided to lie low for a week or two. As Leap suspected, Nox had ordered the school printing press to be shut down, effectively putting the Talamh Tribune out of production. Rina had been furious when she'd heard the news, and had offered to call in a favor with one of her media friends so they could continue printing. But Mavlyn had nixed the idea, pointing out that doing so would only endanger more families if Nox traced the pamphlets back to the new press.

"I'm going stir-crazy sitting in this house," Leap declared after two days of hiding out. They'd done pretty much nothing but read and eat, and while Leap enjoyed snacking as much as any fae boy, he was sick of staring at words for hours on end. "We need to get out and do something."

"I agree." Mavlyn set her book aside with a sigh. "We didn't come to Talamh just to squat in an empty house and twiddle our thumbs." She pursed her lips in thought. "Perhaps we should go back to Lochanlee, and see if we can continue the anti-war effort there? I can try to disguise us as water fae, see if that makes them more likely to listen to us."

"We could do that," Leap said, a slow smile coming over his face as an idea came to him, "but I have something more exciting in mind."

He told Mavlyn his plan, and they spent the rest of the afternoon hashing out the details. Once night fell, they snuck out of the house, then traveled across town to Emelie's house, riding on Cirra to avoid the guards patrolling the streets. The city had set a curfew, claiming it was for the citizens' own safety during these times of war, but Leap knew better. Their efforts to educate the public about General Slaugh and Nox had taken root, spreading throughout the city, and Lady Mossi had enacted the curfew to discourage citizens from staging any rebellions at night.

Leap and Mavlyn pulled up alongside Roylan and Rina's house, rapping on Roylan's window to wake him. He hurried to the window and let them in, his eyes wide with delight at the sight of Leap's cloud.

"I had no idea you had a cloud familiar," he said in a hushed voice as they climbed inside. "I thought only Lightning Riders had those!"

Leap shrugged, his insides prickling as he thought of Gale. He tried not to think about what might have become of the older Lightning Rider who had defied Ryker in order to set him and Mavlyn free. "My parents were Lightning Riders," he said by way of explanation, then changed the subject before she could ask him more about it. "We have a plan to stop General Slaugh from launching his next attack. But we're going to need some help. Do you think you can get some volunteers together to assist us?"

"I can definitely try," Roylan said. He sat down on the edge of his bed, eyes gleaming with interest. "But first, tell me what kind of scheme you two are brewing."

After laying out the plan, Roylan enthusiastically agreed to recruit volunteers for Leap and Mavlyn's mission. The three of them agreed to meet on the northern outskirts of Talamh, and Leap and Mavlyn showed up two nights later, their meager belongings packed in case they had to flee the area.

They expected Roylan to arrive with two or three volunteers, but to his surprise, a group of fifteen students were waiting for them at the edge of the woods where they'd agreed to meet. "Emelie!" Mavlyn exclaimed as they landed. She jumped off Cirra and rushed to greet her friend. "I didn't think you would be here!"

"My parents would kill me if they found out," Emelie admitted, "but I couldn't very well stay behind and let the rest of you have fun."

"And neither could we," Tora said, stepping forward. She was there with Lyra and Rina, and Leap recognized most of the other faces from the club meeting Roylan had invited them to. Had that really been almost two weeks ago? It felt like it had just happened yesterday. He shook his head—time was passing way too quickly.

"Did you bring the supplies?" he asked Roylan.

Roylan nodded, hefting a jug of oil in one hand. "Several of these, matchsticks to light them, wire cutters, smoke bombs, and the other tools you asked for." He pointed to the large sack resting next to his feet.

"Great." He glanced skyward, judging the sun's position in the sky. "Let's go. We've got a long walk ahead of us."

The group headed north, sticking to the cover of the trees alongside the road to avoid attention. They walked for several miles before Leap hopped onto Cirra and flew ahead to check on their target. He'd spotted the military camp a few days ago when he'd taken a short night flight to get some fresh air, and after snooping around at a safe distance, had figured out it was a training facility for the new recruits.

Circling the area from a safe distance, he noticed the camp was mostly empty, and spotted the soldiers about a mile north on a training march. They all looked young and green behind the ears—brand new recruits receiving rudimentary training before they were thrown into General Slaugh's growing army.

Encouraged by what he saw, Leap returned to his friends as fast as he could. "There's only a few soldiers at the camp right now," he said, tripping over his words in excitement. "Now is the perfect time to strike."

"Good." Mavlyn gave him a grim nod. "Let's do this."

They picked up the pace, jogging the last mile until they reached the camp. Leap and Roylan went ahead, and Leap used his wind magic to produce a whistling sound to distract the two soldiers guarding the camp entrance. They turned toward the sound, and Roylan and Leap snuck up behind them, putting them both in sleeper holds, then dragging them away from the camp and stashing their unconscious forms behind a nearby boulder.

"That was easier than I thought it would be," Roylan said.

Leap shrugged. "They're probably new recruits too," he said, giving them a pitying look. He knew they would be in deep trouble, but that was far better than sending them off to die in this stupid war.

They checked the perimeter to make sure there weren't any guards they'd missed, then gave the others the all clear. Moving quickly, the group rushed into the camp and got to work, each one armed with a small jug of oil and match sticks. In no time at all, they'd set fire to the barracks and the storage buildings. Leap used his wind magic to stoke the flames high and fast, and watched with satisfaction as they ate through the walls and roofs. All the troop's armaments, equipment, food, and supplies were in those buildings.

"Leap!" Roylan yelled, and he turned to see the earth fae running toward him. "Griffin Riders!"

Leap spun around, and his heart dropped at the sight of four of Lady Mossi's soldiers winging their way here on the backs of the majestic half-bird, half-beast creatures. "Run!" he shouted, amplifying his voice with wind magic. He whistled for Cirra as the others scattered in all directions, and she swooped down from where she hid in the clouds. Gathering his legs beneath him, he leaped into the air and landed square in the middle of his cloud familiar, who whizzed off so they could search for Mavlyn.

He was scanning the area for her when the first of the Griffin Riders caught up to him. "Surrender, boy!" he shouted, aiming his bow at Leap.

Swearing, Leap turned to face the enemy, lashing out with a wind strike to deflect the first arrow. The griffin shrieked, flapping its wings hard as it reared back to keep from being thrown out of the air, and Leap used the opportunity to call lightning from his fist into the sky. He aimed the bolt straight at the Griffin Rider's chest, and it hit with the force of a thunderclap. But the rider only laughed as the lightning sizzled harmlessly across his chest, dispersing like fog beneath the summer sun.

"Foolish child," he spat. "All earth fae armor is grounded against lightning strikes! Your lightning rider magic is useless here."

A second griffin rider joined the first, and the two of them attacked. Leap dodged the first volley of arrows, but the two riders split off to the sides, making it difficult for him to defend. He deflected the first arrow, but the second one pierced his left shoulder, narrowly missing his lungs. Pain lanced through him, and Cirra vibrated in alarm as she sensed her rider's peril.

"No, wait!" he cried as she shot skyward, the world moving around them in a blur. The wind shrieked in his ears as they hurtled away from the camp, Cirra traveling so fast Leap feared his stomach would slingshot out of his throat. Such speeds were dangerous for both cloud and rider, and there was no way the griffins had a hope of catching up.

"Cirra, please!" he shouted. The high winds whisked his words away, but he knew she could hear him just fine. "We have to go back for Mavlyn!"

His cloud familiar vibrated with anger, and she refused to stop. It took Leap an hour to convince her to take him back, and when they finally returned, she would only dip low enough to allow him to see what was going on from a safe distance.

Ignoring the pain radiating through his chest and back, Leap pulled his goggles down, then adjusted them so he could zoom in. The recruits had returned from their march, and were running around the camp, putting out fires and cleaning up debris. But there was no sign of the griffin riders, the other students, or Mavlyn. Heart pounding, he summoned a wind current and sent it down to sweep through the training camp, collecting the conversations and bringing them back to his ears.

"Those blasted kids!" someone seethed, his rage so potent that the hair on Leap's arms stood straight up. "They've destroyed our rations!"

"We should punish them," another soldier growled. "I saw which way their tracks went—they can't be more than an hour north, faster if we took the horses."

"No," said the third soldier, this one sounding older and gruffer than the rest. "We have more important problems to solve now. Besides, the griffin riders captured their leader. She'll be taken to Lady Mossi and put on trial for her crimes."

Leap's stomach turned leaden. He wanted to believe they weren't talking about Mavlyn, that one of the others had been captured instead. But even if it hadn't been her, one of their number had been taken, and if he didn't do something, they were going to be executed.

"Please," he pleaded to Cirra. "Take us north. We have to find the others."

28

Mavlyn

M avlyn groaned as she returned to consciousness. Her ribs ached, her head pounded, and something sharp and uncomfortable poked at her through her shirt, making her skin itch. Cracking open her eyes, she found herself staring at a dark stone ceiling illuminated by the thin sliver of daylight filtering into the room.

It took her several minutes to find the strength to push herself up to a sitting position so she could look around. Her eyes adjusted to the dim light, allowing her to see the room more clearly. She was in a bare bones prison cell, the only comforts within the moldy straw that had been poking into her back, the chamber pot in the corner, and the narrow, rectangular window set into the top of the rear wall, thin and high enough that there was no chance she could use it to escape.

Her memories came rushing back to her then—the military camp, setting fire to the food stores, running from the griffin riders. Leap had been busy fighting off two of them, and she'd held off the other two so the students could escape. She'd used her vines to lash out at the griffins and block the soldiers' arrow strikes, but the two riders had overpowered her, knocking her to the ground with a well-placed kick from one of the griffins.

"That strike should have killed me," she muttered, rubbing the back of her tender skull. They must have gotten her back to the castle and to the healers at lightning speed. But why bother treating her, if Lady Mossi was going to have her executed anyway?

She was just wondering if they would bring her any food or water when the prison door opened and a soldier walked in. Mavlyn's eyes narrowed—she recognized the male as the one of the griffin riders who had captured her. He was tall, with orange hair and green eyes, with the same light, compact build all riders were required to have. Even so, he made himself look plenty intimidating as he came to a stop outside her cell.

"Good," he said gruffly, surveying Mavlyn through the bars. "You're awake."

"By some miracle, yes," Mavlyn groused. She pushed herself to her feet and walked over until they stood a scant few inches away from each other. "It's a good thing you confiscated my seed pouches, or I'd be throttling you through these bars right now."

The rider gave her a withering stare. "I should cut you down where you stand."

"Why don't you?" Mavlyn challenged. She wasn't sure what was pushing her to be so reckless, but something feral had awoken inside her. The exact fate she'd been so fearful of when she'd returned to Domhain was playing out, and now that she was in it, she had nothing to lose. She might as well give these bastards as much hell as she could before they killed her.

"Because we're not barbarians," he growled. "Even war criminals deserve the right to a trial."

"Do we deserve food and water, too?" Mavlyn crossed her arms over her chest. "Because if you don't give me any, I might perish before the trial can even begin."

The two stared at each other for a long moment, hatred sizzling in the air between them. "I'll have it brought to you," he finally said through gritted teeth, "but first, you need to answer some questions."

He opened the cell door, and two prison guards entered the cell, one holding handcuffs. Once secured, they escorted her out of the dungeons and into a small, dingy room with only a metal table and two chairs. She thought the griffin rider would come in, but he left her chained up in there for an interminable length of time, forced to sit in that hard chair with nothing to drink or even a chamber pot to piss in.

By the time he wandered in, carrying a glass of water, she was fuming.

"Sorry for the delay," he said, not sounding sorry at all. He set the glass of water on the table, which she snapped up and promptly drained.

"Is it normal for soldiers to apologize to hardened criminals?" She considered chucking it at his head, but knew the punishment she would get for that would outweigh the very temporary satisfaction she would get.

"No, but that's the thing I can't wrap my head around." His eyes narrowed as he studied her over steepled fingers. "You're not a hardened criminal, Mavlyn. You're a bright young girl from a small village who, by all accounts, has never stepped out of line her entire life. I spoke to Talamh University's Dean of Students—she said your test results were impressive, and that in your interview, you seemed enthusiastic about learning to use your talents to impress others. And to top it off, you're a distant relative of Lady Mossi herself." He leaned forward. "How does someone like you go from all that to being a war criminal in the span of a few weeks?"

"Some things are more important than university grades and pristine records," Mavlyn said. "Like opposing a war being fought for nefarious reasons."

His lip curled. "And what nefarious reasons would those be? Your silly story about Lady Mossi's granddaughter being controlled by a Shadow? I read that article in the paper, and I'd love to know who is feeding you such lies."

"Lies?" Mavlyn said. She was thankful she'd hidden her hands under the table so the officer couldn't see her fists clenching and unclenching in her lap. "Are you really telling me you haven't noticed anything strange about Lady Gelsyne?"

The rider's eyes flickered. "It's not my place to comment on the behavior of my betters, especially to a criminal like you."

"And yet you've noticed something, haven't you?" Mavlyn pounced on his lack of denial. "And what about Lady Mossi herself? Surely it's not within her nature to order her soldiers to raze entire villages, killing defenseless mothers and children. And don't even try to deny it. I came across one of the border villages myself. Not a single person was left alive. And yet you accuse *me* of war crimes?"

A muscle ticked in the soldier's jaw, but Mavlyn plowed on, emboldened by his lack of rebuttal. "As for Lady Gelsyne's possession, I saw it happen myself when I was at Castle Kaipei. You have *no* idea the horror I felt watching that wretched demon pour itself out of King Aolis's dead body and into Gelsyne's." Tears pricked the corners of her eyes at the memory, and she blinked hard, refusing to let the soldier see her cry. "Unlike you, I knew Gelsyne before all this happened. She practically raised me, and she was the gentlest, kindest soul in the village. You can't tell me the fae walking around in Castle Ithir fits that description."

But the rider's eyes gleamed now, like a dire wolf who'd finally sighted its prey. "So you admit you aided the traitor Adara in the death of King Aolis, and yet you expect me to believe everything else you've said?" The rider shook his head in disbelief. "You're mad if you think I'm going to sympathize with you."

Mavlyn sighed, sitting back in her chair. "You can think whatever you want of me," she said, rattling her chains. "We both know your superiors have already put me on the list for the chopping block. I don't know why we're bothering with this conversation."

"Call it a formality." The rider stood abruptly, his chair screeching across the stone floor. "Your trial has been scheduled for next week. We've sent word to your parents so they can make travel arrangements."

Mavlyn's heart clenched at the thought of them. What must they think of her now, especially after the warnings her father had given her? "Will I be allowed to see them beforehand?"

The soldier hesitated. "It's unlikely. But I'll put in a request."

Mavlyn hated that she felt any gratitude toward him for that. "What about witnesses? Will I be allowed to call any?"

"Witnesses?" His lips thinned. "That would be a waste of time. Your crimes are so public and egregious, there's nothing a witness could say to refute them. You'd be better off praying to the Radiants for a miracle."

He opened the door, and the two guards from before stepped in to collect her. Mavlyn's stomach churned with nausea as they unchained her from the table and led her back to the cell, but though many questions battled for attention in her mind, one burned brighter than all the rest.

Why hadn't the soldier questioned her about Adara and Einar's whereabouts?

29

Leap

"I s everyone ready?"

Leap surveyed the faces of the group as they stood inside the dimly lit house he'd broken into. It had been three days since he'd found the remaining students hiding out in the woods, some five miles away from the military camp. It had been a challenge getting them back into Talamh unseen, especially since a few had been injured in the escape, but he'd managed it, and most of them were back with their families.

Most of them had been too emotionally scarred by the ordeal to agree to do another mission, but the five standing before him—Roylan, Rina, Emelie, Lyra, and Tora—had enthusiastically agreed when he'd asked them to help stage a rescue attempt for Mavlyn.

"Ready as we'll ever be." Emelie shifted her weight from one foot to the other, betraying her nerves. Leap was feeling a little anxious about this too, but as the leader, he couldn't show fear. "How many times did you say you've done this?"

"Technically, none, since I've never broken into this castle before," Leap pointed out. "But I've organized and taken part in a couple dozen heists, some with insanely tight security." He glanced at Rina. "Can I see the map again?"

Rina nodded, removing the rolled up parchment from her satchel. She'd used a connection at the city hall to get an old blueprint of the castle, and while Leap knew the document wouldn't tell them about the castle's defenses or secret passages, it was still a helpful guide.

"We're going to be tunneling into this storage shed," Leap said, pointing to a building within the castle bailey. "It's the least likely to have people inside it, especially in the middle of the night." He looked at Nora. "You'll be able to get us through the foundation if there is one?"

"As long as it isn't more than a few feet thick," she confirmed. Tora had the power to manipulate rocks—she could shape and liquify any type of stone, even the hardest of diamonds.

"And you'll be able to tunnel?" he asked Emelie.

"Yes," she confirmed.

"Good." Leap studied their faces one last time, searching for any sign of doubt. But though he knew they were all experiencing various degrees of nerves, the resolute determination gave him hope.

We can do this, he told himself. *You've come out on top with far worse odds, and far less help, before.*

"All right," he said to Emelie. "Lead the way."

The group fell in line behind Emelie as they exited through the back door of the house and into the yard. Just outside, a pair of double doors set into the earth led into a cellar. The room was freezing cold and smelled of damp and rot from years of disuse, and Leap pulled his cloak tight around him as they entered.

Roylan struck a match and used it to light the torch on the wall, and Leap waved his hand once they were all inside, using wind magic to shut the cellar doors behind them.

The torch's flickering light caused the shadows in the room to dance, making Leap shudder. The movement reminded him of Nox and the way her own shadow seemed to move independently, a writhing entity of darkness barely leashed within the confines of Gelsyne's body. He hoped Mavlyn was okay, that her mind was still her own, and that she hadn't been subjected to too much cruelty at the Shadow's hands.

The six of them made a circle in the center of the room, and Emelie stepped into the middle. She crouched on the floor, placing her hand atop the earth, and closed her eyes in concentration. At first, nothing happened, but then the ground began to tremble. The tremors were slight at first, but they grew larger and more insistent, until the surrounding walls shook and dust rained from the ceiling. The others cast nervous glances upward, but just when Leap feared the ceiling might cave in, the earth beneath Emelie's hand collapsed, falling away to reveal a deep hole about four feet wide.

"Phew," she said, wiping a sheen of sweat from her brow. "That was more work than I thought it would be."

"Here." Lyra handed Emelie a hunk of bread and cheese. "Eat this. You need to keep up your strength."

Emelie wolfed down the bread and cheese, then levered herself into the hole. Leap leaned over to see her bracing her hands along the sides and shimmying down. He shuddered as she disappeared into the darkness.

"Be prepared," she warned them. "It's about ten feet down."

The others followed her, and Leap gritted his teeth. As an air fae, the idea of being trapped beneath the earth like this was his worst nightmare. But he couldn't stay behind, not when Mavlyn's life was on the line, so he shoved his fear down, then grabbed the torch on the wall and used his wind magic to float his way down the hole.

The tunnel was wider down here, and Emelie had already used her magic to forge a path, allowing the rest of them to spread out so they didn't bottleneck the entrance. Leap passed the torch ahead to Roylan, who stood just behind Emelie, and he lit the way for the rest of them while she led them. The earth rumbled as Emelie used her magic to shift it aside, and step by step, inch by inch, they made their way to the castle bailey.

Leap tried to focus on keeping one foot in front of the other, on counting his breaths, on anything except how the walls seemed to press in on all sides, and how the shadows loomed threateningly. More than once, he had to wipe off clumps of dirt from the back of his neck, or pick grubs off his hair and arms that had fallen from the walls or ceiling. His skin crawled and he struggled against the urge to scream when something that felt very much like a spider skittered down his forearm. He flung his arm violently, then cursed when it smacked into the wall, dislodging even more earth.

"Are you okay?" Lyra asked, glancing back at him over her shoulder.

"I'm fine," Leap ground out.

Lyra opened her mouth to say something else, but Emelie came to a stop ahead. "The castle wall is just a few feet ahead," she announced. "I'm going to start tunneling down."

Long seconds passed as Emelie worked, the earth vibrating around them, and she told them to hang back while she tunneled farther down. Leap tried not to shift nervously as those seconds turned into minutes, but though he knew it was his fear talking, he couldn't help feeling that this was taking far too long.

"Is everything okay?" he called.

Her answer came, too faintly to hear, and Leap used a thread of wind magic to collect her words and bring them closer. "I've tunneled down twenty-five feet so far and I still haven't cleared the bottom of the wall," she said, her magically amplified voice echoing through the chamber. "I don't know how much farther it goes, or how much longer I can keep this up for."

The group cast worried glances amongst themselves. "Come back up," Rina called down. "The last thing we need is for the tunnel to collapse while your magic is running low. We'll take some time to rest and regroup."

"Here," Leap said, pushing past the others to the front. "I'll help you, Emelie."

He used his wind magic to float Emelie back up to the top, which was considerably more difficult down here since there was no natural breeze for him to use. Relief flooded him as her dirt-smudged face emerged from the hole, and Lyra offered her more bread to munch on while they all sat down, resting their backs against the dirt walls as they brainstormed solutions.

"Do you think you could use your magic to make a hole in the wall?" Roylan asked Nora.

Nora frowned. "Possibly. It depends on how thick the wall is, and also on the wall's structural integrity. I'd need to make sure we weren't tunneling through a weak spot, or the rest of the wall could collapse."

"You can sense the weak spots by touching the wall though, right?" Rina asked.

"I can." Tora paused. "I could also tell you exactly how far the wall goes down."

"Why didn't you say that in the first place?" Leap asked, a little annoyed at himself for not thinking of it. "We should have had you do that first, before having Emelie dig all that way down."

Tora gave him a sheepish look. "I didn't think of it. I guess my nerves got the better of me."

"It's okay." Emelie put a comforting hand on her shoulder. "Let's try it now."

Emelie used her magic to clear a path to the castle wall. The thick stone was a darker color than the above ground section, but still appeared just as solid as the rest of it. Bracing herself, Nora approached it, then placed a hand against the wall and closed her eyes.

"I think—"

Her words cut off as a pulse of magic burst from the wall, knocking them all backward. Leap landed hard on his butt as the earth shook around them, and to his horror, dirt began to rain down on them. The tunnel collapsed, muffling their screams, and the last thing Leap saw was a flash of light before a rock struck the top of his head and everything went dark.

"Leap. You need to wake up."

Leap groaned as the voice penetrated through the fog in his brain. His eyes flickered open, and he stared into a pair of green irises rimmed in gold. His heart lurched, and he nearly collided heads with Emelie as he bolted upright.

A dull pain radiated through his skull, but Leap pushed it aside as he took in his surroundings. He was back in the cellar, his earth fae friends gathered around him, all disheveled and covered in dirt.

"Are you all right?" Roylan asked, but Leap barely glanced at him. His eyes were fixed on Emelie, on those strange eyes, and the faint golden glow emanating from her body.

"You're Kiryan, aren't you?" he croaked.

Emelie—or Kiryan, rather, nodded. "I took over Emelie's body and channeled my magic into her so I could shore up the tunnel and get you all back to safety," he said in Emelie's voice, an unearthly undercurrent in each word. Leap wondered if anyone else noticed when Kiryan possessed a body, or if it was his acute sensitivity to sound and air currents that allowed him to pick up on the nuance. "Roylan carried you back while I made sure the tunnel held long enough for us to return to the cellar."

Leap rubbed the tender spot on his head. "Was anyone else hurt?" he asked, looking around.

"I tweaked my ankle on the way back up," Rina admitted. She leaned against her brother, who had his arm around her, and Leap noted the way she favored her left leg. "But everyone else is fine."

"I still can't believe we're in the presence of an actual Radiant," Lyra said, staring at Kiryan in awe. "Is Emelie aware of what's going on right now?"

Kiryan shook his head. "The last thing she will remember is the tunnel collapsing. This entire incident will be a blank space in her memory, and she will be disoriented once I vacate her body, which I need to do very shortly." He glanced toward the cellar doors above them. "Nox will have sensed my magic, and she will be looking for me. I cannot allow her to catch me."

"What even happened back there?" Nora asked. "What was that magical pulse that caused the cave in?"

"Witchling wards," Kiryan said darkly. "House Ithir must have paid for them to be set into the walls and foundations to repel invasions. You triggered them when you tried to use your stone magic on the wall."

Leap pushed himself to his feet, anger growing within him. "You were able to use your magic to save us. Why not do the same for Mavlyn?"

"I cannot use my magic within the castle walls," Kiryan said sharply. "Not while the Mother of Shadows is in residence, with her claws sunk into so many of the servants and soldiers. I already risked too much as it is to save your group—and if you don't want my sacrifice to be in vain, you should leave this place tonight."

"And abandon Mavlyn?" Leap demanded. "I can't do that."

"I will find a way to help Mavlyn," Kiryan said. "But there is nothing more you can do here, and your talents are better put to use in the Gaoth Aire. Nox is preparing to make her move against the air fae to draw them into the conflict—you must be there to counteract her influence and save your people."

"I don't—" Leap started, but Emelie's eyes went blank, then returned to their normal honey-brown color. Lyra and Nora rushed to catch her as she collapsed to the ground, and Leap held in a sigh.

He knew the Radiant was right, and that there was nothing more he could do for Mavlyn without risking himself. But was there truly anything he could do in the Gaoth Aire, when his own people viewed him as nothing more than a wanted criminal?

30

Mavlyn

The next few days passed in relative silence, broken only by the occasional mutterings of the other prisoners. Mavlyn wondered if they were truly criminals, or if any of them were like her—rebels or protestors who'd been jailed for the crime of speaking out against authority. She wished she could ask, but whenever she tried to speak to the other prisoners, the guard on duty barked at her to shut up. With no one to talk to, or even so much as a book to read, she felt like she was slowly losing her sense of reality.

The only blessing she had was that the guards had seen fit to replace her moldy straw bed with a cot. It wasn't the most comfortable of beds, but at least she didn't have to worry about rats skittering over her while she tried to sleep, or that she would catch some kind of disease. They'd started feeding her as well, a watery gruel that barely qualified as food, but kept the worst of her hunger at bay.

How on earth had Adara fasted for ten days? Mavlyn shook her head at the very idea of going without food for that long. She wondered if the dragons would make her undergo another fast, and how she was faring. She'd caught glimpses of Quye in her dreams—nothing as concrete as the dream visit she'd experienced when Mavlyn and Leap had been searching for her, but enough to know the two were safe and well. The time for her to return was drawing close... but with every day that passed in this prison cell, with no word from Leap or even Kiryan, Mavlyn grew uncertain as to whether she would survive long enough to see her best friend ever again.

Stop thinking like that, she scolded herself. *Stay positive.* Maybe Leap would rescue her at her trial. It was supposed to be held during the city's monthly public tribunal, which anyone in Talamh could attend. She wondered if her new friends would show up, and if so, whether they would try to help her. Then she felt guilty for even expecting them to, when they'd already risked so much as it was.

The door at the end of the hall swung open with a bang, and Mavlyn sat up on her cot as two guards approached her cell. Her skin prickled at the sight of tiny black veins around their blank eyes, and her palms began to sweat as they opened the door and entered the cell.

"S-stay away from me," she said, backing away. These soldiers were clearly under Nox's control, capable of anything. Had she sent them in here to assassinate her before she could speak at the trial? Her spine hit the cold, stone wall, and she whipped her head around, searching for a weapon. But the only thing available was the chamber pot, and she was too far to reach it.

The guards yanked Mavlyn from the wall, then fastened manacles around her wrists and marched her out of the room. Her heart beat a rapid staccato in her chest as they led her out of the prison, and she struggled ineffectually against their grips.

"Help me," she pleaded to the guard on duty as they marched past, but the fae didn't look up from the book he was reading, not even when the guard on her left cuffed her on the ear.

"Shut up," he growled. "No one is coming to help you, so stop your whining unless you want me to gag you."

"Maybe she's into that," the other guard suggested. His grip on her bicep loosened as he began to rub his thumb in slow circles across her skin. "Just let us know if you are, sweetheart. We'd be happy to oblige.

Mavlyn pressed her lips together, and the guards snickered. She kept her mouth shut as they led her up a set of stairs and through a winding maze of hallways. It was the middle of the night, so they passed no one save for the guards on patrol, who merely nodded. Mavlyn cursed the manacles on her wrist as they passed various items that could be used as weapons—a heavy vase, a fireplace poker, a pair of fencing swords mounted on a wall. But even if she could grab them, the guards would knock her out before she could take a swing.

She wished she had Adara's physical prowess. Her friend was strong and fast enough to easily throw these two across the room, manacles or no. But Mavlyn hadn't been born with the strength and speed of a Greater Fae. Her forte was in plant magic, and with the anti-magic manacles on her wrists, she had no way of accessing her powers.

When the guards finally led her into a salon, Mavlyn wasn't the least bit surprised to find Nox sitting on a sofa, waiting for her. She'd chosen to leave the wall sconces and candelabras in the room unlit, using only the flickering light of the fire to see by. A shiver that was part fear, part revulsion raced down Mavlyn's spine as the guards brought her to stand before Nox, forcing her to bear the full weight of the Shadow's gaze. Steeling her spine, Mavlyn stared into the depths of Nox's gaze. It was like looking into a bottomless pit, or the yawning maw of some primordial creature about to devour her, and she tore her gaze away, sensing that if she stared too long, she might fall into that abyss and never return.

"Well, well." Nox clucked her tongue, leaning back against the sofa and recrossing her legs. She wore a black dress with off-the-shoulder sleeves and a long slit in the thigh, revealing far more skin than was appropriate for a lady of Gelsyne's station. "I had no idea the rebel running around my city and spreading such nasty rumors was such a skinny young thing. I suppose heroes come in all shapes and sizes, don't they?"

Mavlyn blinked, caught off guard by the statement. "I'm not a hero," she blurted.

"No, you're not," Nox purred. "You could have become one though, if you'd succeeded in your pathetic attempts to thwart me." She tossed a skein of dark green hair over her shoulder, a slow smile spreading over her face. "The villagers of that little backwoods town you grew up in would have sang your praises when you returned home, and spent the rest of their days telling their children and grandchildren about how you helped Adara, daughter of dragons and fae, child of ice and fire and prophecy, vanquish the Shadow and bring peace back to Ediria again. The historians would have written about you, memorialized your name in the annals of their records. Perhaps you would have even appeared in song and legend."

Nox unfurled herself from the couch, her movements sinuous and graceful and utterly alien. Mavlyn tried to take a step back as the Shadow approached, but the guards held her fast as Nox closed the distance, stopping inches away.

"But you're not going to be a hero," the Mother of Shadows said, her frigid breath ghosting against Mavlyn's face. "I've squashed your little rebellion, and without Adara and her icefire, there is no power in Ediria that will save you from my wrath."

Mavlyn opened her mouth, but whatever she was about to say died on her tongue as Nox pressed an icy finger to the center of her forehead. Her mind went blank as darkness descended around her, and her vision tunneled until all she could see was the yawning abyss of Nox's eyes.

"Now," the Shadow said, her voice reverberating through Mavlyn's head. "Tell me everything that's happened since you and your friends escaped me in Kaipei."

Mavlyn's mouth opened, and to her horror, the entire story spilled out. She told Nox everything—about the secret tunnel they'd used, about how they'd been separated when the water fae had taken Adara and Einar, about how she and Leap had traveled to the Gaoth Aire to rescue Quye instead. She told Nox about what had happened in the Bala Oighr—Adara's failed attempt at the ritual, the battle between her and Dune where both Tamil and the priestess had been killed, and her journey to the Deadlands so she could access the portal and find the dragons. About the mission Quye had assigned to her and Leap, to encourage their fellow fae to rebel against the war effort so Nox couldn't gather the dark power she needed to summon the rest of her cohort. And, worst of all, the names of all the students who had helped her with the military camp raid.

"Interesting," Nox said when Mavlyn finished. She was sitting on the couch again, but even though she was no longer touching Mavlyn, her hold on Mavlyn's mind remained steadfast. Mavlyn tried to open her mouth to speak, to curse the Shadow for mind-raping her, but she couldn't even produce a small whimper. She was a prisoner in her own body. "So that's why the Bala Oighr refused to aid the water fae, even though by all rights they should have sought vengeance against General

Slaugh. Perhaps this is even why the water fae have been slow to act. Kiryan is more wily than I've given him credit for."

Mavlyn struggled to speak, and Nox gave an annoyed sigh. "Say what is on your mind, child."

Mavlyn's tongue popped free from the roof of her mouth. "What do you mean about Kiryan?" she asked. What was the Radiant up to? She'd half-expected him to show up and break her out himself, like he'd done when they were at Kaipei Castle, but there'd been no sign of him.

Nox waved her hand. "According to my reports, he's been running around Lochanlee, spreading anti-war propaganda much like you have here. He won't be coming for you," she added, a taunting smile on her face as she read Mavlyn's thoughts perfectly. "Perhaps he would risk it if you were Adara, but I'm far stronger than Kiryan. I would crush him like a bug the moment I sensed him here, and he knows it."

A pit of despair opened within Mavlyn, and she would have sank to her knees if the guards hadn't been holding her up. "That's right," Nox crooned. A pink flush suffused her cheeks, as if she was experiencing physical pleasure from Mavlyn's misery. "There's no one coming for you, little Mavlyn. The sooner you accept that, the sooner this will all be over."

She turned away then, a clear dismissal, and the guards dragged her away. Mavlyn's body moved on autopilot as they escorted her back to her room—her mind was completely detached, separated from reality by a curtain of darkness. Was this what had happened to Cascada and the other hostages? Adara had told Mavlyn about how Cascada had tried to murder her twice, before they'd discovered Nox had implanted a piece of herself into Cascada's shadow, allowing her to influence the water fae's mind. But according to Adara, Cascada had still been able to speak and act of her own volition. Perhaps Mavlyn would be able to also, when Nox turned her attention away.

The guards returned her to her cell, and Mavlyn laid on her cot for a long time, struggling with her body. Eventually she was able to rise from her cot and pace around, but she still couldn't speak. She also didn't seem to be able to inflict any kind of self-harm—Nox clearly didn't want her killing herself, in case she had more questions. Nausea rose in Mavlyn's throat, and she had to sit down again. She'd never felt so violated in her life, or so helpless.

Desperate to escape the new, horrible reality she found herself in, Mavlyn laid down on her cot and tried to sleep. But when sleep did finally come, it brought visions of death and destruction, of a Fenwood filled with dark, monstrous fae twisted by shadow magic. Of her parents bearing down on her, their eyes wild with madness, smiles bright with sharp fangs and claws black with blood.

She thought she glimpsed Quye's horrified face in the midst of it all, and cried out to her friend for help. But there was no one who could save her from this darkness, no one except Adara.

And Mavlyn knew in her heart she wouldn't live long enough to see that happen.

31

Adara

"Are you ready, Adara?"

I nodded, not looking at Ylena as I took in the landscape sprawled out before us. In the absence of Mount Furian, we'd hiked to the highest point of the island—a dormant volcano that lay still and silent beneath our feet.

It had been a week since Ylena had agreed to help me perform the Umnar, and we'd spent the last seven days on a strict schedule of fasting, meditation, and study. I'd expected to be nervous now that the day of the ritual had finally arrived, but instead, a strange sense of melancholy came over me as I looked out at the island and its inhabitants. I spotted a small group of dragons chasing each other as they flew over the waves, their colorful scales glittering in the sunlight. A few others were down by the docks setting crab traps, and more roamed around the island, socializing, doing chores, or just enjoying the beautiful slice of paradise they'd made their home.

There was no place like this in Ediria, or at least not one I'd ever been to. And there were no dragons back home either, save Einar. This was the only time I would get to experience what it was like to live amongst a dragon clan, and once I completed the ritual, our time would come to an end.

"Are you sure?" Ylena asked. I turned to see her watching me with raised eyebrows, and my cheeks heated as I realized my thoughts must have been written all over my face. "You seem to be elsewhere."

I shook my head, pulling my mind back to the present. "I just realized that I'm going to miss this place, that's all."

"I would suggest you stay, if I didn't know that keeping you here would break Einar's heart." To my surprise, her full lips curved into a crooked smile. "You've proven to be an asset to the island, and the others have taken quite a liking to you."

"And you?" I asked, only half-joking.

Ylena's expression softened. "You are Daryan's daughter through and through. I'm proud to call you kin."

Tears stung at my eyes, and I blinked them away rapidly. "Thanks, Auntie."

She snorted. "I'm still not sure I want to be called Auntie. It makes me feel old."

I laughed, and just like that, the mood lightened. "We should get started then, before I slip up again."

"Agreed."

Ylena crouched down and slid the bag she was carrying off her shoulder. She pulled out a small clay pot and a wooden flask filled with the herbal drink she'd brewed beforehand. "Normally I would have had you drink this and then ascend the volcano on your own," Ylena said as she poured the contents into the pot. "But given that you're only half-dragon, I thought it best that I supervise you, in case something goes wrong."

I nodded, watching as she used a flame to reheat the liquid.

Within minutes, a strong, earthy smell began to waft through the air, underscored by herbal notes that were somehow both sweet and bitter. My skin prickled with nerves as she handed the pot to me, and I swallowed hard as I took it in my hands, staring at the dark contents bubbling within.

"Whenever you're ready," Ylena said gently.

I closed my eyes and took slow, deep breaths, visualizing my intended outcome like Ylena had taught me. An image of the ice dragon I'd seen in my last trance formed in my mind's eye, but this time, her glittering blue form was curled up, her eyes closed in sleep.

The beast was inside me, waiting for me to wake her.

All I had to do was drink the potion, and it would begin.

I opened my eyes, then downed the contents of the pot in one go. The hot liquid hit my empty stomach hard, and I doubled over, nearly throwing it up. Ylena was by my side in an instant, her hand rubbing slow circles across my back.

"Breathe, Adara. Breathe."

I did as she said, focusing on her touch to keep my mind off the nausea. Eventually, my stomach settled, and I assumed a cross-legged position facing the ocean. Ylena set out the tools she'd brought on a leather cloth in front of me, then settled in a similar position, far enough away to be unobtrusive, but close enough that she could still observe. Her presence faded away as I focused on the undulating waves, my mind entranced by the patterns until they were all I could see.

I didn't know how long I stayed in that trance, but eventually, I became aware of a tingling sensation along my hip and the side of my thigh. The world shifted around me, everything turning hazy, and an image began to unfurl in my mind's eye, a pattern the likes I'd never seen before.

Hardly aware of what I was doing, I hiked up the skirts of the dress I wore, exposing the flesh beneath. My skin was burning now, lines of fire etched across the surface that hissed at me like a living thing. I wanted to claw at it, to tear it off, but I ignored the instinct, instead reaching for the knife Ylena had left for me. In one quick motion, I slashed my left palm open. Blood pooled in the wound, but it was not like the blood I usually shed when I was injured. This blood was gem-bright, shimmering with iridescence and thick like ink.

I put the knife down, then reached for one of the needles next. It was about twelve inches long, with an impossibly thin point, but Ylena had already showed me how to use it, so I grasped it confidently. I dipped it into the pool of blood in my palm, then pressed it into the skin covering my hip, following the pattern that blazed there.

Pain burst from the puncture, so sharp and bright I nearly dropped the needle. But it dissipated almost immediately, and the burning sensation on my skin lessened a little as well. Gritting my teeth, I dipped the needle back into the 'ink', then tried again. There was another flash of pain, but in its wake, the burning receded again.

I continued on like this, dipping and stabbing over and over until my entire existence was reduced to the tiny, but intense, explosions of pain. The process was both painstaking and excruciating, and echoes of the past danced around me. The children who'd teased me growing up, the mother who'd loved and raised and sacrificed for me, the king who'd killed my father and tried to enslave me, the dragon who'd fought for me. They all tried to drag my attention away, but I refused to give in, keeping my gaze firmly on the task.

Slowly, the pattern began to emerge, taking shape across my hip and thigh. Flames and snowflakes swirled up and down my skin, coalescing into the shape of a dragon. My breath caught as her wings and spikes took form, as her tail thrashed and her fangs gleamed and flames spewed from her open mouth.

Wait. Was this my imagination, or was the tattoo actually moving?

I inked faster, feverishly stabbing the ink into me again and again as I rushed to complete the pattern. Not even the pain was enough to deter me as I worked, filling in the edges, adding little flourishes. I let out an excited whoop as I completed the last line, and the tattoo glowed, a fiery blue that filled me with pride.

The glow brightened, growing bigger and bigger until it rose from my skin and took shape before me. My breath caught as the dragon from my vision floated before me, far larger and more lifelike than before. Her entire body was made up of crystal blue scales that looked like shards of ice, the spikes jutting from her head and along her spine gleaming like icicles on a fresh winter morning. Her eyes were the same cornflower blue as mine, and they burned fiercely as the two of us stared at each other.

Mine, she seemed to say, though no words echoed across the space between us.

"Mine," I agreed.

I got to my feet and approached, ignoring the throbbing in my leg. The dragon lowered her head as I placed my hand atop her brow, right between her eyes. Energy pulsed between us, and I gasped as light began pouring from my skin—the same golden light from my last vision. The dragon's form turned incorporeal again, swirling around me as she merged with the energy, turning it from a deep gold to the same fiery blue that had burst from the tattoo earlier.

This was the true icefire. The power that would allow me to destroy Nox once and for all, and save my mother.

The icefire spread all around me, until it filled my entire field of vision, burning away all the other images. Power pulsed through me, and I lifted my head to the sky and roared with the need for release. As I did, my body began to shift, flesh and bones turning liquid and spreading out in all directions. Panic threatened to take hold, but I let the feeling pass through me, embracing the rush as I changed for the first time.

When the light finally faded away, I looked down at myself. Looked at my powerful legs, my icy scales, the iron-hard claws protruding from my digits. I craned my neck to stare at my wings, fully extended, and the spikes running along my spine that led to the long tail snaking out behind me.

I gave the tail an experimental whip, and sent a small boulder flying down the mountainside.

"Hey!" a familiar voice snapped, and I turned to see Ylena standing next to me. Her hands were propped on her hips, and she seemed torn between exasperation and amusement. "Watch what you're doing, Adara. You have to remember that there are other living creatures around you."

"Sorry," I said, or tried to. Instead of words, a strange, croaking sound echoed from my mouth.

Ylena laughed, her eyes sparkling. I noticed the sky behind her was still dark, the palest hints of dawn just beginning to lighten the horizon. "Try speaking with your mind instead," she suggested. "Think of what you want to say, but aim the words at me, like you're tossing them in my direction."

I did what she suggested, blurting out the first question on my mind. *"How long have we been here?"*

"Three days." Ylena reached with both her arms overhead, her back popping as she stretched. "It's a good thing I remembered to bring food."

My stomach rumbled at that, and she laughed again. "Here, why don't we fly down together and get you some breakfast. I'd say you've earned it."

Ylena transformed into her own beast form, a burgundy dragon with golden eyes. She ran a little ways down the volcano, then kicking off with a powerful flex of her back legs, wings snapping out to catch the updraft. I followed her lead, a little nervous at first, but some hidden instinct flared to life, taking over like muscle memory. I copied her movements exactly, and a thrill raced through me as I leaped into the air with my wings fully extended, catching the updraft just like she did.

"*Very good,*" she said, her voice crystal clear in my head. Her eyes shone with pride as she hovered in the air before me. "*Now, beat your wings and angle your body like this.*"

Ylena showed me some basic maneuvers, how to turn and dive, how to speed up or slow down both when gaining altitude or during a descent, and a few other things. My dragon instincts allowed me to copy the movements well enough, but after fifteen minutes, I began to flag. It had been over a week since I'd eaten, and three days since I'd slept.

Sensing my exhaustion, Ylena led me back to the village. The sun was just beginning to crest the horizon, but even so, several people were up and about, and they pointed excitedly as they saw our approach. By the time we landed, a large crowd had gathered, with Quye and Yaggir at the front, beaming.

"You did it!" Quye squealed, darting forward. She grabbed me around the neck in a fierce hug, heedless of my sharp spikes and scales. "You've finally become a dragon!"

"She was always a dragon," Yaggir said, a little amused. His eyes gleamed as he looked me up and down. "But now, everyone else knows it, too."

Ylena shifted back into her bipedal form, then coached me through the process as well. For some reason, it was harder to shift back—my inner dragon, who was finally free for the first time in nearly twenty years, was reluctant to relinquish control. The two of us were the same person, yet somehow not, and only after promising her a long flight did she finally relent, allowing me to return to my body.

"Phew," I said, swaying on my feet a little. Yaggir caught me as I stumbled, slinging my arm over his broad shoulder and taking some of my weight. "That was a little scary. I thought she wasn't going to let me change back."

Ylena laughed. "We all go through that during our first shift," she said, patting me fondly on the shoulder. "Now come. Let us eat."

The dragons gave me a small breakfast to break my fast, which I devoured eagerly before returning to my bed and promptly crashing. I awoke at sundown to find that the dragons had prepared a massive celebration feast, roasting several wild boars they'd hunted while I'd undergone the ritual.

"Amazing," Quye said, tracing the edge of my new tattoo. I wore a high slit dress that exposed most of it, and it gleamed in the firelight as we sat near the bonfire. "Do you have any talent for drawing? This is a work of art."

"None at all," I said, shaking my head. "The pattern just appeared on my skin, and I followed the lines."

"That's how it is for all of us," Diyani said, dropping onto the log next to ours. She studied my tattoo for a long moment, then lifted her gaze to my face. "Have you had a chance to test out your icefire?"

"No." I dropped my gaze to the golden cuff around my wrist. It was nearly full to bursting with icefire, having collected all the energy that exploded out of me during the Umnar. "We don't have any shadow creatures here, so there's nothing I can test it out on yet."

"Hmm." Diyani stared at the cuff thoughtfully. "May I see it?"

"Sure," I said, though I was a little taken aback. I hadn't removed it since Einar had given it to me, and the lack of weight felt a little strange. I watched carefully as Diyani fastened it around her own wrist, then turned her palm face up. A flame ignited in the center of her hand, and I sucked in a sharp breath.

This wasn't the usual reddish yellow fire, but the same fiery blue I'd conjured earlier.

Diyani was using icefire.

"Yessss!" Quye squealed, jumping to her feet. She punched the air triumphantly and did an excited little dance. "I *knew* the other dragons would be able to use it."

A group gathered around us, and they took turns passing the bracelet around. Ylena appeared as well, and she watched impassively as the dragons tested the primal stone out. All of them were able to conjure a flame, but no one was more delighted about this than Yaggir.

"That's it," he proclaimed, handing the cuff back to me. "I'm coming with you."

"You're what now?"

"You heard me." He crossed his arms over his chest. "I'm coming back to Ediria with you."

"Not alone, you aren't." Diyani elbowed him. "I'm coming too."

"What? But you—"

Diyani leaned forward, her eyes burning into mine. "I've thought about what you said, about the dangerous enemy you and Einar are facing. You have proven yourself to be one of us, and Einar is a blood brother to me. I won't let the two of you fight for our homeland alone. I'm coming with you."

"I'll come too," another dragon announced, stepping up. His name was Keenan, and he was barely an adult, his facial hair still patchy, his limbs too long and gangly for the rest of his body. "I've always wanted to know what our homeland was like."

"Oh no, you won't!" His mother grabbed him by the ear and dragged him backward. "You're not to go through that portal. It's too dangerous!"

The young male protested, but his words were drowned out as several other dragons volunteered. I glanced helplessly at

Ylena, torn between gratitude and hesitation. "Are you okay with this?"

She didn't answer at first, and the others grew silent, waiting for her to speak. She slowly scanned the crowd, meeting each of their gazes and the rainbow of emotions—excitement, anger, fear, and everything in between. The only sound that could be heard was the crackling bonfire and the waves crashing against the surf in the distance.

"I won't lie and say that I'm happy about it," she finally said, "but Diyani is right. Einar needs help, and while I cannot abandon my position here, if there are those among us who are willing and able to go, I will gladly allow it... so long as their families are in agreement."

She gave Keenan a pointed look, who sulked in response. The parents who'd been listening gave sighs of relief, and hastily dragged their children off to bed while the ones who'd volunteered cheered. As they began to talk excitedly amongst themselves, Ylena laid a hand on my arm.

"I am leaving my people in your care," she said in a low voice. "Are you ready to lead them, unflinchingly and without fear, into this battle?"

"I am," I said, for once without hesitation. I wasn't sure if it was because I'd had a full meal and ten hours of sleep, or if it was the newfound power flowing in my veins, but my previous fears seemed to have vanished. My entire being brimmed with power and purpose, and I'd never felt more ready for anything in my life.

"Good." She pulled her hand away, but the hard gleam in her stare pinned me to the ground. "Keep them safe, Adara. Your icefire may be powerful, but it won't make them invincible. Make sure the sacrifice they are about to make is not in vain."

Einar

By the time I made it across the border and into the Gaoth Aire, I was exhausted. Even with the boost of energy I'd gotten from the hot springs, the flight was arduous and fraught with danger, the shadow creatures out in full force at night and hungry for a meal. It had taken everything I had to fight them off, and when I finally made it to safety and found a mountain cave to take shelter in, I'd collapsed, falling into a deep and dreamless sleep.

A blizzard hit in the middle of the night, and I was forced to hunker down in that cave for three days, using my dragon fire intermittently to melt the snow piling up outside the entrance. By the time the snowstorm passed and I emerged, I was so hungry I could barely see straight.

Leaving the primal stones hidden in the cave, I took off, desperately searching for food. There was nothing in the immediate area, but a few miles east, I found a mountainside littered with mountain goats. The animals panicked when they saw me coming, jumping from one precarious ledge to another in an attempt to get to safety, but I plucked two of them from their perches with my claws and devoured them whole, then grabbed another before the rest fled.

Satiated, I took a moment to rest, then went in search of a place to bathe the weeks of dirt and grime off my body. I lucked out, finding a hot spring a few miles away from a mountain village, and after circling the area to make sure there were no nearby predators, I shifted into my bipedal form and waded in for a long soak.

I was half-asleep when a shadow fell across me, blocking out the weak winter sunshine. Opening my eyes, I startled at the sight of a shepherd standing over me, wearing heavy robes and a thick fur cloak, a staff clutched in his burly fist. I nearly attacked him, but our eyes met, and I froze at the familiar green and gold irises staring back at me.

"Kiryan." I relaxed into the water again, but only a little. I hated the way the Radiant always seemed to sneak up on me without warning. "What is it?"

Kiryan squatted by the hot springs, bringing himself closer to eye level. A sense of unease began to spread through me as I looked closely at his features, which were pinched with worry. "Nox has captured Mavlyn and tortured her for information. She's scheduled for a public trial in a few days' time, after which she'll be executed."

Kiryan's words hit me like a punch to the gut. "Is there anything I can do?" I said, getting to my feet. Steam rose in thick curls from my bare skin as I climbed out of the water and hunted for my clothes. "Perhaps if I leave now, I might be able to—"

"If you go to Domhain now, you won't make it back to the

portal in time to open it for Adara," Kiryan interrupted. "She is the priority, Einar. You must not forget that."

"But there must be something we can do, at least to stop her from being killed." I raked a frustrated hand through my hair. "Can't you break her out, like you did for us in Kaipei?"

Kiryan shook his head. "The only reason I helped you in Kaipei is because Nox was still adjusting to her new body and too weak to attack me," he said grimly. "My presence in this world is the only thing keeping the balance of light and darkness from tipping—if I were to enter Castle Ithir now, she would strike me down and tip the balance in her favor, and then all our plans will be for naught."

"And what about Leap?" I demanded as I pulled my clothes on. "Was he captured as well?"

"No, thankfully. He attempted to rescue Mavlyn, but after he was almost caught, he prudently fled the area. I told him to return to the Gaoth Aire and convince his uncle to aid in our efforts to defeat Nox."

"I can't believe this." Guilt and horror gnawed at my insides. Mavlyn was Adara's best friend. She would be absolutely devastated if they killed her. "There has to be something we can do."

"Adara will have the power to save Mavlyn," Kiryan said. "You must bring her back, then fly her to Domhain as fast as you can if you hope to spare her life from Nox's wrath."

"When is Mavlyn's trial?"

"In four more days."

I did some quick calculations in my head. "I don't see how that's possible," I said, hating every word that came out of my mouth. "Adara isn't due back for another three days. Even if I fly as fast as I can, I won't be able to make it all the way to Talamh."

"I know," Kiryan said. "That's why I've come, to give you a boost."

"A boost?"

"Yes." He glanced around, his brow furrowing. "Now, where are those primal stones you collected from the mines?"

33

Leap

Leap's heart sank as he saw smoke rising from the village at the base of the mountain. Taking Kiryan's advice, he'd said goodbye to his earth fae friends and left Talamh just before dawn. He hoped to find safe passage back into the Gaoth Aire before nightfall hit and the snowstorms became impossible to navigate.

Kiryan was right, he thought, hovering on Cirra just beneath the dense layer of iron-colored clouds blanketing the skies. Snow fell around him in thick flakes, and only the continuous breeze he'd generated to circulate around his body kept the frozen water from soaking into his hair and clothes. Nox might not be able to send General Slaugh and his troops into the Gaoth Aire, but they could attack the border villages, just like they'd done to the water fae. There were only a few exposed villages like this one, but his Uncle Oren couldn't stand by and allow Slaugh to wipe them all out. He would send Lightning Riders to retaliate.

Is that wrong, though? Leap wondered. It was all well and good for Kiryan to tell them they needed to stay out of conflict, but that didn't mean they could sit by and do nothing while General Slaugh spilled fae blood with impunity.

Leap pushed his goggles down over his head, then adjusted them so he could get a better view of the burning village. He half-expected to find it deserted, like the last one he and Mavlyn had run across, but a jolt of surprise hit him as spotted a battle taking place only a few hundred yards from the village outskirts.

"Take us down," he ordered Cirra, his heart beating harder. She did as he asked, speeding toward the conflict, and as they got closer, Leap was able to identify the two groups by their armor. The larger group of soldiers were earth fae, judging by their dark-colored armor stamped with House Ithir's crest, while the others were air fae soldiers. Leap's stomach lurched in his chest as he saw Ryker in the fray, spinning his javelin through the air around him as he beat back the earth fae soldiers, and for a heartbeat, he considered telling Cirra to turn around.

But he couldn't leave his fellow air fae at the mercy of General Slaugh's soldiers just because his evil cousin was amongst them. That would make him no better than Ryker himself.

Leap raised his hand toward the sky, calling on the storm energy already brewing in the air above them. Lightning sprang to his palm, and he allowed a massive charge to build up in his hand, then concentrated a smaller amount of it into the tip of his finger.

The soldiers all glanced up as he approached, and the air fae whooped at the sight of his cloud familiar. Leap pointed his forefinger at one of the fae and shot off a lightning charge, aiming for the soldier's head. The strike hit him right between the eyes, and his body convulsed, but Leap didn't wait to see him fall. He fired shot after shot, aiming for their faces each time. Some of his strikes hit their armored helms or shoulder plates instead, which, as he'd learned from his encounter with the griffin riders, were grounded against lightning strikes. But enough of them hit their mark that the earth fae panicked, running in all directions to avoid him.

Emboldened, the air fae gave chase, using their air magic to shove or trip up the earth fae so they could finish the enemy. Ryker was in the lead, and he threw his javelin with deadly precision, skewering two soldiers at once. But the throw left him wide open, and another soldier tackled him to the ground before he could retrieve his weapon.

"Squalls," Leap growled. He swooped in low on Cirra's back, then reached down and grabbed the offending earth fae, lifting him into the air. The soldier yelled as Cirra shot up into the sky, arms flailing, and Leap dropped him, allowing gravity to do the rest of the work. The din of battle covered the sound his body made as he hit the ground, and Leap moved on, helping the air fae pick off the rest of the enemy soldiers.

Only when the last of them were dead did Leap return to where his cousin had fallen. He found Ryker exactly where he'd left him, a dagger sticking out of his shoulder and his hair matted with blood. His eyes were closed, his chest rising and falling with shallow breaths, but he managed to crack one raptor-yellow eye open and glare at Leap.

"Finally returned to your people, have you, traitor?" he spat, blood dribbling from his lips.

Leap rolled his eyes, resisting the temptation to plant his boot on his cousin's chest. "Ungrateful as usual," he muttered, then shouted, "is there a medic here?"

"No, but I have enough training to bind his wound while it heals," a soldier said, stepping forward. He was a lesser fae with close cropped white hair and scarred, pale blue skin—a little scuffed up from the battle, but no worse for wear otherwise. "Apologies in advance, my Lord," he said as he knelt beside Ryker, pulling a roll of gauze from his pack.

Ryker cursed colorfully as the soldier removed the dagger from his chest, and nearly clocked the fae on the jaw. "Watch what you're doing, idiot!"

"Knock it off," Leap snarled. He pushed his boot against Ryker's neck and knocked him back down, taking no small amount of satisfaction when his cousin choked. "I saved your life, and this soldier is trying to help you. Can you stop acting like a log of harpy dung for five minutes and be grateful?"

The other air fae soldiers watched the exchange with open mouths, but Ryker only snarled back. "Grateful?" he said through bloody teeth. "Why should I be grateful to you for abandoning us?"

"Abandoning you?" Leap cried. "You tried to—"

"I'm sorry," the soldier treating Ryker said, sounding torn. "But could you please remove your foot from Lord Ryker's neck, and could the two of you stop yelling at each other? I can't clean or bind his wound in this condition."

The two cousins glared murderously at each other, but Leap backed off, and Ryker settled down so the soldier could do his work. Leap knew his cousin would survive the wound just fine—as a Greater Fae, he could heal most injuries. But it would heal faster if it was properly bound and treated.

"What are you doing here?" Leap asked once the soldier had finished. "Did Uncle Oren tire of your spoiled ass and put you on border patrol?"

"No." Ryker curled his lip as he got to his feet. At seventeen years old, he towered over Leap, his raptor-yellow eyes filled with cruelty as he curled his thin lips. Yet even though Ryker was older, his lean body packed with muscle Leap hadn't yet developed, Leap no longer felt the gut-wrenching fear his cousin used to strike in him. "I came here because I heard a rumor Tempest was spotted near this village."

"You're out here searching for Tempest?" Leap asked, taken aback. That was the *last* thing he expected to come out of Ryker's mouth.

"Of course I am. She's my sister. Unlike the rest of our family, I haven't given up on her yet." He looked around at the remaining air fae soldiers and the carnage strewn about the snowy field, and let out a deep sigh. "I wasn't prepared to find a troop of earth fae soldiers burning down the village when I arrived."

His shoulders drooped, and pity stirred inside Leap despite himself. "You should send the soldiers into the village to check for survivors," he said. "I'll search the surrounding area for Tempest."

Ryker glared at Leap. "How do I know you won't use this as an excuse to run off again?"

Leap whistled, and Cirra zipped down from the sky, skidding to a halt right behind him. "If you're that concerned, you can come with me. Just don't cry to me if Cirra launches you off her back for being an asshole."

Ryker snorted, but he agreed, giving his soldiers the order to search the village before joining Leap on Cirra's back. "She was supposedly spotted over there," he said in a terse voice, pointing toward a grove a mile east of the village.

Cirra led them to the area, which was thickly wooded enough that they were forced to search on foot. The moment Leap stepped beneath the canopy of trees, a chill raced over him, and the hairs on his arms stood straight up.

Next to him, Ryker shuddered. "Do you feel that?" he asked, his voice hushed.

"Quiet," Leap hissed back. He moved on silent feet, gathering electrical energy into his body from the surrounding environment without actually calling lightning to his fingers. The crackling sound would give them away to whatever entity was lurking in these trees.

For once, Ryker didn't argue. He followed Leap's lead, clutching his javelin tight as they swept the area. The forest was far too quiet, and as they moved deeper and deeper, the chill turned into something dark and sinister.

A hissing sound caught his attention, and he turned just in time to see a figure leap from a thicket. Ryker and Leap dove out of the way, in opposite directions, and whirled around to confront their assailant. The figure was fae in appearance, with long, dirty silver hair, a torn gown, and skeletal features. Her eyes were completely black, dark veins scattered across her deathly pale skin like an inky web of malice. She snarled at them, baring a mouthful of fangs.

"Tempest!" Ryker cried, and Leap's mouth dropped open in shock. *This* was his long-lost cousin? Ryker's grip slackened on his weapon, and he took a step toward her, his face an almost comical mask of part horror, part joy. "It's really you!"

"Yessss," she hissed, surprising them both. She gave Ryker a smile that was full of sweet venom, her eyes gleaming with malice as she flexed her claws. Leap had assumed she was a mindless monster, but while shadow magic had obviously poisoned her brain, she still possessed her intelligence. "It's been a long time, brother. Come, and let me feel your embrace after all these years. I've missed you."

A heartbeat passed as Ryker and Leap looked at each other over Tempest's head, torn about what to do.

And then she pounced.

34

Adara

I arose before dawn two days after the feast, feeling more at peace with myself than ever.

"You seem different," Quye noted as we dressed and packed our belongings. "More centered, if that makes sense."

I nodded as I folded my cloak and stuffed it in my pack. It was still far too warm to wear here, but I imagined it would still be winter when we returned to Ediria. "It feels like a missing piece of me has finally clicked into place," I told her. "Which, in a literal sense, it has."

Quye nodded. "I felt the same way when I went through my own Coming of Age ritual." Her gaze drifted to my leg, where the Umnar tattoo rested just beneath my leggings. "When I connected with my animal form, a floodgate opened within me. I'd always been able to hear whispers on the wind, but they were faint, and I could rarely control which ones spoke the loudest to me. After the ritual, I felt connected to the universe for the first time, like I finally understood my place within it."

"Exactly." I turned my palm up and allowed a small flow of icefire to pool into it. It wasn't quite the same as regular fire—its form was more liquid, almost like magma at first, before it unfurled into tongues of matter similar to flames. My beast lifted her head inside me, checking for danger before settling contentedly once more. I no longer doubted my role in this war of shadow and light, no longer felt sad or guilty about not fitting comfortably into any of the boxes the others had tried to put me in.

I was a daughter of dragons and fae. And I would live and fight and die on my own terms.

A knock sounded at the door, and Yaggir poked his head in. "Are you ready? Everyone is waiting to send us off."

We shouldered our packs and followed Yaggir to the same beach we'd arrived at. Sure enough, the entire village had risen from their beds to see us off. We spent the next twenty minutes exchanging heartfelt hugs and words with everyone, some of which brought me to tears more than once.

"I really do wish you were coming with us," I told Ylena as I embraced her. "I'm not ready to let you go yet."

Ylena smiled. She removed a gold ring from her pinky finger, set with a tiny, star-shaped diamond, and set it in my palm. "Take this with you to remember me by," she said, curling my fingers around it. "My place is with my people here, but a piece of my heart will always be with you."

I swallowed hard against the lump in my throat, wishing I had something similar to offer. An idea struck me, and I pulled a knife from my belt, then took a lock of my hair and cut it, only a few inches from the root.

"May I?" I asked, reaching for a lock of hair framing Ylena's face.

Ylena seemed a little taken aback, but she nodded. I think she expected me to cut the piece off her hair as well, but instead, I deftly braided my lavender-blue locks through her dark, reddish brown hair, threading the contrasting hues until they blended seamlessly in the morning sun. Someone appeared at my elbow, offering a bead, and I used it to secure the braid at the bottom.

"There," I said, stepping back to admire my handiwork.

Ylena rubbed the braid between her fingers, admiring it too. When she looked up at me again, I was surprised to see her eyes sparkling with unshed tears. "You will make a wonderful mate to Einar," she said, her voice thick with emotion. "May your flame shine ever brightly."

"And may yours never go out."

I turned away to find Orga, the elderly dragon, conversing with Quye. "It's too bad you're not staying longer," she said, clucking her tongue. "I was looking forward to watching you translate the rest of that diary, especially since the author's name was so similar to my grandfather's."

"Trust me, if we weren't running out of time, I would have begged Adara to let us stay longer," Quye said. A thoughtful look came over her face. "When you were telling me stories of your grandfather, didn't you mention he had a deathly fear of spiders?"

"I believe I did." Orga gave Quye a puzzled smile. "Does that have something to do with the diary?"

"It could be nothing... but Pyros mentions in the diary that his plans to test out the spell were delayed because a spider egg sack hatched in his study. Thousands of the tiny critters skittered all over his desk and workspace. He almost burned the whole room down in his terror, and it took him a week to work up the courage to enter it again!"

Orga snorted. "That sounds exactly like something my father

would have done. He set our gardens on fire on more than one occasion, but unlike the fire fae, we weren't on friendly terms with any water or earth fae to help us undo the damage. It was quite a nuisance!"

"I can only imagine," Quye said, somewhat distractedly. I could see the wheels turning in her mind, and a sneaking suspicion formed in the back of my own. I waited for Quye to voice the thought aloud, but she only said, "Thank you, Orga. You've been so very helpful over these past few days. I'm going to miss you."

"I'll miss you, too." Orga embraced Quye with her spindly arms. "Perhaps you'll visit in my dreams after you solve the mystery and tell me all about it, eh, seer?"

The elderly dragon tapped her on the nose, and Quye grinned. "I'll see what I can do," she said, giving her a wink.

Finished with our goodbyes, the dragons retreated to the edge of the beach, giving the rest of us room so we could shift into our beast forms. I lifted my head to the sky as I allowed the change to ripple over me, transforming into my dragon form. This was the tenth time I'd done it, having practiced the transition multiple times, yet I felt the same thrill that shot through me the first time. I wondered if it would ever change, or if all dragons experienced this sense of electrification whenever they let their inner beasts out.

Soon enough, the surf was filled with dragons, scales of every hue glittering in the morning sunlight as we flexed our wings and thrashed our tails. Quye climbed upon my back, settling just behind my shoulder blades. We'd done a test flight yesterday, and had discovered that unlike with Einar and the other dragons, she experienced no adverse effects from touching my scales. I wondered if this meant I hadn't inherited the same protections against fae magic the dragons had...but then again, since I could wield fae magic, I supposed that made a certain amount of sense.

The journey back seemed to take forever now that I was ready to go home. I pushed myself as far and as fast as I could, the other dragons keeping up without complaining, but even so, we were forced to stop and rest for the night. We slept on the bedrolls we'd packed under the starry night sky, dreams of Einar and his warm, loving embrace cradling me through the night, and continued our journey with the rise of the sun.

It was mid-afternoon when we reached the rolling, hilly landscape where we'd entered this world for the first time. A buzzing sensation started up beneath my skin, and I felt a tug in my chest—the bond guiding me to the portal's location.

"Adara!" Yaggir's sharp voice echoed in my head, tearing my attention to the present. *"Incoming attack!"*

I whipped my head to the left to see a swarm of dragons flying in from the east. There were only a dozen or so, less than our number, but these dragons were older, their massive forms bigger and stronger than ours. A burst of adrenaline rushed through my veins, driving away the exhaustion, and my inner fire roared to life as I prepared for battle.

"Who are you?" I shouted, pushing my telepathic message to the incoming group.

"You know who we are," a voice snarled in my head as the dragon at the head of the group glared at me. *"Thanks to you, we are now fugitives, forced to fight for our lives every night as the God-King's men hunt us!"*

"And what does that have to do with us?" Diyani sneered, drawing up alongside me. *"We aren't the ones who were dumb enough to engage in your little charade."*

"Play stupid games, win stupid prizes," Isador chimed in.

"Please don't tell me you're actually considering attacking us," I said.

The enemy dragons stopped about three hundred yards away, the imposter scanning our group. We outnumbered him two to one, and though hesitation flickered in his eyes for a moment, I could tell he wasn't going to back down.

Well, neither was I.

Before the dragons could make the decision to attack, I shot forward, closing the distance faster than a loosed arrow. Before he could swerve aside, I opened my mouth and blasted him not with fire, but with a wave of pure ice. His roar of agony was cut off as ice crystals encased his entire head, and before the other dragons could react, I spun, smashing my spiked tail straight into the side of his head.

The dragon's head shattered into a million pieces, scattering across the wind like glitter. The rest of his body hovered in the air for a heartbeat, then plummeted to the ground. It hit the earth with a thunderous boom, creating a deep crater that rippled outward for a good quarter mile. Dust and smoke billowed up from the impact, clouding the air below us, and everyone froze, their breaths suspended in the air.

I took advantage of their momentary shock to retreat to the safety of my group before the other dragons could react. I fully expected them to attack, to avenge their fallen leader, but instead they sized our group up again, weighing their options. They weren't the only ones gazing warily at me either—the dragons on my side were staring at me, too, witnessing what I was truly capable of for the first time.

A tiny voice in my head whispered at me to shrink away, to make myself smaller so the others would forget that I was different. Instead, I puffed out my chest and spread my wings wider. I'd spent all of my childhood trying to blend in, wishing I was someone else, and I was done with that. I was a daughter of dragons *and* fae, and I would embrace both sides of my heritage unapologetically. Now that I'd finally merged with my inner beast, a primal part of me had awoken, one that would do whatever it took to protect my loved ones. Killing the leader in cold blood like that might seem cruel... but cutting off the head of the beast, as it were, was the best way I could think of to ensure minimal bloodshed.

If anyone here had a problem with that... well, they knew how to leave.

"Leave now, unless you'd like to meet the same fate as your leader." The enemy dragons glanced toward the crater on the ground, the dust finally clearing enough to see the imposter's dead, mangled body lying within. "This is your only warning."

Without a word, the enemy dragons turned and left. We watched them go, their winged forms shrinking into the distance, and only when they were out of sight did I let out a sigh of relief.

"Squalls," Quye said, and I started. I'd completely forgotten she was still atop me! "You sure know how to finish fights before they start, Adara. You've really come into your own."

"Yes, you have," Diyani said, and I turned to face the others. Every single one of the two dozen dragons looked at me with respect and admiration in their jewel-toned eyes. *"We are proud of you, and honored to follow you into battle against the shadow creatures."*

"That means more than I can say," I said. A sense of pride and validation filled my chest, filling me with strength and courage for the challenges ahead. *"Now, let's return to Ediria and finish this once and for all."*

35

Einar

My breath echoed harshly in my ears as I climbed the steps of the passage leading from the temple into the heart of Mount Furian. Kiryan had filled the primal stone hanging around my neck with Radiant magic, giving me a much-needed boost. But even with that infusion of energy, I'd barely made it back here in time to open the portal.

"Come on," I told myself as my legs trembled beneath me. I braced my hand against the wall and pulled in a deep breath of sulfuric air, wishing Quye could be here to purify the air like she'd done the last time I'd traversed the passage. As a dragon, I could withstand the scorching air and the poisonous fumes, but that didn't make it pleasant to endure.

I closed my eyes and turned my attention inward, toward the bond. I could feel Adara on the other end, her anxiety thrumming, and it pushed me onward, giving me the strength to climb the last hundred steps to the entrance. She was worried she'd missed the timing, that the portal wouldn't be there, that she wouldn't be able to come back.

I couldn't let her down.

My legs buckled as I stepped onto the stone bridge that spanned the heart of the volcano, and I collapsed to my knees against the hard surface. A sea of magma hissed and bubbled below me, and to my exhausted mind, it almost sounded as though it was scolding me for stopping now, when I was so close. Gritting my teeth, I crawled to the center of the bridge, then reached into the pouch at my waist and pulled out the other primal stone Kiryan had charged for me. I placed it on the ground, then sliced my hand open, dripped my blood onto it, and recited the ancient chant from last time.

The bridge rumbled beneath me, and the portal opened with a violent burst of energy that sent me flying backward. My claws and wings sprouted, and I used them to stop myself from falling into the abyss, gouging my fingers into the stone and spreading my wings wide to catch the stiff breeze generated by the open portal. I planted myself in the middle of the bridge again, a safe distance away, and held my breath as I waited for Adara and Quye to return.

One minute ticked by, then two, then five. Anxiety bubbled inside me, and I glanced at the primal stone fueling the portal. Its bright white light was dimming—what would happen if it shut? Would I have to fly back to the Gaoth Aire and find Kiryan again, then come back? And would Adara still be waiting on the other side if I did?

Come on, Adara, I called through the bond. *Come back to me.*

As if summoned by my very thoughts, Adara stepped through the swirling violet vortex. My heart swelled with joy and relief at the sight of her, disheveled and scuffed, but gloriously alive. Her entire being glowed with power, and I leaped to my feet, my body buzzing with renewed vigor.

But before I could rush toward her and scoop her into my arms, Quye stepped out of the portal behind her... along with another dragon.

"Yaggir!" The name of my deputy burst from my lips, my shock cutting through the roaring winds that whipped through the room. I took another step, then stopped again as another dragon, then another, and another came through the portal. My knees buckled again, but I barely felt the pain as I hit the ground and stared open-mouthed at the growing crowd before me.

"Hello, my love." Adara knelt before me, a tender smile on her face. She lovingly cupped my cheek loving, and as she swiped a thumb across my sooty skin, I realized I was crying. "I brought you a surprise."

"I'll say," I croaked, barely able to speak around the lump in my throat. I wanted to pull her into my arms, to kiss her like I'd been dreaming of doing every night since she'd left, but the portal snapped shut, drawing my attention away. I looked over her shoulder, struggling to comprehend the sight of the two dozen dragons standing before me. I knew almost all of their faces—Yaggir, Diyani, and Isador had been my closest comrades in the army, but I'd served with most of the others. The few I didn't know were young and fresh-faced, their Umnar tattoos newly inked on their skin, and I realized they had to have been born in the new world.

Yet they'd left the safety of their homes and followed Adara and Quye back here. To me.

"You look like you've seen a ghost," Diyani said, arching her brows at me. She crossed her arms over her chest as she looked at me. "Aren't you happy to see us?"

"Of course he's happy to see you," Quye smirked. "He just wasn't expecting it. He also looks like he's about to die of exhaustion. Give the poor guy a minute to take it all in."

I opened my mouth to say something, but Adara grabbed my

face and kissed me. A firestorm of emotions exploded as our lips touched, and I gasped as a rush of energy flooded into me from the bond, burning away the fog of exhaustion and revitalizing me. My arms banded around her, and I crushed my mate into my chest as I kissed her back with everything I had. All the pain and fear from the last few weeks evaporated beneath the scorching passion that flared within us both, and I lost track of time as I soaked it all in—her scent, her touch, the taste of her mouth and the salt of her tears. I hardly registered the dragons whooping and cheering in the background—in this moment, she was the only thing in my world that mattered.

"I missed you more than words can say," she said in my mind, her nails digging into my shoulder blades as she clung to me. Pure delight filled me at the sound of her voice in my head—a sound I wanted to hear every day for the rest of my life.

"I missed you too." I nipped at her bottom lip, uncaring of our audience. *"I can't wait to see your dragon form."*

She grinned, pulling away. "And I can't wait to show it to you," she said aloud.

"Show him what?" Yaggir asked saucily. "Are the two of you going to complete the bond here? Shall we give you the room?"

I rolled my eyes as I pushed myself to my feet, helping Adara up along the way. "You're just as impertinent as you always were," I said, striding across the bridge. The two of us grasped hands, and I pulled him in for a hug.

"And you're just as big as a softy as *you* always were," Yaggir said, hugging me fiercely. "It's good to see you again, old friend."

My heart felt like it was going to burst with joy, and I was nearly overcome by the urge to hug everyone who had come through. "Why have you all returned?" I asked them. "Don't you know the dangers here?"

"We do," Diyani said, "and we couldn't let you face them alone. Besides," she said, giving Adara a sly smile. "Your future mate isn't the only one who can use this new power. We discovered we can wield it too, using the primal stones."

I stared at her, uncomprehending. "What?"

"It's true," Adara said. I turned to see her tapping the primal stone on the cuff wrapped around her bicep, and as I looked closer at it, I noticed a violet iridescence swirling within the gem. "I accidentally filled this stone to the brim when I unleashed my power during the Umnar, and I let the other dragons test it out. They were all able to draw on the magic within and produce icefire."

"This... this changes everything." I hefted the pouch of primal stones, glancing at Quye. "Is this why you asked me to gather these things?"

"Of course," she said, a little smugly. But the self-satisfied look in her eyes faded as worry crept across her expression. "There's something wrong. I can feel it."

Guilt slammed into me as I remembered the reason I'd rushed here in the first place. "Let's get back to the temple," I told her. "We'll debrief each other, then discuss next steps."

Once back in the temple, Yaggir set most of the dragons to work, ordering them to clear away the debris and prepare temporary quarters. While they toiled, Adara, Quye, Yaggir, Diyani, and I found a quiet place away from the commotion, so we could hold a council of sorts.

Adara and Quye told me about their journey through the portal, the civilization they'd found on the other end, and how the dragons there had integrated themselves into society as false gods. I wanted to thrash Yaggir when he admitted he'd been part of the group that had ostracized Ylena and the others, but Adara assured me he'd more than made up for it—without him, she would have never found Ylena and the others, and likely would have never survived the God-King trial, either.

In turn, I told the others about what I'd found searching for the ruins, and also about Mavlyn's situation. "We don't have much time left to rescue her," I told Adara and Quye, who were stricken by the news. "Her trial is scheduled to happen any day now."

"I can't believe this." Adara scraped a hand through her hair. "What was she thinking, going to Talamh and starting up a rebellion right underneath Lady Mossi's nose?"

"I'm the one who told Mavlyn she needed to go to Domhain and champion the anti-war effort," Quye said miserably. She seemed even more distraught than Adara. "It's my fault that she's in this situation."

"I understand your desire to rescue your friend," Diyani interrupted. "But what about the situation here in Hearthfyre? Should we not be working to clear out the shadow creatures and establish a proper base here from which we can fight?"

"That will take months," Adara argued. "Mavlyn doesn't have that kind of time."

"Besides," Quye added, "clearing out the shadow infestation here in Hearthfyre isn't the priority. They are only a symptom of the larger problem. Stopping the war and defeating Nox is the only way to vanquish the shadow creatures for good. We can kill two birds with one stone by rescuing Mavlyn and taking out the Mother of Shadows at the same time."

"Then it's settled." Yaggir clapped his hands against his thighs. "We will go to Talamh."

"Very well," Diyani said. "But I expect you to help us rebuild Hearthfyre when all this is finished."

"Of course." Adara smiled. "I intend to make Hearthfyre my home when all is said and done."

"You do?" I asked, more than a little surprised. "I thought you would want to return to Domhain with your mother."

She reached for my hand and squeezed it. "I love my mother, but she is my past, and you are my future. I want to build that future here with you, and honor my father by creating a newer, brighter Hearthfyre where all are welcome—dragons and fae and everything in between."

I squeezed her hand back, struggling against the temptation to pull her into my lap and kiss her again. "How long will it take you to charge the primal stones?" I asked instead.

"A day."

"All right." I turned to Yaggir and Diyani. "Tell the others. We leave at dawn tomorrow."

36

Leap

I t took everything Leap and Ryker had to subdue Tempest. As a Greater Fae who was much older and stronger than them, she made a formidable opponent, and the fact that Leap and Ryker were trying to capture rather than kill made it that much more difficult. But Leap finally knocked her unconscious with a lightning strike, then bound and gagged her so they could take her back.

"I hope you didn't fry her brain with that lighting strike," Ryker panted as he carried her out of the forest. "You almost killed her, Leap."

"She almost killed us, five times," Leap snapped. If she hadn't been severely malnourished, Leap wasn't sure they would have survived at all. "We're lucky to be alive. And forget lightning—her brain is clearly damaged by shadow magic. She must have been attacked by creatures in the area."

They returned to the village, where the soldiers were waiting on them. As Leap had half-expected, there were no survivors, but the soldiers *had* found an apothecary, and among the supplies was a deep sleeping draught. Leap forced the contents of a full bottle down Tempest's throat, then packed the rest of the bottles away in his bag.

"What are you doing?" Ryker asked as he hefted Tempest's body onto Cirra's back.

Leap gave Ryker a withering look over his shoulder. "I'm taking her back to Uncle Oren, you idiot. What do you think I'm doing?"

"You're not going alone," Ryker said, ignoring the jab. "I'm coming with you."

Leap folded his arms. "And what about the rest of your soldiers?"

"The soldiers can take care of themselves." Ryker bared his teeth. "The only reason we came out here in the first place is to find Tempest, and I'll be damned if I let her out of my sight now that we have her."

"You are unbelievable." Leap took a step toward Ryker, his teeth bared. He swept one hand toward the field, where the dead soldiers were strewn about. "These fae sacrificed their lives to help you on this quest, and you're going to leave here without even burying them? Or making sure your wounded are taken care of?" He shook his head. "I feel sorry for House Reatha, knowing that one day they're going to have a shit stain like you as their leader."

Ryker snarled, but before he could launch a fist at Leap, the soldier from before stepped forward. "It's all right," he said, giving Leap a pleading look. "Let Lord Ryker return with you, please. We can take care of things here."

Leap looked into the soldier's eyes, and saw the unspoken words there. The soldiers hated Ryker nearly as much as he did, and wanted to be rid of him. Leap would be doing them a favor by taking his cousin off their hands.

"Fine." Leap raked a hand through his spiky hair, then turned away. "Hurry and get on, before I changed my mind."

Even with Leap and Ryker using their combined wind magic to clear a path through the snow storms, it still took them two full days to reach Angtun. Between battling the winds, taking shelter in caves for the night, forcing sleeping draughts down Tempest's throat, and dealing with Ryker's constant criticisms, Leap was ready to throw himself on one of the city's gleaming spires and end it all right then and there.

The lighting riders guarding the city entrances paused at the sight of Leap, but as soon as they realized Ryker and Tempest were with him, they allowed him through. An escort was assigned to them, and they were brought directly to the palace, where Tempest was handed off to the healers.

Leap was so exhausted that all he wanted to do was collapse into bed. But as he expected, his Uncle Oren summoned them into his study, refusing to give them the chance to eat or clean up first.

"This is a first," his uncle growled, pacing in front of the fireplace. Leap and Ryker watched him silently, unused to seeing Lord Oren exhibit this kind of frenetic energy. The leader of the Gaoth Aire usually kept his emotions tightly controlled, but the air around him crackled with power, so much so that various objects in the room levitated every time Oren got too close to them. Leap would have found it amusing if the situation hadn't been so dire. "I've never been so conflicted as to whether to reward or punish someone under my command, never mind *two* someone's."

"Do you think maybe you could feed us while you decide?" Leap suggested. He wasn't trying to be snarky, but after three days of hard travel with very little rest, he was feeling light-headed. "I think we've earned some food, seeing as how we brought back Tempest safely and all."

Uncle Oren snapped his fingers at a servant, who scurried from the room. "Tell me how you found her, and why she is in this condition," he ordered Leap. "You've been running around the entire country—I know you know something about all this."

"I'm the one who tracked her down," Ryker said stiffly. "I've been sending out scouts for weeks to scour the borders, and one of them reported seeing her near that village. Leap just swooped in at the very end. *I'm* the one who did all the hard work."

Lord Oren's raptor eyes flashed, and a bolt of lightning streaked across the sky outside the study window. "Your sister is lying in the infirmary, her body riddled with shadow infection, and all you can think about is getting proper credit for finding her?"

His words snapped through the air like a whip crack, and Ryker took a step back as though Oren had physically struck him. "I didn't mean it like that," he said. "But I—"

"But nothing." Lord Oren's lips thinned. "You disobeyed my orders and left the safety of the city. Officer Kil sent a battle report to Gale ahead of your arrival—If Leap hadn't shown up, you would have been killed, and I would have lost *both* of my heirs." He turned to Leap, dismissing Ryker. "Now, tell me why my daughter is in this condition."

The servant came back into the room with a platter of sand-wiches, and Leap told Uncle Oren everything between mouth-fuls of meat and bread. He explained that Nox had planted a piece of her shadow into all the hostages, and his theory that the shadow magic had reacted badly with Tempest, turning her into this monstrous creature. He also told Oren about Nox's master plan, and that instead of rising to the bait of General Slaugh's attacks, they should evacuate the border town and villages, and do everything they can to avoid the conflict.

"You're suggesting we sit back and do nothing?" Ryker scoffed incredulously. "That we just hide out in the mountains and allow this Nox to get away with what she's done to Tempest?"

Leap ignored Ryker. "We have to wait until Adara completes the ritual," he insisted to his uncle. "If we attack now—"

A knock on the door interrupted him, and a healer entered the room. "Apologies for the interruption," she said, "but I wanted to update you on Tempest."

"Yes." Uncle Oren returned to his seat behind his desk. "Speak. How is my daughter?"

"She is severely malnourished," the healer said, "and her entire body is riddled with shadow taint. We have tried giving her everbright potion, but the potion is meant to be used as a preventative, not a cure, so it hasn't done much. Her mind has almost completely been taken over by the shadow taint, and she nearly killed two of our healers when they removed her restraints to do an examination. We've been forced to sedate her again for our own safety."

Uncle Oren clenched his jaw. "Is there nothing that can be done to make her more comfortable, at least?"

"Other than sedating her, no." The healer shook her head sadly. "We are feeding her just enough to ensure she doesn't waste away, but if we give her too much food, we won't be able to contain her. She's too powerful, and the shadow taint makes her resistant to normal magical restraints." She hesitated. "May I speak plainly, Lord Oren?"

"Yes."

The healer swallowed. "I know how much you love your daughter, my lord. But she would not want to live on in this condition, and I don't believe it's in her best interests to force her. If you wish, we can give her a stronger sedative. One that will allow her to peacefully pass on and free her from this torment."

The silence that descended upon the room was so thick and oppressive, Leap thought he would choke on it. It was like sitting in the middle of a thundercloud right before it released a storm.

"Thank you," Lord Oren finally said. Leap didn't think he'd ever heard his uncle speak so quietly. "You may leave us."

The healer bowed, then hastily retreated, shutting the door behind her with a soft click. Lord Oren steepled his fingers, staring into the fire for so long, Leap wondered if he'd been dismissed, too.

He was just about to leave the room when his uncle finally spoke. "You said Adara went to find someone to help her complete the ritual. If she does, and she gains this icefire power, will she be able to cure Tempest's affliction?"

"Yes," Leap said, even though he wasn't sure that was true. But he did know that if his uncle believed Adara was his best bet for Tempest's survival, he would do everything in his power to support her.

"Very well." He met Leap's gaze. "Then I will tell the healers to keep Tempest alive until Adara returns."

"And the border villages?" Leap asked. "You're going to evacuate them?"

"No. I will send reinforcements to guard the villages. I refuse to cower before General Slaugh. He will pay for what he and his Shadow have done to my daughter, and to my people."

"But—"

"No buts. This matter is closed." Lord Oren picked up a piece of parchment from his desk. "I received a letter from Lord

Prentis offering to form an alliance against House Ithir, and I am going to accept. Between the might of our combined Houses, we will show Lady Mossi and her nephew that we are not to be trifled with."

"Good." Ryker's eyes gleamed. "I am happy to join the cause, Father."

"You will do no such thing," Oren snarled. "Unless and until Tempest is cured, you are my only heir. You will remain here at Angtun, and keep things running here."

"And what about me?" Leap asked. He hoped his uncle would let him go so he could find another way to stop Nox. Maybe he could travel to the water realm and convince Lord Prentis to back down. Or find Einar and see if the two of them could take another crack at rescuing Mavlyn.

To Leap's great surprise, Lord Oren smiled. "You will join the Lightning Guard as a cadet officer."

"A cadet officer?" Leap said in a strangled voice. Panic rose up inside him, and he struggled not to choke on it. "But I'm not of age!"

"Correct," his uncle said, "but your unique position and your knowledge and experience with the enemy is more than enough to make up for that. You'll be assigned a squad of four, subordinate only to me, to use as you see fit either in the battle against Nox or to assist Adara when she returns." He nodded toward the door. "Now go get some rest. Your first day begins tomorrow."

37

Mavlyn

For the next three days after meeting with the Mother of Shadows, Mavlyn was consumed by endless suffering. The darkness Nox had infected her with tried to take over her mind, attacking her relentlessly with horrific visions of black-eyed demons that scraped her insides raw with their vicious teeth and claws. Mavlyn knew what they wanted—for her to give into the pain, to succumb, to let the darkness numb her so it could take over her body and make her do Nox's bidding.

She thought of her friends—of Adara, navigating a strange new world and trying to convince fae-hating dragons to help her. Of Einar, who was all alone in the Deadlands, waiting for her to return. Of Leap, who had to be worried out of his mind, and of Quye, who was counting on her to keep Nox at bay until Adara could return. They were the only reason she kept fighting, kept getting back up every time the horrors in her mind tried to knock her down.

But her strength flagged with every blow she absorbed, and as the days passed, she knew she wouldn't be able to hold out much longer.

Hiding behind a gnarled, blackened tree, she watched the hulking monster that stalked through her mind, searching for her so it could tear its claws through her gut once more. Retreating, she wished desperately for a place to hide where they could not follow. A sacred haven in her mind where dark thoughts and entities could not tread, and where she could lay her head and rest.

Something flickered in her peripheral vision, and she turned to see a path snaking between the blackened trees. It glowed faintly, and she took a hesitant step toward it, worried that she would be spotted. When the creature didn't immediately notice, she crouched low and took another, then another, hope rising in her chest when the path began to glow a little brighter.

A roar echoed through the dark forest behind her, and she picked up the pace, abandoning her pretense at stealth. Her breath sawed in her chest as she pumped her legs, gooseflesh rippling across her skin as shrieks of rage ripped through the air. But the path grew brighter, a light appearing ahead, and she seized on that vision of hope, clinging to it like her life depended upon it. She refused to look at the multitude of eyes upon her, refused to turn even as she felt hot, fetid breath on the back of her neck. Refused to do anything but run, run, as fast as she could toward that light.

Claws slashed at her back, and Mavlyn cried out as white-hot pain burst along her spine. With one last ditch effort, she flung herself forward, across an invisible threshold and into the light... and found herself stumbling into a verdant grove filled with sunlight.

Panting, Mavlyn stared at her surroundings, hardly able to believe what she was seeing. A ring of ancient trees surrounded her, and though she could see the dark forest lurking beyond, the shadows could not penetrate into this space. A small pond filled with fresh water sat in the middle of the grove, a flat rock perfect for sunbathing laying right next to it. Golden-feathered birds nested in the boughs of the trees, serenading her with a gentle melody that soothed the ragged edges of her abused soul.

Warily, Mavlyn lowered herself onto the rock, watching the gaps beneath the trees in case any monster tried to come through. But though she occasionally saw something shifting beyond the grove, nothing tried to follow her through. She couldn't even hear the shrieks and growls from before, even though they'd filled her ears only a few heartbeats ago.

The sound of a door clanging jerked her attention back to the present, and she opened her eyes to see two guards marching into her cell. "Get up," one of them snapped, grabbing her roughly by the arm. "It's time to take you to the trial."

The guards hauled her out of the cell, and though Mavlyn was still unable to speak, she no longer felt trapped in her mind. Instead, she felt safe, protected, as if she were still in that grove she'd discovered in her dreams. She wrapped that feeling around her as the guards marched her out of the castle and loaded her up into a prison wagon. Five other prisoners were chained to the benches inside, all in various states of distress. But Mavlyn couldn't feel any of it, even when the wagon came to a stop outside the city plaza, which was already packed with fae.

"How are you so calm?" one of the other prisoners whispered as they disembarked. "Don't you know what's about to happen?"

"I don't think she's all there," another prisoner muttered. "Look at how her eyes are unfocused."

"Lucky bitch," someone else grumbled. "Wish I could do that."

Mavlyn wished she could speak, that she could tell them

that she *was* still present and aware. But really, what good would that do? The guards herded them to the left of the stage that had been set up toward the back of the square, where Lady Mossi was already waiting, seated upon a grand throne in the middle of the platform. To her right was Nox, and on her left, Mavlyn recognized Avani, one of the hostages that had covered their escape from Castle Kaipei. Pity welled within her as she realized Avani was being held by the same shadow taint Nox had infected her mind with. She wondered if Avani had been able to retreat the same way Mavlyn had, but the thought evaporated as she faced the crowd and found her parents watching her, their faces stricken with anguish.

"Mavlyn!" they shouted, waving frantically at her. "Mavlyn, be strong, baby! We're here for you!"

Mavlyn tried to smile, to wave back, to make words come out of her mouth. But even from within the safety of the grove in her mind, the shadow geas Nox had set upon her held fast. She would not be able to speak unless the Mother of Shadows spoke to her first.

Mavlyn watched as the other prisoners were brought up, one by one, to face trial and sentencing. The city barrister informed the audience of their names and the crimes they were accused of, and each prisoner was allowed to come forward and defend themselves. One or two of them had hired a barrister to defend them on their behalf, but most were too poor to afford it. Some of these people were genuine criminals—thieves, fraudsters, and con artists—but others seemed to be regular citizens, accused of petty things like loitering, disturbing the peace, and even trespassing. Mavlyn didn't understand why Lady Mossi was hearing such minor cases. Didn't she have anything better to do?

When it was finally Mavlyn's turn, she walked up the steps, still wrapped in the blanket of serenity she'd draped around herself. Looking out across the crowd, her heart lurched as she noticed groups of students scattered throughout the crowd and along the edges of the square. They all held anti-war protest signs, their identities hidden by clay masks painted with lotus flowers, olive branches, and other symbols of peace. What were they doing here? Didn't they realize the risk they were putting themselves at, showing up while she was on trial?

"The criminal who stands before you now is Mavlyn of Fenwood. She has been accused of sedition and spreading propaganda by undermining House Ithir with her anti-war and anti-draft protests."

The crowd burst into excited chatter as they realized who Mavlyn was—the person behind that scandalous anti-war article in the Talamh Tribune, and who had staged that daring protest outside the recruitment office. Several witnesses came forward to testify against Mavlyn, some of them students who had been at Roylan's club meeting, others from the recruitment office, or who had been in the square when she and the others had been handing out those leaflets.

"Well?" Lady Mossi demanded, once the last witness had finished. "What do you have to say for yourself? Do you plead guilty to the charge?"

Mavlyn's tongue finally loosened, and she realized Nox had released the geas. She felt a pressure on her mind, tasted the words Nox was trying to force her to speak, but she swallowed them down as she looked into Lady Mossi's eyes and squared her shoulders.

"I plead not guilty."

Lady Mossi scowled, and Nox's black eyes flickered with surprise. Mavlyn felt the pressure in her head intensify, but she wrapped the mental blanket around her tighter, refusing to allow the darkness to touch her. "How can you claim such a thing when so many witnesses have come forward? Are you accusing them of perjury?"

"No," Mavlyn said. "They are telling the truth. Just as I have been trying to tell everyone the truth about this war, about the Shadow sitting on your left who has poisoned all your minds and is trying to drag the kingdom into a civil war so she can destroy us all." She wished she could turn and face the crowd, but though she could speak, Nox had a tight hold on the rest of her body. "I am not the one committing treason, Lady Mossi. You are."

The crowd gasped, and Lady Mossi's face mottled with rage. "I hereby find Mavlyn of Fenwood guilty of treason against House Ithir and the realm of Domhain," she spat, banging the staff of her office against the stage floor. "She will be executed in three days' time for her crimes against the state."

The crowd erupted at this, some of them cheering, while others yelled in protest. Mavlyn could hear her parents screaming and crying underneath it all, and her heart ached at the pain she was putting them through. The guards moved to take her away, but Nox held up her hand, and they halted.

"If you name your co-conspirators," she said, "I will allow you to say goodbye to your parents."

The pressure in Mavlyn's head shifted, as though Nox was rummaging around in her brain, trying to force her answers to the surface. The names of the students who'd helped her burned a hole in her tongue, and she nearly released them as her parents sobs grew even louder in her ears.

Instead, she held Nox's gaze and smiled. "I have no co-conspirators. The idea was mine, and mine alone."

Nox's lips thinned, and she ordered the guards to take Mavlyn away. As she passed her parents, who tried to reach out and touch her, she retreated back into the safety and comfort of the grove, allowing it to soothe the guilt and anguish that would have otherwise overwhelmed her.

The Mother of Shadows could take her away from her allies, her friends, her parents. But at least she couldn't take away this.

38

Adara

Filling up the primal stones took more effort than I expected. I was lucky the dragons had thought to pack extra rations and share them with me, or I might not have managed it. But eventually, I filled all two dozen of the stones Einar had brought, and gave them out to all the dragons.

Yaggir had demanded we do a test run to make sure they worked, so I led him, Einar, and four other dragons out of the temple. Sure enough, there were shadow creatures lurking outside, and they pounced, eager for what they saw as an easy meal. The primal stone on my arm flared in response, and I had to hold myself back from attacking the creatures myself.

Instead, I stood beneath the temple portico and watched as Yaggir, Einar, and the others charged into the fray. They wore their primal stones on cords around their necks, and the gems flared to life, lighting up the night sky with bursts of reddish-blue color.

The dragons gleefully conjured icefire in their hands and hurtled them at the shadow creatures, looking for all the world like children having a snowball fight. The creatures screamed and fell to the ground as the icefire hit its mark, and I watched carefully as the magic raced across flesh, fur, and hide. I half-expected the icefire to incinerate them, but to my surprise, it sank into their skin instead, leaving them unharmed. Plumes of steam began to rise from their bodies, and their monstrous features began to recede.

"I'll be damned," Yaggir breathed as one of the creatures staggered to its feet. It was a Flamehorn—a large, deer-like animal with a crown of fire antlers circling its head. My breath caught in my throat—I'd only ever seen these in illustrations, never in the flesh. "It reversed the taint!"

The others looked at each other, their eyes shining, and I felt a swell of emotion in the bond from Einar. I knew how much this meant to him—when he'd helped Kiryan seal that portal, he'd never expected to see the glory of his homeland restored. And even when he'd been told that my power would give us the ability to do it, he hadn't dared to allow himself to believe.

Until now.

The animals raced off into the hills, and I watched them go, torn between hope and sadness. I knew they would be reinfected with shadow magic and turned back into monsters, but there was nothing I could do to prevent that. I had to hope they would stay alive long enough for me to defeat Nox, so I could use my magic on them to return them to their normal forms, this time permanently.

Now that we'd vanquished the shadow creatures, we returned to the temple to tell the others what happened. The dragons were ecstatic, but though Quye seemed happy, her subdued enthusiasm reminded me of Mavlyn's predicament.

"We need to leave now," I told the others, interrupting their celebration. "Pack up your things and shift into dragon form, and remember, do not use your primal stones unless it's absolutely necessary. I don't have the energy to fight and also refill all your stones."

After a brief logistics discussion, we packed up and headed out. For stealth purposes, we decided it would be best if I shifted into full dragon form so I could carry Quye, but that the others would fly in half-dragon form. Even if we stayed above the cloud cover, it was far more difficult to conceal a pack of two dozen full-grown dragons than it would be if they remained in their bipedal forms.

Einar flew alongside me in dragon form, helping me correct my flying techniques as we traveled. Flying alongside him was a dream come true, but the dire situation that lay ahead of us tempered my joy. We flew as fast as we could, avoiding shadow creatures and other threats whenever possible, and in two days, we landed in the closest forest, about five miles away from Talamh's outskirts.

It took precious time, but Quye and I foraged the necessary ingredients, then brewed a potion to hide the dragons' distinctive eye color and darken their skin. I didn't have time to brew enough for everyone, so we agreed that Einar, Quye, Yaggir, and Diyani would accompany me, while Isador and the others stayed back and waited for our command.

"I don't like the idea of giving myself fae features," Diyani complained after they'd all downed the potions. Her striking gold eyes were muddy brown now, and her tanned skin had darkened to a beautiful ochre that offset her brilliant violet hair. "How long is this supposed to last?"

"About a day," Einar told her. "Adara did this to me too the last time we visited Talamh, and she also put this strange putty on my ears to make them pointed."

"You're not going to do that to us too, are you?" Yaggir asked, rubbing the rounded tips of his own ears.

I rolled my eyes. "It's not like the putty doesn't come off, but no—we don't have time for that, so make sure you wear your hair down, and keep your hoods up whenever possible." We were traveling in the dead of winter, so it wouldn't look suspicious for us to cover our heads.

We said our goodbyes to the other dragons, then walked the five miles to the city gates. "It's too early for the city to be this busy already," Quye said as we entered Talamh through the eastern gate. Groups of people were hurrying up the street, their voices pitched high with a kind of anxious excitement. "I'm going to fly ahead and see where they're going."

Before I could argue, Quye transformed into her owl form in a flash of light, winging her way ahead of us. Noticing an abandoned newspaper sitting on a café table, I snatched it up and flipped to the front page. My heart dropped into my chest at the headline printed across the top in bold words "ANTI-WAR REBEL SCHEDULED FOR EXECUTION ON MONDAY."

"Blast it," Einar swore, reading over my shoulder. "That's today!"

We broke into a run, heading for the city center plaza, where the execution was scheduled to take place. The closer we got, the thicker the crowds grew, forcing us to elbow and shove people out of the way in our haste to get to Mavlyn.

"This is impossible," Einar growled as we got caught in a bottleneck at the plaza entrance. "We need to get to higher ground."

"Let's go this way." I grabbed his hand and pushed our way through the crowds and to the left. Yaggir and Diyani followed on my heels, watching our backs as we entered a narrow alley. The guards on duty were so preoccupied with the massive influx of people that they didn't notice us, and to my relief, the alley was deserted. We shifted into our half-dragon forms, wings unfurling from my back, scales rippling down my extremities to cover my forearms, hands, and feet, and flew up to the roofline.

Quye joined us on the roof and shifted back into fae form as we laid flat against the snow-covered tiles to avoid the guards. "They've already got Mavlyn up there, along with a group of prisoners," she hissed as we peered into the packed square. Sure enough, I spotted Mavlyn standing off to the side of the stage, bound in heavy iron chains at the wrists and ankles. She stood next to ten other prisoners, but while they all appeared to be in various states of distress, some staring apathetically at the ground while others sobbed and wailed, Mavlyn didn't show any emotion at all. She stared blankly ahead, and while I was too far away to see the look in her eyes, I had a hunch that they would be completely empty if I could.

"She's been infected by shadow taint," Einar growled. "Look at the lines on her neck and wrists."

"But why hasn't it reached her eyes?" I asked. I'd expected them to be black, like the other shadow-tainted fae and creatures I'd encountered, but they were still green. "Is she resisting somehow?"

"The Traveler's Grove," Quye breathed, dawning comprehension spreading across her face. "That's where she is."

"What?" Diyani screwed up her face. "What are you talking about? She's standing right there."

"There's no time to explain," Quye snapped as we watched the executioner walk onto the stage. "We need to act, now."

The executioner carried a wicked-looking axe, and two guards followed behind him, bringing a low stone table and a large bucket. My stomach lurched as they set them in the center of the stage—the prisoners would rest their heads on the stone, and once the executioner swung his axe, they would tumble neatly into the bucket for easy disposal. "We need a distraction, *now*."

"Diyani, Yaggir," Einar said. The two nodded, then launched themselves into the sky, beating their wings hard to gain altitude as quickly as possible. They transformed into their full dragon forms mid-flight, and the crowd looked up as the two majestic beasts cast long shadows across the square. Their excited murmurs turned into screams of horror as the dragons dive-bombed them, opening their mouths to spew jets of flame through the air. They aimed them just high enough to avoid the crowds, but some of the buildings caught fire, smoke rising from the walls to curl into the sky.

"Don't let them kill anyone!" I barked at Quye, then jumped off the roof with Einar, snapping my wings out to catch an updraft. As Quye used her wind magic to snuff the fires out, Einar and I made a beeline for the prisoners. Most of the guards were too pre-occupied with evacuating the gathered crowds and shooting at the dragons, but one of them spotted us, and I hissed in pain as an arrow tore through my left wing. Gathering a ball of fire in my hand, I hurled it at the guard to distract him while Einar flew low, snatching Mavlyn up in his arms.

"*Incoming!*" Yaggir warned, his telepathic voice echoing in my head. I turned to see a dozen griffin riders winging their way toward the square from the palace, armed with crossbows. "*We'll cover your retreat—get out of here!*"

The two dragons engaged the griffin riders as Einar and I flew out of the plaza, Quye following us in owl form. Two of the griffin riders peeled away from the group and tried to follow, but to my surprise, four more dragons dove from the clouds to intercept them, raining fire as they went.

"*Diyani called them for reinforcements,*" Einar explained, grabbing my hand and pulling me away as I stared open-mouthed at the aerial battle taking place right before my eyes. "Now let's go!"

I tore my gaze away from them, and we flew onward, pushing ourselves hard. This time, no one made any attempt to follow us, and we made it back to the forest in one piece, though my wing still bled and my muscles shook with exhaustion.

"Sit down," Einar said as the remaining dragons crowded around us. He gently laid Mavlyn on the forest floor. "You've done a lot of flying these past few days and your body isn't used to it yet. You need to rest."

"Is this her?" one of the younger dragons asked. He stared at Mavlyn's too-pale face, at the blackened veins crawling across her skin, a troubled look in his eyes. "She doesn't look too good."

"I need to help her." Shrugging off Einar's hand on my shoulder, I crawled on my hands and knees across the dirt, ignoring the exhaustion in my trembling muscles. Mavlyn's chest rose and fell with steady breaths, and she didn't stir when I took her hand in mine. She'd somehow fallen asleep during the journey, and if not for the obvious signs of shadow taint riddling her body, I could have convinced myself she was taking a nap.

Closing my own eyes, I drew on the power from the primal stone, using it to shore up my flagging strength. Icefire rushed into my veins, the burning cold energy filling me with renewed vigor. I carefully pushed that power into Mavlyn's body, gradually spreading it through her system to drive out the taint while trying not to overwhelm her.

At first, nothing happened, but after a few minutes, black steam began to curl from her skin. She bucked violently in my arms, and Quye and Einar moved in to hold her down by the hips and shoulders so she wouldn't hurt herself. My heart ached as I watched my best friend tremble from head to toe, but I forced myself to continue, to keep the icefire flowing into her until the black veins disappeared and a healthy color returned to her skin.

Finished, I sat back and wiped a sheen of sweat across my

brow. "That was far more difficult than turning the shadow creatures back," I said.

"That's because Nox implanted a piece of herself into Mavlyn," Quye reminded me. She stroked Mavlyn's face, brushing a sweaty lock of auburn hair away from her forehead. "You need to eat and replenish your strength for the battle ahead."

I shook my head. "I can't eat now, not while Mavlyn is still in this condition." My gut churned with worry as I looked upon my friend's comatose form. "Why is she still like this? Why hasn't she woken up?"

"Don't worry about that," one of the dragons said, stepping forward. I glanced up, then jolted at the sight of Kiryan's golden-green eyes staring at me out of the dragon's face. "Quye will bring her back. The rest of you need to head to the Plains of Geelan now, before it's too late."

"The Plains of Geelan?" Einar asked. "Why?"

"Did you not think it strange that Nox wasn't there to preside over Mavlyn's execution, and that there were so few griffin riders and guards to respond to the dragon threat?" Kiryan countered. "There's a reason for that. Lady Axlya and Lord Oren have formed a military alliance against House Ithir, and Nox, Lady Mossi, and General Slaugh have marched their forces out to meet them."

An icy chill rippled through me as the impact of Kiryan's words hit me. "The final battle," I said, my voice hollow. "It's about to begin."

"Yes," he said. "Nox is about to rip a hole between worlds. If you don't stop her now, you will lose everything."

39

Mavlyn

Mavlyn sat on the flat rock by the pond in the center of the grove, tracing patterns across the surface of the cool water with her toes. She knew today was her execution day, and that the guards had already brought her to the square along with the other prisoners, but she'd decided not to participate in the last day of her life. She would stay within the sacred grove in her mind and enjoy her final moments in peace.

Mavlyn wondered if she would even notice when she died— if she would feel the pain of the executioner's axe at all, or if the landscape of her mind would change. What was the afterlife like? Would she join the Radiants and become one of them, or would she become an earth spirit instead, merging with the land so her magic could continue to fuel the flora and fauna who lived there? She hoped Adara had made it back, that she and Quye were safe, and that they would prevail. She had done everything she could to stall and distract Nox—the rest was up to her friends.

A flicker of movement distracted Mavlyn from her musings, and her head snapped up. Fear pulsed through her for the first time in days as she saw a figure approaching, and she jumped to her feet, fists balling at her sides. Had Nox's shadow taint grown strong enough to breach the protection of the Grove? Or was this a spirit, come to claim her soul now that she was finally dead?

The figure stepped between two of the trees and into the sunlight, and Mavlyn's breath left her in a whoosh. It was Quye, dressed in a long, ivory gown that highlighted every curve of her tall, willowy form. Her riotous white curls formed a halo around her heart-shaped face, and the star-shaped birthmark on her cheekbone seemed to wink as she smiled.

"Hello, Mavlyn," she said, her silver-blue eyes twinkling.

The two raced toward each other, colliding in a tangle of limbs and emotions. Mavlyn kissed her fiercely, burying one hand in Quye's curls as she snagged the other around the Oracle's waist and pulled her in. Their hearts pounded against one another, beats perfectly in sync, joy and relief singing in their blood.

"I can't believe it," Mavlyn said, pulling back to look into Quye's eyes. Tears ran down her cheeks, but she couldn't bring herself to remove her hands from Quye's body long enough to wipe them away. "Is this another dream? Or are you back in Ediria?"

"A bit of both." Quye smiled. She leaned in and kissed the tears from Mavlyn's cheeks, her lips featherlight. Desire rushed through Mavlyn like wildfire, and she had to resist the urge to crush her mouth against Quye's again. "Adara and I made it back through the portal, and we came to Talamh to stage a daring rescue. Snatched you right from beneath the executioner's nose and everything."

"So I'm not dead?"

"No." Quye tweaked Mavlyn's nose. "You're just in hiding, which is understandable. Adara healed you, but she had to run off with the others to the battle, so I stayed behind so I could wake you up." Quye gave her a wry smile. "It took me a while to break through all your mental defenses. I'm proud at how well you've protected yourself."

"The battle?" Mavlyn asked. Her heart dropped as the implications of those words sank in. "Does that mean I've failed, and that the civil war is happening?"

"You haven't failed," Quye said firmly. "You did everything you could, and you held Nox off until we returned." Her tone gentled as she added, "I know the grove is a safe and comfortable place. But it's time to return to the real world."

Mavlyn sighed, stepping back from Quye. "I know," she said. "But I'm going to miss this place."

Quye smiled. "The Traveler's Grove will always be here, now that you've found it. You can come back any time." She offered Mavlyn her hand. "Come with me."

Mavlyn cast one last glance around the Grove, taking in the sanctuary that had protected her from Nox's influence. She took Quye's hand, and their surroundings dissolved around them, evaporating into darkness. Taking in a deep breath, she opened her eyes to find herself in another forest, this one much more mundane. Quye knelt on the ground next to her, and a few feet away, leaning against the tree, was a male with ruby red irises she didn't recognize.

"Oh good," he said, pushing off the tree. He stretched his arms over his head. "I was beginning to think she'd never wake up."

"Who are you?" Mavlyn asked, puzzled. She scanned him

from head to toe, taking in his strange clothing. Her gaze snagged on the tips of his rounded ears, and her mouth dropped open. "Wait a minute. You're a dragon?"

"Yes." He gave a long-suffering sigh. "I should be on the battlefield with my friends, but Adara ordered me to stay behind and guard you two."

"Adara and I brought a few friends back from the new realm," Quye explained. "They've agreed to help us fight Nox in exchange for being allowed to reclaim Hearthfyre when the battle is over."

"Do you think the other fae Houses will allow that?" Mavlyn asked.

Quye shrugged. "It'll be hard for them to argue against it, should we actually win."

"Should?" the dragon demanded. "Are you saying there's a chance we won't?"

"Of course there's a chance we won't," Quye huffed. "Either Adara will succeed, or Nox will spill enough fae blood to bring in her fellow Shadow generals and combine their magics to rip a hole between the spirit realm and the fae realm. I've seen both outcomes in my visions."

A shudder rippled through Mavlyn, sending a spike of anxiety through her. "We should go to the battlefield."

She tried to stand, but her legs buckled almost immediately. "You're not going anywhere," Quye said, placing a steadying hand on her shoulder. "You need to rest."

"I've been 'resting' for at least a week in a jail cell," Mavlyn protested, even as lethargy crept over her. "I can't just sit here and do nothing while our friends are fighting for the future of our world!"

"You aren't going to do nothing." Quye said. "Yaggir will go, and you and I will stay here and discuss this." She reached into her pack and pulled out a leather-bound notebook.

Mavlyn wanted to argue, but the scholar in her perked up when Quye opened the book to reveal yellowed pages and cramped, faded handwriting. "What is this?" she asked, peering closer to read the script.

"It's a journal written by a fire fae scholar," Quye said, her eyes twinkling. "And you are going to help me use it to end the longest conflict in fae history, once and for all."

40

Lord Prentis

Prentis stood at the top of a knoll as he surveyed the twenty-thousand troops gathered below. All were outfitted with the shining, flexible armor of the water fae. About five thousand were calvary, mounted on kelpies and armed with spears, while the infantry had been given iron-tipped swords and knives.

"You did well to gather so many on such short notice," Lady Axlya said. She stood next to him, clad in battle armor that was both practical and elegant, with swirling water designs etched onto the breastplate. Her cerulean hair was hidden beneath the golden helm she wore, the visor flipped up as she surveyed the battlefield. Prentis wasn't sure if he was annoyed or relieved that, at the very last second, she'd chosen to take command herself. He flicked his gaze to the toxic purple storm clouds brewing above the battlefield and tried to ignore the queasy feeling they caused. He sincerely hoped they wouldn't be forced to use them.

Prentis shook his head. "It would have been better if we'd had a few more weeks to prepare them." Most of the soldiers were battle-tested, but about a third of them were new recruits, more familiar with pitchforks and quills than they were with swords and spears. And many of the ones who did have battle experience had not tested in quite some time, not since the dragon-fae war had ended all those years ago.

"I thought so too, but I could not convince Lord Oren of the same." She tipped her chin to the western end of the battlefield, where Lord Oren and his army of air fae—who were far better trained from all their years patrolling the Gaoth Aire against shadow creatures—waited. The air fae lord surveyed the plains from atop his golden cloud familiar, his Lightning Guard spread out behind him in formation. Lightning crackled across the sky, betraying Oren's emotions—though his expression was as stoic as ever, the fury within him was coming to a head, ready to be unleashed. "He wants vengeance against Slaugh for what happened to Tempest, and we stand far more of a chance against Slaugh if we ally with him than we do if we stand aside and wait for the earth fae to slaughter him."

Prentis clenched his fists at his sides as he stared at the south end of the battlefield, where General Slaugh, Lady Mossi, and Gelsyne waited. He didn't know what to think—Mossi had her griffin riders, and Slaugh had his Shadow Guard, but while General Slaugh's army was mostly filled with fresh-faced recruits, they still outnumbered the water and air fae armies combined. And to make matters worse, Slaugh also controlled the air and water fae that were part of the late King Aolis's Shadow Guard, all of whom were Greater Fae.

"We should have listened to Adara," he muttered.

"What?" Lady Axlya snapped.

"We should have listened to Adara," he repeated, his voice

rising along with his temper. He jabbed his finger at Gelsyne. "I remember Gelsyne from her days as Olette's Lady-In-Waiting. That female is not the same fae, and you know it. She's clearly been corrupted by shadow influence, just like Cascada. If we'd taken her warnings about this Shadow seriously, we wouldn't be in this predicament now."

"That may be so, but Adara isn't here." Lady Axlya narrowed her eyes at him. "If she had done her duty and married you, instead of running off with her dragon lover, we wouldn't be here either. Now enough of this," she said, cutting off Prentis before he could argue further. "We've made our bed, and we *will* dominate it."

She dug her heels into the sides of her kelpie and charged down the hill. Pressing his lips together, Prentis spurred his own mount on, ten other cavalry soldiers falling in to flank their matriarch as she headed to the middle of the battlefield. The others came out to meet them, Lord Oren and his Lightning Guard on the backs of their clouds, Lady Mossi and General Slaugh on the backs of griffins and accompanied by a cadre of griffin riders.

"Your fiancée doesn't care to join us?" Lady Axlya asked. She cast a scornful glance at Gelsyne, who had stayed back with the rest of the Shadow Guard. Prentis's eyes narrowed as he took in the shadow she cast, which was far bigger than her willowy form warranted.

"Why should she?" General Slaugh sneered. A cruel smirk curved his mangled lips as he took in the size of their opposing armies. "What a pathetic showing. You two might as well surrender now."

"I'll surrender after I've cut your depraved heart from your chest and shoved it down your poisoned throat," Lord Oren snarled. "Our armies are more than a match for yours, and my lightning riders are far superior in battle to your silly little Griffin Guard."

"Perhaps," General Slaugh said. "But we have an ace up our sleeves, don't we, Lady Mossi?"

He turned to his aunt, who snapped her fingers. The earth rumbled beneath them, and Prentis's jaw dropped as thirty or so massive creatures rose from the ground, forming a line in front of the earth fae army. They were fifty feet tall, with moss-green hair and granite skin, their fists the size of boulders and their legs thicker than the most massive of tree trunks. They bared their jagged, irregular teeth, and Prentis could physically *see* the wave of terror that rippled through the water fae army at the sight of them.

"Giants," he croaked. "You summoned the giants."

"Of course I did." Lady Mossi smiled at the dumbfounded look on his face. There was something vacant about her stare, something that reminded him of the look he would sometimes see in Cascada's eyes when she'd first returned to Usciete. "They answer to me just as all creatures of the earth do. And they will crush you, Lord Prentis, unless you lay your arms down."

"Oh please." Lady Axlya threw back her head and laughed. "Do you think we're going to be scared off just because you have a few lumbering oafs with pea-sized brains in your army?" She flashed a smile that was all teeth and no joy at Lady Mossi. "I've brought down giants in battle before, Mossi, and I will do it again if it means the choice between losing some of my soldiers or giving my lands up to you."

"Very well," General Slaugh rasped. His dark eyes gleamed with bloodlust as he eyed Lady Axlya, and Prentis had to resist the urge to rip him off the back of his griffin and kill him right there. "Prepare yourselves."

Slaugh and Mossi turned their griffins about and flew back to their troops, and the others did the same. As they returned to the knoll, Prentis glanced back over his shoulder to where Gelsyne stood. A small smirk played across the curve of her lips, and Prentis's stomach clenched. There was something wrong with all of this, some game she was playing that no one else seemed to be aware of.

If only he had time to figure out what it was, and how to stop it.

Lord Oren lifted his hands, and a tremendous thunderclap shook the sky—his equivalent of blowing a war horn. The air fae responded at once, and the other armies followed suit, charging into battle. Lightning and griffin riders clashed in the air, and both ground and sky shook as elemental magic was unleashed by all sides. Wind howling, earth rumbling, water hissing, all while the giants stomped on fae or crushed them between their fists.

This is madness, Prentis thought as he cut down earth fae after earth fae. For all of General Slaugh's prowess as a military leader, his soldiers went down far too easily, and he didn't seem to care too much about directing them. Rather, he was focused on Lady Axlya and Lord Oren, directing his shadow guard to keep them preoccupied. Fae soldiers of all races littered the battlefield, but far more earth fae blood soaked the ground than anyone else.

Why was Slaugh throwing his soldiers away?

Prentis was yanking his sword out of a dead soldier's body when he noticed a young lightning rider with spiky hair peel away from the others, a group of four more riders in tow. The unit headed straight for Gelsyne and Lady Mossi, who stood in the shadow of a cliff. Lady Mossi, to his surprise, was standing with her hands by her sides, staring vacantly, while Gelsyne's eyes were closed, her mouth moving as if in prayer. Four Shadow Guard soldiers formed a semi-circle in front of them, and they sprang into action as the lightning riders tried to attack.

"Help them. Before it is too late."

The voice echoing in Prentis's head was not his own, yet he didn't think twice. Calling a group of cavalry soldiers to him, he urged his kelpie around the fray, heading for Gelsyne. He didn't know what kind of villany she was up to, but he was damn certain she wasn't praying to the earth spirits for victory.

He was nearly there when a massive red gorilla barreled through a group of soldiers and leaped through the air. Prentis swore as General Slaugh collided with him in his animal form, knocking him off his mount. The two of them tumbled through the grass, and Prentis screamed in agony as the beast smashed him into the ground. Roots burst from the earth, wrapping around his limbs as the gorilla roared, rearing back to punch him. But before he could make contact, a bolt of lightning hit him square in the chest, sending him flying.

Panting with pain and fear, Prentis tore at the roots binding him to the ground. One of his soldiers rushed to help him to his feet, but Prentis resisted his efforts to pull him away from the fighting.

"My lord, you're badly injured," the fae tried to say, but Prentis wouldn't hear of it.

"I don't care," Prentis snarled, pushing the soldier's hands away. His ribs were on fire, but they would heal—he was a Greater Fae, after all. He glanced toward the lighting riders furiously firing bolts at the shadow soldiers, wondering which one had saved him. "We have to get to—"

His words died in his throat as he turned to Gelsyne, who raised her hands. An inky black shape swirled in front of her, slowly taking on the shape of a monstrous figure with a bull-shaped head and multi-pronged horns. It stood on two hooved feet, and six forked tails lashed the air behind it.

Lady Mossi continued to stare vacantly into the distance, and dread rose inside Prentis as he realized what Nox's plan was. He shouted a warning as he ran toward Lady Mossi, but his cries fell on deaf ears, and the Shadow reared up and swallowed her right before his horrified eyes.

41

Adara

With no time to lose, we took to the skies in dragon form, Einar by my side while the other two-dozen dragons spread out on either side of us in perfect v-formation. My breath sawed in my lungs as I pumped my wings as hard and fast as I could, heedless of my protesting muscles. I couldn't afford to slow down, not even for a moment. Not when the very world hung in the balance.

The plains of Geelan soon came into view, a vast expanse of open terrain that seemed to stretch on forever. From a distance, it was beautiful, with a backdrop of rolling hills and low mountains, but that beauty was marred by the battle raging below. The water fae had taken position near a shallow river that wound its way across the plains, the air fae encamped in the shadow of the mountains, and the earth fae scattered throughout the fields, makeshift fortifications and trenches dug into the ground.

Smoke rose from burning tents and structures, and as we drew closer, the sound of magical blasts filled the air. Steel glinted in the sunlight as earth, air, and water fae alike engaged in armed combat, and elemental magic flickered through the air as they hurtled spells and projectiles at each other. My heart hurt at the sight of so much carnage. The very thing that we had fought so hard against was coming to pass.

"Adara!" Einar barked, and I whipped my head around as panic ricocheted through our bond. *"Look, to the west!"*

I followed his gaze, and my heart stuttered in my chest. Nox and Lady Mossi were standing at the base of a knoll, and next to them was an enormous shadow creature with wicked-looking horns, cloven hooves, and forked tails. I only beheld its true form for a split second before it unraveled into a shapeless, inky black cloud. It reared up, then descended upon Lady Mossi, engulfing her completely.

A roar of fury and denial ripped from my throat, shattering the sky around me. I tucked my wings and dove, Einar and the others following close behind, and the battle came to an abrupt halt as the fighting fae all looked up to see who was approaching. Cries of fear and alarm filled the air at the sight of the dragons, a sight none of them had seen in two decades, but I barely paid them any heed. I had to get to Lady Mossi, had to stop that infernal creature before it took over—

Nox snapped her head around to face me, then raised her hands. The air around her hands began to swirl, coalescing into a dark, electric current crackling with malevolent energy. With a swift motion, she flung her hands out, hurling the shadow magic at me in a wave of dark energy. Though I was immune to the effects, the pulse of magic still slammed into me, sending me flying backward and crashing into several of the dragons behind me.

I righted myself in the air again, but it was too late now. Lady

Mossi's body had absorbed the Shadow completely. I could see it in the blackness that filled her eyes, and the way her hair darkened from its usual sage green to a black tourmaline. Her lips stretched into a wicked grin as she looked me up and down.

"This is the little upstart who's been giving you so much trouble?" the Shadow asked, addressing Nox. "She doesn't seem like much."

"She isn't, but she's backed by Kiryan, making her a bit of an annoyance." Nox's upper lip curled as her black gaze flickered to mine. I wondered if my mother was aware of any of this, or if she'd retreated into her own mind to escape the fact that she was a prisoner in her own body. "We'll need to eliminate her if we want to conquer this world."

"So it's true!" a familiar voice shouted, and I turned to see Prentis standing only a few dozen yards away. He was flanked by a half-dozen elite water fae soldiers, his face red, sword drawn and bloodied, chest heaving with exertion as he glared at Nox. "You really are a Shadow! Adara was right all along."

"Of course she was," Nox said sweetly. "I'm very thankful you all were too stupid to listen to her, or else I might not have succeeded in bringing you all here." She frowned at me. "It's too bad that Tempest was attacked before she could make it to Angtun, and that you and Kiryan thwarted my attempts to use Cascada as a plant. I was planning on using Oren or Axlya as the third avatar... but that's all right." She turned an avaricious glance toward the crowd. "I've got the perfect back up in mind."

"*Who is that?*" Einar asked, and my heart dropped as I followed Nox's gaze to where a massive red gorilla stood. He looked a little different than the last time I'd seen him, sporting a large, singed pattern of fur on his chest, but I'd recognize him anywhere.

"*It's General Slaugh.*"

As if he could somehow hear me, General Slaugh turned in

our direction. His black eyes were glassy as they locked onto Nox's face, and his expression went slack as she entered his mind.

"Come to me, my shadow soldier," Nox cooed. "It's time to fulfill your destiny."

Slaugh took a step toward her, but jumped back as a lightning bolt struck the ground directly in front of him. Nox snarled, jerking her gaze up at Leap, who glared defiantly at her.

"I never thought I'd be defending General Slaugh," he said, "but over my dead body are you taking him."

"That can be arranged." Nox raised her hands and shot a bolt of shadow magic at him. Leap and the other Lightning Riders scattered, but Einar and I dove straight for Nox. I opened my mouth as icefire barreled up my throat, fully intending to unleash it on her and end this once-and-for-all.

But I was so focused on my goal that I didn't notice the giant until he stepped in front of me.

"Adara, watch out!" Einar cried, but it was too late. I slammed into the giant's chest at full speed. Pain radiated through my body as several bones broke upon the impact, and the giant let out a roar. He grabbed me, but Einar intervened, blasting the giant's head with fire. The giant released me, and I plummeted, my wings struggling and failing to hold me aloft.

Isador and Diyani caught me before I slammed into the ground, carrying me a safe distance away and depositing me at the base of another hill. Though I knew it would be painful to do so, I shifted into my half-dragon form, knowing that the physical change would force my body to heal. The pain was excruciating, and I collapsed to my knees on the hillside, panting hard.

"What do you want us to do, Lady Adara?" Diyani asked as she crouched above me, shielding me with her body.

I scanned the battle before me, trying to get a sense of my bearings. Einar had successfully fought off the giant, and he was now fighting General Slaugh, using his fire magic to keep the general from going to his mistress. Nox and her Shadow companion had retreated farther behind their lines, and I spotted them just in time to see the one in Lady Mossi's body raise its hands and send a wave of shadow magic rippling over the earth fae army. Dismay filled me as the earth fae began morphing into shadow creatures—mindless minions who would fight to the death and beyond, turning all their victims with each bite and scratch of their claws into the same soulless monsters.

"I need you and the other dragons to use the icefire primal stones to burn out the shadow taint in the armies," I told Diyani. Even now, the earth fae shadow soldiers were ripping into the water and air fae, infecting them with Nox's poisonous magic. *"It's already spreading, and if we don't stop it now, every soldier on this battlefield will become a shadow creature."*

"What about the Shadows?" Isador asked.

"Let me worry about them."

I rallied my strength as the last of the pain faded, and the three of us took to the skies, heading back to the battlefield. Diyani and Isador flanked me for a few brief moments before veering toward the lines where the earth and water fae armies clashed. Leap, Lord Oren, and the other Lightning Riders were relentlessly attacking the giants, and Einar was still fighting Slaugh, who had shifted back into his fae form. The general seemed to have grown twice his usual size, shadow magic oozing from his pores as he held his own against Einar with a combination of shadow and earth magic. It was obvious Nox was fueling him through their connection—the only way to stop him was to stop her.

"Oi!" Leap pulled up alongside me. He was sweaty and disheveled, but still gave me a crooked grin. "Need someone to watch your back?"

"Always." I grinned back at him, my heart swelling with affection.

Leap shadowed me from above as I flew over the battlefield, heading toward Nox. He used his lightning strikes and wind magic to fend off attacks from the earth fae below, giving me freedom to make a beeline for the two Shadows. Nox's eyes widened as she saw me coming, and she fired bolts of shadow magic in our direction, trying to knock Leap from the sky.

"Go!" I shouted at him as he swerved to avoid the attacks. "Help the other Lightning Riders. I've got this."

Leap looked torn, but he did as I said, veering away from Nox's line of fire. The other Shadow was too preoccupied with directing the earth fae army—the dragons were doing a good job of purifying the soldiers with their icefire amulets, forcing the Shadow to make more—so she had no choice but to face me on her own. I conjured a ball of icefire as I raced toward her, but just as I threw it, shadow wings burst from her back, and she took flight, narrowly avoiding the blast.

"You'll need to do better than that!" she shouted, circling around behind me. I turned in time to see her fling a rope of shadow magic at one of the giants, lassoing it by the wrist. The great creature lumbered toward me, its shadow-blackened eyes brimming with hatred, and I cursed as I flew sideways, narrowly avoiding its grasp.

"Coward!" I shouted, shooting another blast at her. "Getting others to do your dirty work instead of fighting yourself!"

"But of course." Nox alighted on the giant's shoulder, stroking her hand down its craggy cheek. "Why work harder when you can work smarter? A queen doesn't waste energy swinging her own sword when she has soldiers to fight for her. She uses her superior intellect to direct them in battle."

"Queen?" I scoffed, dodging the giant yet again. "Of death

and destruction, sure. But you don't know the first thing about how to lead living, breathing people."

"I have no interest in leading living, breathing people." Nox flicked an imaginary speck of dust off her shoulder. "They hold no value to me aside from the life energy my shadows and I will harvest from them, once we take control of your world."

I tried to blast Nox with icefire again, but although she dodged it, the ball of magic hit the giant square in the shoulder. The creature roared, stumbling back a step and crushing several fae underfoot as the magical blue flames raced across its body. A minute later, its eyes cleared, and it blinked in confusion as it turned this way and that.

"Stupid beast," Nox snarled. "Attack her!"

But the giant wasn't listening, too entranced by the battle raging around it. It began to walk toward its fellow giants, and I took advantage of the opportunity to close the distance between me and Nox, weaving in between her blasts of shadow magic. Her eyes widened as I reached out to grab her, but right before I made contact, a cloud of shadow magic burst from her, temporarily blinding me.

When it cleared, I had my fist around the front of her dress, and she had hers around the handle of a knife.

But the knife wasn't pointed at my throat.

It was pointed at *hers*.

"If you make one move," Nox said, a feral gleam in her eyes —no, my *mother's* eyes—as she spoke, "or summon so much as a flicker of icefire, I will slit your mother's throat here and now. She will die, and I will take General Slaugh's body while she bleeds out in your arms and everything you hold dear crumbles to dust."

I froze, my heart lodging in my throat. "No," I croaked, struggling for breath. This couldn't be happening. I couldn't have come this far, only to be told that in order to win this battle, in order to defeat Nox, I would have to lose my mother.

"Yes." Nox smiled, her confidence growing as she sensed my weakness. She pressed the knife into her throat, sending a trickle of black blood flowing down the column of her neck. "You have to make a choice now. What's it going to be, Adara? The world, or the person who loves you most in this world, who sacrificed her life for you? The one person you set out on this quest to save in the first place?"

"How dare you?" My body began to shake, and I fought against the urge to let go. I couldn't do as Nox asked. I couldn't release her. Yet how could I kill my mother to defeat her? Why were the spirits asking such a cruel thing of me?

"Mother," I whispered, so faintly I could barely hear my own words. "Mother, if you're in there still, please do something. Anything."

Nox cackled at that, a diabolical sound that sent shivers down my spine. "Gelsyne can't hear you," she sneered as more blood dribbled down her neck. "That spineless twat is too busy cowering inside the back of her mind to—"

Nox's words cut off mid-sentence, and she slid her wide-eyed gaze to the hand holding the knife. Hope surged within me as I saw what she was seeing—her hand was pushing the knife away from her neck, millimeter by millimeter.

The Mother of Shadows was wrong. Gelsyne—Mother—hadn't given up. She was still fighting. And so would I.

Nox scowled, and her hand trembled as she tried to re-exert her control over the knife. Before she could take control again, I grabbed her wrist and squeezed as hard as I could. Her hand opened reflexively, and as the knife clattered to the ground between us, I opened the floodgates of my magic and poured every ounce of icefire I had left into her.

42

Lady Axlya

L ady Axlya gritted her teeth as she watched the battle play out before her. She'd wanted to use her poison rain to take out the giants, but Lord Oren had already sent his Lightning Riders in to fight them. The giants were immune to lightning strikes, so the riders resorted to trickery, using their superior speed and wind power to trip up and confuse the giants so they could lead them away from the battlefield. Meanwhile, the Shadows had turned the entire earth fae army into shadow creatures, and now the infernal creatures used their teeth and claws to infect their enemies and turn them to their side.

She felt useless, unable to offer her soldiers any aid, any advantage to help them in the battle. The only reason they hadn't been annihilated was because of Adara's dragons, who were using a strange blue fire to fight off the shadow-infected earth fae.

To think that the welfare of her people depended on the

good graces of dragons! She never thought she would have seen the day.

"Lady Axlya." Prentis shoved his way through her guards to get to her, then bent over and leaned his hands on his knees, panting. His normally neat hair had come free of its queue, sticking out in all directions, and his face was smudged with dirt and blood. "This can't go on. You have to do something."

"What do you suggest I do?" Axlya snapped. It was unusual for her to speak with temper, but Prentis had struck a nerve. "I can't use the poison rain without hurting our allies, and—"

"Forget the poison rain!" Prentis shouted. His cheeks turned pink with anger as he jabbed a finger behind him to where Adara was facing off against Nox. The Mother of Shadows roped a giant into defending her, and Adara dodged its attempts to crush her, her blue dragon wings flapping furiously behind her. "Adara needs your help! She was right about everything, about Gelsyne's true nature, about the Shadow's plan, about the icefire power!"

Even as he spoke, Axlya watched as Adara hit the giant with a blast of icefire. The strange magic purified the creature on the spot, and after a few moments of dazed confusion, it lumbered away. Much as she wanted to, Axlya couldn't deny the truth before her own eyes. Adara was their only hope—the only one with the power to purify their world of shadow magic. And should she fall...

"Please, Lady Axlya." Her eyes flickered to Prentis, who was on his knees now. The pleading look in his blue eyes hit her like a blow to the gut—she'd never seen him beg for anything in his life. Not even the throne that had once been his by right. "We've turned our backs on Adara for far too long. Help her now, before it's too late."

A burst of light ripped Axlya's attention from Prentis, and she looked up to see a brilliant blue glow illuminate the sky.

Adara and Nox were at the center of the pulsing light, the latter's head thrown back in a scream as the icefire purified her from the inside out.

Everyone else's eyes were glued to the spectacle, so no one noticed the other Shadow had stopped what it was doing. That as the blue glow around Adara and Gelsyne began to fade, the Shadow possessing Lady Mossi was coming in for the kill. And Adara didn't have the strength to fight her.

43

Adara

Nox threw back her head, an unearthly scream ripping from her throat as the icefire raced through her. I held onto her for dear life as black mist began to evaporate from her body. It wasn't just shadow magic I was erasing—it was the Shadow itself that had taken root inside my mother, masquerading as an earth fae these past weeks as it drove the kingdom of Ediria headlong into a civil war.

A multitude of voices echoed in my head, some shouting threats and curses, others whispering dark promises and temptations. All begging, pleading, negotiating with me in some way or form to let go, to stop, please, just STOP!

But I held on to the memory of my mother, to her smiles and laughter and tight, warm hugs. And I kept pouring the icefire into her, until the voices were gone, until her body stopped trembling, until there was nothing left but the soft, comforting blue glow around us.

Exhausted, I brought us to the ground, the weight of my wings no longer able to hold us up. Mother's lashes fluttered as I alighted at the top of the hill, and for the first time in what seemed like forever, she stared back at me with full awareness. Her emerald eyes were heavy, but they were fully her own, not a trace of Nox's dark presence lurking with in.

"Adara," she said, and my heart soared to hear the raspy cadence of her voice. "You did it."

A fierce and incandescent joy burst to life within me, obliterating all the pain and grief and fear of the past few months. I hugged my mother tight, burying my face in her shoulder. "I've missed you so—"

A shadow fell over me, and I looked up just in time to see the Lady Mossi charging toward me. A small army of dire wolves, boars, and fae-stags ran alongside her, all twisted into hideous beasts by shadow magic, all frothing at the mouth and ravenous for my blood. Gorge rose in my throat as I realized I didn't have the energy left to fight her, that Einar and the other dragons were too far away to intervene.

Shoving my mother behind me, I braced myself for the impact. But at the last second, Lady Axlya jumped in front of me, shielding me from the onslaught. She threw up her hands, and my eyes nearly popped out of my skull as she unleashed a literal tidal wave from her palms, conjured out of thin air.

The massive ocean wave slammed into theShadow, sending it tumbling end over end across the field and scattering the shadow creatures. I knew there was no way that it would stay down for long; it was already struggling to its feet. But instead of rallying herself for another attack, Lady Axlya crouched in front of me, then removed the gemstone torque from her throat.

"Here," she said quietly as she placed it around my neck. The three large stones, set at intervals along the length of the golden plate, flared with power as the necklace settled against my skin. The moment that happened, Axlya's face sagged, fine lines and wrinkles appearing along her face, neck, and arms as her skin turned paper-thin. "Take the energy from these primal stones and finish this."

"I... but..."

"Do it."

I sucked in a breath, and the energy from the primal stones rushed into me, as if they'd merely been waiting for an invitation. This was not the burst of energy I'd received from my father's primal stone, but a supernova exploding inside me, ready and willing to annihilate anything and everything in its path. I struggled to contain it as the Shadow came to a stop before us, dark magic crackling in the air around Lady Mossi's body.

"Well, well," the Shadow purred. "You are already on your knees. Should I take this as your official surrender?"

I said nothing, allowing it to grab me by the hair and haul me upright. "Well?" it snarled. "Where is your fearsome power now, girl?"

"It's right here," I said, and slammed my palm into the center of its chest.

Even though I knew it was the Shadow I was fighting, I still felt a sense of vicious satisfaction as several of Lady Mossi's ribs cracked. Grabbing her by the neck, I held her against me as I flooded her body with magic. Lady Mossi thrashed and screamed as I drained every ounce of power from Axlya's primal stones, converting it into icefire and flooding her body with it. Black mist billowed off her in thick waves, nearly choking me, but I held fast, crushing her against me as I burned every last trace of evil inside her.

The moment she sagged against me, I dropped her to the ground, my arms reduced to leaden weights. I would have collapsed as well if Einar hadn't appeared out of thin air, catching me before my head could hit the ground.

"There," he murmured, cradling me against his chest. The steady thrum of his heartbeat soothed me along with his smoky scent, wrapping around me like a blanket. "It's all right. I've got you."

"B-but what about..."

"She's fine. But you've drained yourself beyond all limits, and you need to sleep now. Relax now, princess, and let us take care of the rest."

He kissed my forehead, and I surrendered to the abyss of sleep.

44

Lord Oren

L ord Oren watched from atop the hill on his side of the battlefield as Einar cradled Adara's unconscious body in his arms. He shook his head in amazement as the earth fae soldiers stumbled about, befuddled looks on their faces as the shadow magic cleared from their brains. The girl had actually done what she'd set out to—used her strange hybrid magic to defeat the Shadows. The prophecy was, at long last, fulfilled.

Oren wondered what the late King Aolis would have thought if he knew fulfilling the prophecy would involve bringing the dragons back. He watched as the beasts retreated from the battlefield to form a ring of protection around Adara and Einar, as well as the fallen Axlya, Mossi, and Gelsyne. An uneasy feeling spread through him as Lord Prentis marched up to the dragons and demand entry to retrieve his aunt. What were they going to do now that the dragons had returned? Had Adara vanquished one enemy, only to bring back another?

"Uncle." Leap pulled up alongside him on the back of his cloud familiar, his pale face smeared with blood and dirt. Oren narrowed his eyes at the streaks of green dye still marring his nephew's spiky white hair. "Gale has ordered our soldiers to clear our dead and wounded from the battlefield. Do you have any directives for us, or are we free to retreat?"

Oren opened his mouth to answer, but a movement in the air caught his attention. He turned just in time to see two dragons in their half forms lifting a fae from the battlefield. A spike of adrenaline rushed through his veins as he recognized their captive—it was General Slaugh, the earth fae soldier's red hair flopping about as he thrashed in his captors' grip and tried to escape.

Oren thought the dragons would bring Slaugh back to Einar and Adara, but to his surprise, they headed toward him. He said nothing as the two dragons—a male with red dreadlocks and a female with bright purple hair—landed before him. They shoved Slaugh to his knees in the bloody grass, keeping their clawed hands wrapped around his upper arms.

"You filthy, brain-rotted lizards!" Slaugh hissed through his teeth. "Let me go!"

"Lord Oren." The female spoke over Slaugh as though she hadn't heard him. "We bring you the enemy you came here to vanquish, compliments of General Einar and Princess Adara, to do with as you wish."

Lord Oren raised his eyebrows. "You're giving Slaugh to me?"

The male nodded. "We know what he took from you, what he did to your daughter. We know what it's like to want justice for your loved ones, to want to mete it out with your own hands." He released Slaugh and shoved his foot into the middle of the general's back, pitching him forward into the dirt. "Do with him what you will."

The two dragons stepped back, and Oren took a step

forward. He expected Slaugh to fight back, to make some show of resistance. But the general did nothing as Oren fisted his bright red hair and pulled his head back to face him.

"Well?" he hissed, his raptor-yellow gaze boring into the general's. "What do you have to say for yourself? What justifications do you have for what you have done to my daughter? To the havoc you've wreaked across these lands, all for the sake of your own gain?"

Slaugh clenched his blocky jaw. To Oren's surprise, tears sprang to his good eye, tracking down the ruined flesh of his face... and as he followed them, he realized the black veins that usually covered the general's skin had vanished.

The shadow magic Nox must have given him was gone.

"Nothing," he said hoarsely. "I have no justifications for what I've done. I submit to whatever punishment you wish to mete out."

Despite himself, pity stirred within Oren. He'd seen first-hand what shadow magic corruption could do to a person—had witnessed it in Tempest when Leap and Ryker had brought her back. A tiny part of him wondered if killing Slaugh was the right thing to do. Was spilling his blood enough to atone, or if he should be forced to live with his sins and spend the rest of his life atoning for them.

But then his gaze flicked to his nephew, who stood just feet away, watching. Leap said nothing as he waited, but the rigid set of his jaw and the hatred burning in his silver eyes told Oren all he needed to know.

"You are not a victim," he said, his thunderous voice rolling across the landscape. He drew the knife at his belt, and the blade glinted in the dying sun as he held it high. "You were fully cognizant when you made the choice to side with the darkness, and now you will pay the price."

Slaugh opened his mouth, and Oren plunged the dagger

straight through his heart. The general choked as blood poured down his chin, and Oren held him fast, watching as the light left his eyes. Only when they went completely dark did he let him go, flinging his body so that it tumbled down the hillside and landed in the trampled grass.

From the earth he came. And to the earth he would return.

"Give my regards to Einar and Adara," he said to the dragons. "They are welcome in Angtun anytime."

The unspoken request for Adara to come and cure his daughter hung unsaid in the air, and the dragons nodded. Lord Oren watched as they flew away, then turned to Leap to give him marching orders.

Justice had been served. It was time to go home.

45

Lady Mossi

"Grandmother. Grandmother, can you hear me?"

Avani's soft voice penetrated Lady Mossi's mind, like a shaft of light piercing a grimy window. She opened her eyes to see Avani kneeling next to her, her hands clasped tightly around Lady Mossi's. Her heart thudded in the chest at the sight of tears in Avani's eyes—this was the first time her granddaughter had shown genuine emotion since she'd returned from Castle Kaipei.

"I'm here." Lady Mossi squeezed Avani's hand back and used it to pull herself into a sitting position. Looking around, she saw she was in her private tent. "What's going on? Did... did I..." she trailed off as she tried to make sense of the muddled flashes of memory playing through her mind. She remembered Adara using a strange blue fire on her, remembered trying to kill her.

"No, you didn't kill Adara," Avani said gently, reading Mossi's thoughts as if she'd heard them aloud. "Lady Axlya stopped you, then gave Adara her primal stones so she could drive the Shadow from your body."

"Shadow demon?" Lady Mossi shook her head. There was something familiar about that... and then she remembered Mavlyn, remembered the article in the Talamh Tribune, the trial. "That girl was telling the truth? Gelsyne really was possessed?"

"Yes," Avani said grimly. "She used her shadow magic to turn me, Cascada, and Tempest into her personal agents, then sent the three of us back home so we could do her bidding. With her so close by, I was unable to do or say anything without her permission, but I knew I was under her control." She laid a hand on Lady Mossi's shoulder. "Her influence on you was more subtle, more insidious, because you are so much more powerful than I am. By the time she had a hold on your mind, you didn't even realize she was in there. That's why you're having so much trouble remembering the events of the past few weeks."

Lady Mossi rubbed her temples. A headache was brewing inside her skull, but she tried to fight it off, tried to grasp for clarity. "And Slaugh?" she asked. "Was he a pawn as well?"

"Not exactly," Avani said. "He knew what he was getting into when he agreed to join King Aolis's shadow guard, and willingly helped Nox by setting the stage for Adara to kill King Aolis. Nox tried to possess him, but he fought back and kept her imprisoned inside him. When Adara killed Aolis, she unwittingly freed Nox so that she could possess Gelsyne instead, who was powerless to fight back." She shook her head sadly. "Adara has freed her of the taint, but she has yet to wake up. We fear she may never recover."

"This is my fault," Lady Mossi said, her voice wooden. The full horror of the last three weeks sank in as she realized the severity of what she'd done. "I should have realized that I was not myself, should have listened to my instincts when I noticed something wasn't right with you and Gelsyne. Instead, I let my greed and my desires blind me, and I betrayed my own people." She buried her face in her hands. "How are they not calling for my head right now?"

"They were," Avani admitted, "but Adara spoke up in your defense and explained that Nox corrupted your mind and forced you to do her bidding."

The well of guilt inside Lady Mossi pooled even deeper at that. She'd betrayed Adara when she'd come to her help, yet the dragon-fae hybrid had spoken up in her defense, had *saved* her from the Shadow.

"What of Lady Axlya and Lord Oren?" she asked Avani. "Did they survive?"

"Lord Oren did, but Lady Axlya did not. The toll the battle took on her body, combined with her advanced age, was too great. General Slaugh also perished—Einar subdued him, and Lord Oren finished him off to avenge Tempest."

Lady Mossi laughed bitterly at that. "I suppose that leaves Adara as the only worthy candidate for the throne," she said. "Not that I'm complaining. She's proven herself more than worthy."

"Actually, Adara has stated that she doesn't want the throne," Avani said, her lips curving with amusement. "She's taken over Castle Kaipei, but only temporarily. As soon as the dragons have rebuilt Hearthfyre, they will relinquish Kaipei."

Lady Mossi was silent for a long moment as she absorbed that information. "I should relinquish my seat as well," she finally said. "I don't deserve to rule, not after everything I've done. You should take up the mantle in my stead."

"No," Avani said firmly.

"No?" Lady Mossi stared at her in shock. "But... haven't you always wanted to rule?"

"Yes, but you are the oldest House ruler to survive the battle, and your wisdom and experience are sorely needed if we hope to rebuild the kingdom." Avani smiled. "You will retire someday, Grandmother. But today is not the day you run from your throne."

Lady Mossi gave a watery laugh. When had Avani grown so wise? "You're right," she said, throwing off her blanket and rising to her feet to face the dawn. "Today is the day I redeem myself."

46

Adara

S oft, feather-light kisses pressed against my forehead, stirring me from consciousness. I opened my eyes and stared into a pair of golden ones, molten with tender affection that swelled my heart and sent tingles racing through my blood.

"Good morning, princess," Einar purred, nuzzling my nose. We were in bed together, I realized, in one of the royal suites I'd claimed as my own after arriving in Castle Kaipei. Einar and I had brought the rest of the dragons here to rest and recover, and after a long day of settling everyone in, we'd retreated to this room, where I'd promptly passed out after a much-needed bath. "Did you sleep well?"

"Very." I stretched my arms over my head, pressing my breasts into Einar's chest. He purred, sending vibrations from my heart straight into my core, and when I clenched my legs in response, they cinched his hips. "So well that I didn't realize you'd wormed your way between my legs," I added, arching my eyebrows.

Einar chuckled. "I'm not sure 'worm' is the word I would use," he said, pushing his hips into mine. I gasped as he ground his hard length against my core, and my entire body throbbed in response. My dragon lifted her head, and for the first time she spoke, a single word that echoed through my head.

Mine.

Seizing Einar's head, I pulled him down and kissed him the way I'd been aching to kiss him since I'd stepped through the portal and left him behind. He growled, seizing my jaw and angling it just right so he could work his tongue against mine, licking into my mouth with a ferocity that set me on fire—literally. Our nightclothes burned off in a flash, leaving us skin-to-skin.

"I've waited so long to do this," he groaned, pulling away from my mouth so he could trail kisses down my jaw and throat. I moaned as he forged a path straight down my body, stopping to lavish attention on my nipples. He teased the sensitive peaks, alternating with nips of his teeth and lashes of his tongue until I was a writhing mess beneath him.

"Einar, please," I whimpered as he moved lower, trailing open-mouthed kisses across my abdomen. He stopped just above my mound, gently nudging my thighs apart, and I shuddered as he blew a stream of hot air against my core. The throbbing between my legs increased, and I reached for his shaft, desperately needing to fill the ache.

"Uh-uh." He intercepted my hands, then hiked my legs so the backs of my knees rested on his shoulders. Encircling my wrists with both of his hands, he pinned them to the bed, then buried his face between my thighs and dragged his tongue up my slit.

I cried out as a pulse of pleasure radiated through me, more intense than anything I'd ever felt. My hips instinctively lifted, pressing into his eager tongue, and I gripped the bedsheets for dear life as he used his tongue to work me into a frenzy.

"There you go," he growled as I bucked against him. His words vibrated through my core, nearly pushing me over the edge. "That's it, princess. Come for me."

His name exploded from my mouth at the same time I did, the orgasm hitting hard and fast. I tried to pull away, but he grabbed my hips and pinned them to the bed. Relentless, he licked and sucked, pulling orgasm after orgasm until the sheets were drenched and I was nearly delirious with pleasure.

"Please," I gasped, my vision dancing with colors. I wasn't entirely sure where we were anymore, or how much time had passed. "I can't take anymore."

He lifted his head from my core, and the scorching look in his eyes set me aflame all over again. There was something so unbelievably sexy about him looking up at me from between my thighs, mouth glistening, gaze feral, his hair a wild mess from how hard I'd been gripping him.

"You can," he said, his voice brimming with wicked promise. "And you will."

He rose onto his knees, using one hand to spread my legs wider and the other to grip his shaft. A savage hunger rose inside me as he pumped his hand up and down the thick length, and I closed my hand around it above his, wanting to feel it too. His eyes flared, and he changed his grip so that he was guiding my finger. Together, we rubbed the tip of his shaft along my folds, and moaned in unison as he coated himself in my wetness.

"Are you ready?" he whispered.

The question hung in the air between us, and I knew he

wasn't just asking if I was ready to have sex. He wanted to know if I was ready to complete the bond, to be mated to him, body, mind, and soul. To forge a connection that not even death itself could break.

"Yes," I answered. I had never been more ready for anything in my life.

He surged forward then, filling me with a single stroke. I'd heard there was supposed to be pain the first time, but if I felt any, it was eclipsed by an explosion of sensation. My fingernails dug into his back as I groaned, feeling myself pulse around him. The sensation of having him inside me for the first time was like nothing I'd experienced before—it was hunger and satisfaction all wrapped up in one enticing package.

Einar held still, watching me carefully for any sign of discomfort. In response, I slid my hands down his back and cupped his ass, pulling him deeper into me. His golden eyes ignited, and he grabbed my hips, working his shaft into me with slow, purposeful thrusts that hit a hidden spot inside me. Pleasure began to build, like pressure inside a keg, and I held on for dear life as he pushed me closer and closer to the breaking point.

"Give it to me," he growled. *"Now."*

His words triggered another explosion of pleasure, and this time, a floodgate opened up inside me. A maelstrom of emotion and sensation rushed through me, and as the pleasure multiplied, I realized I was experiencing both my orgasm and Einar's at the same time. The experience blasted me straight out of my body and into the ether, where color and sound blended seamlessly together. Our souls briefly became one, and for the first time, Einar's entire past folded out before me. I experienced the timeline of his life in the span of a heartbeat—his parents, his childhood, his triumphs and failures, his hopes and fears—and he experienced mine. My heart swelled with more love than I thought possible, and for a few achingly poignant moments, I genuinely couldn't tell where I ended and he began. It was as if we'd been woven into the weft and warp of the universe, and the sense of peace and belonging, of knowing exactly how we fit, was like nothing I'd ever known.

Then it faded away, until I was back in my body again, and Einar in his. We lay in a tangle of limbs and sheets, the only sound in the room our breaths as we tried to calm our racing hearts.

"I can't believe we waited so long to do this," I said, and he laughed.

"We can do this as many times as you want." He lifted his head, and even though I was pleasantly exhausted, the look in his eyes had my body humming all over again. He was just lowering his mouth to mine for another kiss when a knock sounded at the door, distracting us both.

"Lady Adara," Diyani's voice called through the door. She seemed to have the sense to know what was going on, and not open the door. "Your mother is awake. And she wants to see you."

I almost rushed from the room right then and there, but Einar reminded me we were both sweaty and smelled like sex. The idea of showing up in that condition to see my mother was sufficiently mortifying to bring me back to my senses, and I called for a bath, then dressed in a simple gown.

I asked Einar to wait outside, then entered Mother's room, my heart in my throat. I braced myself, unsure of what condition

I would find her in. But though she looked a little wan, and thinner than usual, she was sitting up and seemed fully aware and present. There was no sign of the Shadow in her eyes, and her hair had lightened to its normal moss-green color.

"Adara." Her eyes lit up at the sight of me, filling with tears. "Oh, my sweet girl!"

I flew across the room and into her arms, kneeling by the bed so as not to put my weight on her. "Mother," I sobbed, pressing my face into her chest. "I'm so glad you're back."

We clung to each other for a long while, happy tears spilling down our cheeks as we laughed and cried all at once. "It's so strange to be in control of my own body again," Mother finally said, giving me a watery smile. "For a time, I thought it would never happen. It took everything I had just to hold onto my sense of self."

"I never doubted you," I said, squeezing her hand. "You're too strong to let anyone erase you. Even the Mother of Shadows."

My mother shook her head. "No, you are the one who is strong. You saved me...you saved everyone, even though you were thrust into all this madness with very little time to prepare or wrap your head around any of it." Her face fell. "That's my fault. I shouldn't have hid the truth from you, shouldn't have lied about your heritage or forced you to wear that amulet. I thought I was doing the right thing, thought I was honoring your mother's wishes."

"You were," I said, giving her a gentle smile. "I know I was angry at the time, but if I've learned nothing else, it's that the universe works in mysterious ways, and everything unfolds the way it does for a reason." I glanced toward the door, where Einar waited on the other side. "Speaking of the universe... I have something to tell you."

The door opened, and Einar stepped into the room. "I

remember you," Gelsyne said slowly, sitting up straighter. "You're the dragon general. Prince Daryan's best friend."

"I am." Einar smiled, threading his fingers through mine as he came to stand next to me. "And I'm also your daughter's mate."

47

Leap

Leap sat on the balcony railing outside his suite in Castle Angtun, staring out at the city of spires as he contemplated the events of the last few days.

He'd never imagined he'd go from scrounging as a thief through the streets of Wynth to fighting in battle as a Lightning Rider, taking down giants and facing down Shadows alongside his closest friends. And he definitely never thought he would be living in Angtun again, sitting in his childhood room as he stared out at the city's spires and contemplated what he wanted to do next.

He knew he couldn't go back to his life of thieving and racketeering. Those occupations had given him some useful skills, skills he had begun using, and wanted to continue to use, for good. And while he'd initially joined the Lightning Riders so his Uncle Oren would give him the authority and resources he needed to help Adara, he realized he wanted to continue walking the path his parents had tread. Not just because it would make them proud. But because it gave *him* purpose.

It's also strange to be on good terms with Uncle Oren, he thought as he swung his legs back and forth over the railing. He and his uncle hadn't fought once since the battle, and the old coot had even backed him up once or twice when Ryker tried to make snarky comments during state meetings. He and his cousin would never love each other, but things were tolerable now. With time, they might even become pleasant.

Leap was about to hop off the railing to head back inside when he spotted two figures flying in the distance. At first, he thought they were harpies, but there was no way harpies would dare travel this close to Angtun, so he slipped his goggles over his head and zoomed in for a closer look. His heart leaped in his chest at the sight of two dragons—one ruby red, the other ice blue, their scales throwing off rays of rainbow light in the morning sun.

Leap whistled for Cirra, who pulled up in record speed. He jumped on her back and the two of them zoomed off toward the western gate to meet the approaching dragons, who shifted into half dragon forms so they could land outside the electric gate.

"Hello," Adara said, stepping up to greet the guards on duty. "My name is Adara, and this is Einar. Lord Oren—"

"Let them through," Leap ordered, hopping off Cirra's back. He stepped forward and pressed the golden ring on his finger to the metal arch that served as the gate portal. An enormous sense of satisfaction filled him as the electric force field powered down. He still couldn't believe his days of breaking and entering were over, that his Uncle Oren had given him a gate key, even though all lightning riders had them.

"Leap!" Einar grinned, and to Leap's surprise, he rushed forward and scooped the air fae boy up into a hug. "I never thought I'd be so happy to see you, street rat."

"Likewise, old man," Leap shot back, though he was grinning too. Einar put him down so he could hug Adara next. She smelled a little different, a sweet, smoky scent clinging to her skin that reminded him of pinewood burning on a winter night. "You seem happy," he told her. "Like you've found a missing piece of yourself."

"I did." She beamed, sending a look to Einar that was full of pure love. He gave her a tender smile in return and Leap blushed, feeling like he was witnessing a private moment. But the look faded away, replaced by a grave expression as she turned back to him. "How is your cousin?"

"She's holding on," Leap said grimly. "Do you want me to take her to you, or do you need to rest first?"

"No, we're fine," Adara said. She squared her shoulders as she looked toward Castle Angtun. "Take me to her."

The three of them flew to the castle, Leap on Cirra's back, while Adara and Einar used their wings. It was surreal to watch her soaring alongside him, bat-like wings of powder blue flapping effortlessly behind her, as if she'd had them all along.

Leap wondered if she would take the throne—with the powers of flight, fire, water, and her herbalism knowledge, it was almost as if she were a child of all four races. For all the bickering between the three remaining Houses about her qualifications, she was clearly the best fae for the job.

Lord Oren was waiting for them just inside the grand entrance. The guards must have alerted him to Adara's arrival. "Welcome, Adara and Einar," he said in his rumbling voice. His expression was as stoic as ever, yet Leap caught a flicker of anxiety in his raptor-yellow eyes. "The healers have prepared Tempest for you."

"Excellent." Adara and Einar inclined their heads in a show of respect. "Please lead the way, Lord Oren."

The group walked down the long hall and through the

courtyard maze, flanked by guards on both ends. A frigid wind whipped through the air, and it felt to Leap as though it were ushering them forward, pushing them along the path toward the infirmary tower where Tempest was staying. They climbed the steps to the top floor, and the guard at the head of the group knocked briskly.

"Come in," the healer called, and they entered. The room wasn't big enough for all of them to fit, so most of the guards save two waited outside in the hall. Leap's gaze flicked to one of the large windows set in the circular walls, and he caught Gale's eye, who hovered outside on his cloud familiar along with three of their comrades. The older rider gave him a subtle nod, and Leap turned his attention back to his cousin, satisfied that, should anything go wrong, they had security covered from all angles.

Tempest lay on the bed, eyes closed, breathing shallow. Since Adara had vanquished Nox and thereby removed her influence on Avani and Tempest, Tempest's disposition had improved. She was no longer a crazed, unthinking beast, driven by madness, but she wasn't herself, either. The shadow taint still remained, running up and down her paper-thin skin as blackened veins. It was a testament to her strength that Tempest had held out this long.

Ryker was also in the room, holding Tempest's hand as he sat by her bedside. Though Leap still couldn't stand the bastard, he had to give him credit—Ryker hadn't left Tempest's side even once since she'd returned to the castle. He pressed his lips together as he took in Adara and Einar, clearly conflicted about having dragons so close to his sister... but also knowing they were the only ones who could help.

"Is she still sedated?" Adara asked the healer.

"Of course she is," Ryker snapped. "Did you expect us to keep her awake and force her to suffer?"

"She didn't ask you, boy," Lord Oren barked. He was on edge, Leap realized, his hopes for Tempest on tenterhooks now that Adara had arrived. "If you can't speak respectfully to Adara, then you can leave the room."

Ryker stiffened. "I'm not about to leave Tempest alone in a room with dragons."

"Then shut your mouth and let the adults talk," Leap suggested. "Or I'll toss you out the window myself."

Ryker glowered at Leap, but since he was outnumbered, he elected to follow his younger cousin's advice. Adara turned to the healer expectantly, who had been watching the exchange with a look of apprehension on her face.

"She is still sedated," the healer said. "The shadow taint has been painful for her to endure, and she still has fits and tantrums, so it's easier on everyone to keep her in this state."

"All right." Adara approached the bed and took Tempest's free hand in hers. "You may want to let go," she warned Ryker, who was still holding Tempest's other hand. "I'm about to pump your sister full of icefire, and if you're holding onto her, you're going to feel it too."

"Will it harm her?" Ryker demanded, not budging.

"No," Adara said. "But it's still fire, and it's going to be painful."

For a heartbeat, Leap actually thought Ryker would refuse out of sheer spite. But it seemed his cousin didn't believe in needless suffering—at least not on his part—so he reluctantly released Tempest's hand. Leap grabbed a chair from the corner and slid it behind Adara, who sank gratefully into it, her wings shifting a little to drape across the chair's back.

"Let's begin," she said softly.

The others gathered around the opposite side of the bed, where Ryker still sat, to watch the process. Leap felt a ball of nerves gather in his throat as Adara lifted Tempest's hand and clasped it in both of hers. Their joined hands began to glow, faintly at first, then brighter and brighter, until Leap had to glance away before the fiery blue light seared his eyes.

He watched as the fire spread from Tempest's hand, down her arm and torso until it rippled across her whole body. Ryker cried out as black smoke began to rise from her body, in thin streams at first, then thicker ribbons. At first, Leap worried it would fill the room and suffocate them. But then he noticed the ribbons of smoke evaporating—they only curled up a few inches into the air before dissipating. The icefire wasn't just driving the shadow magic from Tempest's body, but purifying it as well.

Tempest bucked and thrashed as the icefire did its work, and Einar and Leap held her down to make sure she didn't fall off the bed and hurt herself. Leap flinched as the icefire licked at his hands as he grasped Tempest's ankles—the sensation was uncomfortable, like laying his hands on a hot stone on a summer's day. But it wasn't actually burning him, so Leap gritted his teeth and held on.

Eventually, his cousin's body stopped shaking, and the last of the smoke curled away, dissipating into the morning sunlight. Everyone in the room let out a collective sigh of relief when Adara released Tempest's hand.

Slowly, Tempest's eyes fluttered open.

"She's awake!" Lord Oren crowed, his voice filled with utter delight. Without a care, he shoved Ryker aside and grasped his daughter's hand. "My daughter, can you hear me? Do you know who I am?"

Tempest blinked up at him, her silver eyes adjusting. "Papa?" she rasped, her voice rough with disuse. "I... where am I? What am I doing here?" She pushed herself up onto her elbows, her eyes going wide as she scanned the room and its inhabitants. "Am... am I back in Angtun?"

"Yes," Ryker said. For once, there was no hint of cruelty or derision in his expression, only relief and affection as he looked at his older sister. "You're finally back, Pest."

Tempest laughed even as the others in the room raised their eyebrows at the nickname. "Good to see some things never change," she said fondly. Her eyes narrowed a little as she beheld Adara. "I don't remember much over the last few weeks, but I do remember you. You're the girl from the prophecy. I... did you save me?"

"I am." Adara nodded. "But I was just returning a favor." She took Einar's hand in hers again and squeezed it tight. "If not for you, Avani, and Cascada, my friends and I would have never made it out of Kaipei alive. I owed you a great debt... and now, I hope, that debt is paid."

The door opened, and Quye burst into the room, Mavlyn at her heels. "You're back!" she squealed, hurtling to Tempest's side so she could fling her arms around her cousin.

"All right, all right," the healer said, a little crossly now. "That's a little too much excitement, I think. Everyone except family, out. Tempest needs time to recover."

While Leap was definitely considered family, he chose to shuffle out of the room along with Mavlyn, Adara, and Einar, giving Tempest and the others their privacy. They retreated to Leap's tower, where they happily munched on tea and sandwiches while they sat by the crackling fire.

"So," Leap said around a mouthful of bread. "What's the plan now that we're done fighting Shadows and we no longer have to convince these morons to stop killing each other?"

Mavlyn snorted at that. "Well, Quye and I are traveling back to Wynth tomorrow," she said. "She's already spoken to Lord Oren and gotten his blessing for me to live there with her... and she's also negotiated that she's allowed to start taking trips around the country, though she has to do so with an armed escort." Mavlyn raised her eyebrows at Leap. "She was hoping you and your squad would be willing to serve as her personal guard."

Leap started. "I'd have to ask Uncle Oren... but I would love to." The chance to make Wynth his home again, this time legitimately, and with family and friends by his side, was far too good of an opportunity to pass up. "What about the succession?" he asked Adara. "Are you taking the throne? You've already taken the castle."

"No," Adara said. "The castle is a temporary haven until we're able to clear out Hearthfyre and rebuild enough homes for the rest of the dragons to live in. Then we'll all be moving out. As for the succession..." she smiled, tilting her head a little. "If you want to know more, you'll have to come to the summit next week."

"Summit?" Mavlyn asked. "What summit?"

"I've called the House heads together for a summit to discuss Ediria's leadership and its future," she said. "Einar and I have come up with a plan that we think everyone will be satisfied with, and I hope you will all be by my side when I present it next week."

"Of course," Mavlyn said. "I would be my honor."

"And mine," Leap agreed. "But, as your friends, I still think it would be better if we knew what we were walking into. You know, in case it's a stupid idea and we have to brace ourselves for another civil war."

Einar snorted at that. "If this causes a civil war, then Ediria deserves to fall apart," he said, then winced when Adara elbowed him in the ribs.

"Don't jinx it!" she scolded him, then leaned forward on her elbows. "All right. I'll tell you. But you have to promise not to breathe a word to anyone else..."

48

Einar

O ne week later
I sat next to Adara at the massive round table in the council chamber—a room that had not been used since King Aolis had taken the throne. The table was so large it took up most of the space in the room, but even so, it was barely big enough to seat everyone who'd answered Adara's call to attend the summit.

Each of the House heads had arrived—Cascada and Prentis representing the water fae, Lord Oren with Tempest--who had been named as his successor--and the Oracle, and Lady Mossi with Avani and Mavlyn. Mavlyn sat between Quye and Mossi, a choice Adara had made deliberately to make Mavlyn more comfortable. Even so, it didn't seem like she held any ill will toward Mossi—the two of them had exchanged very cordial greetings upon entering the room.

"All right," Adara said, raising her goblet to quell the chatter in the room. My heart swelled with pride and admiration as I looked at her—she was dressed in a flowing gown of shimmering blue-green silk, cinched at the waist with a silver belt and adorned with silver beading at the neckline that glimmered in the light. The gown was airy and light, yet it still flowed with a certain regality, and her lavender hair was styled in loose waves that framed her beautiful, determined features. "Let's get down to business. As you know, I've called you here to discuss the succession."

"Yes, we know," Lady Mossi said. "Though I admit I'm not sure why you bothered. I expected to be called for a coronation ceremony instead."

"Would you have come?" Cascada asked from the other end of the table. Her tone was only mildly acerbic—she'd mellowed out since being released from Nox's influence.

"Of course I would have," Mossi said stiffly. "While I still think the earth fae should eventually be allowed to rule again, I admit it would be a disgrace for one of us to take the throne now, given that we allowed ourselves to be manipulated and used as pawns in the Mother of Shadows' grand plan for destruction." She inclined her head to Adara. "I owe you a great debt and an apology for all the wrongs I have committed against you. You have more than earned my House's fealty."

"And ours as well," Prentis chimed in. "I should have never agreed to go along with Lady Axlya's plans to force you into marriage with me in exchange for our help. We should have supported you unconditionally."

"This is all very touching," Lord Oren drawled before Adara could respond, "but perhaps you might let the lady actually tell us what her plan is, before you all pledge your undying loyalty to her?"

The others glared at him, and Adara stifled a laugh. "I thank you for your heartfelt apologies," she told them, "but Lord Oren is right. I haven't come here to tell you that I'm taking the throne. In fact, my intention is to abolish the Kingdom of Ediria altogether."

The water and earth fae sucked in shocked breaths, but Lord Oren only smiled. I wasn't exactly surprised, given that he'd already threatened to pull out of the alliance. "You can't just disband the kingdom!" Mossi cried. "Our existing infrastructure will fall apart! We'll have to negotiate a new set of trade agreements and laws!"

"I think that's a small price to pay in exchange for giving each realm its autonomy back," Adara said gently. "Besides, I'm not suggesting we go back to the way things were before the alliance. We would become a republic, where the House heads rule together with regular council meetings and voting sessions."

"And not just voting amongst the elite," Mavlyn chimed in. "The lesser fae will also have a say. We need to create a system that represents the needs of all the people, not just the Greater Fae."

"I don't know about that," Lord Oren groused. "There is such a thing as too many cooks in the kitchen."

"Perhaps, but even restaurant customers get to vote—with their wallets, if not their words," Adara pointed out. "Just because the lesser fae don't have as much magic doesn't mean they don't have value. We must find a way to include them."

"What of Heathfyre?" Lady Mossi asked. "How is that land going to be divided amongst the Houses?"

"It's not," Adara said. "I claim Hearthfyre on behalf of the dragons. The land is rightfully ours, and the dragons deserve a home, especially after coming back to Ediria and risking their own necks to help save you all."

"No one is arguing that the dragons deserve a home," Cascada said. "But there are only a few dozen of you. Surely you don't need an entire realm! And there is still the matter of the fire fae—"

"About that," Quye interrupted, holding up a finger. A slow smile spread across her face as all eyes in the room turned to her, and she pulled out a notebook from a pocket in her robes. "I went exploring around the ruins in Hearthfyre, and found some very interesting journals and ancient texts. It turns out the dragons didn't kill the fire fae at all. They are actually their descendants."

The room exploded into chaos at this, and I cast Adara a hopeless look. I'd hardly believe Quye's theories myself, even after she'd shown me everything. Could these fae really be expected to?

"Have faith," she said to me through the bond. She sent a pulse of reassurance down the connection, and my nerves eased a little. *"The others may not like what Quye has to say, but they do respect her as the Oracle. They'll come around eventually."*

"How could the dragons possibly be descendants of the fire fae?" Lord Oren snapped. "Everyone knows they arrived in a hail of meteors!"

"Because the fire fae were dabbling in foolish magics," Quye said. "They found and modified an ancient witchling spell and summoned the dragons from another realm, intending to tame them and use them in warfare against the other three Houses." She smirked a little. "However, the magic backfired very badly, and instead of the fire fae bonding to the dragons as master and slave, they created a soul bond where the two became one." She pulled out an ancient notebook and waved it in the air. "This is a journal written by a fire fae scholar that I've been translating. The author's name is nearly identical to the grandfather of one of the dragons I interviewed while Adara and I visited them in their new realm, and the two of them have personality quirks that are far too similar to be coincidental."

Quye spent the next few minutes reading a few passages from the book, passages that backed up her claims, then allowed the leaders to pass the book around and examine it for themselves.

"How would you describe what it was like when you shifted into a dragon for the first time, Einar?" she asked me once they were finished looking at it.

"It felt as if a hidden beast inside of me had awoken for the first time," I said, thinking back to that day. "That beast is both me and not me. Our urges are often at odds, and it sometimes feels as if I have two different personalities inside me."

Adara smiled. "That sounds about right to me, too." She brushed a hand across the side of her leg, where her Umnar tattoo was. "I'm still trying to figure out how to live in harmony with mine."

"Exactly," Quye said. "Dragons are dual creatures—they have the soul of a fae, and the heart of a dragon, combined in one body. That's why all the fire fae in Hearthfyre disappeared, why there wasn't a single dead body found. They merged with the dragons and were reborn as different beings, the memories of their previous lives erased."

A heavy silence blanketed the room as the House heads contemplated this. "So you're saying the war we fought against the dragons, the thousands of years of bloodshed, was all based on a misunderstanding?" Lady Mossi finally asked.

Quye gave her a sympathetic smile. "I wouldn't feel too bad," she said. "The fire fae brought this upon themselves by trying to summon and enslave a race of beasts that they intended to use to conquer the other realms. If they'd succeeded, the war still would have happened. It just might have ended a lot sooner."

"But there is no question now that Hearthfyre belongs to us," I said. "And as the only ones with the ability to clear out the

Shadows and make it habitable again, we *have* earned the right to live there."

"I agree," Lord Oren said simply. "I acknowledge Hearthfyre as its own kingdom, as well as your and Adara's right to rule it as you see fit. I only hope we can negotiate proper trade agreements, so the rest of the kingdoms might once again benefit from the use of primal stones."

"Of course," Adara said. "We would be more than happy to trade primal stones in exchange for your help in healing the land." She shifted her gaze to Lady Mossi. "I would be especially grateful for your assistance in establishing farm and grasslands again."

"Well, I..." Lady Mossi seemed flustered, but Avani laid a hand on her grandmother's arm.

"I think I speak for everyone in the room," she said with a smile, "when I say that we are more than happy to negotiate. All in favor of acknowledging Hearthfyre as a fourth kingdom of the new Edirian Republic?"

All the House heads raised their hands. And just like that, after thousands of years of fighting, the Dragon-Fae War finally came to an end.

49

Adara

Two years later.

A warm hand slid down my outer thigh, sending tingles through my body and waking me from a deep slumber. Stirring, I opened my eyes to find Einar snuggled up to my chest, one arm wrapped around my waist while he used his free hand to trace the outline of my Umnar tattoo.

"I was wondering if you would wake," he said, a twinkle in his golden eyes as he looked down at me. His hair was a rumpled mess, and I reached up to run my fingers through it and smooth it back into place. "You're very sensitive here, you know."

I squirmed a little as he tickled me, a laugh bubbling up from my chest. "I'm sensitive everywhere," I said, wiggling out of his arms.

"Come back here," he complained as I rolled out of bed.

"No." I reached for the blue silk robe draped over the back of my lounging chair and shrugged it on, then walked to the balcony doors. "I want to see what's going on out there."

Einar grumbled under his breath as I pushed open the doors and headed outside into the fresh air. It was late morning—I'd slept in quite a bit—and an early summer breeze toyed with my hair, lifting it from my shoulders as rays of sunlight caressed my cheeks.

I leaned on the railing as I surveyed the royal family estate, which Einar and I had nearly finished rebuilding. Kaipei Castle was still our main residence—it was close enough to Hearthfyre's border that it was easier for us to stay there, since we spent a lot of time traveling both around Hearthfyre and between the realms. Not to mention the monthly council meetings we were required to attend.

But we came to this estate as often as we could, which had become both my sanctuary and my center of learning. When I wasn't tending to the estate or meeting with the other dragons, I was buried in the library, reading up as much as I could on the history and customs of the people I now ruled.

My chest swelled with pride as I took in the blossoming gardens and, beyond the newly constructed walls, the rolling fields filled with growing crops and small herds of game animals. An azure lake dotted with fishing boats glittered in the distance, and pristine white clouds scooted across the clear sky.

All of this had been made possible through the new Edirian republic, which had reforged the alliances between the realms. In exchange for copious amounts of primal stones, the air fae had cleared the ashes from our skies, the water fae had purified our springs and lakes, and the earth fae had revitalized our soil, making it possible to plant new crops. Yes, Hearthfyre still had its volcanoes and flowing magma rivers, but between my icefire and the help of the other fae, we'd made it habitable once more.

"You've done fine work here," Einar said, coming up from behind me. The bond hummed with pride and affection as he wrapped his arms around my midsection and nuzzled the side of my neck.

"*We've* done fine work," I amended, lacing one of my hands through his. A movement caught my eye, and I glanced down to find the estate's gardener—an earth fae—tending to the rose bushes. Now that the war was over, fae could travel freely between the realms, and it made my heart swell with happiness when some relocated here. It had taken a year for that to happen, but it had been a huge step, a sign that the fae were truly beginning to accept the dragons as not just their neighbors, but their friends.

"I could never have done this without you," I said, turning in his arms so I could face him. I hopped up onto the railing so that we were eye level, and brought his face to mine until we were nose-to-nose. "I may have brought the dragons back, may have even given them icefire so they could help me win this war, but it was *you* they came back for. Your golden heart and selfless leadership that inspired them to cross back through that portal to fight for a land that had rejected them. They support me, and this alliance, because of their trust in you."

"Perhaps." Einar brushed his lips against my forehead, and there was something about that tender gesture, even after two years together, that made me want to melt into his arms. "But they never would have acknowledged you as queen if you didn't deserve it, my love. That you pledged yourself to Hearthfyre, dedicated yourself to the future of dragonkind, when you could have become the queen of Ediria, has earned you their undying love and respect all on their own, even without me as your mate."

The fierce look in his eyes sent heat rushing through me, and I had to look away before I gave in to the urge to kiss him.

"Are we going to work on the guest wing today?" I asked him. "Mavlyn and Quye have been asking to come visit."

"Yes," Einar said, scooping me up in his arms. Desire pulsed through the bond—both his and mine—and my heartbeat picked up in anticipation as he walked back into the bedroom. "But first, you're going to let me have my way with you again."

I squealed as he tossed me onto the bed, and before I knew it, he was on top of me, hands fumbling with the ties on my robe as he kissed the breath out of me. Passion flared between us, fierce and wild as ever, but as he moved down my body, spreading my thighs, a thought occurred to me.

"Einar?" I asked, lifting my head.

"Mmm?" he rumbled against my inner thigh, and the vibrations sent such an intense rush through me, I almost forgot what I was going to say.

I gripped the sheets as I looked down at him. "After we finish the guest wing, there's an urgent project we need to get started on next."

He raised his head now, his brow furrowing as he met my gaze. "And what project is that going to be?"

I grinned. "The nursery."

THE END

Thank you very much for reading Caged in Shadow! Make sure to join the mailing list at JasmineWalt.com so you can be notified of future release dates, and to receive special updates, freebies and giveaways!

P.S. Did you enjoy this book? Please consider leaving a

review. Reviews help authors sell books, which means they can continue writing sequels for you to read. Plus, they make the author feel warm and fuzzy inside, and who doesn't want that? ;)

And if you'd like to read more Jasmine Walt books, turn to the back of this book for a list of her other works!

ABOUT THE AUTHOR

NYT bestseller **JASMINE WALT** is obsessed with books, chocolate, and sharp objects. Somehow, those three things melded together in her head and transformed into a desire to write, usually fantastical stuff with a healthy dose of action and romance. She also writes under Jada Storm.

Her characters are a little (okay, a lot) on the snarky side, and they swear, but they mean well. Even the villains sometimes. When Jasmine isn't chained to her keyboard, you can find her practicing her triangle choke on the mats, spending time with her family, or binge-watching superhero shows. Drop her a line anytime at jasmine@jasminewalt.com, or visit her at www.jasminewalt.com.

ALSO BY JASMINE WALT

Of Dragons and Fae

Promised in Fire

Forged in Frost

The Baine Chronicles Series:

Burned by Magic

Bound by Magic

Hunted by Magic

Marked by Magic

Betrayed by Magic

Deceived by Magic

Scorched by Magic

Fugitive by Magic

Claimed by Magic

Saved by Magic

Taken by Magic

The Baine Chronicles (Novellas)

Tested by Magic (Novella)

Forsaken by Magic (Novella)

Called by Magic (Novella)

Dragon Riders of Elantia

Call of the Dragon

Flight of the Dragon

Might of the Dragon

War of the Dragon

Test of the Dragon

Secret of the Dragon

Her Dark Protectors

Written under Jada Storm, with Emily Goodwin

Cursed by Night

Kissed by Night

Hidden by Night

Broken by Night

The Dragon's Gift Trilogy

Written under Jada Storm

Dragon's Gift

Dragon's Blood

Dragon's Curse

The Legend of Tariel:

Written under Jada Storm

Kingdom of Storms

Den of Thieves

Made in United States
Orlando, FL
21 February 2024

43946257R00269